]

a

Sky

ALSO BY RENITA D'SILVA

Monsoon Memories
The Forgotten Daughter
The Stolen Girl
A Sister's Promise
A Mother's Secret
A Daughter's Courage

Beneath an Indian Sky

RENITA D'SILVA

bookouture

Published by Bookouture in 2018

An imprint of StoryFire Ltd.
Carmelite House
50 Victoria Embankment
London EC4Y 0DZ

www.bookouture.com

Copyright © Renita D'Silva, 2018

Renita D'Silva has asserted her right to be identified
as the author of this work.

All rights reserved. No part of this publication may be reproduced,
stored in any retrieval system, or transmitted, in any form or by
any means, electronic, mechanical, photocopying, recording or
otherwise, without the prior written permission of the publishers.

ISBN: 978-1-78681-310-7
eBook ISBN: 978-1-78681-309-1

This book is a work of fiction. Names, characters, businesses,
organizations, places and events other than those clearly in the
public domain, are either the product of the author's imagination
or are used fictitiously. Any resemblance to actual persons, living or
dead, events or locales is entirely coincidental.

For my father, Cyril D'Silva, for stories and laughter, walks and equations, dust storms and tickle fests. Who introduced me to the magical world of fiction by gifting me my very first storybooks. With all my love.

Part 1

Friends

Chapter 1

Mary

Culmination

England, 1936

'Iris, you're nearly there. Follow Mary's lead. She's got it,' Mary's aunt says.

Mary, startled by the uncharacteristic pride in her aunt's usually cool voice, loses her step and trips.

'Mama, surely you don't want me to fall in a heap in front of the king?' Iris snorts and Mary joins in her cousins' laughter from her sprawl on the marbled floor of the great ballroom of the house she shares with her aunt, uncle and cousins, seizing this chance at respite from the relentless practice of the complicated curtsey they are required to execute while being presented at the king's court as debutantes. Mary, along with her cousins, has been looking forward to it for ever – it's practically all they have talked about for years, since Mary's aunt told them about her own coming out at the royal court – and this is the frenzied culmination, the last few heady weeks before they come out before the king.

'You need to get this right,' Mary's aunt declares, mouth set, lips dipping in a frown. She has come to watch them practise, which is making her daughters and her niece all the more awkward and clumsy. 'You're being presented at court in twelve weeks.'

Mary's cousins groan, but she can see the excitement in their eyes, mirroring the anticipation, the palpable, pulsing expectation she herself feels.

She curtseys with renewed vigour, breathing in the scent of lavender and beeswax, polish and perspiration, the ornate, wide-paned windows framing a gleaming emerald morning musical with birdsong, fingers of light dancing patterns on the floor.

'That's it, Mary, perfect.' Her aunt smiles and Mary tastes well-being on her lips, like hot mouthfuls of marshmallow-speckled chocolate on a winter's night, orange flames cavorting on the coals in the fireplace.

'Now that Mary's done it, can we be excused, please?' Rose asks sweetly of her mother.

'Not until each of you execute a curtsey just like Mary's,' her mother replies.

Mary's cousins groan in unison once again.

'The seamstress is coming to discuss the alterations to your gowns this afternoon. Your curtsey needs to do your dresses justice,' their mother says, hoping, Mary can see, that this will urge her daughters into action.

Mary beams as she pictures the diaphanous white chiffon and lace gown she is to wear draping her in a graceful swirl, making her look grown-up and sophisticated and beautiful. She pictures herself walking down the wide staircase of the palace with her cousins, being presented to the king as her aunt was many years ago, executing the perfect curtsey.

As she takes in her aunt, by nature aloof, but engaged enough by the debutante ball to urge her charges on to get their curtsey just right, smiling appreciatively – a rare event – at Mary's flaw-less curtseying, she thinks, *I don't imagine that I have ever felt this happy and excited, that I have ever looked forward to something this much. I will be coming out with my cousins at court, continuing a tradition that has been carried out by generations of Brigham women. My heart is fit to burst.*

*

After tea, they ride through town, nodding at acquaintances, the scent of burgeoning blooms, the giddy hope of spring and new life, budding liaisons, the promise of parties and fun in the sweet air.

'Ah, there's Lady Winthrop. I'd like a word,' Mary's aunt declares.

The carriage grinds to a halt, horses whinnying, and Rose nudges Mary. 'Mama is compiling a list of eligible men for us to set our sights on this season. Lady Winthrop is the fount of all gossip – she knows who has title but no money, whose name is associated with unsavoury women, whom to stay away from and whose attentions are welcome.'

Mary watches her aunt conferring with Lady Winthrop and once again, she experiences that oddly jolting thrill of contentment and expectation, of being just where she wants to be while at the same time knowing that her life is heading in exactly the direction she wants it to go…

In a few weeks, she will come out as a debutante alongside her cousins, at the king's court. She will have a wild season of parties and balls, one in her name – her aunt has promised a ball in honour of each of her charges: her three daughters and her niece. Mary and her cousins will be feted and courted and in time, an eligible man from the list her aunt is compiling, who makes Mary's heart race and her pulse flutter, will propose to Mary and she will accept. She will marry her beau with her aunt and uncle's blessing and move into a house as grand as, if not grander than, the one she currently lives in.

Love, family, a husband and, in time, children; a household of her own to manage. It is all Mary has ever wanted. What she has been looking forward to all her life.

Chapter 2

Sita

Mud Cakes

India, 1925

Sita picks up one of the mud cakes that she's spent the last half-hour fashioning, having painstakingly mixed the powdery earth with the stagnant, dead-fly-and weed-infested water from the pond until she had squidgy balls that have dried in the sun to fist-sized pellets.

She takes aim at Giri, the son of the cook, Savi, who is snoring gently, stretched out on a low-slung branch of the mango tree that arches over the pond.

Giri is her only friend, besides her brother, Kishan, who is out with their father doing something important – Sita had deduced this from Kishan's self-important swagger as he followed in their father's wake.

'Can I come too?' Sita had asked and they had both looked at her as if she had committed a grave offence, even Kishan, who's supposed to be on her side.

Her father's mouth had thinned as it does during those rare times he looks *at* her instead of right through her, as if her very presence was disappointing to him.

'No,' he said, just that one word, final as a train door closing, whistle blowing, signalling departure.

Sita had turned away before her father and Kishan saw her upset, and had run to find Giri, something she had been expressly banned from doing: 'No more gallivanting with servants' children, boys especially!' Her mother irate, her voice stern and weighty at the word 'boys'.

'You agreed to a running race,' Sita had complained, knowing she'd win hands down, which was why, she supposed, Giri showed no indication of moving from his perch on the branch.

'I'm not in the mood for racing – I'm tired. I was drawing water from the well for Ma – I carried six pails to and fro without spilling a drop.' Giri's voice thick with pride, looking at Sita as if expecting her to congratulate him on his achievement.

'You're tired after carrying a few pails of water?' she scoffed.

'How many have *you* carried then?' Giri asked, stretching languidly on the mango tree branch.

'Ten at a stretch and I didn't spill anything either.'

'Liar,' he said, eyes closed, a smile on his lips. 'You're not allowed to.'

'Too right. I'm not allowed to do anything at all, including playing with you. I'd like to study, like Kishan, but I'm not *allowed*.' Her mouth hot and bright and burning with stored-up frustration and resentment.

But Giri was not listening; he was already asleep, whistling snores escaping his slightly open mouth, the tart tamarind breeze gently rocking the branch upon which he slept, his bare feet skimming the sluggish water, making the mired sludge ripple and swirl.

Annoyed, Sita kicked at the earth, dust rising in a gritty cloud, sticking to her clothes, stinging her eyes. And that was when the idea of making mud cakes came to her…

Her mother thinks Sita is with her governess and her governess thinks she is with her mother. The perfect plan.

'Ma wants me for something,' she had told her governess, having another excuse ready in case she saw through this one. For when was the last time her mother had needed Sita for anything other than to tell her off?

But the governess had just nodded and gone back to fashioning flower garlands with jasmine picked from the garden, with which she would adorn her hair.

Sita had breathed in the milky-sweet fragrance of jasmine and success and escaped, encountering her father and Kishan on the way.

Hot air sputters from Giri's slightly open mouth. His hands are slack by his sides. How he can sleep dangling from a branch, so deep and restfully, Sita has no idea. Doesn't he feel the mosquitoes biting, the flies circulating, the heat causing a moustache of perspiration to form under his nose, applying a sheen to his face? The air smells of stale water and baked earth, tasting damp, of sweat and anticlimax.

A butterfly, bright yellow with blue-gold wings, alights on one of the mud cakes drying beside the pond.

She adjusts the one in her hand, takes aim and fires.

Splat!

It hits Giri right in the face, dislodging the droplets of sweat above his lips. He startles, and then he is falling in the dirty water with a great big splash, his sleep-befuddled gaze meeting hers and, just before his face disappears underneath the water, hardening with resolve.

She turns to run but she is too late.

A wet hand, reeking of brine and algae, grabs at her and the next thing she knows is the shock of the water, warm but not warm enough, the slimy taste of it in her mouth, the wet sticky feel of mud squelching and sifting beneath her feet as they angle for a grip.

'You...' she cries as she walks slowly out of the water, her clothes sodden and unwieldy, tendrils of weeds caught in her hair, stroking her dripping face.

And that is when the carriage drives past, her father and her brother staring at her with matching stunned expressions – but in her father's eyes is the addition of outrage.

Chapter 3

Priya

Cliché

London, 2000

Priya waits in the dark, populated by the hushed breathing, anticipation and excitement of friends and well-wishers. In the heaving, eager darkness, someone sneezes.

'Shhh,' someone else cautions. 'He's coming.'

A giggle, quickly stifled.

Then, Jacob's footsteps on the stairs. But wait. Is there one set of footsteps or are there… two?

His key in the lock.

Fumbling.

As always.

Priya smiles.

'I'll be away for your birthday, I'm so sorry, Jacob,' she had said. 'I'll make it up to you when I get back, I promise.'

And her husband, understanding, 'Don't worry, sweetheart. After fifteen years together, we can postpone birthday celebrations by a couple of days. We've earned the right.'

She had convinced him.

And now they wait, she and all of his friends, *their* friends. Did he really think she would miss his forty-fifth birthday?

More fumbling. Why does he always do this?

She tastes the keenness, the animation colouring the air in the room. The tense impatience as Jacob's friends draw in breath, ready, waiting.

He steps inside.

She switches on the lights.

'Surprise!' Laughter, vibrant relief as held-in breaths are released all at once in jubilant shouts.

Then, as eyes adjust to light, as they make sense of what they are seeing…

Calls of 'Happy Birthday' and 'Surprise' stilling on lips.

Gasps, indrawn breath. Stunned silence.

Jacob's dumbfounded gaze taking in the crowd, finding hers and immediately slinking away.

He is not alone. A nubile nymph draped across his arms like a scarf.

The older woman jilted in favour of a younger usurper. The much-married wife discarded for a virginal mistress.

'I try to be original at all times. My pet hate – clichés,' Priya has said countless times, in interviews and when people compliment her on her unorthodox, hard-hitting documentaries.

And now, she is one.

She is a living, breathing cliché.

Chapter 4

Sita

Shame

1925

'Do you know where I found her?' her father roars, dragging Sita up the steps and through the front door, into the dining room where her mother sits, sipping cardamom tea and biting into a pakora.

Her mother stops mid-bite, her eyes widening in horror at the sight of her bedraggled daughter, her waterlogged clothes dripping puddles all over the house.

'Swimming in the pond with the cook's son,' her father barks.

Her mother's eyes widen even more at her father's words and along with outrage, Sita discerns something else in her expression. Shame. On Sita's behalf.

'I wasn't—' Sita begins.

'Quiet,' her father bellows.

Sita's father's default stance is to ignore Sita; her mother is the one who chastises her for her transgressions, which is nearly every day, as Sita can't keep track of all the things girls are not supposed to do. Which is why now, along with dread, Sita experiences a sliver of terrified excitement at finding herself so brazenly in the glare of her father's raging censure.

'I... I'll deal with this.' Sita's mother is uncharacteristically subdued, so unlike her usual strident self.

'You better,' Sita's father snaps. 'She cannot be allowed to make a spectacle of herself. We will never get her married off if she insists on destroying her reputation in this way… If word of what she was doing gets about—'

'It won't,' her mother says, quickly. 'I'll make sure of it.'

'It is imperative she makes a good match. As it is I'm still paying off debts incurred when we had to repair that roof destroyed when she was born…'

'It's not—' Sita begins, shivering in her pond-drenched clothes, shifting her weight from one foot to the other, the puddle of stinking water on the floor around her squelching wetly.

'Not a word,' her mother says sharply.

Sita bites her tongue, tasting slime and pondweed, her stomach revolting and nauseous, wanting to vomit, to rid herself of the foul taste in her mouth and the angry ache in her heart.

That evening her mother comes into Sita's room. 'Your governess is fired. She was too mild with you, allowing you to get up to all sorts.'

'She wasn't—'

'You'll have a new governess, starting tomorrow, someone who will see through you to that wilful nature you cannot seem to keep in check.' Her mother takes a breath. 'You're not to play with Giri, or any other boy for that matter. If we catch you with any of the servants' sons again, the servants will be fired and it will be your fault.'

'Why can't I—'

'Quiet or we'll get you married right now.'

The words of protest die in Sita's throat. She doesn't want to get married, not now, not ever. Living under her parents' roof is bad enough but marriage, living with a strange man in a strange household, abiding by his rules, sounds even worse.

'I've written to the wife of the deputy commissioner in the neighbouring town. They have a daughter some years your junior,' her mother says. 'You've managed to sever every one of the friendships I've tried to foster with girls from good families around here—'

'That's not my fault,' Sita says hotly. 'They don't want to play any of the games I suggest. All they want to do is host tea parties for their dolls.'

'That's exactly what girls should do instead of playing rowdy games like you do. Oh, Lord Vishnu, of all the daughters I could have had…'

Her mother starts up the lament that Sita has heard a thousand times and she lies back down on her bed, burying her head in her pillow and wishing she could shut her ears too, for although the sound is muffled, she can still hear her mother all too well.

'But hopefully you'll take to this girl.'

'How much younger is she?'

'Three years or so, I think.'

'Just a baby then.' Sita sniffs derisively.

'I couldn't find anyone your age. You've alienated them all. Their mothers won't speak to me. They think themselves lucky to have dutiful daughters who'll make good marriages when their time comes. But I'll prove them wrong. You'll make a good marriage yet. You are more beautiful than all of them put together and that counts for something.' Her mother snorts. 'Anyway, the fact that this girl is younger might work for both of you. As long as you don't make her cry like you did the last girl I introduced you to…'

I hate her already.

'You have the kind of character that will land you in trouble if not reined in.'

If I did everything you wanted of me, Sita thinks, but has the sense not to say out loud, *I'd die of boredom.*

'That's why we're so strict with you. It's for your own good.' Her mother's voice softens.

I am in hell, living a life of daily monotony. How is it good for me?

Sita longs for the freedom her brother is allowed. Like him, she would like tutors instructing her in mathematics and the sciences, teaching her English to read and write, not just to speak. But instead she has to learn to sew and dance and sing and keep house, activities she has no interest in.

Every girl her mother has forcibly foisted on her, hoping they'd be friends, has been accepting of this fate.

But Sita cannot be the docile, meek child her parents expect. She cannot be happy with this life, her days spent grooming for marriage. After marriage she will be answerable to a man just as her mother is to her father. Where is the freedom? Why won't her mother listen when Sita tries to point it out? Why does she want for Sita what she herself has to endure, a life of doing what her husband wants, abiding by his decrees of what's best for her and for her children? The only control Sita's mother has is over the servants and even then, her father has the last word. Why do men have such power? Why do they get to decide what women must do? Why do women put up with it?

I will be different.

And yet, she can't while she is with her parents; her father intent on Sita making a good marriage, her mother imposing obedient girls on her, hoping their sweetness will rub off.

I will run away and create my own destiny where I'm not answerable to anyone.

'You will behave, set her a good example,' her mother is saying. 'You will be friends.'

Chapter 5

Mary

Tea Party

England, 1936

It is on a glorious spring afternoon, during an unremarkable tea party like a thousand such others she has attended over the years, that Mary's world changes direction, abruptly and without warning.

The previous day, she was in the morning room when her aunt, opening her letters, which had been brought to her, as always, after the breakfast dishes had been cleared, looked up at her husband over the top of her glasses.

'Andrew, Major Digby is coming to tea tomorrow. I trust you haven't forgotten.'

'I haven't, my dear,' Mary's uncle murmured, not looking up from his newspaper.

Rose, the eldest of Mary's three cousins, groaned. 'Mother, I've been invited to Lady Bramworth's card party tomorrow. Must I be present?'

'Yes, Rose.'

Lily, the youngest of Mary's cousins and closest to her in age, nudged Mary under the table, nodding at Rose, who was scowling darkly into her teacup, and Mary bent her head to hide her smile.

If she had known then what was to come perhaps *she* would have been the one scowling.

But she had sat at the table beside Lily, across from Rose and Iris, the smell of marmalade and toast and tea, the flavour of an ordinary morning, looking out at the flower beds, the mist-kissed lawn glowing honeyed in the mellow morning light, pigeons pecking at the grass, birdsong heralding the new day, blissfully unaware that fate was about to shock her out of her complacency, her assurance of her place in the world…

Major Digby is a bumbling old man, with a habit of saying, 'Quite.'

The tea is laid out in the glasshouse, it being one of those rare, cloudless English spring days. The gardens sparkling, daffodils smiling in the sunshine, unashamedly resplendent as if intent on shrugging off the memory of frostbitten winter.

'My daughters, Rose, Iris and Lily, and my niece, Mary.' Her aunt makes the introductions.

'Quite.' Major Digby squints short-sightedly in the general direction of Mary and her cousins.

Mary's uncle leads Major Digby to the table. 'How are you finding England, old chap? The civilian life?'

'This is all quite smashing, but once one has been in India…'

India… A flicker of something stabs at the edges of Mary's consciousness.

'I can't quite settle, I'm afraid,' Major Digby is saying. 'I'm thinking of going back.'

Mary feels nauseous, the air in the room suddenly heavy and close, pressing upon her so she is breathless.

'Aunt, please may I be excused?'

Her aunt gazes at Mary with a curious expression that she cannot quite place, before nodding. Mary slips outside, taking in huge gasps of air, fresh and smoky, tasting of grass and budding fruit. She gazes at the neat lawns, the perfectly positioned flower beds, and gradually her racing heart settles, the nausea easing.

She's had several of these turns over the years. They come without warning, and during those times, she needs to be alone, somewhere safe, ordered; the library, the garden…

'You're of a sensitive disposition,' her cousins have soothed.

'Nothing to worry about,' her aunt has maintained in that clipped way of hers.

And yet…

This feeling of being rocked, unsteady, as if the very earth beneath her will give way at any moment. The ache in her head, pressing, as if caving in to the weight of something… important. And yet elusive.

Some mornings she wakes with that feeling, a heavy head, her pillow wet with tears. She is aware of having dreamed during the night, vivid dreams, splashed with colour, hot and bright, but just out of reach in the ice-tipped brightness of day.

She shakes her head to clear it and walks back to the glasshouse. Her hand on the door, about to push it open. But… Major Digby's voice. Speaking her name…

'Mary is quite the image of her mother,' he is saying.

Major Digby knew her parents?

Mary stops in the doorway, knowing she shouldn't eavesdrop and yet unable to help it.

'Richard couldn't string two sentences together without bringing Mary and Peggy into the conversation.'

That feeling again, as if her head is going to explode.

'Digby, old chap,' her uncle is saying, 'best not bring it up in front of Mary. She doesn't…'

Approaching footsteps, on the other side of the door, coming too fast for Mary to act. Giggling, rustling, the door wrenched open.

Iris's stunned face as Mary startles into the room.

'Oh, I'm sorry, Mary, I—' Iris begins and then, 'You're shockingly pale. Are you quite all right?'

Mary ignores her cousin, her attention fixed upon her aunt and uncle and Major Digby seated at the table, her aunt's face blanched, her uncle's expression grim. Only Major Digby completely unaware, finishing off his cucumber sandwiches, his eyes lighting up as the servants come in bearing jam pastries and cream buns, lemon tarts and chocolate cake.

'I...' Mary gathers saliva in her suddenly parched mouth, screwing up her eyes against the brilliant honeyed light of the glasshouse that is assaulting her eyes, her head feeling as if a giant hand is squeezing it, 'I... My parents...'

'Shame what happened,' Major Digby says. 'Quite the crying shame.'

The fusty odour of onions and dust and sweat, the sun hot on Mary's face, the shocked collective gasp of a thick press of people, followed by howls of upset – all this ringing in her ears as Mary's feet suddenly give way, as her head caves in to the pressure that's built up within, just before soothing blackness envelops...

Chapter 6

Sita

Small Rebellion

1925

'Don't fidget,' Sita's mother says, slapping at Sita's hand as she pulls at an errant gold thread peeking out of the elaborate sari her mother has insisted she wear.

Sita is hot, sweaty, itchy. Her head hurts from having her hair pulled back into an intricate hairdo by her mother's maid. It feels sticky and smells strange, of the amla oil massaged into it to make it behave as it was subjugated into an ornate plait, which was then weaved into a bun. She can feel strands of it coming loose. She can feel *herself* coming loose. She wants to pull off the sari, wear her old but comfortable ghagra and dance in the orchard in the shade of the coconut, mango and guava trees, her governess – the old one whom Sita adored for she could fool her so easily, and who was fired after Sita was caught in the pond by her father – snoozing in the banana grove, the fruity breeze wafting her sparse greying hair all over her face.

'You will behave when we get there, be nice to the girl, not make her cry like you did the last young lady I introduced you to.'

'She was talking nonsense and when I corrected her, she—'

'Well, keep your mouth shut and be good this time. If you can convince your father you have a nice young lady for a friend instead of keeping company with servant boys, he'll not insist on marrying you off quite so soon.'

Sita turns away from her mother, glancing at the passing scenery, their carriage spraying an additional layer of dust on tired, red-coated bushes. Girls younger than her, huge, hungry eyes and tattered clothes, help their mothers light fires, stir pots outside the huts dotting the roadside, while their brothers climb trees and chase each other across the road, jumping out of the way of the carriage just in time.

The unfairness of it is a gasp in Sita's throat, a permanent angry lump in her chest. Why is it okay that boys can do what they want, play and create havoc and they are smiled at indulgently, while girls have to behave, do as they're told, no matter what class of society they hail from?

'Here we are.' Her mother's voice sounding unimpressed, intruding into Sita's imaginings.

The gateman smartly opening the gates for them, the grounds wide and long and wild.

'Why is this place so unkempt? I thought sahibs took care of their properties and given this is the deputy commissioner's residence, I was expecting…'

Her mother's voice tails off. She is unable to find words with which to outline her disappointment.

The chaotic colour of the courtyard, everything growing profusely and without order, appeals to Sita. *So many places to hide. If that girl bores me, I'll escape here until it's time to go home.*

A peacock runs away from their advancing carriage, a squawking flutter of kaleidoscopic feathers.

'Even the drive is not maintained.' Her mother sniffs as the carriage rattles over stones. 'I don't think this is…'

But then the house comes into view, sprawling and impressive in size but desperately in need of repainting and care, and once again her mother leaves her sentence half-finished.

As they approach the house, a little girl jumps off her perch on the veranda wall, dusting down her dress before peering at the carriage, a mixture of anxiety and excitement on her face.

She's tiny, practically a baby. Sita wants to complain out loud but her mother is already in a foul mood so she decides against it.

Shiny brown hair, the undulating, glorious caramel gold of the sea at twilight holding the ebbed day, cascades in waves down the girl's back, allowed to be free, unlike Sita's, which is always rigidly manipulated into tight plaits that make her head ache – another way she is subjugated, for why can't she be allowed to let her hair down; it is *her* hair after all. But, 'Only wanton women let their hair free,' her mother declares when Sita complains. And to the maids, 'Tie it up, tightly does it.' But, by the end of the day, Sita's hair escapes the confines it is enslaved in anyway, a bit like how she herself longs to, and it is her small rebellion. 'I lost my ribbon,' she says. Or, 'It just came off.'

A single ribbon adorns this girl's hair, vibrant red, tied in a bright bow at her forehead, contrasting beautifully with the vivid brown gold of her hair. Her dress is immaculate, her face shiny clean, her socks pulled up to the same height on both feet and not sagging even a little.

Sita hates her on sight.

The girl is noting the progress of their carriage, her gaze eagerly searching, hands clasped together as if in prayer.

Sita looks away before the girl's eyes can meet hers. It is a mistake as her gaze collides directly with her mother's ominous one.

'Be good,' her mother bites out. 'This is your last chance.'

The carriage comes to a stop and her mother gets out, accompanied by her maids, one of whom dusts off her mother's sari, a new gold and maroon affair resplendent in the sunshine, completely overshadowing the girl and even the peacock, who, joined by his friends, has been following the carriage at a safe distance.

Sita's mother pats her hair into place and the jewellery choking her neck and arms, sparkling and glinting in the sun, chimes a musical tune. Her mother's other maid bears gifts meant for the girl's mother – a basket of fruit, a sequinned shawl, a box of freshly prepared Indian sweets.

'Come, you have to get off.' Sita's maid, who has been brought along by her mother, nudges her.

Sita reluctantly steps out of the carriage, aware of her mother's exacting gaze and the girl's curious one upon her, studiously ignoring both.

'Your hair has escaped your plait already!' her mother hisses. 'And that sari is falling off your hips. How could it have come undone?'

She turns and snaps at the maid, 'Fix her hair and sari, quick,' and the maid scurries to do her bidding. 'Good job I asked you to come along. Don't leave her side and make sure she's on her best behaviour.'

Sita turns away from her mother, pretending she is deaf. Her maid tags along, holding Sita's sari up so it doesn't drag in the dust. 'Stay still a moment, so I can tuck it in,' she pleads, but Sita pays her no heed, taking in the surroundings, the messy and yet gloriously blooming garden, the fruit trees, the pineapple bushes, the fragrant air smelling like a feast.

'Smile,' her mother bites out, but Sita, once again, disregards her, her face set in a mutinous scowl. Bad enough that she is here, forced to interact with a little girl years her junior. She will not smile and appear happy too.

'Oh, hello.' A scruffy-haired woman, her feet unashamedly bare and dirty, wearing a flowing dress smudged with dust and a wide, warm smile that encompasses both Sita and her mother, appears on the veranda.

Sita watches her mother take in the woman's untidy appearance, her lips thinning to the point of disappearance, and feels the smile that has evaded her since they left home blossom on her lips.

I don't think Ma will be pushing my friendship with this girl for much longer.

'I hope I haven't kept you waiting. The cat just had kittens and I went to have a look and lost track of the time…' The woman speaks softly, breathlessly. Unlike her daughter, she hasn't taken any care over her appearance, but like the garden, it is haphazard and yet works. Sita decides she likes her, much more so than she does her daughter, if only for showing that she doesn't care for convention, that she is happy enough in her own skin not to care about what her new visitors might think of her.

The woman, completely oblivious to Sita's mother's censure, smiles pleasantly at her. 'Won't you please come in? We will take tea in the courtyard at the back. Mary, do show… er…'

'Sita,' Sita's mother prompts, her voice short.

'Thank you. Mary, do show Sita around.' The woman turns to go indoors, gesturing for Sita's mother to follow.

Sita's mother shoots Sita a glance that encompasses a whole conversation before disappearing inside in the wake of the girl's mother, followed by her entourage of servants, who look as out of place here as Sita's splendiferous mother does.

Her mother is ill at ease, Mary's mother's casual appearance having wrong-footed her, Sita can see.

Good, now you know what I feel like, Sita thinks as Mary comes forward and smiles winsomely at her.

Sita pointedly ignores her, scuffing her feet, getting dust all over her sandals and sari skirt, her maid sighing in frustration beside her.

'I'm Mary. How do you do?' Mary says, trying to capture Sita's gaze.

Her voice is soft and diffident and somehow that annoys Sita even more.

She turns away, arms crossed, looking at the house with its peeling paint and unloved facade, a frown of disdain on her face. Beside her, her maid nudges her gently, trying in this way to convey to Sita to obey her mother, not to be rude.

Sita ignores her too and the maid huffs, standing a distance away, biting her nails. Sita knows the maid is worried about what will happen when her mother finds out that she has not followed her command and the maid has not made her do so.

Out of the corner of her eye, Sita sees the little girl's face crumple; she seems on the verge of tears.

Sita is about to speak to her before she cries when the girl takes a deep breath and, bringing her palms together, rubbing them as if gaining comfort from them, says, all in a rush as if she has been holding the words in and they are impatient to be released, 'You're absolutely beautiful, like a princess from my *Arabian Nights* book.'

Sita is so surprised by this sudden gushing speech that she cannot help but meet Mary's gaze.

'Your eyes are so unusual. Like liquid gold. I've never seen that colour on anyone before,' Mary declares, hands still clasped together, expression earnest.

And Sita feels something she has rarely experienced: embarrassment. She is dishevelled, she knows, her hair crowding her face, her sari trailing behind her, her feet dusty, and yet this girl finds her beautiful. Nobody has been so wholeheartedly complimentary about her – the other girls she has been (briefly) introduced to (none of them wanting to continue the association), have been damning of her: 'You're so messy, why don't you behave like a girl?' (Sita has been equally damning, if not worse, but that's another story.) Sita's mother's compliments always come with an admonishment and an addendum: 'You're beautiful, but…'

She wasn't expecting this from a girl she has snubbed so thoroughly and rudely.

As she is busy revising her opinion of the girl, a servant comes onto the veranda bearing glasses of lime juice adorned with sprigs of mint and sweating with condensation, syrupy rasgullas and freshly cooked samosas, piping hot, disgorging steam.

The servant sets the tray down and she and Sita's maid chat animatedly in the shade of the guava trees lining the drive.

Mary picks up a glass and sips at her juice.

'You own books?' Sita asks.

Mary sets her glass down, carefully. 'Yes. Storybooks and encyclopaedias. But I love fairy tales best.'

Sita picks up her glass, takes a sip. It tastes bitter green, of envy. This girl, so casually mentioning her cache of books while Sita is not allowed to read, to learn. The warmth she felt for Mary of a minute ago replaced by resentment, the boiling ache of injustice. She does not want to speak; she wants to turn away, but curiosity gets the better of her. 'Is that *Arabian Nights* book you mentioned a fairy tale?' *Arabian Nights*. She rolls the exotic words around on her tongue. What she wouldn't give to own an *Arabian Nights* book, slip it easily into conversation!

'Well, yes, of a sort…' The girl scrunches up her nose. 'Don't you own books?'

I don't own anything. I am owned, Sita thinks sourly. The only books she has are stolen from the pile of books her brother no longer uses. They were to be sold but Sita had seen them before the maid had time to take them into town. She had pilfered just enough so as not to make a dent in the pile, arouse suspicions. They are in English.

Sita has been taught to converse in English – 'A skill you'll need when you're entertaining or invited to formal events.' But her parents do not deem it necessary for her to be taught to read or write in English. She has hidden the stolen books under her bed where her maid does not venture and has taught herself, painstakingly, to read them although there are many words she still does not understand.

She has opened her mouth to rebuff the girl, end this conversation, when – commotion.

A greyish brown, furry body streaks along the side of the house and into the bushes in front of them. There's a scuffle and a rustle, furious scurrying and squeaking and then a… a *mongoose*, of all things, sidles up to Mary, setting a dead snake down at her feet.

Mary screams. 'How many times do I have to tell you not to do this?'

The mongoose slinks peevishly away, back round the side of the house.

And again, Sita is completely taken aback by this girl, her opinion of her doing an about-turn once more.

'That mongoose… it understands what you say?' she asks, staring at the dead snake in fascination.

'It's my pet,' Mary says.

'Your pet?'

'Papa wanted me to have a mongoose for a pet when he realised I was scared of them.'

'And you aren't scared now?'

'I am, of course. It insists on bringing me gifts of snakes and lizards, among other things. Even a bird once! And sometimes they're alive! Although badly bruised…'

Sita laughs, delighted.

'Would you like to see my pet zoo?'

'You have a pet zoo?' Sita's eyes widen in wonder.

'My parents want me to love animals and not be scared of them.' Mary shrugs, as if it is of no consequence, while Sita stands there, fascinated and envious in equal measure. Mary is scared of animals so she is given a pet zoo! She owns a variety of books. Her parents clearly dote on her and are not just putting up with her until she is married and gone. They want her to improve herself, not just prepare for marriage…

I will make my own destiny, instead of getting married and being beholden to a man like my parents want me to. I will have a house full of books and a pet zoo.

'I have books about animals too,' Mary is saying.

Sita forgets herself enough to declare, 'You're so lucky.'

Mary's face lights up in a glowing smile that seems to encompass her whole body.

She's not so bad, Sita concedes. It prompts her to relax her guard, be honest with this girl. 'I love books. But I'm not allowed to learn; my parents say no man wants a clever wife.'

'Wife? Surely that's ages away.' Mary's nose scrunching up in befuddlement. 'You're older than me, but not *that* old…'

'Exactly.' Sita rolls her eyes. 'Anyway… I've taught myself to read using my brother's books.'

Mary's eyes widen. 'You have?'

'Some of the pages had pictures and I vaguely understood what the words accompanying them meant. I flicked through the books and found where the words had been repeated and was able to guess at the meaning of the sentences. Now I can read most of the words.'

Mary's mouth is open in an 'o' and her face bright with awe. 'You're amazing,' she says, with such conviction that once again, Sita is filled with a peculiar mix of embarrassment and pride and delight. No one in her life before now has been so openly admiring of her, looking at her as Mary is doing, with unabashed regard. Sita finds it a strange and yet wonderful feeling. To be liked, looked up to, admired.

Mary comes up to her and slips her small dainty arm through Sita's.

Across the veranda, Sita sees her maid pause in mid-conversation with Mary's maid. She sends a pleading glance Sita's way as if to say, 'Don't shake it off. Be nice.'

Mary leans close to Sita. 'Come, let's go to my room. I'll lend you my dictionary – you can look up words you don't understand in it. And you can borrow any of my books that take your fancy.' Her breath hot and sweet, smelling of mint and eagerness. 'After, I'll show you my zoo.'

Sita surprises herself as much as her maid by allowing herself to be led by this younger girl, a thrill blooming in her heart at Mary's words: *You can borrow any of my books that take your fancy.*

'I think we're going to get on very well indeed,' she says and Mary glows.

And just like that it is decided.

They are friends.

Chapter 7

Priya

Madness

2000

After the fiasco of a birthday surprise, after everyone leaves, Priya retires to the bedroom, expecting Jacob to console her, to apologise, to plead: 'I'm sorry, Priya, my love. It was one moment of madness.'

But Jacob, her husband of fifteen years, the great love of her life, stands in the doorway to their bedroom like a stranger, and says, 'I… I'll leave now.'

She lies there, her head buried in the pillow until the door closes, his footsteps recede and it is silent again, the silence devastated, as different from the expectant, excitement-infused hush of friends waiting in darkness to surprise Jacob as it is possible to be.

Priya spends the next few days pacing in a state of stunned upset. She cancels all her appointments and projects, not up to facing her crew, all of whom had watched Jacob arrive with the bimbo. They know Jacob and like him – his firm invests in Priya's film production company. Much as Priya loves the freedom of only making documentaries that interest her, working for herself and not being affiliated to any one network (which would mean having to abide by their rules and their ideas of what to create), it makes for a very uncertain life. There are times – extremely rewarding, although few and far between and, sadly, not any recently – when everyone wants her latest documentary and all the networks bid for it. There are others (these more common) when it is the opposite and all the investment and hard work that has gone into making the documentary goes down the drain. Those times, it is Jacob who is her cheerleader – he believes in her completely, even when she is hard-pressed to believe in herself, when she is ready to give up.

Jacob had been the one to rouse her, encourage her, in recent times when her documentaries, each new one of which she was convinced would be her 'breakout success', had failed to garner interest.

Priya has cherished Jacob's absolute confidence in her; he is her staunchest supporter, her greatest fan. He loves her.

Doesn't he?

Priya paces and she rages, choking on great sobs of salty anger.

She tortures herself with images of her husband with that woman, a girl really, her svelte body, her supple skin. Is he with her now while Priya stalks their empty home, the silence incriminating, resounding, shocked, hurt?

She strips in front of the mirror, critically eyeing her body, cellulite-ridden, with its bulges and sags.

She gives herself a stern talking-to: 'He's the one in the wrong. Why are you making yourself small because of his actions? You're better off without him.'

She recalls the heady days of courtship – when he had wooed her with (bad) poetry: 'You inspire the poet in me!'; when he whisked her away on impromptu holidays; when he took the day off and they stayed in bed, lost in each other – and she cries some more.

Then the anger arrives afresh and she bemoans all the years she has wasted on him, her youth given to him, the feckless infidel.

She picks up the phone to call him, but stops herself just in time. *He* should be the one calling. *He* is in the wrong. She will be dignified. She will wait and when he begs to come back, remorseful and grovelling, she will give him a piece of her mind and, once he has reiterated just how much he loves her, avowed how he cannot live without her, once he has apologised for his mistake, his one lapse, once he has been suitably penitent, she will take him back.

When one of her friends had complained about her philandering husband, Priya advised, 'Leave him. You deserve better. If Jacob ever did that, I would lose him in an instant.' Smug in the knowledge that Jacob would never do so. He loved her, only her. They were happy together. She was enough for him.

Although she didn't want to, mean to, Priya had judged her friend even as she felt sorry for her. She was obviously not giving her husband what he wanted. She was failing him in some way. Otherwise why had he strayed? And if her friend was happy in her marriage, why didn't she know what her husband was up to?

Now, Priya rues her hasty judgement, her smug superiority.

Now she understands that you don't always know what goes on in a marriage, least of all your own. You think you are happy and that he is too. You aren't perfect but then neither is he. Of course you've been tempted to cheat once or twice. But he is your soulmate. He is the one to whom you have committed your forever. And so you squash the temptation and you think – if you think at all – that he's doing the same. That for him too, you are his soulmate, his forever.

She rages. She wails. And despite herself, she pines.

Finally, two endless days after the debacle of the surprise birthday party, he calls.

She debates whether to leave it, even as her traitorous heart jumps.

I will make him grovel. I will be dignified.

At the tenth ring – she knows that at the end of the twelfth, it will go to voicemail – she picks up.

'Hello?' Congratulating herself on the ice in her voice.

He is abashed. Hesitant. 'I… I was wondering if I could come round, get a few things.'

Come round, get a few things. What does this mean? Isn't he going to apologise? Isn't he going to beg to come back?

'Priya? You there?'

She clears her throat. 'Yes.'

'Can I come tomorrow after work?'

So he's going to work? While for her the world has stopped spinning on its axis, for him it has gone on just the same as before.

She is tempted to say no, even as her heart somersaults at the thought of seeing him. She has missed him – his arms anchoring her at night, his solid presence keeping nightmares at bay. His smell as familiar as her own.

'Around seven?' he prompts.

She wills her voice to work. 'All right.'

'See you then.'

No, 'I love you'. No, 'Sorry for what I put you through'.

Anger, white-hot, bites again. She nurses it.

Chapter 8

Sita

The List of Things That Girls Should Not Do

1925–1926

'Ma, I would like to see Mary again.'

Sita's mother's hand stills on its way to her mouth, the laddoo in her hand crumbling. She sits up straighter, perusing her daughter.

Sita has chosen this moment after careful consideration, her mother still drowsy from her post-lunch nap, partaking of her mid-afternoon snack: freshly prepared sweets dripping in ghee and ginger-infused tea. This is usually when she is at her most languid.

Please say yes, she thinks but she keeps her face expressionless, not wanting her mother to know how much she wants this.

'I didn't much like the mother. She's too easy with the servants, which is why their house is so dirty, the garden wild. Being the deputy commissioner's wife, she needs to uphold certain standards, but she appeared not to listen to my suggestions – in fact, at one point, I thought she was nodding altogether too vigorously and discovered she was dozing!' Her mother's voice rises in a scandalised squeak.

Sita swallows down the chuckle tickling her throat, the smile pulling at her lips at the image of Mary's mother, with her bare feet and her absent-minded air, falling asleep in the midst of her mother's earnest, endless advice.

And again she thinks, *I like her.*

'Mary is very well behaved,' Sita says. 'And her room is very tidy.'

It had surprised Sita, how perfect Mary's room was, with its rows and rows of books, and not a thing out of place, in direct contrast to the rest of the house, which was packed with lovely things but no order whatsoever, everything placed as if an afterthought.

'You're very neat,' Sita had said.

Mary had glowed then, although Sita had not meant it as a compliment, only an observation.

'I like order,' Mary had said. 'My parents let me do what I like. They grew up with many rules and they didn't like it, so they want me to be free of them.' She had bitten her lower lip. 'I do wish though that they would set *some* rules. I feel a bit lost without them.'

'You don't know how lucky you are!' Sita had cried. 'I am snowed under with rules. It seems there is *nothing* I can do without breaking one, nothing *fun* at least.'

And Mary had beamed. 'I like you, Sita.'

Just like that. No conditions. No one had ever liked her so genuinely and guilelessly. Nobody had given of their affection so easily.

'You make my life seem so wonderful,' Mary was saying, wistfully.

'It *is*. You have a room full of books. You have no rules that you must follow. You have a pet zoo. What more could you want? If you're so enamoured with rules, stay one day at my house and you'll come screaming back to yours, I promise.'

Mary had laughed, a sweet cascading peal of delight, and blindsided Sita once again by throwing her arms round her. Sita had stood stiff in her embrace, but oddly, it wasn't *that* bad. If the other girls her mother had tried to get her to befriend had seen her then, they would have been stunned speechless.

*

'Yes, that girl, Mary did have beautiful manners.' Her mother is eyeing Sita with a raised brow. 'And you liked her? You want to play with her rather than the cook's son?'

'Yes.'

If her mother asks why, she has an answer prepared. She will say that Mary is nice, unlike the other girls. That they have common interests: Mary's various exotic pets.

But her mother's gaze drifts to the kitchen, where the servants are giggling over something. 'Get to work!' she yells at them.

Sita swallows the disappointment clogging bitter in her throat. She should be used to it by now. Her parents don't see *her*; they never have, unless it is to chastise her for some code she has violated from The List of Things That Girls Should Not Do, a list that every other girl seems to inherently know, a list she does not like and will not adhere to.

'Can I go to see Mary?' she asks her mother. 'The maidservant who accompanied me last time can take me.'

'Why don't I invite Mary here?'

That will not do: Sita wants access to Mary's books. There was one on paper crafts that had fascinated her, and Mary had said, 'Next time you come, we can make paper boats and sail them in the river.'

'You're allowed to go to the river on your own?'

'I can go wherever I want in town. Everyone knows me and looks out for me. It is quite safe.'

'I'm not even allowed to play in my own garden without being admonished!'

Sita wants to roam Mary's town with her. She wants a taste of the freedom of which Mary has so much.

'Mary may not like it here, being English and all,' Sita says now. 'And in any case, she has invited me back – and her mother did too, when we were leaving, remember?'

'Yes, and she did write to me, asking us to visit again.' Her mother sets down her tea tumbler. 'You'll be good, if the maid takes you? If I get word of any…'

'I will, I promise.'

Sita holds her breath.

'Your maid will be keeping a strict eye on you.'

Sita nods demurely, careful not to overdo it in case it arouses her mother's suspicions. She is almost there.

'I will write to Mary's mother and arrange a day when you can visit. She was such a sweet little thing and goodness knows, a vast improvement on Cook's son. Your father will be appeased.'

Sita hides her smile until she is in her room. She sits cross-legged under her bed, slivers of light invading, showing up years of dust – no maid has ever cleaned here, which is why it hosts Sita's treasure, the cache of books stolen from her brother's pile of cast-offs, the smell of secret knowledge and hidden worlds encased in stories. She opens the book Mary has lent her, painstakingly reading the words using the dictionary that Mary has also allowed her to borrow, wanting to finish the book before she sees her next, so she can return it and borrow another one.

Sita is given permission to meet with Mary once a week.

Sita lives for those afternoons, when she has free access to Mary's stupendous and vast library. After they have played with Mary's pets and read from her books, Mary and Sita jaunt around the town, Mary's mother absent-mindedly waving them off, Mary's ayah reminding them to be home in time for tea.

Sita has made a pact with the maid accompanying her to Mary's house, a girl not much older than herself. She gossips with Mary's ayah and the other servants in Mary's household, and in return, she allows Sita to do what she wants for those few hours. The maid has taken to bringing along spare clothes for her charge to change into, as Sita often gets the set she is wearing stained and dusty, and she has agreed not to breathe a word about the books hidden among the dirty clothes making their way back to Sita's home.

'I'm so happy you're my friend,' Mary says, slipping her hand through Sita's as they walk through town, the townspeople grinning fondly at Mary, calling her 'Missy Baba'.

Sita is envious of the regard they show Mary, the freedom her friend takes for granted and seems to resent.

Coming to Mary's is wonderful, but it is also bittersweet. Seeing all Mary is allowed, all she has, fills Sita with ache and envy. And yet, it is hard not to love Mary herself, so affectionate and sweet, so generous and warm.

Mary's gifts, the dictionary that she has told Sita she can keep, the books she lets her borrow every week, offer a respite from the monotony of home. They allow her to dream, to understand that her time at home – groomed for marriage, bound by rules – although it feels endless, is only an interval. One day she will escape, as she escapes every week to Mary's house, but then it will be for good. She will run away from home and create a life for herself just like Mary's.

In Mary's eyes, Sita sees a different version of herself. Someone who is not a troublemaker and a rebel, but clever, beautiful; someone to be looked up to and admired. Mary's regard reinforces what Sita herself knows – that she matters – and yet finds hard to hold on to against the onslaught of her parents' constant disapproval. It feeds the self-belief that flags when Sita is at home, when she wonders if she will ever escape. Mary looks at her with her bright, admiring eyes as if she can do no wrong and it is a balm to Sita's soul, battered from constant flare-ups with her parents.

'Sometimes I see other girls at parties – we only attend a few, my parents are not invited to many as they are so different from everyone else,' Mary confides as she and Sita walk down the dust-splashed streets of Mary's town.

'What about these other girls?' Sita nudges.

'Well, they have governesses and timetables, they know when to dress for supper, when to go to bed. My parents don't think it's necessary for me to have a governess. My father buys me books, reads to me, my mother tells me stories. I don't have fixed mealtimes – I eat when I'm hungry. My parents urge me to be free, be myself. But I like order, rules. It is who I am, but that is going against what my parents want for me.' Mary takes a deep breath.

Sita stops short and stares at her. 'I should be living your life and you mine.'

Mary smiles widely, rubbing her palms together. 'This is *exactly* why I like being with you. You make me see my life in a new light.'

'Are you friends with any of these other girls you mentioned?' Sita asks.

'The other officers and their wives don't like my parents and their free ways; they don't want their daughters associating with me. When a couple of the girls visited, they left in a few minutes in tears. They were frightened by my mongoose. My parents say I should play with the children from town. But the girls are working either as servants or helping their mothers and don't have time to play and the boys, well, they're too rough.' Mary scrunches up her nose in that sweet way of hers.

Both of us friendless. Not fitting in. Feeling out of place in our lives, Sita thinks. *Much as we are different, we are also alike.*

'You have me now,' Sita says, smiling at Mary.

She grins, her hand slick and trusting in Sita's. 'I have you.'

One afternoon when they are sitting by the riverbank throwing pebbles into the water, a boy approaches them.

Mary smiles at him while Sita ignores him, until he says, 'You're not doing it right.'

'I *am*,' Sita snaps, furious. 'Who are you to tell me otherwise?'

The boy balks at Sita's angry tone, but nevertheless he picks up a pebble and throws it deftly. It executes a few arches over the water, a nimble dance, before sinking.

'Impressive.' Mary's eyes shine as she claps her hands, jumping up and down on the riverbank. A chicken from the huts bordering the water, which was pecking at the dirt of the riverbed, squawks in fright and runs away.

The rope bridge across the river sways and boatmen snooze on their boats as they drift on the current – it is that drowsy time of afternoon. Buffaloes graze in the fields beyond the huts and the air smells of fish and weeds and earth; it tastes of dung and fruit and spices.

Sita refuses to be as easily impressed as her friend.

'I can do it too,' she says, curling her lip in a sneer.

'You can't,' the boy retorts, bold now that he has been able to make his stupid pebble pirouette on the water. 'I've been watching you try for some time – that's my house over there –' jerking his chin towards one of the huts, the saris that serve as doors, each a different colour, contrasting brightly with the hay-topped roofs, flapping lazily in the languorous afternoon breeze.

The boy's cool assertion makes Sita even more determined to prove him wrong. She picks up a pebble and throws it with all her might, swinging her hand as she watched the boy do.

The stone sinks lifelessly, refusing to skim and skip as the boy's had done.

She fully expects him to laugh at her, but instead, he says, 'Here, let me show you.'

And much as it grates on her to have to learn from a boy, the desire to master the skill wins.

*

Over the next few weeks, Amin – for that is the boy's name – takes to accompanying Sita and Mary on their rambles through town.

He waits in the doorway of his hut and when he sees Mary and Sita approaching, he comes skipping out to join them.

Sita loves these excursions, the townspeople smiling genially at them, treating them with respect. She knows it is because of Mary, but she tries not to care. Here, she is accepted. Here, they don't say, 'What are you doing gallivanting about town without a chaperone, with a boy at that?'

When Sita visits Mary next, there's an air of industry in the house, the servants buzzing, everyone busy.

'The commissioner, Papa's big boss, is visiting town,' Mary says.

A host of women are at work in the courtyard, painting a banner that declares in bold letters, 'Welcome, Commissioner'.

'Mama outlined the words for them, because they don't know English.' Mary nods at the women, who smile at her and Sita before returning to their work, heads bent, hands occupied.

'Let's see what's going on in town,' Sita says, and Mary happily links her arm through her friend's.

The town's streets are being swept by women, their sari pallus tucked into their skirts, and Sita, Mary and Amin, who has joined them, walk right into the cloud of dust trailing the sweepers, collapsing in a fit of sneezes.

Bunting is being hoisted up and down the streets to much banter and laughter, colourful insults being exchanged, drying up as they approach.

'When is the commissioner coming?' Sita asks.

'Friday,' Mary says.

'Please can your mother write to mine, inviting me here that day?' Sita asks. 'My mother ought not to know the reason for it – if she finds out I'm here for something other than playing ladylike, demure games with you and picking up some of your beautiful manners, she'll not give permission for me to come.'

On the day the commissioner is to arrive, Sita, Mary and Amin join the townspeople lining the streets, excitement and anticipation, dust and celebration. He arrives in a great big car, a small, balding, sweaty man, waving at everyone, his moustache twitching.

There is a banquet and endless boring speeches, during which Mary dozes off – Sita has to keep knocking her knee to wake her.

It is when the commissioner is setting out on the hunt Mary's father has arranged that Amin (who was not invited to the banquet, but had joined them the moment it finished), says, 'Let's try and see if we can overtake the elephants with our kites.'

They had spent a whole afternoon the previous week making kites, Amin patiently showing Sita and Mary how to build one, but they have not yet had a chance to try them out.

Mary looks unsure, but Sita says, 'It'll be fun,' and Mary finally nods.

They run alongside the elephants, competing to see whose kite rises highest. They are giggling with delight, breathless, when Sita trips, almost falling under the horse leading the parade of elephants. The horse neighs and bucks, nearly dislodging its rider, and the elephants trumpet in outrage, the mahouts swearing as they try to calm them. The procession grinds to a halt, the commissioner's face flushed pink as a pomegranate seed.

If word of this gets home to her parents, Sita will be in so much trouble and her visits to Mary's house, the highlight of her week, will come to an end.

Please, no, Sita prays.

The commissioner's lips have thinned, his eyebrows meeting in a frown, and he looks very angry indeed as he peers first at Sita, then at Mary, who is biting her lower lip, a sure sign she is going to cry, and lastly at Amin from atop his elephant.

Then he roars at Mary, his loud voice at odds with his short stature, 'Who are you? Why are you running about with natives, in this mannerless way?' His bulbous eyes protruding out of his face, his moustache stiffly standing to attention.

Mary starts to sob in earnest.

Her papa, perched atop the elephant beside the commissioner, opens his mouth, but Sita, so angry that she forgets about trying not to draw attention to herself, speaks first. 'You know who she is! She was introduced to you this afternoon. Her name is Mary, and it is her papa who is sitting next to you.' The commissioner's face turns even redder, like an inflamed bruise. But Sita is not finished. 'I'm not just any native, you know. I'm related to the *king*. And Amin and I are Mary's friends. In the sky, kites merge, colourful, and it doesn't matter if they're flown by natives or Englishmen. So why does it matter on the ground?'

Mary stops crying to stare open-mouthed at Sita; Amin is gazing at her too, shock and admiration on both their faces.

Mary's papa smiles at Sita and gives a small nod before turning to placate the commissioner.

The procession finally moves on, but the triumph that replaces the adrenaline thudding in her chest is chased away when Sita finds that her kite has flown off during the furore and become entangled in the branches of the banyan tree at the side of the road.

Amin nimbly climbs up the tree to rescue her kite but it is broken beyond repair.

'I'll make you a new, even better one,' he promises.

Mary throws her arms round Sita, declaring, 'You're the best friend ever and the bravest person in the world!'

But the best reward is when Mary's papa says when he next sees Sita, his eyes shining, 'You are truly something, Miss Sita. Will you do Mary and myself the honour of accompanying us to the panchayat, where the townspeople bring any problems they might have to me? I've a feeling you'll make a great arbitrator.'

No adult, certainly not her parents, has ever paid Sita a compliment like this before. It makes her glow – and, strangely, it makes her sad. And angry. She will never get this approval, this admiration, from her parents. If they had watched her stand up to the commissioner, they would have been mortified, not proud. It fills her with a futile and desperate despair, the realisation that has been creeping up on her since meeting Mary now staring her in the face: she is trapped in the wrong life.

At the panchayat – the townspeople gathering to air their concerns at the field in the centre of town beside the newly installed water tower – Sita and Mary sit on either side of Mary's papa as he listens to the townspeople's problems and settles disputes between them.

The women peruse Sita from behind their veils. 'You're so fair,' they say. 'Almost white.'

And to Mary, 'You're beautiful as a goddess.'

Mary scrunches up her nose. 'I don't think so. In the shrines I've seen, the goddesses have many arms wielding weapons and wide red tongues. But thank you all the same.' She is fluent in their language, and the women laugh.

The panchayat starts and Sita, fascinated, forgets everything else.

This is power, Sita thinks, taking a long heady swig of it. It is addictive, mind-turning. She cannot get enough.

'Your bull trampled through my field, crushing my paddy saplings,' a stocky man yells at the tall, bald man beside him.

'Last year, your children and their friends raided my orchard and stole my entire mango crop.'

'My paddy saplings…'

'My mangoes!'

'How much did your paddy saplings cost?' Sita shouts into the mayhem.

The men fall silent, looking at her.

Then they both speak at once.

'One at a time,' she orders. 'You,' pointing to the paddy man. 'How much did they cost?'

He tells her.

'And your mango crop?' And when the other man replies, 'Well, it's almost the same amount. Is the small difference worth you falling out with each other, being sworn enemies for life?'

The men stand sullen, but someone from the gathered crowd yells, 'She's right.'

'You used to be friends,' someone else calls.

'Your children are in and out of each other's houses,' another says.

'I command you to be friends,' Sita declares.

After much nudging from the crowd, the men reluctantly clap their arms round each other's shoulders.

The crowd erupts in cheers and Sita feels on top of the world. She has talked to grown men and they have listened, done as she said. She has sampled the heady freedom, the exhilarating release of power and loved it. *When I run away into my new life, this is what I want.*

'Miss Sita,' Mary's papa says, his eyes wide with awe and pride. 'You're a better arbitrator than I am. Will you accompany me and Mary to every panchayat from now on?'

And Sita nods eagerly, thrilled, even as she notes Mary's face fall at the look of admiration her father is giving her. Mary's hand, which has been tucked into Sita's, falls away.

'I don't want to attend any more, Papa,' Mary says. 'The loud voices scare me.'

She has all the freedom in the world but she doesn't want it, Sita thinks, despising her friend in that moment. *I do, but I don't have it. How is that fair?*

'You don't want to go to the panchayat meetings, not because you're afraid of the loud voices, but because you're jealous of what your father said to me,' Sita accuses Mary later, when they are alone.

Mary's lower lip trembles and she looks set to cry. 'Yes, I am,' she says in a small voice, surprising Sita, who'd been sure she'd deny it as she herself would have done in Mary's place.

'I'm sorry, Sita. I just… I've always felt that my parents want me to be a different person, someone brave and unafraid to take risks, speak her mind. Someone like you.'

'Why would you think that?'

Mary takes a shuddering breath, fiddling with the seam of her dress. 'My father was so impressed when you stood up to the commissioner. He told me I needed to be more like you.'

'Did he?' Sita asks, a warm glow snaking through her.

'You are the daughter my parents wish they had.' Mary sounds dejected.

She might be mild and hesitant and weak, but she is also Sita's only friend, the one person to see Sita for who she really is, who accepts her and admires her, who gives her the boost (through her wholehearted affection and veneration) and the ammunition (by lending books) to survive her stifling days at home.

'Your parents love you, Mary.' Sita squeezes her friend's hand.

'I know.' Mary sniffs. And then in a voice so soft as to be almost unintelligible, 'But they admire *you*.'

'Mary, can we attend the panchayat again? It is only when I'm with you that I feel I have some sort of control over my life. You give me so many new and wonderful experiences. I live for these afternoons at your house. Please?'

And to Sita's great relief, Mary nods, smiling wetly. 'All right, if it means so much to you.'

Sita and Mary attend the panchayat meetings, Mary flinching from the raised voices, shutting her eyes, clamping her palms on her ears during heated disputes, Sita enjoying them hugely, proving to be an excellent conciliator, basking in the glorious taste of brief, magnificent power and the splendid, transitory embrace of approval from Mary's papa and the assembled crowd.

Chapter 9

Mary

Bruise

1936

Voices. Piercing the fug in her brain.

'Mary? Cousin?'

Her eyes hurt. Easier to leave them shut. To allow the images that have been playing across her lids access.

So many images. It is as if her brain has broken open and is spewing memories, images of the girl she did not know she was…

A town on the banks of a river. Familiar as her heartbeat and yet so different from the life she has been living, the life she has unquestioningly accepted as hers.

A precarious bridge held up by rope straddling a river, women gossiping on its bank, bangles clinking, the clothes they've washed and spread out to dry making the grey rocks chorus in festive colour. Gulmohar and jacaranda and neem trees in glorious bloom. A cow on top of a tower, being coaxed down tenderly by burly men.

Paper boats in rainwater. The menthol flavour of eucalyptus and the creamy fragrance of jasmine, the taste of washed grass and churned mud after the rains.

Three children – two girls, one tall, one small, and a boy – walking down an unpaved road that stretches into the red-hazed, blurry-edged horizon, dirt rising off it in a gold-orange cloud. The smell of baked earth, sunshine, ripening fruit. The slimy, rotting-boots odour of stagnant water. The wide, endless sky, hot white.

'Let's see if we can walk blindfolded,' the older girl, brandishing a handkerchief with which to cover their eyes. She is dazzling, messy curls crowding her face, colourful clothes haphazardly draped across her slender frame, her gaze animated, honeyed amber.

Sita. The name arrives unprompted on Mary's lips. Exotic and yet so *known.* As if it has always been there, tucked next to her heart. Waiting to be uncovered.

'What if we trip over a snake, a cobra, and it bites?' The younger girl speaks and Mary realises, with a start, that it is she as a child! Her dress stained, her feet bare, her hair long and flowing and loose.

Sita gives Mary a look: scorn and disdain. Strangely, it inspires confidence in Mary – *Sita thinks the idea is preposterous so it must be.*

'Nothing will happen; Amin and I will guide you, silly.'

Amin. The boy with them. His dirty face, his wide grin. She knows him too. Like Sita, he is Mary's friend.

My friends.

Mary blindfolded, darkness pulsing before closed lids, her legs taking tentative steps over pebbles and mud, her friends' sweaty hands in hers, showing her the way, indolent afternoon breeze rushing in her ears, the burnt smoke caress of heat and adventure and excitement.

'Mary?' Her aunt's voice.

She opens her eyes, with difficulty, blinking in the harsh sting of light.

Her eyes are open and yet it feels as if she is blindfolded. But here there are no friends; only confusion, hurt, pain, the stark purple bruise of betrayal.

Chapter 10

Sita

Water Tower

1926

Sita and Mary are perched in the branches of the mango tree in the fruit orchard behind Mary's house when there's a bustle of activity, the servants carrying a table out and setting up the tea things, almost right underneath them.

A moment later, Mary's mother, who has been sprawled on a blanket in the shade of the banana trees, reading, stumbles into the house, dusting down her dress, which is mud-stained as usual, patting her hair into place and muttering to herself, 'I quite forgot she was coming to tea…'

'Lady Dunstable,' Mary informs Sita, scrunching up her nose. She is straddling a branch, her face framed by mango leaves, tart, pungent, her legs swinging back and forth under the tree. 'She's here to dig.'

'Dig?' Sita asks, fascinated, marking her place in the book she's reading, thinking, *Never a dull day at Mary's.*

'She comes every so often "to dig for gossip," Mama says. She will go back, take tea with the other ladies and they'll discuss the latest thing Mama and Papa have done that goes against the rules of polite society.' Mary's voice is bitter as the mango twig Sita has been chewing absent-mindedly while lost in the story she was reading.

'"Who cares if they gossip about us. We're happy, aren't we?" Mama says.'

'She's right.'

'*I* care.' Mary's eyes sparkle fiercely. 'I don't want them making fun of our dirty house, Mama's messy appearance. I want the other girls to like us. I want their mamas to like my mama.' She takes a breath. 'I want us to be accepted,' she says finally, softly, sounding defeated.

There's a thud below as one of the chairs the servants are setting out falls down. A peacock cries as it runs to join its fellows, plumage closed and yet glinting blue gold.

'If it matters so much to you, why don't you tell your parents?' Sita asks, curious.

'I have. But they say, "It's freeing not to care what people think, Mary. Growing up, we were both bound by constraints, forced to conform. We want you to be free." But I don't *want* to be free, I want to belong.' She sighs. 'And when I say that, they say, "You belong to us." And Papa tickles me until I can't be cross any more.'

Sita feels a stab of envy and pain. Pure and sharp. 'You—' she begins but is interrupted by Mary's mother, who is saying, gaily, 'This way, Lady Dunstable, we'll have tea in the garden as it's such a nice day.'

Lady Dunstable is dressed in a gown far too grand for afternoon tea, looking extravagant in contrast to Mary's mama's simple attire. Her face powder is blotchy, her haughty face set in an expression of endurance as she sits down daintily at the table beside her.

The peacocks strut up to Lady Dunstable hoping for crumbs as she bites into a cucumber sandwich and she startles, her chair rocking so much it is in danger of toppling.

Mary's mama laughs, sweet bells, and the peacocks scatter with a collective screech.

Lady Dunstable winces, setting her sandwich down. 'This garden is ever so wild, Peggy,' she says, taking a delicate sip of her tea and grimacing as if the tea, like the house and the garden, is not to her satisfaction. 'I can recommend a good gardener, if you'd like.'

'Oh, I wouldn't dream of replacing old Khan. He's been with us for ever.'

'And settled in his ways, I see.' Lady Dunstable sniffs, her lips curling with scorn as she takes in the old gardener, who is pottering among the bougainvillea. 'I wouldn't presume to tell you how to run your household, Peggy, but he's a drain on you. It doesn't do to get sentimentally attached to the staff.'

From among the branches, Sita watches the old gardener's face droop and his shoulders slump – he has understood every word that is being said.

'Come,' Sita says and pulls a startled Mary down from the branches with her, jumping onto the ground in front of Lady Dunstable, dispersing a mini-tornado of dust and making the table wobble and a bit of tea spill from the pot.

Lady Dunstable lets out a little shriek of fright, before sneezing from the dust, and Sita sees Mary's mama disguise her smile by biting her lower lip. Over by the bougainvillea, a burst of joyous pink and orange, Khan straightens up and grins, his brown face creasing in a map of wrinkles.

'Your daughter is becoming quite the junglee. You need to take her in hand,' Lady Dunstable says when she has gathered herself, sending Mary a withering glance, not deigning to look at Sita, as she tries to brush the dust off her elaborate gown with her handkerchief.

Mary's face falls while Mary's mama beams as if she has been bestowed a compliment.

Later, as Mary and Sita are snacking on spiced puffed rice before Sita leaves for home, Mary's father arrives.

'The girls saved me from Lady Dunstable today.' Mary's mama smiles as she recounts the afternoon's events.

'You girls are quite something,' Mary's papa says, smiling kindly at both of them. Then, to Sita, 'So, what would you like to be when you grow up, Miss Sita?'

Sita doesn't have to think about it. 'I want to make a difference, change the world.'

Mary's parents' eyes light up. Mary sees it too and Sita notices her toying with the food on her plate.

'But my parents have other plans. They want to get me married.'

'Married? Surely not yet?'

'I've been groomed for marriage since the day I was born. I would love to learn, but they think a woman with too much book knowledge will put suitors off. I'm spirited enough as it is without books giving me more ideas, my ma says. I have a governess and I've been taught some rudimentary accounts and the basics for how to interact with servants and keep house. It's only made me thirst for more...' Although she's been accompanying Mary's papa and Mary to the panchayat, Sita has never had a chance to talk leisurely to either Mary's papa or her mama before now. There's always so much to do while at Mary's house. But now she is finding that, just like at the panchayat, it is so novel to have adults pay attention, listen as if what she says matters. Sita doesn't want to stop.

'But you can read books in English? I've seen you,' Mary's mama says.

'I taught myself to read.' Sita tells them how. 'It was easier once Mary lent me her dictionary.'

Mary's parents exchange glances and when they look at Sita again, their expressions are of admiration, awe. Mary pushes her plate away, her face small.

'Anyway, I'm not going to get married even if it is what my parents want.'

'And how will you achieve this?'

'I'll run away from home,' Sita declares definitively. She has a plan in place – she will steal the dowry her father is saving for her. It is in the safe in his study. She knows where the key is kept, behind the little temple to Lord Vishnu in the puja room. After all, if she is not going to get married, there is no need for that dowry.

'But Sita, that will not do. The world is a big place and…'

What Mary's mama is saying is right, she knows. Sita hasn't planned beyond stealing the money and escaping to the city. And she *is* a tiny bit scared when she considers that eventuality. But… 'I have to. My brother will be going away to school soon and then my home will be even more of a prison than it is now. And I cannot see my married home, if I go along with my parents' plan for me, being much better…'

'Would it help if we were to speak with your parents?' Mary's father asks.

Mary turns away from Sita, arms crossed, lower lip trembling. Sita pays no notice, her heart warm and aglow. Here is an alternative to running away, which, if she is to be honest with herself, is daunting. Perhaps if Mary's parents, the deputy commissioner and his wife, were to speak to her parents, they *might* be convinced to allow her to learn and not get her married off quite so urgently.

'We've been invited to the palace for a celebration next month. We will write to your parents, ask them if we can drop by for a visit on the way.'

'Your friend Mary's parents have written to ask if they can come for a visit,' Sita's mother says, a few days later, her voice grim. 'What have you done?' Scowling at Sita over the top of the letter.

'Nothing,' she says, indignant. 'I've been good.'

'Hmm… Your manners have improved considerably since you started going to Mary's. You no longer climb trees or swim in the pond with the servant boys.'

If only you knew what I get up to at Mary's. Now I have that one day of freedom, I don't mind being tied here as much. And I have the books Mary lends me to read.

'They say you can go to theirs for tea while they're here. Why?'

'Mary is very shy. She likes her own environment.'

Her mother nods. 'I need to plan the menu for when they come. Let's see…'

For once, Sita is glad her mother doesn't really care enough to cross-examine her, see through her. She goes to her room, where she laughs in sheer relief before escaping into the world of the latest book borrowed from Mary.

'Let's have a boat race! We can launch our boats from the rope bridge,' Sita announces on the day Mary's parents leave for Sita's house to talk her parents into allowing her to learn. Sita wants something to do that will distract her from the nerves gnawing at her stomach, choking her throat. Hopefully a boat race will take her mind away from dwelling on the outcome of the meeting between her parents and Mary's.

Will her parents heed Mary's and agree to delaying Sita's marriage, to getting a tutor for her while Kishan is away at school? Every time she envisions being able to read freely instead of doing it furtively, a thrill travels up her body.

'Are you sure it's safe to go on that bridge?' Mary asks, her face troubled.

Sita holds on to the rope and arches her upper body over the rickety bridge, her legs lifting off the ground, only her hands holding her up, the wind buffeting her and rocking the bridge, so she feels weightless, as if she is flying. 'See, it's safe as anything.'

The bridge wobbles precariously, and Mary shivers, even as she gazes in admiration upon Sita.

'Come now, Mary,' Sita urges. She calls Mary by her given name, while everyone in the town, including Amin, refers to her fondly as Missy Baba (which also makes Sita envious – the regard the townspeople have for Mary, the love they bestow on her as a given). 'If it can take my weight, it can take yours.'

'I'm not brave like you, Sita.' Mary's gaze awed, mirroring Amin's as Sita pirouettes and the bridge dances above the river.

'You are, too. You just don't know it.' Sita knows Mary will come round to doing as she asks in a minute. She just needs coaxing, like usual. Amin is always the first to come round to Sita's way of thinking – Sita is the acknowledged leader, especially since the incident with the visiting commissioner – and Mary follows soon after. 'Come on. Didn't we spend the last half-hour making boats so we could sail them?' Sita lets go of the rope, stamping her feet, the bridge swaying like a pendulum in response.

Amin wipes his hands on his grimy vest and, turning to Mary, holds out a dirty palm. Mary seems to come to a decision then. She swallows and grabs his hand, shutting her eyes and trusting Amin to lead her onto the bridge, biting her lower lip to stifle the scream that Sita can see wants to escape.

'Mary, how will you cheer your boat on if your eyes are closed?' Sita commands once Mary's on the bridge.

Mary opens her eyes and Sita sees her take it all in: the three of them standing high above the river, the water rippling beneath, the tart, tamarind-flavoured squall pushing and pulsing at the bridge. Her eyes widen in wonder and she beams.

And seeing the delight on her friend's face, Sita laughs, the curls that refuse to be subjugated into plaits twirling around her face. 'Isn't it glorious? This is why I love coming to you.'

'You can be too pushy for words, Sita,' Mary declares. 'But I put up with your forcefulness because it's down to you that I've met Amin, my *true* friend.'

Sita's eyebrows shoot up, and she is surprised by how hurt she feels.

'Don't look so upset!'

'I'm not…'

'I'm only teasing.' Mary's eyes twinkle mischievously. 'Amin is ordinary. Like me. But you, Sita, you are… beautiful and fearless. Feisty. Untamable. Unafraid of anything. Like my mongoose. Always ready to take on a snake or any predator, no matter how dangerous.'

Sita grins, inhaling lungfuls of fresh, sweet air tasting of friendship and happiness, and Mary laughs. Amin joins in.

'This is why I love you, Sita,' Mary declares. 'Only you would take being compared to a mongoose as a compliment.'

'What do you want to be when you grow up?' Sita asks as they prepare to launch their boats, picturing Mary's parents even now convincing hers to allow Sita to learn.

'A boatman,' Amin says at once, nodding at the boatmen calling to each other across the silvery expanse, their backs gleaming with sweat, their boats drifting lazily on the water.

Sita frowns. 'But boatmen live in huts…'

'What's wrong with that?' Amin asks, gently.

Sita tries not to show her disapproval at Amin's lack of ambition, turning to Mary instead. 'Mary, what do you want?'

'I want to marry a handsome man, like Papa, and have many children. Not one only, like me, although Papa and Mama say I'm perfect, which is why they didn't want more.'

This time Sita cannot help herself. 'Your parents let you read, they are planning to educate you and you want to get married?'

'W-why do you sound so cross?' Mary stammers.

'You could be anything you want to be, Mary. You could make a real difference.' Sita's voice is rising with passion. Sometimes she wants to shake Mary until she sees sense.

She is all set to give her a piece of her mind when Amin asks, 'What do *you* want to be?'

'I want to change the world, make a difference. I want girls to be equal to boys.' Her voice pulsing with zeal.

'But you're better than boys, everyone knows that,' Amin says.

Sita laughs and Mary joins in, the tension of a minute ago dissipating, best friends again.

It is hot, that humid torpor that means rain is imminent. The air heavy with slumber. Thick and dreamlike. The silver sheets of glinting water below them whisper secrets to the fish, scales glittering and winking, bright flashes in the sunlight.

'Go, SS *Maharani*!' Sita cheers her boat on with fierce determination, as if, by the sheer power of her encouragement, the flimsy, sagging paper boat, which is dithering and falling behind, will gain a second wind and win. 'Go!' She stomps up and down the bridge in frustration, the crows sitting on the ropes flying away, squawking in shock.

'Careful, we'll topple into the water at this rate,' Amin says, as he and Mary hold on to the rope for dear life, just as a man runs past them on the bank, yelling, 'My cow!'

They exchange puzzled glances.

'What's happened?' Amin calls to the man.

He barely pauses in his running, his voice a lament, 'My cow, my Nandi.'

'Let's find out,' Sita says and then they are running, off the bridge – Mary curious enough to forget to be afraid – and up the riverbank, across the mud road, raising dust in their wake.

They follow the man, joined by other townspeople, some of them rubbing sleep from their eyes – they were enjoying their afternoon siesta.

A big crowd is gathered at the newly installed water tower that takes pride of place at the field in the centre of town.

And at the top of the tower is a cow, peering down at the assembled crowd from beside the railings and mooing mournfully.

'My Nandi,' cries the man standing directly beneath the cow at the base of the tower. 'She's my livelihood. I don't have fields, and her milk feeds my family – by selling it I get by. What to do now, oh, what to do?'

Sita, along with Mary and Amin, watches, spellbound, as a couple of men climb to the top of the tower and try to urge the cow down the steps, but she resists, mooing piteously.

'How did she get up there?' Sita asks Amin, who is next to her, wonderingly.

Amin only shrugs, both he and Mary squinting up at the cow, Mary's hands clasped together as if in prayer.

Sita is so caught up in the drama that it takes her a while to understand that someone is chanting 'Missy Baba', insistently, repeatedly. That everyone has stopped looking at the cow and is looking at Mary instead. That even the cow is not howling any more.

'What is it?' Sita whispers.

Or does she? Her voice seems to have stopped working all of a sudden.

Mary is also mute, staring wordlessly at her ayah, who has suddenly appeared, along with the servants from Mary's house; the whole household is here, it seems, including Sita's own maid, looking aghast.

They have been crying.

At the sight of Mary, fresh tears run freely down their faces.

'Don't worry, the cow will be fine,' Mary murmurs, but Sita can see the terror that is taking over the incomprehension on her face. The terror that has seized Sita's heart in a vice.

They're not here about the cow.

Mary's ayah scoops her up in her arms although she is too old to be carried.

'What's happened?' Sita finally discovers her voice, surprised to find it is trembling, broken.

Over her ayah's shoulder Mary's petrified gaze meets Sita's.

'An accident. On the way to your parents' house.' Mary's ayah glares at Sita, swollen, tear-spattered lids, red, bruised eyes. Is Sita imagining the accusation in her voice? 'The sahib and memsahib are both gone.'

'Gone?'

Sita is not sure who speaks. Her throat is suddenly dry, sore.

'Dead.' A whisper but it resounds in that space, the hot press of people, the odour of onions and sweat, the blinding sun, the trapped cow's piteous calls.

And into the shocked silence, a child's voice, taut with pain. Mary's finger pointing right at Sita, 'Oh, Sita, why? Why did you have to make them go? If it wasn't for you they'd still be alive.'

Chapter 11

Mary

Ordered World

1936

'You lied to me,' Mary says.

She is in the library, her favourite room in this house, which she has always assumed was the only home she has known. But now, after Major Digby's visit, and the ambush of memories that has left her reeling, reminiscences of a different life in a country across the world, she doesn't know what – if anything – to believe.

How much of what she remembers is true? And surely they must be true, these vivid images that assault her without pause, so real that she can smell the heat, taste the spices, feel the sweat dribbling down her back, arching along her brow? And if they *are* true, then how could she have forgotten them so completely, blocked them so thoroughly up until now? And on the heels of confusion, anger, bitter red...

'We didn't lie as such...' Her aunt, standing behind the desk, beside her husband. So collected and remote.

Fury, fiery orange. 'I believed my parents died in the war when I was a baby, that I never knew them...'

Even as she speaks, Mary chokes on the overpowering flavour of shock and grief, Ayah's scent of fried onions and perspiration as she clasped Mary to her (Ayah – that word returning to her along with memories of the warm woman, her childhood companion whom she loved so much); the piteous moos of the cow stuck atop the water tower; the hot press of people rushing to comfort her, a whole town offering her love; Amin's hand squeezing hers, his face raw and stunned, eyes sprouting tears, the first time she'd seen him crying, her friend who was always smiling; Sita's dazed expression. Sita...

Mary, her words dripping with pain, 'Oh, Sita, why? Why did you have to make them go? If it wasn't for you they'd still be alive.'

Sita's face crumpling...

Mary shuts her eyes tight against the stabbing wound, dormant for so long, that has reignited now and flares and burns with passion.

Her aunt is saying, 'You were lost and grieving and traumatised. You would not speak and if anyone mentioned India you would shut your ears and sob. So we stopped talking about India, bringing up your past, and somehow along the way you came to believe that your parents had died here, during the war.'

Rage, white, blinding, giving her, quiet, biddable Mary, the means to challenge her aunt. 'You're saying *I* lied to myself? If so, then why didn't you set me right, why allow me to believe an untruth all these years?' She hates the tremor in her voice.

'It was just easier...'

And once again, fury igniting in Mary the courage to stand up to her aunt. 'For whom, me or you?'

'For almost a year after you came to us, you refused to speak at all.' Her aunt's voice uncharacteristically soft.

And again a memory. Mary on the ship to England – the bewildering journey she'd been forced to make.

'The journey home,' everyone declared.

She opened her mouth to protest, to say that *India* was home, but no words came, the aroma of onions and sweat and heat and loss smothering her as the last image of her parents bloomed in her mind's eye: her mother in her travelling cloak, dancing eyes, brown curls escaping her hat, bright blue, clashing with her pale yellow dress, bending down to kiss Mary, her smell of talc and roses; her father lifting her up and wheeling her around, lime and tobacco and comfort, his stubble grazing her cheek.

Mary's voice had disappeared, like her parents. They were in an accident and inexplicably, *gone*. They had said goodbye to her as always. 'See you soon,' as always. 'Have fun,' as always, eyes twinkling.

And that was it.

She wouldn't be seeing them again. How to equate this supposed truth with the mother and father so alive and real in her head?

And that is why she had made up her mind to stay inside her head. To not speak; for if she did, the world she had fashioned for herself, where her mother and father were alive, just away, would be shattered and she'd be left with this one, where nothing made sense. Where she was on a ship on high seas bound for a country that was supposedly 'home' but where she had never been, leaving everything familiar behind, even the name she was known to the townspeople by: 'Missy Baba'.

Her chaperone, Miss Devon, was nothing but kind – urging Mary to eat, holding her when she woke, whimpering, from nightmares into a world that was another nightmare, with nothing familiar in it, nothing loved. Miss Devon didn't push her to talk and yet, Mary couldn't quite warm to her: she was not Ayah. And just by being there, she represented everything Mary had lost.

Mary blinks, coming back into the present, the high ceiling of the library, the ink and paper perfume of knowledge.

'Any inadvertent mention of India or your past and you would retreat into your shell, become morose, refuse to eat, to engage.'

Another image: standing at the base of the steps leading up to the grand house, *this* house, the estate surrounding it stretching away, encompassing shiny green lawns, tidy flower beds, with tennis courts beyond.

The air, tasting of outdoors, green and fresh, stroking her cheeks with icy fingers.

It was summer, Miss Devon had said, but the sun in England was lukewarm. Not angry and tempestuous and passionate, like in India, arousing a response from you in the form of sweat, plastering your clothes to your body. The sun here seemed diffident. It barely shone, much of the time hiding timidly behind clouds.

Like me, Mary had thought then. *Papa and Mama wanted me to be like the sun in India, bold and fiery, but I am more like the sun here.*

Her parents had wanted her to break rules, defy them and rise above them, but Mary preferred the rigidity and structure imposed by the rules. She longed for boundaries – they made her feel safe, giving her leeway to push against them, knowing they were there to stop her going too far. And as she looked at the clean, perfectly maintained grounds of her aunt and uncle's home in England, the plants neatly contained in their arbours, everything ordered, following a pattern, sticking to a rigid code, she had felt, for the first time since she was uprooted from her home, her life, something other than sorrow – a tentative flutter of hope in her grieving, battered soul.

'You spent most of your time here, hiding from the world, from all of us,' her aunt says, waving her hand around the library.

Now that the dam blocking her past has burst open, Mary is able to recall her first few days in England. The confusion, the upset, the grief… The only thing that kept her going was rules, order, the comfort she derived from the structure to her life.

Although she couldn't speak, put into words her befuddlement, her ache, she learned what was expected of her very quickly. Here, in this ordered world, with its blessedly rigid code of conduct, there was only one *proper* way of doing things. Mary, undone and grieving, grasped at these rules, using them as a bridge across the crater that had opened up inside of her since the loss of her parents and her home and all she once knew, using propriety as a crutch. But all the while she was racked with guilt, as if she was betraying her parents in some crucial way.

After meeting Papa's family in England, she understood that perhaps she was like them. The family who had disowned him.

'Do you miss them?' she had once asked Papa when she was a child.

'Hmm…?'

He had finished reading to her – a book about family – and she was drifting off to sleep. He looked so out of place, sitting in her small chair, among her neatly arranged bookshelves, her colour-coded toys, with his wild hair, his crumpled shirt, his wise, kind eyes.

'Other parents have to nag their children to clean their room, whereas yours is always perfect, Mary,' Papa was fond of saying. He chuckled when he said it but she had sometimes wondered if perhaps he wanted her to be more like those other children.

'Your family in England?' she prompted.

He rubbed his eyes. 'Sometimes, yes.'

'I would miss you very much if I lived thousands of miles away, Papa,' she had said.

His eyes shone even as he smiled. 'I know. And I do miss them. But I felt stifled there, Mary. Propriety mattered more to my parents than anything else. They were sticklers for rules, bound by tradition. Everything had to be done right.'

I'm like that, Mary had thought. 'Papa, I…' *Do you feel stifled by me?* she wanted to ask. *Will you leave me too, one day?* But the words stuck in her throat, a briny lump.

'Marrying your mother was the last straw for them. But marrying your mother, coming to India, was the best thing I ever did.'

'Why didn't they want you to marry Mama?'

Papa had rubbed an arm across his eyes again. 'It's late, Mary. I'll answer your questions tomorrow. Sleep now, goodnight.'

It took her a long time to fall asleep that night, and when she woke the next morning, she had deliberately pulled all her books to the floor, but although she tried to shut the door on the mess, she couldn't bear to leave her room in that state and spent the next half-hour tidying them again.

'During your first week with us, I came upon you, huddled here, in the library,' her aunt goes on, 'clutching a book to your chest and rocking with upset. The book and your clothes were wet with tears but they kept on coming, endless.'

And there it is, clear as anything, a memory: herself in the library, her refuge, with its vast collection of books providing entry into other worlds far away from her disjointed, fractured one. She had found a tome with her father's name on it, *Richard Brigham*. She had brushed her hand over the letters, touching the words written by him, the pages her father had handled once, when he was a boy himself. It was a book about India, conjuring images she had tried to forget – dust-swathed, rain-freckled green fields, the river swelling in the monsoons, the boatmen's haunting song, her parents, their cool bungalow, Ayah's chapped, beloved, soothing hands, the garden with its mango, jackfruit and guava trees, the snake that had once crawled into her toy box and which had been attacked by the mongoose she kept reluctantly as a pet even though she was scared of it, Amin and Sita, boat races and kite flying, laughter and childhood and innocence, happiness.

She shut her eyes against the barrage of tears. Yet still they came. And then she was sobbing, sitting in the library, the yellow must-and-knowledge scent of books, the green lawns visible through the window, cool air caressing her face, the taste of another country in her mouth.

'We removed every single one of your father's books. We made the library Richard Brigham- and India-proof,' her aunt is saying. 'We thought,' she adds – she sounds strange: helpless, pleading and defiant all at the same time, a tone Mary has never heard her prim guardian use before – 'not mentioning your past, erasing all evidence of it, would help you move on, settle into your new life.' She takes a breath. 'You were struggling, Mary, sinking into grief. We did what we thought best.' Her voice crisp now, defiance winning.

During those first days in England, memory, fickle and unreliable, assaulted at the oddest times – while she was riding in the grounds with her cousins, the air smelling of summer, cut grass and pine cones, perfumed with honeysuckle and flavoured with birdsong, the laughter of her cousins, her pony snorting as she galloped, her eyes closed and the taste of overripe, fermenting apples on her lips – devastating her afresh, showing her up as a traitor to the memory of her parents. Here she was, living the life they had resented with the family who had disowned her father, who had not wanted him to marry her mother.

And so to survive, Mary entombed her memories, systematically wiping away all thought of, longing for, ache pertaining to her childhood in a scorching, dust-spattered, untamed country.

And if some mornings she woke with her pillow wet with tears, the taste of salt and sweat, humidity and yearning on her lips, she ignored that too, pushing open her window and taking a deep, bracing breath of the frosted blue air of the country that was now home.

Her aunt is saying, 'And then one day, almost a year after you had arrived, you started talking. And it was as if your past in India had not happened.'

In England, Mary's days were full: being tutored by governesses, going for strolls on the lawns, taking tea with distinguished visitors, taking the air in carriages in the park, visiting friends, having new gowns made, buying bonnets, pianoforte lessons, sewing, reading in the library and, finally, bed.

And in this way days passed. Years passed. A lifetime created between the girl she is now and the girl she had been. She was part of a new family that, in time, became the only family she knew. An English girl in an English home, burying a colourful past.

'As time went by, you came out of yourself. You blossomed. But you had episodes when a smell, a word, triggered something – a fragment of the world you were suppressing. We all held our breath then but you were fine. Until Major Digby.' A skein of bitterness seeping into her aunt's cool voice. 'I suppose it had to come some time. You couldn't have gone through life repressing what had happened, although we hoped—'

'I would like to see him again.'

'Excuse me?' Her aunt looks surprised.

Mary has, for all these years, done everything that has been expected of her. She has been dutiful, feeling indebted to her aunt and uncle, and never once challenged them, asked anything of them.

But now, she doesn't feel any obligation to her guardians, her mouth hot and burning with the sting of hurt and deception.

'Major Digby. I would like to meet with him.'

'Are you sure…?' Her aunt sounding hesitant for the first time.

'Yes.' She is sharp, short. Not quite able to forgive her aunt for lying to her. 'And I would like my father's books, please. I think I am ready to read them now.'

Her aunt nods, once, and it is Mary's turn to be surprised at how easily she has capitulated. 'I will have your father's books returned to the library. And we will invite Major Digby to tea next week.'

Chapter 12

Sita

Great Escape

1927

Sita hides among the gunny bags, trying not to gag from the pungent tang of manure and pulses assaulting her nose. She has managed over the course of the last half-hour to sidle up to the grime-stained window and peek at the kaleidoscopic, hypnotic world carousing past her, her head and mouth covered by the bags, never mind the stench.

Noise, busyness. Porters carrying luggage, vendors calling out their wares. The British sahibs in their pressed suits and gelled hair, with their assortment of servants hefting bags and sundries. The memsahibs in their flowing dresses and elaborate hats in eye-catching colours – Sita spies a veritable garden of flowers on one hat, a cornucopia of fruit on another, attracting flies even though they are fake. The memsahibs are exotic blooms wilting in the harsh Indian sun, their pale faces dotted with sweat, their rouge collecting in messy clumps, looking harassed and fed up as their maids locate their carriages.

Sita watches sari-clad ladies, heads covered by veils and yet commanding, their entourages following. Their men up ahead with their own lot of servants.

The third-class passengers crowd their compartments, angling for a foothold, pushing and shoving to get inside.

'So cramped we can't even breathe, inhaling each other's sweat,' Kishan's servants, who travelled up to the school with him when he stayed there for a week to see how he liked it, have told Sita, when she has quizzed them.

'Don't you feel sick?'

'We do, but what can you do?' They had shrugged, taking huge gulps of the creamy, cardamom-spiced tea provided by the cook. 'And at every station, we had to fight our way out of the crush and supply the master with tea and food.'

'At least then we could fill our lungs with station air,' one of the other servants said, shoving a laddoo the size of Sita's fist into his mouth. She watched in fascination as, in two bites, it disappeared, not a crumb spilling.

'Yes, but afterwards we'd have to fight to get back in again, try and claw some space in which to stand nose to nose with someone else until the next station.'

Initially Sita's plan was to travel in the third-class carriage. But hearing this, she had changed her mind. She is glad that, serendipitously, the carriage she climbed into transports goods (from the smell she thinks it is horse food; it stinks of hay and dung and pulses), and not luggage, for surely she would be found out by one of the many servants hauling bags inside, or indeed crushed to death by flying baggage – she has witnessed the servants just chucking it in when their masters are not watching.

Sita bunches her fists in frustration. She wants to be on the platform, mingling with the crowds. As it is, she watches furtively, unable to resist the scene before her, her eyes staring out from among the gunny bags.

Beggar children wearing rags, sunken, hungry eyes, some carrying babies although children themselves, their hands stretched out for coins, pass beneath her window.

Steam escapes the kiosk where people mill about drinking coffee, honey-sweet with thick milk skin floating on top – Kishan has described it to her often. 'There's nothing quite like station coffee, Sita – I don't know what they put in it. At any rate, Savi at home cannot recreate it. I have described it to her and she has tried. It is served in these small tumblers, no bigger than my middle finger, and over too soon.'

Sita's stomach rumbles hungrily even though she is nauseous from the gag-inducing smell of the gunny bags.

'Thief!' someone cries and there is sudden uproar. One of the beggar children has stolen a samosa from the kiosk and is running past Sita's window, a gang of men following.

Escape, Sita thinks. He is fast, nimble, weaving between legs, overturning luggage, the memsahibs cross and berating their servants for their possessions being spread all over the dirty station floor.

After a bit, Sita sees the men come back without the beggar boy, and breathes a sigh of relief.

She too will be caught sooner or later. And then she will be in big trouble. But…

Since Mary's parents' death, her life has been unendurable. No prospect of getting away from home, no weekly visits to Mary, no freedom, no books borrowed from her friend to alleviate the monotony of her days.

Mary's accusation when they found out about her parents' accident – the last time Sita saw her – had hurt more than Sita will admit, even to herself.

'Oh, Sita, why? Why did you have to make them go? If it wasn't for you they'd still be alive,' her best friend had cried, her voice raw with pain.

'She didn't mean it,' her maid had consoled on their way back home, as Sita sat shell-shocked beside her.

But in the interminable weeks that followed, Sita couldn't help wondering if there was some truth in Mary's words. After all, Sita's father always maintained: 'You brought bad luck when you were born and I'm still paying for it.'

Her mother never failed to remind her: 'You have the kind of character that will land you in trouble if not reined in.'

Mary's parents, who were going to convince Sita's parents to allow her to learn, to not get her married so urgently, were dead. Mary had left for England...

And when her brother prepared to leave too, to go away to school, so Sita would be left at home with just her parents and their single-minded agenda for her – her father, she understood, was actively looking for suitors for her – no prospect of joy, of lightness, of books, even Kishan's cast-offs, she made up her mind. She would go with Kishan to his school, beg him, once they were there, to allow her to stay. She knew he would capitulate – although her parents were immovable, unimpressed by her pleas, her brother, at least, cared for her, having always felt guilty about the different, superior way he was treated.

This was a much better plan, she decided, than running away into the unknown. At least this way she had an ally in her brother; and, feeling fragile after losing Mary and her parents, she needed one.

Hence this – her great escape. She hopes she won't be caught and punished, but even if she is, the experience itself, after days of mind-numbing boredom at home – made even more intolerable since the freedom she'd sampled when with Mary – is worth it.

A vendor walks by her window, selling toys. Wooden dolls with beautifully woven garments.

The train hisses and steams, it judders and grumbles like a toddler preparing to throw a giant tantrum.

She is struck by a sudden qualm. *Should I have let Kishan know?*

But if she had told him in advance of her planned escapade, he would have talked her out of it. Kishan is a supportive big brother, but he's a stickler for rules.

She will surprise him at the next station when the train stops and there is no immediate danger of being caught and made to go home – she will peek into every first-class carriage until she finds her brother. He is travelling with his mathematics tutor, a gentle, kind man – she is sure she can convince both of them to let her travel with them to the school. After that she's sure that together, she and Kishan can come up with something… Kishan *has* to stick up for her. She deserves this much.

Move, she urges the train. Once it's moving, she'll feel better, and the anxiety and nausea gagging her throat will hopefully ease.

She scans the platform for the guard. There he is, a portly, puffed-up man, holding a flag, a whistle in his mouth. Why is he not blowing the whistle, waving the flag?

Come on!

A vendor hawks groundnuts; she can almost taste their smoky, nutty flavour on her lips. Another chops onions and chillies, and adds them along with a small mountain of tomatoes to a pail of puffed rice, spicing it liberally with a fistful of chilli powder and squeezing a couple of limes over the concoction.

Sita watches families sitting on their luggage, opening tiffin boxes and tucking into rotis wrapped round spicy potato, and her stomach rumbles some more. A vendor cooks puris, golden balls puffing in the sizzling oil, which she knows will go poof when bitten into, oily steam escaping as the round ball collapses into doughy perfection.

A family comes by, the father and son up ahead, mother, her head covered by a veil, leading a small girl of around three, who peers curiously into Sita's carriage. The little girl's eyes sweep over the gunny bags and before Sita can duck for cover, the girl's inquisitive gaze makes contact with hers. The girl startles, her face crumpling as she tries and fails to make sense of a pair of tawny eyes peering out of a mass of gunny bags. She starts to cry, pointing, and Sita hides, pulling the gunny bags completely over her head. She can just about hear the girl's wails among the station clamour, her mother consoling her.

Move, train, before someone else sees me and raises the alarm.

And then, a familiar voice. 'Miss Sita, where are you?'

Her maid.

Followed by the more strident tones of her governess, who falls asleep after her midday meal, snoring with her mouth open, so it takes all of Sita's considerable willpower not to stuff something into her mouth – an insect, perhaps – or to plug her nostrils, from which fine hairs emerge, shivering in the sonorous exhalations that escape her nose. 'You're here, we know it. You left your shawl behind in the carriage.'

Oh no, she thinks. *How silly of me.* She had slipped in beside her brother's cases when the servants were occupied with something else, congratulating herself on her ingenuity. But she had climbed out in an almighty rush, deftly darting into the station before the servants came to see to the cases. She had forgotten all about her shawl.

'Where are you? We've spoken to the guard and the train won't move until you make yourself known.'

The scent of gunny sacks and frustration. The ache of not being able to go to school like her brother, just because she is a girl.

And she desperately needs to use the lavatory.

Sita pushes off the sacks and stands up, her legs cramped from squatting for so long. She dusts down her clothes and comes to the door of the carriage on faltering feet.

So much for her adventure, her great escape.

Her mother's maid and her governess are walking up and down the train carriages, peering into windows. She waits, the taste of salt and defeat in her mouth, feeling faint from tiredness and upset. She breathes in the scene around her: bustling people, their expressions veering from anxious to bored to impatient to excited, all going somewhere – unlike her.

Her maid spots her first. 'There you are!'

Then they are running towards Sita, her maid agile, her governess lagging, tripping on her heavy, laboured tread.

Up ahead, the little girl who saw Sita hiding, in her mother's arms now, meets Sita's gaze as she stands at the door to the carriage and gasps, dissolving in fresh tears.

Kishan must be in his compartment, unaware of the commotion Sita is causing. He will go away to school, soak up knowledge *she* is desperate to gain.

She *hates* the sheer injustice of it.

The governess and maid have caught up with her now and try to get her off the carriage, down the steps.

People are turning to stare and point. The guard ambles over, whistle in his mouth, his uniform stained with sweat, his face shiny with it. The beggar children sidle away from him, out of sight.

And behind the guard, her brother, worry and shock playing on his face to see her emerge from a train carriage when he thought he'd said goodbye to her at home. She feels a burst of hope. All is not yet lost. Kishan can sort it out, perhaps even persuade her governess into allowing Sita to go with him…

'Sita! What on earth are you doing here?'

'I want to go to school with you,' she pleads.

'Your brother's school is only for boys,' the governess says, panting from the unaccustomed exertion of running, scorn in her voice.

Oh! Sita hadn't even thought to check. She has made so many mistakes. If only she had talked with Kishan, shared her plan with him, she would have found this out.

Nevertheless, she juts her chin out. 'Then I want to go to a girls' school.'

'You don't know how lucky you are that your parents are even hiring me to teach you to keep house – other girls do not have this privilege, they're married as soon as they come of age. Your parents have indulged you and you repay them like this?'

A crowd has gathered around them now, and they nod in agreement at the governess's words.

'This train won't start unless you come away,' her governess scolds.

'Oh no!' people in the crowd mutter. 'If it's late leaving, it will be *very* late arriving – it always seems to lose hours on its journey,' they grumble. 'Get a move on, girl,' they nudge.

The guard huffs, looking pointedly at the station clock.

Sita looks to Kishan. 'Please,' she entreats her brother, 'I don't want to go home…'

But Kishan's face is wavering and is that impatience she sees in his eyes?

'Sita, you're not a child any more. You'll be married soon. You cannot carry on like this.'

Sita recoils as if slapped. First Mary, her best friend, turning on her. Now Kishan, parroting their parents' words.

A flash of guilt on her brother's face, replaced almost immediately by a flush of embarrassment at the other passengers' hectoring. He is discomfited at the scene Sita is causing, piqued, like the other passengers, that she's holding up the train. He wants her gone, she understands, so he can embark upon the next stage of his life unencumbered.

'I hate you.' Sita sniffs, tasting anger and betrayal on her tongue, salty violet.

'Come.' Her governess pulls at her hand, none too gently.

It is too much. Disappointment and hurt and upset rise up Sita's stomach in a bilious green wave and she is sick, wiry strands of phlegm, freckled with last night's rice, undigested because of sleeplessness due to excitement, spewing all over her governess's mud-stained sandals, Sita's dream of going to school and learning alongside her brother spattering her governess's feet.

Chapter 13

Mary

Precious

1936

Mary dreams of India, of the town that was her playground, where she roamed free, with a bossy, beautiful girl and a boy with a cheeky grin and dust-stained face. Ayah, bangles tinkling, the music of anklets, her gentle voice singing haunting lullabies in the language Mary learned before she learned English. Having her siesta alongside Ayah on a mat on the veranda, tasting Ayah's fantastic dreams, the fruit-tipped breeze making Ayah's sari pallu, with which she covered her face, dance. Cook's maid humming bhajans in a falsetto. The taste of Cook's rice pudding. Mama: liquid almond eyes, the way her whole face softened when she looked at Mary, the way she said her name, as if it was a gift, precious. Papa: the twinkle in his eyes when he smiled at Mary, letting her try on his hats, his smell of lime and tobacco, sitting on his lap and feeling loved. Humid heat. The fresh pink taste of watermelon. Mango juice running down her chin. Sunshine.

She wakes shivering, lukewarm sun failing to pierce the dour awning of rain-distended clouds. She wakes in England, tasting India in her mouth, after years of keeping her past buried, her childhood at bay…

*

'Are you quite all right, Mary?' her cousins chime.

You knew all along, she wants to yell. *You all conspired against me, hid my past from me.*

But they are not at fault, not really. They were only doing what they thought best. Nevertheless, it hurts. She thought she knew her place in the world. But now, she is not so sure.

Who am I?

Am I the demure, reserved English girl who takes solace in rules, who is looking forward to coming out at court, to getting married and running a household of her own? If so, then I'm doing a disservice to my parents, who wanted so much more for me.

This is why she had blocked her memories as an orphaned, grieving child, she understands. To avoid this dichotomy that tugged at her. The dilemma of trying to identify with the girl her parents had wanted her to be while also recognising the person she really was inside.

She stands at the window, suddenly claustrophobic in the vast house, looking out at orderly lawns, neat clipped hedges, the orangery with its resplendent glass dome, and recalling dusty roads churned to slush in the monsoons. Dancing in the rain, face tipped to the showering clouds, the aroma of wet mud and ripening fruit, the warm earthy flavour of happiness.

'Mary?'

The taste of dung and dust, hair in her mouth, flying all around her face – the memory so vivid. She can see herself in the bullock cart, the bulls' curved horns at odds with their placid eyes – Sita had convinced one of the townspeople to give herself, Mary and Amin a ride. Sitting atop the mound of hay, the three of them feeling like kings; Mary had had a rash from the hay afterwards and Ayah had to slather her in lotion.

Mama sewing in her armchair of an evening as light seeped from the sky and mosquitoes cavorted despite the flares of strong-smelling herbs the servants had lit to dissuade them, while Papa read to Mary, perched on his knee sipping hot cocoa. Her papa's rumbling voice in her ear, the delicious taste of chocolate and contentment. A coconut falling off the tree with a thud, the birds nestling among the fronds squawking their uproar at this interruption. Papa taking a break from reading to sip his glass of whisky, sunset amber, the world mellow and perfumed with evening, cooling dust, ripe fruit, roasted spices, smoke from the water being heated for Mary's wash puncturing the sky, which looked like Cook's rainbow cake, layers of marshmallow pink and jellied orange and soft cerise and a blushing red.

Once, in the thick heat of summer, Papa had declared it too hot to sleep indoors. The servants had carried Papa and Mama's bed into the garden, setting it down under the mango and tamarind, lime and guava trees. The three of them had squeezed onto the one bed, under the mosquito net, the stars winking above them. There was a dust storm that night and they woke to grit flung by a capricious wind upon their bodies, into their mouths. They had rushed indoors, the servants carrying their bedding, sand stinging their eyes.

'Mary?' Iris's arms round her.

She opens her mouth, but no words emerge.

Her cousins look mortified as she turns away, failing to hide her tears. They lead her to an armchair, fetch hot, sweet tea, make a fuss of her. They are being kind, but now that the memories are ambushing her, all she wants is for things to go back to how they were before. She wants not their soft arms round her, their smell of rose water and compassion, but her mama's arms, her ayah's. Her papa's soothing voice, the way it softened when speaking to her. Her friends' – Amin and Sita's – sweaty hands in hers as they planned their next adventure. She wants, after years of living a different life, a life that has brought her happiness of sorts, a life she has liked – even loved – to go home.

Home. The thought startles her.

India was home, once upon a time. But since then, this house, which spurned her father because he didn't conform, has been home. Her cousins, aunt and uncle, her family.

So why now, when the sadness she buried along with her memories is making itself felt, is she thinking like this? Feeling this longing for something that's over, a way of life that disintegrated that hot afternoon by the water tower, the stranded cow mooing piteously, lost and disorientated, like Mary when she learned that her parents were gone...

Chapter 14

Sita

Invisible Thread

1927

Sita was born during a storm that uprooted trees and killed several people. It caused a giant wave of water to wash up to shore and took several lives and livelihoods, houses and livestock with it.

'It was the biggest storm of our lifetimes,' her mother had said, nodding portentously, and her many servants – one fanning her, the other supplying paan, yet another massaging her legs (which seem to be perpetually aching, although she never walked much) – all nodded a beat after, as if they are puppets being controlled by an invisible thread pulled by Sita's mother.

Her mother always sits in the same place, on a comfortable armchair in the dining hall with its view of the kitchen, her feet resting on a pouffe. From this seat, her throne, she orders everyone about: servants, children. Sita's mother is always frowning (except with regards to her husband), always displeased and, most times, this displeasure is directed at her daughter.

As now.

Looking at her mother's face, purple as a ripe aubergine, Sita wishes she was on the train, which left in a puff of steam and grinding wheels, whining machinery, as soon as she disembarked, sighing as if in relief to be rid of her.

From the kitchen drift aromas of lunch – frying dough and lentils and something sweet, milky. Sita's stomach – empty of its contents after she disgorged them onto her governess's feet – rumbles loudly. She is dirty – she wants to wash the train's grime, steam and coal and gunny sacks, the faint whiff of manure, off her body. But first she must endure her mother's anger.

As she waits for her mother's rage-swollen mouth to form words heavy enough to impose upon Sita the gravity of her crime, Sita's mind drifts, offering a respite from her upset at her brother's perfidy and the hopelessness that has taken her body captive, that is threatening to leak from her eyes and make her legs wobble, her whole body judder and shake, her teeth rattle.

'When you were born—' her ayah would say.

'Yes, I know, there was a storm.' Sita would cut her ayah off.

'It doesn't do to be impatient. Let me finish,' her ayah would admonish affectionately as she oiled and plaited Sita's hair in the shade of the banana trees in the somnolent haze of late afternoon, Sita squinting up at the unrelenting sun and finding it hard to imagine a rainstorm.

'The wind croaked and screamed, echoing your mother's cries, and the tamarind tree fell on the house.'

'What?'

Sita turned to face her ayah, earning a gentle rap on her temple with the comb the woman was wielding. This was the first she had heard of a tree toppling onto the house.

'What have I told you about sitting still while I comb your hair?'

'But Ayah, this is important! Why did nobody tell me before, when it has to do with *my* birth?'

'Do you want to hear the rest or not?'

'Yes!'

'Then sit still.' Her ayah smiled warmly as Sita sat very straight and attentive. 'Your ma was safe – she was at the other end of the house. It was the servants' wing that was destroyed.'

'Oh!'

Ayah lowered herself onto the soft bed of fragrant leaves beside Sita.

'Thankfully no one was hurt; all the servants were attending to your mother. There was an almighty creaking and the loudest crash you can imagine. But at that exact moment, you arrived, purple and screaming. Even while your parents were celebrating you, they were bemoaning the damage to the house.'

'So is that why Ma says I was trouble from the day I was born?' Sita had asked and her ayah had cackled loudly, agitating the crows perched upon the branches above them.

'The priest at your naming ceremony decreed that a cost would be extracted for any good fortune where you were concerned.'

'Now I understand why Baba always complains that I cost him dearly, that he's still paying for it, in addition to saving for my dowry.'

Her ayah had gathered her close. 'Don't mind him, he's joking.' Her voice soft and melty as a rasgulla, syrup and comfort.

'He's *not*. He's always angry when he looks at me. I know why now.'

Kishan had arrived then. 'Savi has made peda. If you don't come quickly, I'll finish it all.' Twisting her arm, pulling her along. 'You're nothing but trouble and I have to put up with it.' Expertly imitating Ma's voice, the put-upon moan she employed when their father was around.

Sita had burst into peals of laughter, in danger of choking on Savi's divine peda, milk and sugar dissolving in soft creamy puffs in her mouth.

Now she stands before her mother, awaiting punishment, hollow with the ache of her brother's rejection. His gaze, as if she was a nuisance, a burden, so like their father's when he deigns to look her way. Sita had thought, after Mary left, that at least she had her brother on her side… Now she understands that she cannot rely on anyone.

'You're from a good family; we're related to the king.' Her mother has found the words she wants to say, her fury-inflamed mouth spitting them out. 'You cannot, *will not*, behave in this way again.' A breath, then, 'By creating a scene in public, you have compromised your chances of making a good match…'

Great, Sita thinks.

'We cannot allow this to continue. Before you alienate every suitor in the country, we have to get you married. Your father has been making enquiries, but we were dithering in the hope of interest from some of the nobler houses. But as it stands, we will go with the suitors who have shown interest.'

'Wh-what do you mean?'

'You'll be married to the suitor whose horoscope matches yours most closely, hopefully within the next few weeks. Until then, you'll continue with your music, singing and dance lessons, although I've a good mind to stop everything. The teachers will come here in the mornings, but your governess will accompany you everywhere, chaperone you. You will not go anywhere on your own again.'

The governess smiles at Sita, without joy. A mere lifting of her lips to acknowledge what the mistress is saying. Sita ignores her as her mother's words sink in.

Although she's known all her life that this is the fate her parents have envisioned for her, she's never fully believed it; although in recent weeks her mother had mentioned that they were looking for suitors for Sita, she secretly hoped that it wasn't true, that her parents were using marriage as an empty threat. Surely they wouldn't give her to a strange man without her consent, against her will?

But she's been wrong all along and the truth is the taste of bile, vomit-green, coating her throat.

Married within the next few weeks…

She thought there could be nothing worse than being stuck at home without the possibility of freedom. Turns out there is.

At least home is a prison she knows. She has her well-worn, much-read books under her bed, including the dictionary and the copy of *The Wind In The Willows* from Mary.

Sita's stomach threatens to revolt again, although there is nothing in it but helplessness, and a growing, gnawing rage. She bites her tongue until she tastes blood. She hates her parents, she hates her governess, she hates her life. She fiercely pushes away the tears of desperation and despair blooming in her eyes. She will not cry.

She swallows, speaking past the angry, wretched lump in her throat, pleading with her mother for the first time she can recall. 'Please, Ma. I don't want to get married.'

Her mother's voice softer, almost gentle, 'This is for your own good, child. It does not do to be so spirited. It only leads to problems.'

'How is getting married for my own good?' Sita's voice tight with frustration.

'You need the protection of a man, Sita—'

'I don't need *any* man to protect me,' she bites out. The governess raises her eyebrows at this proclamation.

'You've only ever lived at home, a sheltered life. You don't know how ruthless the world is.'

Angry tears spring in Sita's eyes, hot and fiery. 'I've only ever lived at home, been so sheltered, not because I want to, but because you've forcibly kept me here. I want to experience the world, ruthless or not. I want to see what I'm missing out on.'

'This is exactly why we want you safely married.' Her mother's voice sharp, losing all of its softness.

'How is getting me married the answer?' Sita asks again, her voice a plea. How can her mother not see how miserable she is? Surely mothers are supposed to gauge their children's pain?

But then, her parents have never paid attention to her except when she demands it through what they deem as mischief. She is a burden to them – although she has covertly, wishfully, hoped they'll prove her wrong, show her that they care, *listen* to her instead of ignoring her or being outraged by her actions and opinions.

But now she knows. The truth acrid in her mouth, burning in her chest. Her hopes and dreams don't matter, not unless they tally with what her parents want for her. She is not a person in their eyes, just a duty to be executed.

Surely enough, 'One day you will thank me,' her mother says, turning away towards the kitchen. 'Bring my tea and snack,' she calls imperiously to the servants standing by, waiting. They fluster to attention and, just like that, Sita is dismissed.

Sita has a memory of when she was very little, seated on her mother's lap, laughing with her. She is not sure if it is memory or her fanciful imagination, but sometimes, in the dark of night when she cannot sleep, frustrated with her life, or lack of it, when hot sweet tears that are not given rein during the day leak out and stain her pillow, she brings out this memory – or dream – and it always comforts her.

Sitting on her mother's lap, so wide and capacious and comforting – her mother's scent of jasmine and the gooseberry oil she uses on her hair. Her mother's touch, security and warmth. Her mother's indulgent smile.

It can't be a memory. When was the last time she smiled at you, let alone indulgently? the practical side of her whispers. But the small part of her wanting soothing shushes it, continuing to picture the memory, or fantasy...

'You're my princess.' Her mother's whisper warm in her ear.

'I don't want to be a princess, I want to be a… a queen.'

Her mother's laughter starting deep in her chest and exploding out of her mouth in infectious chuckles.

Ma doesn't laugh.

Shush.

When she finishes laughing, Ma says, 'You can be whatever you want to be, my clever little girl.'

'Promise?'

'I promise.'

Sita, trying and failing to sleep, at odds with her life, gathers this memory/dream close and imagines it is her mother holding her. Loving her unconditionally. Loving her despite Sita not being the daughter she wants – meek, biddable, without an original thought.

That is the only happy memory – if it is one – that Sita has of her childhood.

The rest are all of arguments, strife, anger. Her father's thin lips, his looking right through her, his grumbling about her dowry, of how he had to fix the servants' quarters, the cost she extracted from him at birth and is still extracting.

'You want me gone,' she's wanted to yell, countless times.

But she is afraid to say it, in case he replies, 'Yes, I want rid of the burden of you.'

'Oh, Sita, why? Why did you have to make them go? If it wasn't for you they'd still be alive,' her best friend had cried, her voice raw with pain.

'Sita, you're not a child any more. You'll be married soon. You cannot carry on like this.' Her brother, turning against her.

Her mother: 'You have the kind of character that will land you in trouble if not reined in.'

Her father: 'You brought bad luck when you were born and I'm still paying for it.'

I will run away before my parents can get me married. And this time, I will *succeed,* Sita vows, even as she wants to lie down in a corner and bawl. *I will make my own luck. And it will be* good *luck. I will prove everyone wrong.*

Chapter 15

Mary

Patterned China

1936

'You knew my parents in India…' Mary says.

Major Digby looks at her over the rim of his teacup, 'Quite. Splendid chap, Richard.'

Mary shuts her eyes and tries to summon her parents. But, despite the memories that haven't stopped overwhelming her, she finds she cannot remember their voices; that their features are blurry in her mind's eye.

She has claimed all of her father's books, returned to the library by her aunt at Mary's request, running her hands over her father's handwriting, his untidy notes in the margins, in a bid to summon him more vividly. She is angry at herself for suppressing her parents' memories, but she understands that at the time, grieving and stunned, starting a new life thousands of miles away with strangers, it was the only way she could cope…

'You're quite the image of your mother,' Major Digby is saying.

He knew them, a version of my parents that I don't. He can picture them in a way I cannot. Her eyes fill without warning and she blinks, looking down at her plate of crustless cucumber sandwiches and her tea in its patterned china cup.

Her uncle rescues her, talking into the awkward pause. 'I say, old chap, you're thinking of going back to India?'

'Quite. I used to do some work, you see, with the nuns. They run schools for orphans of servicemen and the like. I'd quite like to go back to working with them.' He smiles kindly at Mary. 'It must have been quite appalling, losing your parents at a young age. But you were quite lucky, as it happens. You had someone to take care of you. Others are not quite so fortunate.'

Mary stares at him, open-mouthed, until Rose kicks her under the table.

What he says is true – a revelation. Since Major Digby's previous visit returned her past to her, she has been angry, upset, blaming her aunt, uncle, cousins, blaming herself.

But… she has never once looked at the bigger picture.

She is so very lucky, she thinks, looking around her, seated at the long table in the glasshouse, the gleaming, polished cutlery, the servants bringing in cakes and cream pastries and jam tarts…

My parents wanted me to be more like Sita. To grab life, experience it, not allow it to pass me by. They wanted me to do something with my life. Make a difference.

And as Major Digby tucks into cake, Mary's thoughts, which have been all over the place since the onslaught of her childhood memories, crystallise and she knows, with sudden clarity, just what she must do.

Chapter 16

Sita

Throne Room

1927

Sita is bored. Incredibly, interminably bored.

The durbar goes on and on, showing no sign of ceasing. Royalty and landowners in their finery being presented to the king. The great hall of the palace winking and shining with all the wealth on display. Servants fanning dignitaries, tending to their every need, circulating with drinks and snacks, bowing and obsequious.

Sita has been looking forward to this all week – a break from routine, from having her governess watch her every move, from monotony. And it was interesting, for a while. Different at least. But now, here too she is bored.

As promised after her foiled escape attempt, her parents have been busy arranging her marriage. And simultaneously, secretly, Sita has been planning her escape. This time she will not leave *anything* to chance. She's stolen the money set aside for her dowry – she did it the day after her mother informed her that she would be married to the suitor whose horoscope matched hers best; it was then that it finally dawned on her that her parents' threats to get her married were not empty but very real. Lord Vishnu had looked askance at her as she took the key to the safe from his shrine, tiptoeing into her father's study when she knew him to be out and her mother and the servants, including her governess, partaking of their afternoon siesta. The money, boldly stolen, is sitting beside her books under her bed, waiting for her escape to the city. Once there, she'll enrol at a girls' school – she's heard there are missionary schools for girls in the city, run by nuns. Now it's just a question of choosing the best time to run away.

When the invitation to the palace arrived, Sita, curious to visit, had decided to wait until afterwards. Now she's having second thoughts. The royal durbar is not all that different from the pujas her parents have conducted at their home, the same protocol and grave solemnity, the only change being that here, everything is on a more ostentatious scale.

Sita is even jaded by the grandeur of the Throne Room where the durbar is being held – this is how her mother had pronounced the words when they had received the invitation, 'Throne Room', both capitalised, her voice dripping with barely contained excitement.

When she first entered the room, Sita had gasped in wonder, taking everything in. Great stained-glass windows filtered rainbow light into the room, reflecting off the dignitaries' ostentatious jewels, making everything glow in an ethereal saffron light. She had marvelled at the polished floor, adorned with intricately patterned carpets, at the light shining off the carved tiles. She had ogled the grand throne housing the king, with its winged arms, arced gilded back with the royal crest engraved upon it, its gleaming upholstery. Seated to the king's right, on another throne, almost as grand, was the British Resident to the kingdom, looking stiff and hot, sweat running down his pale skin. On the king's left, the crown prince.

The play of light from myriad chandeliers on the tapestries and sculptures, the paintings gracing the baroque walls, the curved, inscribed ceiling, the esteemed guests in their dazzling best, each trying to outdo the other – it had fascinated Sita for all of half an hour. Now she twists and turns so much that her mother slaps her hand.

'Don't fidget,' she admonishes in a loud whisper.

They are in the women's section, in a winged alcove that sits above the room, an internal balcony, ringed by whispering velvet curtains. The perfume of luxury and sandalwood and talc, the swish and rustle of expensive saris, gold-embroidered and heavy and insanely uncomfortable.

If Sita bends forward and turns her head slightly to the right, she can see her father, seated among noble relatives of the king, behind the English nobility and kings from other kingdoms come to pay their respects.

Sita's father sits stiff and straight, his moustache, of which he is fiercely proud and which he oils every day without fail, quivering every so often when air from the fans the servants are wielding strokes his face – the only part of him to move.

When Sita was very small, she had watched in fascination as her father's manservant polished and tweaked his moustache, buffed it to a shine.

'Can I help?' she had asked and her father had startled, yelling, 'What are *you* doing here?' The manservant's hand had slipped and the polish had gone all over her father's cheeks, so he looked fierce but shiny.

Sita had smiled and her father had roared, 'You find this amusing?'

Sita had run away, as fast as she could, and burst into tears in her ayah's arms, and only the cook's special milk pudding, thick with plump raisins, could still her hiccuping sobs.

In the middle of the hall a dance troupe performs to music concocted by a band of musicians, but hardly anyone pays them heed; the eclectic strains of harmoniums and veenas, tablas and sitar and santoor, the chimes of anklets and the clinking of the bangles of the dancers, serve just as background to the main event – the king's blessing.

Around Sita, other young girls sit quietly and bashfully, hands in their laps, not a hair on their heads awry.

Sita, in contrast, is already unravelling. Her new, bought for the occasion, crimson and gold sari is coming untucked. Her hair, neatly subjugated into a plait by her maid, is collecting around her face in oily clumps, reeking of the amla oil that her maidservant has massaged into it.

The jewellery her mother has insisted she wear is itchy. Every so often, gusts of blessedly cool air reach her face from the large fans – painted with elaborate scenes of godly battles, presumably from the scriptures – wielded by the maidservants here in the women's section; but they are not often enough for comfort. She can feel the face powder – another thing she didn't want to wear but her mother wouldn't compromise on – running along with sweat down her face.

She has counted the number of crowns on show; she has allocated, in her mind, the prize for best-dressed king – the prince of their kingdom, sitting by the king's side, winning.

'Is the prince allowed to win, if the prize is for best-dressed king?' Kishan would have asked if they were playing together like they used to, once upon a time, before he left for school and everything changed.

She closes her eyes and wishes her brother and the sting of his betrayal away. She shifts in her seat, breathing in the fug of perfume and self-importance, sweat and celebration. The other girls, even the little ones, sit to attention, strands of jasmine in their hair, gold bangles twinkling on their wrists. They appear decorous, rapt, well behaved.

'Stop it at once.' Her mother's heavy, moist hand on her thigh. Sita had not even realised she was jiggling her knees. Sweat patches spread in wide circles from the armpits of her mother's best sari blouse, the shimmery peach of a summer sunset now stained deep orange. Her face is shiny; she looks as uncomfortable as Sita feels. She must be missing sitting in the airy dining room, having her legs massaged while drinking ginger- and cardamom-infused tea and snacking on pakoras as she keeps a beady eye on the servants.

'Ma, I'm feeling sick.'

Her mother's gaze piercing, as if scouring the very depths of her daughter's wayward soul. She knows that Sita has quite the talent for being sick at will, something Kishan used to envy back when he and his sister were allies.

'Find a washroom, clean your face while you're there – your face powder is running – and come back straight after. Do not loiter,' her mother barks in a hoarse whisper.

Sita doesn't need to be told twice. There's no governess with her today – only family were invited – so now she's finally on her own, for the first time since her ill-fated escape attempt. She revels in the freedom of not having her governess's hawk eyes recording her every action, her heavy tread trailing her every move. Her books, those salvaged from Kishan's pile and a couple from Mary, are gathering dust under her bed, next to the bag of money – her dowry stolen from the safe in her father's study – waiting for her great escape. Her only governess-free time is the hour in the afternoons when the governess is enjoying her siesta and she assumes Sita is having a nap too – which is not nearly enough time to read and there's always the danger that the woman will wake and come looking for her – and at night, when Sita daren't risk the light from her candle being seen and her secret hoard discovered.

Sita skips down the stairs, soft carpet sighing beneath her feet. She slips out of the Throne Room, past the circulating servants and the assembled dignitaries and into the corridor, this too magnificently tiled and carpeted, flanked by elaborate pillars and topped by a decorative, domed ceiling, wider than the biggest room in her house and stretching, seemingly, to infinity, feeling free at last after what seems like years of being trapped.

Sita ambles through the magnificent and apparently never-ending rooms, linked by the boundless lavishly carpeted corridors of the palace – and this is only the ground floor. Ornate curving stairs lead to the upper floors but she doesn't have the time to explore every nook and cranny, although she wants to. She has a limited window before her mother sends one of the servants, circulating with sweetmeats and rose sherbet, in search of her.

How magnificent to be king, to be the person everyone answers to, to set the rules, decree what must be done and how it must be done!

The palace is a treasure trove of wonders. She enters a room and gasps, taking a few steps backward. A tiger staring at her with beady eyes, mouth open, teeth bared. A lion beside the tiger, poised to strike, or so it seems to Sita. It is a heart-stopping moment before she realises they are stuffed. Animal skins adorn the walls, stuffed heads – bison and deer, leopards and other animals she cannot name – regard her coolly, glassy eyes glinting.

There are rooms with paintings of grim-looking, ostentatiously dressed, crowned men, yet others overflowing with sumptuous furniture and antiques, richly carved chests, silk hangings and exquisite mirrorwork, jade and ivory and quartz, clearly from different countries, accumulated over the years, brought back from travels. Tapestries adorn the walls, elaborate tales depicted on them. Swords and shields vie with palms and ferns. Jewelled screens dripping pearls and emeralds, stained glass creating rainbows on the plush carpets and soft rugs. Ornamented throws. Thrones galore. Window seats with velvet cushions. Fountains in the middle of rooms, in the shape of mermaids and animals, marbled and sequinned with jewels, the water burbling and sparkling in the light angling through the panelled, domed windows. The entire ceiling a beautiful, intricate painting.

She hears the gentle susurration of water coming from the opposite end of a room, the sound different from the gurgling of fountains – this one more continuous, smoother. She gently pushes open the heavy, carved door at the far end and is confronted by a magical courtyard, ringing a pool, summery aquamarine, a quiet haven in the midst of the palace, bright with golden light from the sky above – an open space indoors, the palace rising magnificent all around. The courtyard has tables and chairs, divans and chaise longues scattered amidst palms and ferns. There are even birds: parrots and mynahs, a couple of peacocks, crooning and twittering. A small temple floats at the centre of the pool, a shrine to Lord Vishnu.

Sita slips off her sandals, bought especially for this occasion to match her sari but now dusty and dishevelled, like the rest of her, she is sure, and sits at the edge of the pool, dipping her feet in the cool water. She wants to stay here for ever but she is conscious of time passing – her mother will be sending a search party soon.

If I was ruler, she thinks, lying down, her feet in the water, *I would spend all my time here.*

She could fall asleep here, under the brilliant blue awning of sky, but instead, she reluctantly sits up, slips her sandals back on and crosses the courtyard, randomly opening another door, wanting to quickly explore the other rooms, see if she can find another secret courtyard like this one. The furniture in the rooms she passes is so luxurious and sumptuous that she is afraid to sit on it. There are shrubs in decorative holders, elaborate, bejewelled lamps. There are sofas and armchairs, writing desks and display cases showing off all sorts of treasures.

Sita had thought her house big and luxurious, but this... This is on another level altogether.

She commits everything to memory to recount to herself later, when she is back to being bored. Her life is usually colourless – no escapades, no fun, nothing. But today, she can pretend she is someone at home here, in possession of all this. She can do whatever she wants, for she is the ruler, her word law.

How wonderful that would be. I wouldn't be accountable to anyone. Even my parents, who treat me like I don't exist except when I do something they don't like, would have no choice but to listen to me. Ha!

She giggles, the sound echoing in the splendorous room with chequerboard floors – dance hall? function room? – that she finds herself in.

She pushes open the door to yet another room and gasps, enraptured – for this one is filled, floor-to-ceiling, with books. Armchairs scattered around, fern trees, writing desks – and the books. Books everywhere.

She doesn't want to leave the room but, once again, she's aware of the clock ticking. All this knowledge and she cannot access any of it – torture. Should she steal a book? It is so tempting. Just one book – nobody would miss it, surely? But where would she put it? She can't tuck it into her sari skirt – her sari is unravelling as it is.

What is the punishment if one is caught stealing royal property?

She touches one of the books. As she does so, a curious sound filters into the sombre room with its dizzying aroma of ink and knowledge.

She jumps. Has she been caught out? She takes one step, two, out of the room and into the corridor. Listens.

Again that sound filtering in through the door to her left, distant but distinct: like a cheep, but not quite. A bird? Too loud, surely? Now a low growl. And was that a purr? A menagerie, somewhere near.

Sita has always wanted a pet. She has wanted to learn to ride a horse, but of course: 'Not ladylike!'

'But the British princesses and noblewomen ride!'

Her mother's lips disappearing, her face a thunderstorm. 'You're not British. Your suitors will not want a tomboy who rides horses.'

'Why should everything I do have to please a man? Why can't I just do something to please myself, for a change?'

'Oh Lord, why didn't I get a biddable girl?'

Another high-pitched cheep. What makes such weird sounds? Perhaps an exotic bird. The growls and the purrs? Dogs? Cats?

What will she find, she wonders as she pushes open the door, ornate and gold-rimmed, carved with likenesses of gods and ridiculously heavy, from behind which she can hear the sounds.

And then she is outside, breathing in the smell of spices and earth and sun and freedom and grass and splendour and sweets and a feast. She has exited the palace through one of the side doors round the corner and to the right of the main entrance. From here, she can see cars and carriages still arriving up the long drive, dislodging sumptuously garbed dignitaries in front of the marble steps leading up to the main entrance of the palace. An orchestra stationed near the entrance plays the royal anthem – Sita wonders if it is the same one who played for her parents and herself upon their arrival. If so, aren't they tired? Servants attend to the alighting noblemen and women, one of them offering a cool drink and a snack, another leading them inside.

But Sita's attention snags on them only briefly. The door she has come out of leads to sprawling grounds at the back of the palace, stretching away as far as the eye can see. There are lawns and fountains, bandstands and a variety of exotic gardens, tennis courts, pools, the water bedecked with lotus flowers and fountains and floating temples.

Peacocks roam free in what looks like a fruit orchard, parrots and other striking birds with multi-hued plumage flitting among the branches. Chattering monkeys swing from trees and even walk boldly across the never-ending lawns in groups, near where – Sita blinks once, then again – men walk sleek, polka-dotted animals on leads. Cheetahs!

Sita watches, mesmerised. Awestruck. Then she is running across the grounds, straight for the cheetahs. As she nears, one of the beautiful animals opens its mouth and makes that curious cheeping sound. Birds fly off the trees in a graceful arc, a couple of intrepid monkeys who have dared to come close run away and somewhere, dogs bark plaintively.

The air smells of adventure and excitement as Sita comes to a stop beside the animals, her sari unravelling even further, her hair completely escaping the plait it has been subjected to. She doesn't care. She is fixated by the creatures. Sinuous and lithe, exuding a charged, barely contained energy.

The men walking the cheetahs, who wear the liveried uniform of the king's servants, look curiously at her as she gathers her breath and asks, 'May I touch one?'

They open their mouths to reply but before they do…

'No, you may not,' an imperious, youthful voice states from behind her.

Sita turns towards the young man who has spoken, his hands folded across his chest, lips curling in a sneer as he takes her in. Like her, he is decked out in finery, the jewels on his person glinting in the sunlight, but unlike her, he is impeccably dressed.

'Who are you to tell me what to do?' Sita asks, setting her hands on her hips, legs apart, in the stance she adopts when she stands up to her governess. She has had quite enough of being told what to do by the adults in her life, she will not take orders from a strange youth too.

She sees the men guarding the cheetahs recoil in shock at her daring. They are standing to attention in the presence of this young man. Perhaps he's someone important. Well, so is nearly everyone at the palace today. And honestly, she doesn't care – she's had enough of being made to feel as if boys are superior just by reason of being boys.

'I am the prince,' the boy says, 'and I can put you in prison for being so insolent.'

'Ha,' Sita scoffs. 'There are a hundred princes here today. And if you *are* the prince of this kingdom, you should be inside with your father. However, I *know* that you are not. I've seen the prince and he looks nothing like you.' She almost adds, 'I awarded him the prize for best-dressed king, so I know you're not him.' But that is none of this boy's business.

'You're extremely impertinent. Whose daughter are you? I'll tell my father and he'll ban you.'

'Ha, so you've no power at all, except to tell tales.'

The boy goes red as the rubies winking on his neck. 'How dare you! I can set these cheetahs on you, you know. My men will do as I say.'

She smiles. Pushes her head back and stands up to her full height (which isn't much and doesn't look very dignified anyway, she knows, what with her unscrambling sari, her scuffed sandals, her wayward hair). 'Go on then, why don't you?' Gauging that this boy is all bluster and no action.

'Set them free,' the boy barks at the men holding the cheetahs, who've been watching the exchange worriedly, their eyes flitting from him to Sita.

The men hesitate.

For the first time, a sliver of fear tickles Sita's spine.

'What're you waiting for?' the boy snaps. 'Set—'

'If you're the prince then who was the young man beside the king?' Sita asks the boy, who is staring at the men handling the cheetahs in disgust and fury.

'My twin brother – older by a minute, which is why he gets to be king and I do not.' There is a world of bitterness and frustration in the boy's voice.

Sita has gone and landed herself in big trouble. If she somehow escapes this situation unscathed, what will be the consequences of what she has done? Does being disrespectful to a prince mean their family will be blacklisted or worse?

So what if they are? she thinks then, her fear disappearing in a defiant burst. *I'm going to run away in the next few days. What do I care?*

'Do you think setting the cheetahs free is a good idea, especially when your father is hosting a durbar?' Sita asks, her voice cool. Her parents want her to marry someone like this, an arrogant fool with not a smidgen of sense, and to spend her life obeying her husband just because he is a man even if what he says is nonsense.

'How dare you question what I want to do? Who are you anyway, little squirt of an impudent girl?' the prince explodes.

His words incense Sita, righteous fury flooding her body.

'My father is your father's cousin,' she snaps. 'And if you set the cheetahs free, they'll upset the guests, cause havoc and ruin your father's durbar. Do you want that, you—'

Thankfully anything else she was about to say, which would have made her cross the boundary from mere audacity to high treason, is interrupted by another voice, this one soft and tinged with amusement. 'She's right, you know, little brother.'

They both whirl round. The prince who won Sita's best-dressed king award is standing there, smiling at Sita.

'You speak sense, girl.'

Finally, someone who respects what she is saying rather than discounting her because of her gender! A prince at that!

'What's your name?'

'Sita.'

'I think I just heard someone call for you on my way here.' He turns to his brother. 'Our father wants you in the Throne Room at once.'

'Why send *you*?' The prince who was threatening Sita frowns at his brother. 'Couldn't one of the servants come get me?'

'They've been trying to find you for the past half-hour! In the end, I decided to help them out before one of them was sacked. I knew I'd find you here. And I wanted a breath of air anyway – it's claustrophobic inside.'

'Tell me about it,' Sita says, again without thinking, and the best-dressed prince explodes into delighted laughter while his brother huffs and walks away, with an angry scowl at her: 'I'll be telling my father about you.'

'Don't worry about him, he's all talk. Although you shouldn't have roused him. He has a hell of a temper. And he doesn't forget easily. I'm afraid you've made an enemy.' The best-dressed prince's eyes sparkle at her.

What do I care? I'll have run away to the city before he does anything about it. And so, she says, 'I've a hell of a temper as well. Even without your intervention, I'd have rescued myself. I've got myself out of trickier situations. But thank you, anyway.'

He laughs long and loud, wiping at his streaming eyes. He has a hearty laugh, rowdy and infectious, not princely at all.

It is a novel experience to have someone enjoy her outspokenness and not take offence at it.

The cheetahs strain on their leads.

'All I wanted was to touch one.' A wistful note creeps into Sita's voice as she looks at the animals.

'Go on then.'

Before he can change his mind, she gently strokes the back of the cheetah nearest her. Its skin is deceptively soft and furry, but she can feel the muscles beneath rippling with latent power.

'We take them on hunts. They run faster than the wind. It's beautiful to watch.' Then, 'I'd better get back and you should too, or you'll be in trouble with your mother – I think it was your mother I saw calling for you – as well as with my father.'

She looks up at the prince. 'So your brother will make good his threat?'

'Are you worried?' He raises an eyebrow. 'I thought you were well able to rescue yourself from tricky situations.'

'Ha! Do you want me to grovel?'

He laughs again. 'I've never met anyone like you. You're so refreshing.'

'I've been called many things, but not *refreshing* before. I sound like a drink – lime sherbet.'

He chuckles some more.

She has never before spoken so lightly and easily and for so long to a young man – she quite enjoys it and *he* seems to as well. 'You don't behave like a prince.'

'How does a prince behave then?'

'You're not puffed up with self-importance.'

He bursts out laughing again. 'I don't think I've ever laughed this much in such a short space of time. You're quite something, Sita.'

'First I'm refreshing, then I'm quite something. You're very good with words.'

He guffaws, tears of mirth streaming from his eyes.

The cheetahs are getting restless.

'Have you had your fill of the cheetahs?' the prince asks, swallowing the last of his laughter.

She nods, surprised and pleased that he has considered her. This man is not at all pompous, like she imagined a prince would be. He is courteous and considerate and, most of all, unfazed by anything she says. It is freeing to be able to talk effortlessly with someone (although she would never have guessed it would be a prince), and for them to be so accepting of her – she has missed this since Mary left.

'Do take them away,' the prince says to the men.

Sita watches the graceful loping walk of the beasts as they're led away, transfixed.

One day, I'll own one. Or perhaps more. A stable full.

'Sita!' The angry, raised tones of her mother's voice drift down to her on the wind, along with the scent of frying dough, ghee and sugar.

'Goodbye, nice meeting you, Prince…' Sita says hurriedly as, in the distance, she spies her mother scanning the grounds for her absconding daughter.

What is his name? She is sure her mother mentioned it as she was reading out the invitation, but as usual Sita was not paying heed. If she had, then she would know of his twin too and would perhaps not have got into the trouble she did just now…

'By the way, before I go,' she adds as she gathers the trailing ends of her coming-apart sari, 'you won the best-dressed competition, although your hair needs a bit of work.' She points to his unruly quiff, which is standing to attention atop his head, refusing to lie neatly down in the style it was intended to adhere to.

He chuckles as he attempts to smooth it down. 'What competition?'

She nods in the general direction of the palace. 'I was so bored in there – I don't know how you endure it – so I made up a competition for best-dressed king. You won, although you're a prince.'

'I have good people advising me on my wardrobe,' he says, grinning.

'Be sure to thank them,' she calls as she runs across the grounds, towards the palace and her mother, building herself up to endure her disapproval, even as the prince's laughter follows her, musical and unruly, keeping time with the song of the birds and the chatter of the monkeys, who scoot up the trees as she runs past.

Chapter 17

Mary

Remembering

1936

'What do you mean, go to India?' Her aunt and uncle pin Mary with their equally astounded gaze, her uncle's customary indifference and her aunt's coolness both replaced with shock.

Mary has requested an audience with her guardians and they are in the library surrounded by knowledge, her father's books now returned to their rightful place on the shelves.

Mary takes a deep breath. Since she has been coming to terms with the truth of her past, she has been questioning her guardians' decision, however well meant, to allow her to repress her memories so completely, to let her believe a lie. It gives her the courage to stand up to them, put forward what she wants to do; something she would never have done before, instead meekly going along with what had been decided for her. 'I feel it's something I have to—'

'Mary, we've been understanding and patient, given you've been ill…'

She bristles. 'I've not been *ill*, I've been remembering.'

'We even invited Major Digby back so you could ask him about your parents. But all this nonsense about going to India…'

Mary takes a deep breath, biting her lower lip until the urge to cry out in frustration and anger passes. She has to remain calm. For her plan to succeed, she needs her aunt and uncle's approval.

'…especially when you're being presented to the king in a few weeks,' her aunt is saying.

Mary's coming out at court, her first season, her plans for her future…

But whose plans are they exactly? In wanting to come out as debutante, choose an eligible man from the list her aunt has prepared, marry and run a household of her own, whose ambition is she satisfying? Hers? Or her guardians' on her behalf?

Since recollecting her early years in India, Mary has felt lost, fragile. She cannot trust anything or anyone, least of all herself. She thought *this* was her life, that she didn't know any different. But now she finds that she had a whole other life in another country, which would have continued had her parents not died so tragically, and that her parents had wanted something different for her: they had wanted her to be free. They would have considered her aunt's plans for her – the plans Mary has wholeheartedly embraced, wanted, dreamed about – to be the opposite.

Perhaps this is why her memories have chosen to return to her now – to stop her making a mistake.

But… the coming-out ball and the future following on from it that she has pictured for herself doesn't feel like a mistake. A very big part of her yearns to wear the flowing white chiffon and lace gown whose pattern she has carefully selected and enthused over, and perform a flawless curtsey for the king when presented at court. She wants to be admired and courted. She wants to attend balls and parties and choose, from the eligible men who will woo her, the most suitable one to marry.

And yet another, new part of her that has emerged since her memories returned, the part that recalls her parents – her mother who did not care what she wore, who went everywhere barefoot and dishevelled, her father who wanted Mary to be free of constraints – is ashamed at the frivolousness of her dreams, their narrow self-indulgence.

In accepting what her guardians want for her – what she has unquestioningly assumed *she* herself wants – she is doing the opposite of what her parents hoped for her.

Going to the ball, doing what is expected of her here in her aunt's house is the easy way out, the choice she would *like* to take. And this gives her pause.

Is she settling for something rather than truly wanting it?

What does she really want?

She doesn't know. She thought she did but in the span of a few days her world has turned on its axis.

Who is she?

She wants to find out. And the only way to do so is discover the girl she once was, come to terms with her, visit the country where she was born, collate memories of her parents, bring them alive in this way, even if it means giving up the presentation at court, which she has been looking forward to, postponing her coming out. It is a wrench but also the brave thing to do, the right thing.

It is something, she knows with absolute conviction, her parents would have been proud of.

It is the *only* thing to do…

'I *am* going. I'll be working at a school run by nuns.'

'*Working?*' Her aunt's voice shrill.

'This way I can repay the cost of my passage. You've already done so much for me. You've given me a home and included me in your family and I'm very grateful…'

You also lied to me by keeping the truth from me.

'You are not travelling to India, an unmarried young girl—' Her uncle finally speaks, at the same time as her aunt says, 'It's not about the money—'

Her uncle clears his throat. 'You know, of course, that your father... uh... your grandparents...' He pauses, looking up at the portrait of Mary's grandparents, hanging opposite the desk behind which he is seated. It is hard for him, she can see, to speak of things that are otherwise never mentioned. 'They disowned your father as they were displeased by his choice of wife – they had someone else in mind.'

Someone like her uncle, from a good family but penniless. He had married her aunt and gained this house, which should by rights have been her father's. Mary does not begrudge him, or her aunt, any of it. Her father was happy in India. But she does begrudge them allowing her to forget all about her childhood, her parents, her life before coming to England.

Mary woke this morning haunted by India, as she has been doing every morning since her childhood returned to her. She dreamed of her parents, of Sita and Amin, the river, the rope bridge, the water tower, so vividly that she woke feeling the hot press of humidity and sweat, the taste of spices and dust on her lips, so real she could smell her mother's jasmine and talc, her father's tobacco and lime.

She woke with yearning and ache, nostalgia and grief, the flavour of loss, spicy mauve.

Major Digby knew her parents, a version of them that she never saw, child that she was. When he spoke of them, he briefly brought them alive for Mary.

She wants to go to India to experience for herself the country that reveals itself to her in her dreams. She wants to meet people who knew her parents and herself as a child, collate their memories with hers and create a picture of her life back then.

At the same time, she wants to stay put and continue as before, practising her curtsey, looking forward to her coming out at the king's court, alongside her cousins. She wants the season of parties and balls, musical evenings and masquerades that she has been looking forward to all year.

And the only way she can justify continuing with her life here, the life she was sure she wanted and a huge part of her still wants, the life she has been looking forward to, is by going back.

If, after years of pushing her past away, she embraces it, perhaps the guilt that has plagued her since her memories returned, not only for having forgotten her parents but also for living the life they despised, in the house from which her father was banished, and enjoying it, will ease, and she will be able to return to England and live the life she has envisioned for herself here, without feeling tormented that she is letting her parents down.

How to put this into words so her aunt and uncle will understand?

Her aunt and uncle have looked after her the best they can. Her aunt is a cool, reserved woman for whom appearances matter above all else. This is why, Mary suspects, she took Mary in, in the first place – to quieten the talk that would have arisen had she refused to acknowledge her brother's orphaned child. She treats Mary the same as she does her daughters, with remote, aloof affection. But now, as she looks at Mary, her reserve flustered by her niece's declaration, that tilt of her chin, that sideways glance – Mary sees her father in her.

Perhaps Mary has always seen an echo of her father in her aunt, without really acknowledging it, and this is, among other things, why she has come to love this distant, somewhat icy woman.

'Although they disowned him, your grandparents set aside money for your father, a substantial amount, in fact. We thought it could be your dowry...' Her uncle loosens his tie, clearly uncomfortable discussing money and, especially, her father.

'What your uncle means to say,' her aunt says, her voice having resumed its regular, even keel, 'is that you don't have to feel beholden to us. You have means of your own.'

RENITA D'SILVA

Mary looks at her guardians, stunned, as what they are saying sinks in. She is not indebted to them, she has money of her own to do as she pleases, to travel to India.

'But Mary,' her aunt's voice crisp, 'what your uncle and I would like for you, as for your cousins, is to come out at court as planned and make a good marriage. So no more talk of India.'

Her aunt's assumption that Mary will fall in line with her plans irks her, although, to be fair, it's what she has always done up until now.

I will not do everything I am told, not any more. 'I *am* going to India, Aunt,' she says, softly but determinedly.

Her aunt and uncle exchange looks and as Mary waits for their response, she looks about the library that houses her father's books. Since her aunt returned them to the library, Mary has read them all and they made her feel as if she was following in her father's footsteps, getting to know the boy he was, the man he grew up to be, through his reading choices. She has pored over the maps she found hidden among them – her father had obviously developed an interest in India long before he decided to go there when he was disowned by his parents.

Perhaps this was where Papa stood when he told his parents he had fallen in love with Mama, and they disowned him, Papa's parents behind the imposing desk, his father sitting on a chair, his mother standing beside her husband, her hand resting on his shoulder, both their faces grim.

Mary tries to picture Papa, his face lit up with love, telling his parents, 'I've met this girl…'

Was he afraid? Or resigned? Defiant? Or hopeful? Wishing they would surprise him, set their intransigence aside, choose their son over their rules?

And when he realised that they wouldn't budge, that he was being banished, did he storm off? Or did he plead with them? Try to make them see his point of view? 'If you just give her a chance, I'm convinced that you'll love her as much as I do.'

Did it only incense his parents more?

There are so many questions, so many gaps in Mary's knowledge of her parents. This is why she wants to visit India, so she can at least fill in some of those gaps.

'Mary?' her aunt asks, voice rising. 'Is this Major Digby's doing?'

Mary hears a gasp from outside floating into the room. Her cousins have their ears glued to the door, she knows. They were curious when she requested this meeting with their parents, badgering her for details that she refused to give.

'You'll find out soon enough, if I'm successful,' she had said.

'Why do you have to be so secretive, Mary?' they sighed, exasperated. 'We tell you *everything*. There is joy in sharing, you know.'

It is true, her cousins are as effusive as she is reserved. She has tried over the years to come out of her shell, to be more like them. But, now she understands that she couldn't share, be open, when she was closed even to herself, with her past a no-go area.

She pictures her cousins elbowing each other out of the way as they press themselves against the closed door of the library to eavesdrop on Mary's meeting with their parents, the beeswax scent of polished wood and eagerness, the servants eyeing them curiously and indulgently as they go about their chores.

When Major Digby was leaving after his second visit (during which Mary had her epiphany about what she must do), Mary had followed him out.

For a brief moment, watching his retreating back, her nerve had failed her. But then she recalled him saying, 'You were quite lucky, as it happens. You had someone to take care of you. Others are not quite so fortunate.' And she called, 'Major Digby.'

He had stopped, turned to squint at her. 'Yes?'

'Could I… If I were to come to India, could I work there? Ideally, I'd like to work where my parents… where we lived. Or near there. You said you worked with nuns. Are there nuns in the area?'

Major Digby had stroked his beard, considering. 'Quite. I will write to you.'

And he had been true to his word.

'My dear,' his letter said. *I wrote to the nuns asking if they had any positions available for you at one of their orphanages or mission schools near where you spent your childhood. It appears there is a girls' school near there, in the kingdom of Hawaldar, under the king's patronage but run by the nuns. And as it happens, they are looking for help. If you are interested, do write to them, and I will too. I have enclosed the address of the school with this letter…*

She had read and reread the letter, marvelling at the fact that there was not a single 'quite' in it, even as she bubbled with trepidation, now that going to India seemed a real possibility and not just a vague plan.

Do you really want this? her conscience had cautioned as she set about composing a letter of thanks to Major Digby.

I don't know who I am any more. I want to reconcile the person I am now with the child I was.

And, resolutely, she wrote a letter to the nuns at the school.

They wrote back and here she is now…

Outside the library window lawns stretch as far as the eye can see. A pigeon sits on the fountain. Flowers nod in the weak sunshine.

She thinks of India, the dust and the heat. The stickiness, the poverty. How when she visited Amin's mud hut one day – Sita had not been there, perhaps it was on one of the days she didn't visit – Mary had squatted cross-legged on the floor and eaten the rice Amin's mother served her on a cracked plate, their only one, reserved for special visitors such as her, while they ate from banana leaves. Mary had been served first – it had embarrassed her, all of them watching her eat.

'It's our way, Mary,' Amin had said. 'The guest eats first.'

Only after she had eaten her fill did the rest of them, Amin included, eat.

'You insisted on refilling my plate, but you and your parents have very small portions. Why?' she had asked, as Amin gulped down his food so he could join her in whatever antics they had planned for the afternoon.

'We're not that hungry,' he had mumbled, his face red, but later, she had watched him wolf down ten stolen cashews from Nandu's orchard, one after the other – she had counted.

It is only now that she understands. There wasn't enough food for all of them plus a guest, so they made sure Mary ate first.

These memories, so very vivid. Arriving fully formed since she has sanctioned them these past few days. And yet, when she tries to hold on to them, pluck them from the recesses of her mind, iron them out and cherish them, try to isolate a particular expression – the look on her mother's face when she smiled at Mary, the nuance in her father's voice when he said goodbye that fateful day when she saw her parents for the last time – they disappear, flickering away, extinguished like the bright wicks of her parents' fleeting lives.

'Mary!' her aunt says. 'What's got into you, child?'

'I…'

And then her aunt does a curious thing. She circumnavigates the desk, takes Mary's hands in hers, Mary's palms sweaty from where she's clutching the letter from the nuns inviting her to stay and teach at their school. She smells her aunt's scent of lavender and bergamot, velvet purple with citrus undertones.

'Have you been unhappy here, Mary?' Her aunt's gaze intense.

'No! I-I…' How to put into words what she feels? That, in the past few days, since she allowed her memories access, it is as if her soul is uprooted, as if she is floating, untethered, and only India, solid, dusty, will ground her. 'I've been lucky to have you all, but many children are not. I want to give something back, do some good.'

'A foolish notion,' her aunt snaps. Then, 'Mary, you can go to India for a visit, if you must, but you don't have to *work* there.'

Again that disdain colouring her aunt's voice at the word 'work', accompanied by a little shudder.

'I can arrange for you to stay with your father's friends.'

Her aunt's offer is tempting. Visiting India, staying with friends of her father's, finding out about her parents this way, sounds appealing.

But… Major Digby has gone out of his way to introduce her to the nuns and they have written to her, offering her a job and accommodation. If she had known about her inheritance, she wouldn't have felt the need to work and support herself in India, but now it's done and, although she's nervous, it feels like the right thing to do…

It's what her parents would have wanted for her: to be independent, to give something back.

'Be free,' her father would say. 'Break the rules. Do things your way.'

She never understood what that meant. But now she thinks that perhaps it is taking a leap into the unknown, doing things that scare you but that you know to be right. It is what Sita would have done… Feisty, devil-may-care Sita, hungry for knowledge. Desperate to escape the binds levied upon her. So envious of the freedom Mary had.

'I would like to work, Aunt,' she says softly.

'You may not look like him, but you're exactly like your father in temperament. He too was dreamy yet passionate, filled with ideas of how he would travel to India and make a difference there.'

Her aunt's voice is bitter, but Mary doesn't notice – she's trying to swallow past the lump in her throat.

You're exactly like your father... Her aunt has given her a gift, one she will cherish.

'I never understood his fascination with the country and its people.' Her aunt gives another shudder.

Mary thinks of Amin, who taught her to look for beauty in little things: lotus leaves capturing raindrops like palms holding blessings, the myriad legs of a centipede, constantly in motion, the way it curled into a ball when touched...

They once found a small wounded bird in Nandu's orchard. A baby mynah, fallen from its nest, its wing broken. They had made a little nest for it, with twigs and leaves, in a hole in one of the mango trees. They had fed it worms. They had petted it and made a fuss of it.

The next day, when they came looking for it, it was gone.

'Is it dead, Amin?'

'No, Missy Baba, it flew away.'

He did not look at her, but at the ground, where he was drawing a pattern in the pebbly dust with his toe.

'But its wing was broken.'

He had no answer to that.

'Some animal must have eaten it,' she had sobbed. 'We should have made a nest for it higher up in the trees.'

Amin had spent the whole afternoon trying to cheer her up. He gave her a bouquet of wild flowers, which wilted in the sun. He danced for her, he sang in his tuneless voice.

She remained morose.

'I can walk backwards in the water, look,' he said when they came to the riverbank. He took a couple of steps, tripped and fell into the water.

He had emerged, dripping, from the river, clutched at his heart and pretended to choke.

'What is it, Amin?' she asked, shocked.

'You smiled,' he said, beaming. 'It gave me a heart attack.'

She laughed then, and his whole face glowed.

*

'Your father had all these books about India and had planned to go there even before he fell in love with that Indian girl.' Her aunt's voice jolts Mary back into the present.

Mary meets her aunt's gaze, her voice stiff with shock. 'My… my mother was from India?'

'She was half-Indian, although you couldn't tell from looking at her. Her father, your maternal grandfather, married an Indian woman and brought her to England. Caused quite the scandal.' Her aunt's mouth curling down in distaste.

This was why Papa's parents were against his marriage.

My maternal grandmother was Indian! This explains my colouring, why I go brown in the sun and not red, something my cousins have envied…

'I lost my brother to India. I will not lose you too,' her aunt is saying.

Her aunt cares. It is a revelation. Perhaps Mary has always understood this, but she has never been allowed a glimpse into the raw depths of her aunt's heart before now.

It is tempting to just stay put. Do as planned before her past ambushed her, make a good marriage, live in a house like this one.

But if she did so, she would never discover the other part of her, make peace with that girl she buried when she came here, put the past, which she has damped down for so long, and which is now persistently requesting notice, properly to rest.

'You'll not be losing me, Aunt,' she says, gently.

'My dear, you have been so looking forward to coming out...'

'I want to do this, Aunt.'

'It is foolhardy, sending you all that way alone.'

'It's quite safe. I'll be lodging in residential quarters in the school grounds, with the nuns.' She holds out the crumpled letter.

Her uncle puts on his glasses, reads it. Passes it to her aunt.

Her aunt looks up at her, gaze searching. 'And this is near where your father...?'

'It's in a town not far from where we... I... where we lived.'

'I'll write to the nuns, find out exactly what the arrangements for you will be. I'll also write to your father's friends in India, asking them about the school and the town.'

'I don't—'

'*I* do.' Her aunt's voice firm. 'If we're to send you to India, I want to make sure you are all right, my dear.' And, her gaze assessing, 'Once I've heard back from the nuns and your father's friends, if everything is above board, then you can go, stay for a year. And then you will come back here and find someone suitable to marry.'

Her aunt is setting out rules for Mary. She feels a welcome sense of comfort. One year is a suitable amount of time to work for the nuns. In that time, she will visit the town where she spent the first few years of her life and she will also try to find out all she can about her parents from people who knew them. She'll try to get in touch with Amin and Sita too.

Her aunt is saying, 'But if it doesn't work out, you can always come back. You don't have to stay a year.'

'Yes, Aunt.'

'If we're satisfied with the nuns' arrangements for you, we'll book you a passage and find a suitable chaperone.'

She thinks of the journey here. Her incomprehension. Miss Devon.

'A chaperone?'

'You may not think you need one, but *we* do.'

She nods, knowing it will not do to argue: her aunt's mind is made up.

'You may leave.'

Mary flings open the door to the library and her cousins topple over like dominoes.

'So?'

'I'm going to India,' she says, tasting the words on her tongue, awe and apprehension, while smiling at the looks of baffled amazement on their faces.

Chapter 18

Sita

The Tales of the Mahabharata

1927

A week after Sita's visit to the palace, where she tasted freedom, albeit briefly – that long, wide room filled with books, the nimble cheetahs, beauty and latent danger, restless in captivity, like her – she is hiding from her governess when she sees the sleek black car turn into the drive.

Sita returned from the palace resolute, all the more determined to run away. She is squandering her time forcibly being taught things she considers pointless, while out there are so many opportunities, so much life to be lived. She cannot stand this existence where the only thing she has to look forward to is swapping one prison for another.

Sita refuses to spend her life yearning for more, bored with her lot, feeling frustrated and angry, her only outlet escaping to better places in her mind. She will not accept more of this yawning, tedious monotony as her fate. She will create her own destiny.

And this is why she is flat on her stomach by the pond, where she knows her governess will not venture as it is beset by mosquitoes and flies, swampy and stinking of mildew and algae and stale water. She is planning the final details of her escape, which, she has decided, will be tomorrow as her parents will be away attending a function to which Sita is not invited. Her bag is packed and waiting under her bed, holding her dowry – the money stolen from her father's safe – but, regrettably, not her books; they will only weigh her down. When she has escaped to her new life, she will buy all the books she wants, she's promised herself.

Lotuses float serenely in the water, frogs squat on the lily pads and serenade the flies, flicking their tongues out to catch them, jumping from one pad to the other with a squelch and a splash.

Mary would have enjoyed the frogs' antics.

Sita misses her friend with a passion, often imagining Mary in England. *How are you doing, Mary? Do you think of me? Did you mean it when you accused me of being responsible for your parents' accident?*

It is afternoon, that heady, languorous time after lunch and before tea, when her governess snoozes, open-mouthed, and Sita is advised to take a nap as well in the sweltering room next to the kitchen that serves as study, thick with smells of lunch: aloo gobi and dal, rice and chapatis, the creamy flavour of sweetened milk, the heady aroma of ghee. Sounds drift from the kitchen, the subdued chatter of servants getting the teatime snacks ready, chopping onions, peeling potatoes, boiling milk with sugar and cashew nuts and raisins for sweets. Every so often one of them forgets themselves and speaks loudly, or giggles, or cries out when they inadvertently burn or cut themselves, only to be shushed by the others, mindful of a sleeping household.

Most afternoons, Sita pretends to sleep and eavesdrops on them. She knows that the kitchen maid is in love with the cook Savi's older son, but that she cannot marry him for they are of different castes. The kitchen maid is always chopping onions and crying – real tears, Sita knows, for her doomed love.

Today, though, Sita wanted to get away from the house, feeling claustrophobic within its confines and restless, as she awaited her escape on the morrow, and so when her governess fell asleep, she had tiptoed past the kitchen window and run all the way down the grounds to the pond, knowing the governess would not think to look for her there.

The only excitement in Sita's life is eavesdropping on the servants' conversations or escaping her governess for a few minutes. But it won't be for long.

Tomorrow, I'm running away to the city and my dowry money might even stretch to booking a passage on a ship to England. Mary, I might come and find you.

She opens the book she has brought with her: her favourite. *The Tales of the Mahabharata*, stolen from her brother's pile of discarded books. Since she is leaving it behind, she thought she might as well read it again one last time. Despite having read it countless times she can never get enough of the action. She likes *The Ramayana* too (also stolen from her brother), not least because the heroine is her namesake, but the *Mahabharata* slakes her appetite for adventure more.

There's a tree by the pond that bends towards the water, its branches dipping into a hammock. She lies down on this and reads, the breeze soughing the branches above her, smelling of heat and dust and afternoon and escapade. The water of the pond burbles gently beneath her and fish stir and water snakes slither and glide within its algae-ridden, stagnant depths.

She is reading about the Pandavas' marriage to Draupadi for the umpteenth time when the car startles her into the present. Its glossy exterior gleams in the sun and she realises, as it drives past, that it bears the insignia of the king.

The king's car, here, visiting unannounced.

Fear takes her heart hostage. Did the younger prince complain to the king as he threatened to? If so, she'll have to escape tonight rather than tomorrow. She feels a shiver of panic at the thought.

Truth is, she is nervous, especially after her last foiled escape attempt, which is why she has put off running away until now.

She *will* do it, but… What if it is not as she imagined? Her parents have warned that the world out there is a scary place and much as she wants to explore and experience it, a part of her is terrified. What if it all goes terribly wrong? Would they ever allow her to come back home?

Sita watches the car go up the drive, spewing dust in its wake, and the hunger she was feeling a minute ago for the chole (curried chickpeas) and bature (puffed buttermilk-infused balls of fried dough) to be served with tea in half an hour disappears.

She has relived her adventure – was it just a few days ago? – when she roamed the palace and stroked a cheetah and stood up to a prince, multiple times in her imagination. She has dreamed about cheetahs, those sleek animals, lithe danger exuding from them. At night, the best-dressed prince's twinkling eyes bloom in front of her closed lids, his joyful mirth colouring her sleep, infecting her dreams.

During the interminable 'deportment lessons', unpacking the day from memory, recalling all the scents and smells and experiences helps drown out her governess's droning voice.

'Sita, concentrate! Your mother is convinced you can yet become a lady and she's paying me to perform this miracle,' the governess had remonstrated, just that morning.

Sita snorted. 'Good luck with it.'

'Good luck to your husband.'

'I'm not getting married.'

Her governess laughed, a mirthless chuckle. 'Good luck with that too.'

'*You* are not married.'

'Not by choice. I didn't have parents to arrange a marriage for me, nor dowry to give to a suitable man.' Skeins of melancholy and bitterness plaiting the governess's voice.

Sita had been surprised by the urge to give the woman a hug, at the very least squeeze her hand.

But her governess squashed the impulse very quickly. 'You don't know how lucky you are, with rich parents who'll settle a good dowry on you, and that beautiful face. You think I chose this career, teaching wayward, spoilt girls like you?'

Sita slips into the house via the kitchen. It is busy and bustling; coconuts being shredded, a mountain of onion, ginger and garlic, coriander and mint being chopped, curries sizzling and bubbling, onions frying, tea being brewed, coconut barfi and laddoos being fashioned, gulab jamuns freshly cooked and dripping oil spread out on trays. They will be served swimming in golden syrup, which is also being concocted. Bature are being fried, chole dished up, green pastes, yellow and red masalas are being ground, an amalgam of smells, spicy sweet.

'There you are,' the cook, Savi, hisses.

'Why the feast?' Sita asks, although she knows, of course. The car…

'The king's messenger is here. We can't let him leave without feeding him.'

'Ah.' Her mother has begun damage control by trying to sweeten the messenger of the king, lessen the impact of her daughter's insolence by feeding him a feast. Too late, surely?

'Quick, slip indoors and pretend you were asleep. Or say you were in the kitchen, getting a drink.' Savi slips her a laddoo and a tumbler of water.

Her mother is in the study, grilling the governess. Her father is there too, pacing. As far as Sita can recall, her father has never graced this room.

I'm in so much trouble.

Clutching the tumbler Savi thrust at her, Sita tries to calm her racing heart. *I'm running away as soon as it gets dark. I only have to brave their wrath until then.*

'What do you mean, she *was* here?' her mother is yelling at the governess. 'She could be anywhere. Is this what we pay you for? You're supposed to be keeping an eye on her *at all times*.'

Sita lingers just outside the room. She'll make herself known soon enough – and then her parents' anger will be directed at her for committing the worst possible infraction, upsetting a prince. What will the punishment be this time?

Who cares? I'll be far away, living my life, shaping my destiny.

'She… she was having a nap,' her bleary-eyed, sleep-flushed governess says, her voice small.

'You mean *you* were having a nap.'

'I—'

'The king has sent word. They… She…' Is that a *thrill* in her mother's voice? It bubbles over with something very like excitement. But *why*?

Time to make herself known.

Sita slips into the room, standing just inside the door.

'There you are,' her governess says, her voice heady with palpable relief.

'I woke and was thirsty. I went to fetch a drink.' Sita holds up the tumbler Savi foisted on her as cover.

Her mother turns. Sita waits for admonishment, suspicion, rage, disapproval, accusation. Instead she smiles.

What is going on?

Over her mother's shoulder, Sita can see her surprise and incomprehension reflected in her governess's eyes. For once, Sita is on the same page as her governess.

'My daughter. A princess!' Her mother's voice uncharacteristically soft and laced with awe.

'Ma?' Is her mother ill? Why is she behaving like this?

Her father is looking at Sita with a strange expression, as if seeing her for the first time.

'The king sent word. He's asked if we will consider giving your hand in marriage to his older son, the heir to the throne,' her mother whispers, as if not quite believing the words even as she utters them. 'If we're willing, your father is to travel to the palace with your horoscope.'

Her father smiles at Sita, something she cannot recall him ever doing before.

She stands there, drink in her hand, blindsided by the glare of her parents' approval. Of *her*!

Her governess stares open-mouthed, eyes shocked, face slack, mirroring how Sita is feeling.

Sita opens her mouth to say, 'I don't want to get married,' but her mother pats her cheek fondly and beams at her.

It renders Sita speechless even as a warm glow starts at the centre of her heart and spreads through her body.

For as long as she can remember, Sita has adamantly told herself that she doesn't want her parents' endorsement; that it doesn't matter to her. But now that she's experiencing it, she realises she's been yearning for it all her life.

She closes her mouth again.

Part 2

Blank Frame

Chapter 19

Mary

Reverie

1936

'Excuse me, is this seat taken?'

Mary startles, jolted from her reverie. She has been sitting on deck, lost in thought, fingering her father's books, the notes jotted down in the margins affording a glimpse into his mind, while she listened to the music of the waves.

The further east they get the warmer it becomes. She is wearing just a shawl round her shoulders, the sea-scented breeze tasting of the past, bringing back memories of another journey, one bearing west; her incomprehension and grief; her bewilderment at losing everything, even who she was – not Missy Baba any more but Miss Mary Brigham.

Whales and porpoises swim alongside the ship. Flying fish jump and dazzle.

She is nervous, apprehensive about what awaits her, beset by doubts.

'You're so brave, Mary,' her cousins had reiterated countless times after she told them of her decision. 'To travel to a country on the other side of the world, to work there!'

Brave. It is a word she heard a lot after her parents' tragic accident: 'You have to be brave now your parents are gone.'

Is she being brave or foolish, travelling to India just to honour the memory of her long-dead parents? To experience life, live it to the fullest, like they always wanted her to? Is this what they meant? She hopes so.

Letters had been exchanged between herself and the nuns, and separately between her aunt and the nuns and between her aunt and her father's friends in India, making sure Mary would be taken care of while in India.

All the while, as she watched her cousins prepare for coming out and the season that she would miss, Mary almost wrote to the nuns saying she wasn't coming.

But then she'd think of her parents, how their eyes had lit up when Sita stated, 'I want to make a difference, change the world.'

Mary didn't get a chance to show her parents that she too could take risks, do things that *mattered*. She would show them now.

But now that she is on her way to the country that she left as a child all those years ago, she is, once again, harangued by doubts. What if it is not at all as she remembers? What if she has romanticised it in her mind and the reality is very different?

She misses England, home, the comfort she has derived from rules and propriety, her cousins, with an almost unbearable ache.

'B… but what about coming out at court?' Rose had asked, aghast, when Mary announced she was going to India. 'You're not planning on missing it, surely? You've been looking forward to it so much!'

Mary had felt a stab of pure upset at what she was giving up – her season, the company of her cousins, the dreams she had spun for the future she had envisioned when she did not know any different. (Mary's coming-out gown is in her trunk, alongside dresses her aunt had had made for the season, as Mary couldn't bear to be parted from them.) But she told herself firmly, *Now I do know different. If I don't reconcile with my past I will forever be torn, lost, a crucial part of me missing.*

She looks at the undulating, whispering water and pictures herself at court with her cousins, curtseying for the king. But even as Mary feels a pang for that girl, carefree and innocent and completely confident of the direction her life was headed, even as she aches for the way of life she has temporarily given up in her quest to find herself, she also pities the girl she was just a few weeks ago – the girl blithely unaware of the undercurrents bubbling and surging towards her, the waves of truth that would overtake her, open her up to the part of herself that she had denied for so long.

She misses her cousins, their cheery voices, their excitement over new dresses and balls and shoes and hairdos and men. But she's also relieved to be away from her aunt and uncle; she has not been able to forgive them for keeping the truth of her past from her, for allowing her to believe a lie all these years.

'Miss?'

She looks up at the man speaking. Tall, handsome, besuited, dark, familiar.

She has seen him aboard the ship, one of the few Indian men who are not servants and who are travelling first class.

'Sorry, I was miles away. The seat is free.' She removes the books she has placed on the chair beside her and sets them on her lap.

It is a fine day and more people than usual are on deck, and the other seats, she knows – she noticed while she made her way here – are all occupied.

Mary herself is seated away from the rest, tucked out of sight in a little alcove she discovered the previous day, with only two seats, placed almost at the very edge of the deck, so if one was to look straight ahead, ignoring the rope, one could almost imagine there was nothing separating one from the water. Often seaspray, salt and warmth, splashes Mary. She doesn't mind, likes it in fact.

She is surprised, and a little peeved, that this man knows of this spot that she has begun to think of as *hers*. She has occupied it since she discovered it, only taking a break for meals, and in all this time she has not seen a soul come this way, and she has enjoyed the solitude. Only her travelling companion, Miss Frances Green, knows of it. In fact, Mary had been keeping the seat for Frances, in case she felt well enough to join her.

Frances is travelling to India to work as a governess and, despite her advanced age of thirty-seven, hopes to find someone to marry. 'The love of my life was killed in the war. We were engaged to be married,' she had said, eyes shining, face pale from the seasickness that had plagued her from the moment they boarded the ship. 'After that for years I didn't want to see or know anyone else, although my mother, bless her, kept urging me to set my grief aside and find someone to marry. I'm ready now. I wish to find a suitable husband in India. I've heard there are far more men there than women.'

Mary hoped for Frances's sake that this was the case. Although she had chafed against the idea of a chaperone – surely she was old enough and had proved herself sensible enough not to do anything untoward? – she had warmed to this woman.

'You're a reader, I see,' Frances had said when Mary had opened up her father's books on the journey to the coast to board the ship – Mary was using them as a front, feeling more than a little awkward in the company of this strange woman who was to travel with her. 'I too took refuge in books after my Alfie died.'

And just like that Mary's shyness disappeared – Frances has that knack, Mary has since discovered, of putting people at ease.

They had had a pleasant conversation about books for the rest of the journey, Mary silently thanking her aunt in her head for this kindness in choosing a companion who also loved books.

'I'm so sorry,' Frances had said between bouts of retching on the first evening on board the ship.

'Please don't worry. Is there anything I can do to help?'

'No, thank you. I just... I need to rest. You're fortunate that you don't suffer from this.'

Frances had tried every possible remedy suggested kindly by other women on board, but none had worked. One evening when she looked fit to faint, Mary decided enough was enough: she needed a doctor.

She had spoken to the captain, who said he knew just the man...

'Thank you,' the man says. 'I like sitting here watching the sun set and the flying fish skitter across the water.'

'I thought only *I* knew of these seats.'

'I assumed likewise and was very surprised to find you here...'

'We'll be competing for these seats, then.'

'There are two.' He smiles.

Mary has taken to spending much of her time on deck; the doctor's pills have finally stopped Frances's sickness but it means she's asleep much of the time. Mary's cabin adjoins Frances's, and whenever she looks in on her she is in bed, resting. Mary has seen the doctor visiting her every so often, and she was surprised that he was Indian and then peeved with herself for being surprised. She has noticed how most of the white people on board treat Indians as second-class citizens. She thinks of Sita and Amin, whom she hopes to meet, her best friends once upon a time in another life. Her beloved mother, half-Indian herself...

Now, as she takes in the man beside her, she recalls where she has seen him before. He is leaning back, eyes closed, long lashes fanning a stubbly face.

'You're the doctor.'

He opens his eyes, smiles at her. 'Most people are shocked. I'm not who they expect when they think *doctor*.' Raising his eyebrows at her as if in challenge.

She blushes. 'I'm not.'

'Aren't you? Don't you agree with the people who think I shouldn't be in first class, that I should not dine with the captain?'

She is aware of another blush creeping up her neck at this man's astuteness – he knows exactly what people are thinking with regards to him. To disguise her embarrassment, she raises an eyebrow, as she has seen Rose do, and imitates the arch tone her cousin employs when she's being playful. 'Dining with the captain! Friends in high places.'

He chuckles. 'I treated him, you see. He was desperately ill the first night with food poisoning.'

'Well, that's a relief. I dread to think how this ship would have taken us to India if the captain was ill.'

He laughs and it is a beautiful sound, bubbly and spirited, like the waves.

It occurs to her that what she is doing is improper, sitting here isolated, talking to, laughing with, a man – an Indian man at that. The girl she was before Major Digby's visit, a stickler for rules and propriety, would have balked. But now, she's surprised to find that the thought thrills rather than repels or cautions.

Now that she has left England and its sheltered awning of rules, boundaries, now that she has decided to be the girl her parents wanted her to be, and has embarked on an adventure so at odds with the girl she was in England, something inside her, the part that reveres rules, wants to abide by them, do what is expected of her, is rebelling, breaking away... Perhaps it is the brine-and-seaweed eastern air, perhaps it is hearing her parents' voices in her head as she reads the books her father loved: 'We want you to be free of constraints, to live the life you choose.'

'I couldn't help noticing your books,' the man beside her says. 'I'm sorry you had to move them.'

His gaze on her lap where her books rest.

She moves her legs closer together, out of habit, hearing the voice of the governess her aunt had engaged for her daughters and Mary: 'Ladies must sit properly.'

Once when Mary had intervened to try to make peace between her cousins, who were having the most awful and noisy argument, Rose had yelled, 'What do you know, goody two shoes? You haven't put a foot wrong in your life!'

That had stung, even more so because Rose was right.

'You like books on science?'

'They were my father's books. But yes, I like science. I read anything.'

'Anything?' A raised eyebrow.

The anger comes from nowhere, it seems. 'You accused me of having preconceived notions just now, Doctor. You seem to have some yourself. You think women don't read?'

Where did that come from? Perhaps it is this man, intruding into her peaceful solitude, his raised eyebrow inviting ire.

He colours, dark skin flushing. 'No, I… That's not what I meant at all.'

She is almost as embarrassed by her outburst as he seems to be by her words. But the new, worldly-wise Mary, who has hijacked the old, pliant girl she is familiar with, says, 'Now we've established that, what books do *you* like to read? Romances? Or don't you read at all?'

If you could see me now, Rose.

The flush on the doctor's face is replaced by a smile, his eyes twinkling merrily. 'What if I said yes?'

'To reading romance? Or not reading at all, which I find hard to believe seeing as you're a man of medicine?'

He laughs and she feels a bubble of reciprocal laughter building in her chest.

She realises that in this moment, the sea breeze caressing her face, salty-sweet and gentle, she is happy. All the anxieties cast aside, of what awaits her, of whether she has made the right decision, leaving all she knows behind. She is sitting with an interesting companion and discovering the spirited self her parents wanted her to be.

Perhaps it is because they are journeying east. Perhaps she had scattered the broken bits of her soul somewhere in the ocean when she was made to leave India and now that they are traversing the ocean again, making the journey back, her soul is being mended by the soothing sea air; it is slowly being pieced back together.

And so she casts aside the propriety that she has always held dear – and it gives her a curious kind of freedom. That word, her parents' favourite. She scatters her doubts and worries in the wind that ruffles her hair, soothing as a parental caress, as she and her companion hold a merry discourse about books and medicine and the suffragette movement and women's rights, until the gong sounds for supper.

Chapter 20

Sita

Partial to Cheetahs

1928

The invitation arrives on a gilded tray, alongside boxes of freshly prepared sweets, gold-embroidered shawls, shimmering saris in softest silk, jewellery and baskets of the choicest fruit. A liveried servant brings it, arriving in a car bearing the insignia of the king.

'We have reason to believe the princess-to-be is partial to cheetahs. You are invited to a cheetah hunt taking place the Sunday after next. Please come to the palace at nine and we will leave from there.'

Princess-to-be.

Sita feels a thrill travel up her spine even as her mother looks up from the invitation, the relief overcoming her reflected in her mother's eyes. They have been waiting for intimation from the palace with regards to Sita's betrothal to the crown prince.

The horoscopes – Sita's and the crown prince's – had been a perfect match and it was agreed that the palace priests would get together and decide upon an auspicious date for the wedding. But several months have passed with no communication from the palace. Sita knows her mother has been worried – she has been snapping at the servants and at Sita more than usual and their relationship is back to its usual prickly footing – the beaming smiles directed at Sita, the benign remonstrance that had of late replaced the angry monologues when she did something unlady-like, no longer in evidence.

Sita has been worried at the silence from the palace too. The dreams she has been weaving, the plans for when she is queen, will they remain as fantasy?

Queen. The power that word entails. *I'll be able to do anything I want! Even my parents will have to bow to my decrees instead of the other way round.*

That room I saw, filled floor-to-ceiling with books, will be mine!

Who'd have thought that there was a solution to my misery that would make everyone happy?

'I didn't know you were partial to cheetahs,' her mother says, a question in her voice.

There's a lot you don't know about me, Sita wants to say. But along with patience, she has learned in the course of these past few months, as she waits on tenterhooks to be wedded to the prince, to hold her tongue.

'I like cheetahs,' she says at last, as sweetly as she is able.

There is a pause during which her mother regards her, eyes narrowed as if willing her piercing gaze to peer into the depths of her daughter's wayward soul. 'Take care to be on your best behaviour. They can always break it off, you know.'

Sita recalls how the crown prince had said, 'I've never met anyone like you.'

And all the doubts she's experienced during the silence from the palace dissipate as she thinks, *He won't. He likes me just as I am*, awash, once again, with the wonder she has experienced since his proposal arrived. The only other person who has liked Sita's outspokenness has been Mary. *What would you think of this, Mary? Of me, princess-to-be!*

Her mother is rereading the invitation out loud, her voice layered with awe and self-satisfaction. Since that drowsy afternoon when the word came from the palace, Sita has been having lessons in queenly behaviour in addition to those on deportment and she has learned these willingly.

She has also unpacked the bag sitting under her bed, waiting for her great escape, and replaced her dowry money in her father's safe – feeling a moment's hesitation, a pang as she gave up her dream of running away, shaping her own destiny, Lord Vishnu eyeing her knowingly as she took the key from behind his shrine.

Now, Sita can endure her governess's admonishments; she actually pays heed to them.

'You can be good when you set your mind to it,' the governess huffs, awestruck by this change in her recalcitrant charge.

Since the proposal from the crown prince, her father has taken to smiling at Sita when their paths cross and it is a shock and a gift, her heart blossoming with pleasure at this uncommon acknowledgement.

When Kishan heard, he had written, 'My sister the future queen! You'll be the best queen this kingdom has ever had, Sita!'

Having her family's approval is a novel experience. It has given her a feeling of accomplishment and despite herself, she has wanted it to continue, which is why she has been so worried at the lack of communication from the palace.

Sita had envied Mary her books, her freedom to do as she pleased, her parents' love, being the centre of her parents' lives. But now, all this and more is within her reach.

She pictures the endless opulent rooms within the palace, that courtyard she had chanced upon with its pool and palm trees. How many other pools and courtyards are dotted around that immense palace? She means to find out.

And now, a cheetah hunt! She takes the invitation from her mother and runs her hand over the gold embossed letters, picturing the lithe animals. *Finally, my life is taking off. Finally, I'm experiencing things. Finally, I am living.*

Chapter 21

Mary

Audacity

1936

Mary and the doctor take to meeting on deck.

Each time Mary meets him, she feels a thrill of anxiety about breaking the rules, mixed in with a sense of daring at the same.

I'm not doing anything wrong, she tells the cautioning voice inside her head. *Just talking.*

Talking, unchaperoned, with a man, an Indian man at that, her conscience chides, and she shushes it, pleased with and slightly shocked at this new, intrepid version of herself that she is discovering aboard the ship.

'Please call me Vinay,' he had said, that first day, as they parted for supper.

Mary had laughed then. 'It's hard to believe I spent the last hour talking to you and did not think to ask your name. Shall we begin again? I am Mary. How do you do, Dr Vinay?'

'Vinay will do nicely, thank you.'

They spend whole days together, apart from mealtimes, and when Vinay has to check on his patients, Frances among them.

He is easy to talk to and brings out a side of Mary she has not known before, one that she decides she likes.

'Why are you travelling to India?' he asks during their second meeting.

'I grew up there, and moved to England when my parents...' She chokes on the lump that surfaces in her throat – she's not used to talking about her parents, after having buried their memory, her childhood, for so long. She clears her throat and tries again. '...when they died.'

'I'm so sorry.'

'It was a long time ago.' The waves jump and tease, cavort and frolic, creating little peaks of frothy foam.

'Losing your parents is never easy however long a time passes.'

She dares not look at him, training her gaze instead on the horizon, where the sky arches to meet the sea, until the stinging in her eyes eases.

'And now, you're going back...?'

'I'm going to teach at a school for girls.'

'Ah, giving something back.'

'Yes, something like that.'

He's quiet, both of them watching the water rippling in the wake of the ship. His silences are soothing. Asking nothing of her but to join him in contemplation.

Mary likes that Vinay is well read, that she can speak to him about anything and he will parry with an intelligent remark of his own. It is the first time she has had the opportunity to talk at length to a man, unfettered by the rules of polite society. It is exciting and it is nerve-wracking, and she periodically has to quiet her conscience rabbiting on about propriety and what is expected of her: *This is precisely why your aunt thought you needed a chaperone.*

But she likes Vinay's company and is not prepared to give it up. For the first time in her life, she understands why people might break rules: the perverse joy, the clandestine excitement of it.

Mary has stopped attending dances of an evening. She would rather sit on deck with one of her father's books, the peachy glow of sunset thick with shadows, the lamps lit on deck casting yellow smears on the navy surge of sea, until she can no longer see to read.

'What are you doing here?' she asks one evening when Vinay slips into the seat beside her after supper.

'I was about to ask you the same question.' She doesn't turn to look at him but she hears the smile in his voice. 'Don't you like dancing?'

'I do. I just don't like the vapid conversation that goes with it.'

'Ah, the lure of the book.'

'What do you mean?'

'No human can converse as wisely and as eloquently as a book.'

She turns to him then. In the gathering darkness, his twinkling eyes, his dark, stubble-lined face. Again that thrill of doing something taboo.

'Don't *you* like to dance?' she asks, flinging his question back at him.

'I do. But today I didn't feel able to brave the strange looks I get.'

'Oh.' What can she say to that?

And then, inspired as she looks at the empty deck, the music floating from the ballroom, competing with the melody of the waves: 'Would you like to dance?'

'Pardon me?'

What are you doing, turning tradition, propriety, on its head?

Mary shushes her conscience, excited at her daring. *I am no longer the girl who wants to toe the line, but rather, one who will draw the line where she sees fit.*

'Dance with me?' she asks, her heart agitating inside her ribcage at her audacity.

'Here?'

He looks at the empty deck, golden pools of light, wet boards with their glossy turmeric sheen. Music and laughter, the clink of glasses, drifting out on the salty sea breeze.

This is not you. You will regret this.

Her conscience gives her a moment of pause.

She looks at Vinay, whose eyebrows are raised, a small smile playing on his face, and bravely, she says, 'Why not?'

Because he is... You are... You are not... She quiets the timid part of her that is scandalised by her behaviour, terrified of the consequences of her uncharacteristically bold actions.

They dance on the deserted deck in the honeyed moonlight. His arm round her, her head resting on his shoulder.

He smells of musk and cologne. A sharp lemon and spice scent. He dances competently. After a while she forgets to be worried.

They dance until the music stops and then they collapse onto their seats, giggling like naughty children.

'Shall I get you a drink from inside?'

'I'm fine.' She really is.

They dance beneath the canopy of stars when the music starts up again, fish gliding under the waves beside their ship.

Her hand in his, slick. The taste of happiness on her tongue.

Beware, the water whispers as it swells and foams. *Beware.*

Chapter 22

Sita

Anthem

1928

The palace grounds are milling with cars and trolleys, carriages and visitors. Servants in uniform emblazoned with the emblem of the kingdom offer guests disembarking at the palace entrance freshly prepared watermelon juice and cashew-nut barfi. Guests are feted with flower garlands and serenaded with the kingdom's anthem.

Monkeys scamper across the lawns, curiously watching the parade of vehicles coming up the long, stately drive.

As their car inches up the drive, Sita can see round the corner into the grounds at the back where she first met the prince and where, now, handlers lead the cheetahs, hooded and sleek, into bullock carts.

There's a sudden commotion, monkeys shrieking and scooting up trees, the ground beneath their vehicle vibrating, as row upon row of stately elephants is led into the grounds. Each elephant has a turbaned mahout sitting proudly in front. A studded gold plate adorns the elephants' foreheads, and atop each beast is a bejewelled, cushioned throne – a howdah – with a domed, ornamented roof.

A thrill travels up Sita's spine all the way to her heart as she takes in the majestic animals, their regal, aloof dignity.

'We're travelling on elephants to the hunt?' she asks.

'It would appear so,' her father says, looking *at* her, not through her like he used to do, a smile on his face.

Sita feels her cheeks flush as they do every time her father smiles at her. It annoys her, how happy it makes her feel, even as she knows that she will never tire of it. She did not realise that her parents' approval mattered so much to her. But it does and she will do everything in her power – and she will have considerable power when she is queen – to keep it this way: her parents happy and proud of *her*.

'We'll most probably be in the howdah with the queen.' Her mother's voice jubilant. 'She's very traditional, so cover your head at all times and look demure.' Her mother's gaze appraising as she takes in the jewels in Sita's hair, her glittering sari, her placid expression, her hands lying sedately in her lap as she has been taught, so at odds with the fiery, tempestuous emotions swirling inside her. Excitement and nerves and happiness – electrifying, bubbling and overflowing.

Sita likes that her mother says, '*Look* demure', knowing full well that not one cell in her daughter *is* demure, that she might now, after months of tutelage, appear so, but that she will never be.

Breakfast is served to the guests by liveried servants – men in one banqueting room, women in another. There are thalis with different varieties of rice, puris and chapathis, aloo parathas and rotis, kulchas and naan, myriad curries in an explosion of flavours, a gourmet selection of sweets – melt-in-the-mouth laddoos and barfis, jamuns and peda, halva and kheer. Plates are refilled over and over. There is music and dance to entertain the guests while they eat.

After the guests partake of the food, there is entertainment. Parrots dressed up as clowns and as acrobats. Parrots mounting miniature wheels and shooting minuscule cannons, dancing and singing, imitating humans with startling accuracy.

At the end there is much applause and laughter. Sita looks up from beneath her veil to see the queen appraising her from underneath *her* veil. Sita smiles. The queen's gaze hardens, lips sealing in a frown, and she looks away.

Chapter 23

Priya

Need

2000

The day Priya is to see her husband again for the first time since the night of his surprise birthday party that descended into disaster she has a long perfumed bath.

Afterwards, she puts on a dress that complements her body, that dips at her breasts and takes inches off her waist.

It is for me, not for Jacob. I want to look my best. She resolutely pushes away the image of that supple body draped around him, that glowing young skin.

She applies make-up, deftly hiding all signs of the grief and upset Jacob has put her through, until the mirror shows her the cool, collected, beautiful woman he fell in love with – well, almost; it is hard to wipe fifteen years away altogether.

When Jacob first met her, she was twenty. Wild, spirited, feisty, ambitious. She was becoming recognised after the hard-hitting, small-budget documentary she made, working from her bedsit, was bought by the BBC and nominated for a BAFTA award. She had offers from all over the world but she had rejected them all and gone it alone, starting her own production company. It was a gamble, but she was young, confident, determined to make something of herself. She has since built up a reputation for producing uncompromising, stark films, not bowing to convention, unafraid to voice her opinion via her work. Despite the lacklustre reception of her last three documentaries, she is someone in her own right. She can and will manage without Jacob's firm investing in her production company. She might have to dissolve her company, go back to producing from a bedsit as she did with her first successful film, but she can still go it alone. She does not need him.

You might not need him, but you want him, her heart cries. *For all your bluster, you have missed him. You will take him back – you know you will. He is the one for you. He always has been.*

They met when Jacob's firm signed up to invest in her production company. He was ten years her senior. Good-looking, sophisticated, smooth-talking, suave. He treated her like she was the centre of his world, the most special person in it. She fell in love quickly and completely. And she has been in love with Jacob ever since. While he has moved on to the next young thing.

She gulps, feeling the melancholy threaten, the melancholy that overwhelmed her after she lost her babies, each of them mere specks in her womb and yet imbued with such hope, loved so very much. She pushes it away, determinedly channelling anger instead, as she has done these past few days.

If she gives in to the darkness, she will not be able to claw back out. Not this time.

Before, even at her worst, Jacob was by her side, helping her cope, urging her out of the miasma of despair that engulfed her. Now she is without her anchor, the man who stood by her, loved her through it all: her upset, her hopelessness, her tears, her rage.

When she lost her babies, when she and Jacob decided not to try any more, it was devastating, but with him by her side, Priya forced herself to face the world, his love giving her the courage to do so. She had gone to a counsellor, more for Jacob's sake than her own, indulging his conviction that it would help, although at the time she had felt *nothing* would.

The counsellor *had* helped, just as Jacob had hoped, and Priya felt able to try to salvage some of her earlier self, make documentaries, all of which bombed.

Each day is still a battle, the urge to pack it all in, to give up, to lie down and cry trying to get the better of her.

Jacob knows this. And yet...

The hurt gnaws and bites. It feels insurmountable.

She looks in the mirror and smiles her best smile, holding it up even when her cheeks ache from the effort. She smiles until the rawness in her eyes eases a little, until they don't give her pain away (although she knows Jacob will see through it in an instant – that is, if he wants to), and she waits for her wayward husband to come home.

Chapter 24

Sita

Procession

1928

Just as her mother predicted, she and Sita are in the howdah with the queen.

This howdah is the second most opulent: 'Capable of taking up to five people, for I like to have two maids with me at all times – the other howdahs, with the exception of the king's, of course, take only three,' the queen informs them as they are helped onto it, the elephant kneeling obediently as they gingerly climb in.

The most opulent howdah is taking the king, the princes and Sita's father as the soon-to-be father-in-law of the crown prince. Her husband-to-be smiles at Sita as she peers from beneath her veil. His twin ignores her, his shoulders rigid.

Once everyone is seated on the elephants, the kingdom's anthem is played by the orchestra and then, with a resounding trumpeting of conch shells, they set off, footmen on horses leading the way, some travelling alongside the elephants and some bringing up the rear of the procession.

It is wonderful being high up on an elephant, seeing the world from this vantage point. Sita sees her awe, her delight, reflected in her mother's eyes. The motion of the elephant is gentle, soothing. This is how it must feel to be rocked in a cradle, Sita thinks.

Once they come out of the gates of the palace, the queen motions to the two maids travelling with her and they undo the ties holding back the translucent gold silk that stands for doors in the howdah.

If it was up to me, I wouldn't close the doors.

But nevertheless, the silk cloth is designed so that one can still see everything, and Sita pushes her veil back and breathlessly takes in the townspeople who have collected by the sides of the road, all the way down the hill, to watch the procession, shimmering through the soft gold cloth.

'Where are the cheetahs?' she asks.

The queen is silent, and it is one of the maids who answers eventually, 'They've gone on ahead, with their trainers. The bullock carts take longer, you see.'

Sita's mother stiffens beside her, very aware, Sita imagines, of the slight and smarting from it. She has been silent since they climbed into the howdah with the queen. Sita understands that her mother is nervous, unsure of protocol, wondering if she should engage the queen in conversation or wait for her to speak.

Sita herself has no such qualms. From now on, she will only speak if spoken to, since the queen will not deign to answer her questions. If the silence stretches, that is fine – there is plenty to see outside anyway. She will not let this rude woman – mannerless, despite being queen or perhaps *because* she is queen – spoil her day.

The queen affords the maid who answered Sita a quick, sharp glance, and then she flicks her veil back and looks at Sita, finally meeting her gaze with an unsmiling one of her own.

Sita knows she must try to play nice, at least until she is married, but she cannot bring herself to, not when this woman is looking at her as if she is a commodity to be inspected to weigh its benefits. Her mother nudges her gently – smile – but Sita meets the queen's gaze steadily, unsmiling, until it is the queen who has to look away.

'I hope you are as beautiful inside as you look on the outside,' the queen says at last.

A compliment? Or an insult?

Sita's mother goes even more rigid beside her. *Can the queen see inside my daughter to her insubordinate soul?* she must be thinking. The thought makes Sita want to giggle.

The queen is waiting for her reply. Sita pauses for a few more beats, just to get her back for ignoring her earlier, until her mother jerks her knee with hers.

'I am,' Sita says, at last.

'I hope you do my son and this kingdom proud.'

'I will.' And then, responding to the persistent nudge from her mother. 'I'll learn from the example set by you.' The words stick in her throat but she chokes them out.

If you're horrible to me, I'll be doubly horrible to you.

The queen smiles, finally, a lifting of her lips, the smile not quite reaching her eyes, which are hard, like chikoo seeds. 'You certainly are diplomatic.'

Sita senses rather than sees her mother's smile. The relief making her mother's body loosen. This is the first time anyone has ever called Sita diplomatic.

'Thank you. I hope to improve by learning from you.' The falsehood flowing easier out of Sita's mouth as she gives the queen a matching mirthless smile of her own, a corresponding upward tilt of her lips.

The rest of the journey passes in silence, interrupted every so often by Sita's mother's attempts at conversation – now that the queen has spoken, she feels she can too, but all her efforts fall flat. The maidservants fuss over the queen, fanning her, passing her drinks. The queen complains about everything: the mahout, the heat, the humid air in the howdah, the bumpiness of the ride. 'What bumpiness?' Sita wants to ask. 'It feels like we are floating. And it wouldn't be humid in here if you pulled back those curtains.' But she exercises her new-found restraint, thinking to herself, *Only until I'm married.*

It is cooler in the forest, dark green fingers of light, dappled shadows frolicking through the trees, the elephants happily crashing through, monkeys hanging upside down among the branches, curious eyes warily regarding them.

And then, Sita's gaze is drawn to a pattern of dots shifting on a tree. Not a monkey. Too big.

'Look!' Sita grabs her mother's arm and they watch in awed amazement as a leopard lying spreadeagled on a banyan branch yawns widely, stretches, leaps gracefully down and disappears into the forest, black spots undulating on a sleek yellow body.

The queen yawns just as widely and lazily as the leopard to show her boredom. Spellbound, Sita ignores her. Her heart thuds with awe.

A bit further along, a black face, furry black body, bounding in the opposite direction to them. A bear!

'This is the most exciting journey I've ever had!' Sita exclaims, carried away.

The queen regards her coolly. 'You haven't lived much then.'

Sita bites down a retort and turns back to the forest, wishing a tiger would appear, jump onto their elephant's back – as they are sometimes known to do – and spirit the queen away.

You'd make a good meal for the tiger. Wouldn't that be an exciting end to an exciting life, Queen, you who say I haven't lived?

But all bloodthirsty thoughts completely leave her mind when she spots a hyena and then another leopard in quick succession, her exhilaration and delight at being here, experiencing this, displacing any annoyance.

This forest is chock-full of wonders and danger and she is glad to be atop an elephant!

After a while, the mahout brings the elephant to a stop at the edge of a river. The other elephants gather around and then they all walk in, dipping their trunks in the water and drinking, some of the water droplets arcing through the air and, despite the cloth covering the howdah, splashing the women inside.

'Mahout! We're being rained upon! Stop…'

But the queen's voice is drowned out by Sita's delighted squeals. 'This is amazing. The most magical experience ever!'

The queen's maids smile indulgently at Sita while the queen scowls as, from the front of the elephant, the mahout calls, 'It's thirsty, Maharaniji. We'll move along in a minute.'

'Well, try not to get us wet,' the queen snaps. And to Sita, 'Princesses don't screech. And they certainly don't interrupt their superiors.'

Sita nods, knowing it is expected of her. How miserable does one have to be to not enjoy this? How jaded? Does *anything* make this queen happy?

She cannot help the wide smile that graces her face, never mind the queen, and her joy is reflected on her mother's face, as the elephants, having drunk their fill, walk gracefully out of the water and into the forest again.

They arrive at a clearing, coming to a stop alongside the other elephants, the forest spread out below them. The cheetahs are here, sitting with their trainers on the bullock carts. They pay no heed to the elephants, their attention focused on the herd of deer grazing below, blissfully unaware of the fate awaiting them.

'I'm tired out and the hunt hasn't even properly begun yet,' the queen grumbles, leaning back in her seat and closing her eyes.

Spoilsport, Sita thinks. *Queen Misery.*

I can see where the younger prince gets his unpleasantness from.

Chapter 25

Mary

A Woman's Reputation

1936

At breakfast, Mrs Alden says, face grim, 'Mary, a word.'

Mary's stomach somersaults and she feels distinctly ill.

Mrs Alden is a round, homely woman, an army wife returning to India after a brief sojourn in England to tend to her ill sister. She was the one who recommended myriad remedies for Frances's seasickness. She mothers everyone on board and has shown a special interest in Mary since Frances took ill.

'Now,' she says, crisply, 'There's been talk.'

'Talk?' Bile ambushes Mary's mouth, the slice of toast she's just had threatening a swift exit.

'Of you getting too close to that native doctor.'

It was only a matter of time until you were found out, Mary's conscience chides.

The side of herself she has only just discovered asserts itself, pushing the anxious part of her firmly aside, and she says to Mrs Alden, even managing a small smile, 'Oh, you mean Vinay.'

'You're on first-name terms, I see.' Mrs Alden sniffs.

She'll tell your aunt. You'll get in trouble, her conscience warns. Once again, she shushes it. *My aunt lied to me. Why should I care?*

To Mrs Alden, calmly. 'He's a friend.'

Mrs Alden's lips thin in disapproval. '*Men* are never friends, my dear, and especially not men like him.'

'What do you mean, men like him?'

'You know very well what I mean, my dear.' Her voice full of scorn.

'Thank you for your advice, Mrs Alden. But I don't see how it concerns you or anyone else.' Mary's voice cool. She realises, with a start, that she's enjoying this. Like the previous evening, dancing with Vinay. Once she successfully quieted her conscience, she had had fun.

And after all, Mrs Alden is not saying anything her conscience hasn't already warned her about.

'A woman's reputation is a precious thing, my dear. I understand you want to get married at some point.'

Her aunt's voice in her head: 'You can go, stay for a year. And then you will come back here and find someone suitable to marry.'

Her aunt, uncle, cousins, her life in England with its rigid boundaries, even her coming out at court and the subsequent season, all seem very far away now.

'I'm only looking out for you, my dear,' Mrs Alden huffs.

'Mrs Alden, with all due respect, I don't think marriage is all it's made out to be.' *Where is this coming from? You want to get married!* 'And talking of reputation, what about those women, your friends among them, who slip in and out of cabins not their own nor those of their husbands? Aren't you concerned for their reputations? Or does reputation not matter once one is wed?'

This ship has a code of rules but there are plenty who don't stick to them, who worm their way around them, Mary has observed. It shocked her at first, but perhaps not as much as the new self she is discovering within herself shocked her, this bold woman intent not only on breaking rules, but unafraid to stand up to the person bringing her to book.

Mrs Alden's lips disappear altogether. 'I'm only looking out for you while your companion, dear Frances, is indisposed.' She sniffs. 'I understand you're an orphan. You want to be careful. It doesn't do to get too close to the natives. Take it from me, I've lived beside them for longer than you've been on this earth, they're nothing but trouble.'

'I appreciate your concern, Mrs Alden.' Mary nods stiffly. It takes all her willpower to bite out the next two words. 'Thank you.'

Vinay is at their favourite spot on deck, as she knew he would be.

'So,' she says, slipping into the chair next to him, feeling able, finally, to breathe again, as she releases to the briny air flavoured with heat the anger she has been damping down, holding in, since her excruciating conversation with Mrs Alden. 'We arrive tomorrow.'

'Yes.' Then, turning to her, 'Excited?'

'Nervous.'

Vinay waits, knowing she has more to say and somehow, to him, she feels able to pour out her heart, this complex swell of emotions.

'I... I have this idea of India, based on my memories. I worry that it may not live up to the burden of expectations I've placed upon it. After all, my parents will still be gone...' She takes a breath. 'What if this is a mistake?' Her voice soft as she articulates her greatest fear.

'It's not a mistake,' he says, and his voice is strong with conviction.

'How do you know?'

'Because you've told me that you already feel yourself changing.' His eyes shining as he looks at her. 'If nothing else you would have tried, done something you felt you had to do. And, most importantly, you're going to be making a difference, Mary.'

Vinay's voice echoing everything she has been telling herself, putting into words what her parents wanted for her. He understands somehow the reason she is doing this, despite her never having spoken it out loud. She feels a rush of affection for him, along with a stab of pain at the thought that they will be parting, going their separate ways, in a few hours.

'Thank you,' she says softly. Then, swallowing down the lump in her throat that seems to have arrived from nowhere, she tries to lighten the mood. 'I was warned against you.'

'You *were*?' He lifts an eyebrow, his eyes twinkling. 'It upsets you?'

Yes. 'Not one bit.'

He laughs.

She opens her mouth and the words drop out of their own accord. 'So we better give them something to talk about. Your cabin or mine?' As soon as she says it, she knows she has gone too far. *What on earth are you doing? Have you gone quite mad?*

But it is out there now. It cannot be unsaid.

Beneath an endless sky, the waves jump and the ocean roars, as rapidly and loudly as her heart. She bites her lip and gathers the courage to look at him, expecting shock, anger.

But there is neither. Instead, a question in his eyes.

The thrill exploding in her chest… *Shall I? Will I?*

He is Indian. You are English.

How can you even consider this? What is wrong with you?

After tomorrow, I'll never see him again.

'Our paths will likely not cross again,' he says, surprising her once more with his uncanny habit of reading her thoughts.

He's considering it, my mad suggestion, my impulsive proposition!

'Yes.' Her heart thrumming, excitement and trepidation.

There's no turning back from this. You're playing with fire. Her exhausted conscience working overtime, drumming out panic-flavoured platitudes.

They have one evening together and she wants to make the most of it. *Doing what you're suggesting is not making the most of it – in fact it is the worst thing you can do.*

She wants to spend it with this man in whose company her doubts about India and what awaits her there vanish, in whose presence she becomes a different, bolder person. This man who has treated her like an equal, discussing books and current affairs with her, the possibility of war in Europe, the certainty on his part and the doubt on hers that India will be independent soon, free of British rule.

Talk, like you've been doing, sitting in your secluded deckchairs. Don't go to your cabin.

I… I want to. Thrilling insolence, the clandestine, forbidden taste of disobedience, oh so sweet in her mouth, winning over the good girl, the dutiful girl, the one who never does anything wrong.

No, you don't. This is not you.

It is *me,* the new, bold self that has taken her over declares, and she says, out loud, before she loses courage, 'Let's go to my cabin,' picturing the end cabin, isolated, Frances next door but fast asleep.

Her heart noisily thrums out a cautioning beat. *No, no, no! Don't do this.*

Mrs Alden's voice: *There's been talk.*

All these ridiculous rules and constraints on women. Society policing and deciding what is good for one, what is right, who is suitable and who is not.

Her parents saying: *We want you to be free of constraints, to live the life you choose.*

Is this what they meant?

Once she returns to England, she will be dutiful. She will live a life framed by rules, conscious of boundaries. She won't cross any lines. She knows this. Perhaps she even wants it.

But not quite yet. Not now she is on a ship bound for India with a man she likes who is looking at her, question and invitation in his eyes.

In this moment, she feels free, reckless, absolutely daring. She feels as if she can do anything. And she grabs that feeling, just as she has been greedily devouring her father's words, the books he once treasured. For a brief while she will be someone else, this bold girl who does not care for propriety, who says fiddlesticks to rules.

A woman's reputation is a precious thing, my dear, Mrs Alden's voice cautions in her head.

She is a modern, well-read woman. She will entertain a man in her cabin if she wants to.

Men are never friends, my dear, and especially not men like him.

Vinay takes a step closer to her, so close she can smell him, smoky peppermint.

What are you doing, Mary? her conscience screams in Mrs Alden's voice.

But it is too late. For she has already taken a tiny step forward, so they are touching...

I don't know any more.

It is wrong.

It feels ridiculously right.

He kisses her goodbye as dawn streaks the sky beyond the porthole virginal white.

And she lies there, glorious and guilty, wild and exhausted, stunned and spent.

Chapter 26

Sita

Winners and Losers

1928

The elephants gather around the clearing and as the cheetahs are unloaded and their hoods removed, Sita feels her excitement rise.

I've been like the cheetahs, held back and reined in all my life. The immense, restrained power of the cheetahs radiating from their poised bodies, pulsing and dangerous.

Sita glances at her mother, who is looking small, deflated, and she is angry with the queen for making her feel so when she was so excited, so looking forward to this. She reaches across and squeezes her mother's hand, surprised by this feeling of oneness, of solidarity with her. Her mother smiles gratefully at her and Sita revels in the act of imparting comfort. Then, Sita turns her attention to the cheetahs. The creatures strain at the leads binding them to their minders, raring to go. She wants to touch the animals, feel the energy, the life force, exuding from them.

Time enough for that.

'This is such a waste of time,' the queen intones, her accusing gaze on Sita. 'I only came once before and only because a visiting English duchess wanted to experience a hunt.' She throws her head back on the seat and closes her eyes, the servants fanning her face obsequiously.

Sita and her mother exchange a smirk when the servants are not looking. Later, on their way home, her mother will say, 'You've finally met your match, Sita. If it was anyone else getting that woman as mother-in-law, I'd be worried, but I've a feeling you'll be fine.' And Sita will smile. Both of them hoping that this will happen, that the wedding date will be fixed soon, so they can start colouring in their dreams with the sparkly paint of reality.

Now, Sita looks out through the cloth door of the howdah, barely able to contain her enthusiasm.

The mahouts are gently talking to their elephant charges, preparing them to chase after the cheetahs. The elephants sense the anticipation in the air, their trunks and tails swinging.

A blink and the cheetahs are off, so graceful and unnaturally fast, sprinting through the scrubland, scattering the deer, the elephants giving chase. The howdah jumping, the queen's eyes flying open, the air electrified, rent with the incredible, violent charge of the kill. Sita feels a buzz she never has before, heady exhilaration and adrenaline as she watches the cheetahs, agile and in their element, doing what they were made for, tasting the fear and the thrill, scarlet iron, on her suddenly dry lips.

Sita's mother shuts her eyes tight, surprising Sita, who wouldn't have thought her queasy.

You've come this far, you have to watch this, she would have urged had the queen not been present.

The queen has given up all pretence of sleep and is peering eagerly out of the silk cloth door, her gaze sparkling with anticipation.

The cheetahs swoop on their prey, fangs ripping skin, teeth cutting into flesh, bright red spurts of blood on yellow hide. Plaintive screams of dying deer razoring the gore-blotched air, triumphant calls of pouncing cheetahs, birds flying from the trees in shocked arcs. Minutes that feel like days, counted out by punctured hearts leaking the last drops of life, pus-stained scarlet, into the waiting mud.

'The kill is the only thing that makes all of this worthwhile,' the queen says once it's over, her assessing eyes spearing Sita.

Sita ignores her, watching the cheetahs being rounded up by their minders, while others collect the carcasses of deer, littered all around, guts and entrails, messy crimson smeared on dusty green, all that remains of the beautiful herd grazing so peacefully a few minutes ago, completely unaware of the danger they were in.

'You seem unfazed by the violence. I would have thought a young woman of your sensibilities would...?'

'It was an experience, watching those magnificent animals do what they're designed for, their poise, their grace as they went for the kill.'

'You didn't feel for the deer? The prey?'

'It's the way of the world. Death and life. Winners and losers.'

The queen's eyes narrow. 'Your mother is sickly green. If she can't stand a bit of carnage, it doesn't bode well for the mother of the future queen.'

Sita juts her chin out. 'Surely running a kingdom well means the only carnage one is subjected to is for sport?' Her mother stiffens beside her. 'Which is why we're here now. Our peaceful kingdom is a credit to you and the king.'

Sita feels her mother relax even as the queen's gaze flashes and hardens, her lips sealing in a thin, uncompromising line.

As the elephants begin their journey back out of the forest, Sita thinks of the endless days, each one as monotonous as the last, that she has spent until now (except for her brief sojourns with Mary and her ill-considered attempts at escape, all of which feel so long ago now), chafing against the restrictions imposed upon her, wanting to experience so much more, to embrace *everything* the world has to offer, keenly aware of the life she could be living, the time she was wasting.

And now, here she is, sitting atop an elephant, looking at the green glowing world, exuding peril and adventure, tinged red with the blood and entrails and dust spread out below, eyes watching the stately procession of elephants from the undergrowth, somewhere in the forest a leopard pouncing on its unsuspecting catch, a lion stretching and baring its fangs, a bear gathering its cub, a herd of water buffalo drinking from the river...

She is experiencing the world, tasting its dizzying, emerald flavour, spiked with danger. What could be more adventurous, more vivid than this?

I'll never be bored again. Not when I am part of this family.

Afterwards, more festivities at the palace. More food and entertainment. The queen circulates, being pleasant. She smiles often and even laughs once or twice. She *can* be nice when she wants to be.

Sita, taking advantage of the spotlight being off her, slips out of the women's banqueting hall, meaning to find the cheetahs, give them a congratulatory pat. Once again, as she had done during the king's durbar, when she met the princes, thus changing the course of her destiny, she roams the opulent rooms of the palace, but this time, along with awe, there is the rush of possessiveness: *One day, it will all be mine.*

She is standing in front of a particularly vile-looking ancestor, Maharaja Bikram, beside whom, in place of the portrait of his wife, there is nothing but a blank frame, when she feels a presence beside her.

'You've managed to escape, I see.'

She whirls round. Her husband-to-be is smiling at her, eyes twinkling.

She is conscious of her uncovered head, her hair loose and tumbling out of the plait it is meant to be secured in. Her cheeks suffuse with colour as she bites her lower lip, suddenly, uncharacteristically shy. 'Yes.'

'I was hoping you would, which is why I've been lurking around here.'

I was hoping you would. She allows the words to settle in her heart, warm it. 'I wanted to see the cheetahs, congratulate them.'

'Did you enjoy the hunt?'

'It was amazing,' she says, with feeling.

He grins widely. 'This is why I persuaded my father to invite you. "It's not a sport for genteel ladies," he said – you see, my mother despises it and generally refuses to come along. But I had a feeling you'd like it.'

'I did! Thank you.'

'My mother wanted to accompany you – although she doesn't enjoy the hunt, she enjoys being left out even less. I hope she wasn't difficult. She can be, when she doesn't know someone well.'

Should she tell him the truth? Well, why not, seeing as she was to be married to him? 'She was absolutely insufferable.'

He laughs, his chuckles echoing down the corridor. 'She'll grow on you, I'm sure,' he chokes out between guffaws.

'I doubt it.'

He laughs even harder.

She hadn't imagined it – he *does* enjoy her boldness; he doesn't mind her speaking her mind even when it concerns his mother.

It is liberating to be with someone who accepts her outspokenness and likes her for it. It makes her come alive, feel invincible. And it is even more exhilarating and, if she is to be honest, a palpable relief that this person is her husband-to-be.

The only part of being queen that Sita has been unsure and apprehensive about is her impending marriage – *if* the wedding goes ahead as planned. She has not been very successful at any of her relationships so far. Her parents have been disappointed in her – although not so much since the prince's proposal. Since he departed for school, her brother's love, too, has come with a condition – 'be biddable, pliant, more ladylike'. Mary liked and accepted her, but she held Sita responsible for her parents' accident.

But this man… He seems to like her for who she is. Marriage to him doesn't seem daunting, all of a sudden.

'You were going to go see the cheetahs?'

'Yes, but I was arrested by this. Why is there no photo of Maharaja Bikram's wife? Her name appears at the bottom of a blank frame – there's a placeholder in place of her photo.'

'In the past, kings never used to display photos of their wives. They kept them private. But don't worry, when you're my queen…'

When you're my queen. Her heart glows.

Careful, her conscience warns, *he might turn on you when you're least expecting it like your brother, like Mary.*

He won't. And if he does, it won't matter, for by then, I will be queen.

But she resolves not to give her heart so easily, to be more wary. Just in case.

A servant approaches, with a message for the prince.

Her husband-to-be smiles apologetically at Sita. 'If you go straight on and out the first door on the left, you'll emerge into the palace grounds. Turn left and keep on going round the palace and you'll come to the enclosure for the cheetahs. Sorry I cannot accompany you.'

He is gone before she can say more, his long strides keeping pace with the servant. Sita watches him walk away, a smile playing on her lips.

Chapter 27

Mary

Words Long Forgotten

1936

India.

The smell: dirt and spices and incense and sunshine and sweat and humidity and something uniquely itself, something Mary recognises. Knows. She takes a deep breath that fills her lungs, recalling words long forgotten, sentences that slip out of her mouth in a language she hasn't used since she left India so many years ago. The language she knew before she knew English, that of Ayah's lullabies and endearments and soothing ministrations.

It is all still here, in my heart. It is all coming back. I am coming back.

Mrs Alden ruins the moment, cornering Mary as she stands on deck, taking in her first glimpse of the country that she left behind as a child in the wake of her parents' deaths. 'There you are.'

Mary eases herself closer to the railings, her gaze on the approaching shore. If her cheeks are flushed, it is because of the heat and not the pressing memories of what she did last night. Can Mrs Alden read on her person what she has done? Is there a subtle change in Mary that the other woman can sense? Is that why she is here now?

Vinay had not appeared at breakfast; his place at the captain's table had been conspicuously empty. He is not among the crush of people on deck angling for a glimpse of shore. The deckchairs, *their* deckchairs among them, have been put away.

'I hope you didn't take my advice the wrong way, Mary. I thought I should warn you, what with the doctor being married and all,' Mrs Alden says.

Mary clutches at the railings to steady herself, wondering if she has heard right. A sudden gust of gritty breeze lashes her face, inciting tears. She fiercely pushes them away, turning to look at Mrs Alden, trying to gauge if the woman is joking.

She is not. Her expression is as earnest and self-important as ever.

'He was in England for his studies and is returning to his wife now. But of course you must know all this, being great friends.'

Vinay's eyes dark with desire the previous night. How he had caressed her as if she was fragile, precious. Only.

With all the willpower she can muster, Mary forces her lips upward in the semblance of a smile, betrayal, acrid violet, stinging her throat, turning the taste of his kisses, which still linger in her mouth, to ash.

Mrs Alden is looking knowingly at her and so she says, 'I do. Her name is... Sita and she is feisty, Vinay said, always ready to take on the world. He has missed her and can't wait to be reunited with her.' The words stabbing her as they leave her mouth, each bitter and heavy with perfidy and remonstrance, salty yellow.

But Mrs Alden is not listening, her attention arrested by Frances, who is making her way towards them, shaky limbs, pallid complexion.

'My dear! How *are* you?' she says to Frances.

Relieved to be free of the woman's discerning gaze, Mary looks at the sea, swelling and surging, like the upset and anguish Mrs Alden's words have ignited within her. It appears to be whispering, *he is married.*

An instinct, the feeling of being watched, makes her turn to her left.

Vinay's eyes resting on her, the knowledge of all they shared the previous night in them.

Liar.

She turns away, catching the flicker of hurt dart across his face. But instead of making her feel better, it makes her want to sob.

She is aware of his gaze on her for a while longer and then out of the corner of her eye, she watches him move away and, in a matter of minutes, he's swallowed up by the throng.

Coward.

She lets out the breath she is holding, not knowing if she's relieved or upset that he has not acknowledged her, come up to her and Frances, made conversation. Should he have? But to what end? They will be parting ways soon, him to go to his wife. Her mouth thick with brine, bruised blue.

On shore, a procession advances towards the water. Dancing, singing, keening, holding aloft a swaddled pallet, which, Mary realises with a gasp that echoes through the crowd on deck, is a body.

She understands that the small sectioned-off area on shore is a crematorium. The body is placed, reverently and accompanied by much chanting, on a pyre of twigs. A lit branch is held to the wood, flames leaping into the sky, bright orange against pewter.

A confetti of ash. The scent of smoke and earth, burning and death.

'I'll never understand the way of these heathens, no matter how many years I reside in this country,' Mrs Alden says, with a sniff.

The jumble of feelings churning inside Mary explodes in blinding ochre rage directed at the woman. 'They have their customs, like we have ours. Who's to say ours are better?' Mary snaps, without taking her eyes away from the shore.

She hears Mrs Alden's sharp indrawn breath. 'Excuse me,' she says to Frances, stiffly, and moves away.

'Was there cause to be so rude to her?' Frances chides gently. 'She doesn't know any better.'

'Well, she should, having lived so long in India,' Mary retorts, blinking back tears at Frances's expression of surprise at her mild-mannered friend's sudden biting sharpness.

'I understand you're nervous, worried about what awaits you,' Frances says after a brief pause, squeezing Mary's hand – an attempt to mollify, which, perversely, makes Mary even more angry and tearful.

'I know you're upset that we are to go our separate ways. But that is no reason to be rude,' her companion continues, unaware of the ire pulsing through Mary that is directed, mostly, at herself.

With great effort, Mary manages a small smile for her friend. 'You're right—'

But whatever else she was going to say is swallowed by Vinay's sudden appearance before them.

Traitor. Liar.

I don't want to see you again.

I want you to take me in your arms and kiss me like you did last night, love my hurt away.

'Miss Green, glad to see you on deck. Are you feeling better?'

'Much better, thank you.'

'I came to say goodbye and wish you both well,' he says and this time his eyes meet Mary's, those same eyes that had looked at her with such tenderness and desire the previous night. There's so much there, so many words unsaid, a conversation encompassing their friendship.

Friendship? Seduction, more like.

She looks away, at the tilt and surge of dirty yellow water.

'I also wanted to return the book I borrowed from you, Miss Brigham.' He holds out a book to Mary.

Frances raises an enquiring eyebrow.

'We got talking while on deck and realised our tastes in reading were similar. Miss Brigham kindly lent me one of her books,' Vinay says.

You're a skilful liar. I'm a fool to have been taken in by you.

He nods once, his gaze devouring Mary, and then he is gone.

I'll never see you again.

'*An Essay Concerning Human Understanding* by John Locke. I didn't know you had that in your collection,' Frances says, peering over Mary's shoulder and reading the title out loud.

'Oh. Ummm...' As Mary scrabbles to come up with a reply, Frances sighs. 'Mary, I'm quite worn out. I'll sit inside for a while if you don't mind.'

'I'll come with you.'

The great hall is empty of people. It looks weary, bereft of the glamour it is imbued with during the evenings, the glinting chandeliers, the sparkling jewels and fine dresses and pressed suits on display. It smells faintly of perfume and bleach, tastes of nostalgia, the memory of old celebrations.

Frances reclines on a chair, stretching her legs out in front of her.

'Are you sure you won't go to the cabin?'

'The cabins are being cleaned, our cases are being brought up now,' she says tiredly, closing her eyes.

When Frances's breathing is even, Mary opens the book.

There is a note inside.

Dear Mary,

'They must often change, who would be constant in happiness or wisdom.' Confucius

'Your heart knows the way. Run in that direction.' Rumi

Thank you for your friendship during this voyage. I wish you all the very best.

Vinay

She tucks the note into the pocket of her dress and strokes the book, running her hand over the cover.

She looks out at the country that houses her parents' graves, her childhood friends, coming inexorably closer.

And, nursing an aching heart, she wonders what it has in store for her.

Chapter 28

Sita

The Public

1928

The cheetahs are resting after their busy morning. They look peaceful, harmless – all the fury of the hunt, the way they had pounced on their prey, sleek muscle and sinew rippling, jaws working, is gone.

'Can I…?' Sita asks the keeper and he leads one out and she strokes the cheetah. It is like a pet dog, but even as she touches it she can feel the muscles moving fluidly beneath. The power in them.

'So, you got your wish after all.'

The younger prince is standing before her, teeth bared in the parody of a smile. His mother's son. He looks like her and behaves like her. Entitled.

All that will change, Sita will see to it. *I've won, not you.*

As if he has read her mind, he snaps at the cheetah handler, 'Who gave you permission to bring it out, allow the public to pet it?'

'I'm not *the public*,' Sita says, unable to resist rising to his bait.

'You're not married to my brother yet. There's still time for my father to change his mind. Until then you are the general public, whatever you might think.'

How she wishes she could wipe the sneer from his face. And she will. In time.

You are like me, ambitious. How it must grate on you that just because your brother was born a minute earlier, he gets the throne.

I know how it feels to taste the sting of injustice. I was denied the education I wanted just because I'm a girl.

And because she feels she understands him, she says, 'You ought not to make an enemy of me.'

He laughs; a humourless, dour chuckle. 'Ha. You think you'll have power when – if – you marry my brother? A mere woman? You think my mother can control anything? Her job was to provide heirs – that was the extent of her involvement in the running of the kingdom. Her usefulness was expended when she gave birth to us. Why do you think she's so bitter?'

Sita bunches her hands into fists in anger and impotence. 'I've spent my whole life railing against the injustices afforded me just because I'm a girl. I will not allow that to continue when I'm queen. I'll be involved in the running of the kingdom. People *will* listen to me, I will make a difference.'

He laughs some more, a cruel cackle. '*If* you marry my brother, that is. My mother does not want Jaideep to marry you; she has a whole host of princesses lined up to take your place – girls with royal blood and pedigreed lineage. She may not have been able to stop your match being fixed and agreed upon, but she's working on stopping the marriage itself. She's managed to postpone it so far, using priests and auspicious dates as an excuse. Who knows, she might just postpone it indefinitely, and my brother will get tired of waiting and marry someone else.'

My freedom, my parents' accolades, knowledge, power, everything I've always wanted is within reach. It cannot be taken away from me now!

She thinks of the queen's knowing, taunting smirk, looking at Sita as if she was the punchline of a joke.

'Someone more suitable…' the prince is saying.

'*I* am suitable.' Sita pushes her shoulders back, standing straight and tall.

The prince laughs without joy. 'Someone,' he says, emphasising every word, 'who will bring their aristocratic connections to this marriage. Not a nobody who hadn't seen the inside of a palace until they were invited here.'

Sita bites her lip, hard enough to draw blood, hot iron, recalling how awed she had been as she roamed the palace that first time.

Did this prince see her then? Or one of the servants, perhaps, who reported back to this man? Are there spies inside the palace? Is she being paranoid?

She looks at the cheetah being led away, passive and calm, giving no indication of the power, the danger, the ruthlessness writhing inside it.

I'll be like that. I'll learn from the cheetahs. Those who underestimate me will do so to their own detriment. You included, prince.

Chapter 29

Mary

Different

1936

Mary disembarks from the ship onto Indian soil, breathing Indian air, thick with grit, feeling different. Profoundly changed.

She has broken the rules and while it was liberating doing so, now, after the fact, she is a welter of emotions. Part of it is being here, in the country where she last was with her parents, secure and sheltered in their love.

But mostly, it is because of Vinay and what she feels for him, what he kept from her, his betrayal giving the lie to everything that went before. Was their friendship all in her mind? Did he care for her, enjoy their conversations as much as she did, or was it all a ploy to seduce her? But the book he gave her, his note – the quotes carefully chosen (she assumes) to ease her apprehension and nerves regarding her impulsive journey to India… Surely she was more to him than just a naive, foolish plaything?

You wanted me to be free, Papa, Mama. But does freedom ache? Does it stab at you with pangs of guilt and heartache? Chastise you with angry remonstrations? Plague you with second thoughts after the fact?

The brave, bold part to her she had discovered while with Vinay has been beaten into retreat, and the girl – woman, for she is one now – who seeks refuge in rules, who stays within the bounds of propriety, has taken control, albeit a little too late.

Mary had considered throwing Vinay's book and the accompanying note into the sea, but when it came right down to it, she couldn't bear to. Instead, she has buried the book, and the note within it, deep in her belongings, resolving to put Vinay and the interlude on the ship firmly behind her – she will not open it, read it, look at it again.

And yet, she angled for a glimpse of him as they disembarked and again as she and Frances bid tearful goodbyes, Mary's tears as much for parting from Vinay as from her companion, and also from the different, bolder self she had briefly discovered but is now too afraid to embrace, shocked by what it had made her do, all she had nearly lost.

During the train journey into Hawaldar and then in the carriage awaiting her at the train station, she looks at the passing countryside – so different from England yet strangely familiar – and images of her childhood ambush her. Memories that had been hovering at the edge of consciousness are now clearly defined, as if she had to come back to India to slip into the skin she had shed when she climbed aboard the ship to England as an orphaned child.

Her father pushing her on the swing he had fashioned in the banyan tree in the courtyard. 'There you go, your feet are almost touching the sky!' The thunder of his laughter echoing her hysterical, delighted and fearful squeals. The scent of jasmine and eucalyptus, the taste of adrenaline.

Sita handling a snake as a dare. The dreadlocked holy man who owned it wore the python like a living, undulating scarf. Promising 'It won't bite', taking a coin for the snake to gyrate across one's body.

Mary had balked as she watched through scrunched-up eyes and bitten lips and clenched fists, as the snake, bigger than Sita, slithered across her body. Sita had stood rigid, lips pressed tight, her expression fierce to hide, Mary understood, her fear.

She couldn't watch and yet she had to. It was the least she could do for her friend, for how courageous Sita was being.

'You're so daring, Sita,' Mary whispered, awed, her voice heady with relief, when the holy man finally took his snake back.

'Your turn next,' Sita had said, and before Mary could protest, the snake was on her.

She remembered the greasy feel of it as it straddled her body, Mary standing stiff with shock and terror. Her horrified gaze had met Amin's and in his eyes she had seen the fear that was slithering up and down her body, much like the python. The snake had opened its mouth wide enough to swallow her whole, and she had bitten her lower lip so hard it bled, the tang of copper and terror. Afterwards, relief and accomplishment had surged through her as Sita beamed: 'See, you're just as daring, you just don't know it!'

The holy man had grinned with a toothless mouth, dripping red gums, paan fumes: 'Brave girl.'

The carriage crosses the road at the bottom of a hill, a huge palace sitting atop it, resplendent and magnificent.

Must be the residence of the king of Hawaldar, Mary muses. The school she will be teaching at, although run by the nuns, is under the patronage of the king.

The palace atop the hill, sprawling, vast, and people living in mud huts at the bottom. Poverty intermingling with great wealth. The land of contrasts that is India.

In the city, as she boarded the train to come here, she saw people protesting. They marched through the streets, shouting, 'We want independence, our country back.'

The British police had charged through the crowd with sticks, dispersing it.

Unbidden, she heard Vinay's voice: 'Soon, India will be run by Indians.'

She tried pushing thoughts of him away, but words from his note to her, his goodbye, echoed in her ears: *Your heart knows the way.*

My heart conveyed me here, to this dusty, sun-scorched land of paradoxes.

My heart chose you, Vinay. And you… you used me.

It is hot, the heat sticky and relentless as the throb of longing and ache in her heart: for Vinay. For the familiar soft green undulating landscape of England. Home. Mary closes her eyes and summons her cousins – they will be in the orangery, Rose writing letters, Lily sewing, Iris lounging in the armchair, daydreaming, a smile playing on her pretty face. If Mary was with them, she would be on the settee, reading.

She does not want to open her eyes, accept the reality of this strange country that is so alien even as it feels familiar. But it is intent on stamping its mark on her, inciting a physical reaction, the hot, unforgiving, foreign sun beating down on her, sweat trickling down her neck, sticking her clothes to her body.

At the outskirts of town, the carriage pulls up at a small brick building sporting a tiled roof and myriad extensions, like waving hands, which seem to have been haphazardly added to it on either side. It nestles within a tumbledown, mossy brick wall, sharing space with a vegetable garden and a profusion of flowers and fruit trees.

The messy abundance of the garden brings back a vivid image of her childhood home, with its hotchpotch flower beds, clashing colours. Her mother walking barefoot among the vegetation, bending down to smell the roses and the jasmine, her bright yellow hat at odds with her red dress. Mary shakes her head to clear the image. Now is not the time.

Young girls sit in the shade of the trees, chanting the times tables.

Their heads turn as one as the carriage grinds to a halt.

The chanting stops as they nudge each other and whisper among themselves, even as they look curiously at Mary.

Mary disembarks, dusting down her dress, self-conscious in the glare of the collective gaze of these children, trying and failing to swallow down the panic that surges, bilious green. What on earth is she *doing* here?

The nun in charge of the girls, kind face, plump, wearing a black and white habit with a great big cross pinned to it, comes up to the carriage, smiling, and without a word encircles Mary in her arms.

Mary, taken aback, stands stiff in the nun's embrace, unsure quite what the protocol is here. Should she hug her back? But wouldn't that be forward given this nun is her employer?

The nun holds Mary for a moment longer, completely oblivious to her confusion. She smells of raw onions and sweat.

Then, 'You must be Mary,' she says, holding Mary at arm's length to beam at her. 'I am Sister Catherine. Welcome, child.'

And, turning to the girls, 'Children, what do we say to Miss Brigham?'

The girls stand up with much rustling and dusting of their clothes. Under the fruit trees, they join hands, look solemnly at her and recite as one, 'Welcome to India, Miss Brigham. Welcome to our school.'

Mary's panic eases slightly so she can breathe. They are just children. Little girls looking for direction, like she was, once upon

a time. Like she is, still. She will try her best to give it to them
– and perhaps by doing so, the part of her that has been flailing,
rootless since she allowed her childhood memories access (perhaps
because of which she did what… no, she will *not* go there), will
be soothed and she will be able to put her past to rest and move
forward again. Go back to England, get on with her life.

A fierce pang of longing assaults her for the cool green order
of home, the comfort of routine, the easy companionship of her
cousins. With difficulty, she pushes it away, smiling at the children,
breathing in the mango- and pineapple-flavoured air.

'Thank you,' she says. 'I'm very happy to be here.'

Chapter 30

Sita

An Audience

1929

The queen requests an audience with Sita and her mother – 'a private durbar', the invitation states.

'Perhaps it is to inform us of the wedding date and liaise with us on preparations for the wedding.' Her mother's voice pulsing with eagerness, as her words give her hope wings.

After the cheetah hunt, as months passed with no intimation of a wedding date, Sita's mother had gone from anxious to nervous to intensely worried.

'What if it breaks off?' she kept saying, wringing her hands. 'Why the delay?' she asked no one in particular, sitting in her chair with its view of the kitchen, the labouring servants, who all turned, thinking she was speaking to them, but hastily returned to work when she scowled thunderously – the prelude to a tirade.

Secretly, Sita too had been on tenterhooks. Now that all her dreams were within grasping distance, she wanted to grab them, taste them.

At night she tossed and turned, unable to sleep, picturing the younger prince's expression when he had said, 'Someone more suitable...' The curling, knowing sneer; the scorn in his voice.

The freedom she had yearned for all her life was within reach, alongside power and respect, the adulation of her parents and an entire kingdom…

And yet, with every day that passed with no communication from the palace, it seemed to move that bit further from her grasp.

Already her father had taken to ignoring her once again, the smiles he had sported recently replaced by frown lines that made him look older, put-upon.

'Perhaps if you had made more of an effort with the queen in the howdah,' her mother had barked, two days ago, 'we wouldn't be here now, wondering whether the wedding is still on.'

Sita, unable to be quiet in the face of her mother's censure and unwilling to admit, even to herself, just how much it hurt given her mother's softening towards her in recent months, shouted back. 'You were in there with me. Why didn't you make nice with the queen? As I recall you were sitting there cowed and quiet, afraid to even smile in the queen's presence.'

The servants sucked in an audible breath and stilled in their chores – the washing and peeling, the chopping and frying, the sieving, the stirring.

'It's this insolence that has landed us in this situation,' her mother yelled, her face purple and engorged, eyes in danger of falling out of their sockets.

'If you mean my being betrothed to the crown prince, then you're right,' Sita retorted. 'And you won't dare speak to me like this when I'm queen,' she had cried as she walked off.

'How dare you! Come back at once,' her mother had screeched but Sita pretended she couldn't hear, just as she pretended that the tears smarting her eyes were because of the dust swirling in from the grounds on the summer-spiced breeze and the tang of onions wafting from the kitchen.

That night she had tried to conjure up the crown prince's face but, try as she might, she couldn't, although she could clearly see the cheetahs, their wild brilliance, and the palace with its secret courtyard and its treasure-filled, boundless rooms…

She wanted to own those animals, lay claim to that room full of books, among others, so badly that she could taste the hot, iron tang of her yearning in her desperate mouth, touch her longing with her fisted fingers.

These dreams, within reach and yet not quite, were dazzling and she was blinded by them. But what frustrated Sita most was not being in control of her destiny. Before her betrothal, she'd been planning to take charge of her future, make something of herself, by running away. All that was halted by a new avenue being offered, a new way to achieve freedom – becoming queen.

But this meant being dependent on the palace and the elaborate game being played out with her, Sita, as the gambling pawn: the king and Sita's betrothed on one side, the younger prince and the queen on the other. And until the winning side was declared, she was left dangling.

And now, this invitation. From the queen.

It is *something*. And yet, not quite what Sita was expecting.

Is the queen summoning them to the palace to tell them the wedding is off, wanting to gloat?

For if the wedding date was fixed, wouldn't it be the king meeting with Sita's father? Why is the queen calling for Sita?

The younger prince's words: 'You think my mother can control anything? A mere woman?' echo in her ears.

When did you get so negative? Chin up, Sita. It's not the end of the world.

But it will be. She wants this so much.

She hates that her dreams are at the mercy of the whims of the royal family, that her fate is so flimsy to be decided by someone else – the story of her life so far.

When I am queen it will be different. I'll decide my own fate, the direction I want my life to take. Nobody will dare dictate to me, bend me to their will, force me to do things I do not like.

When I am queen... If I am queen...

Will I be queen?

The queen's durbar is taking place not in the Throne Room, but in another room, just as grand, in the east wing of the palace.

'You're the girl everyone's talking about,' a woman, dripping gold and wearing far too much face powder, says, catching up with Sita and her mother as they are led through the vast and ornate corridors of the palace to the room where the durbar is being held.

Despite her explorations that fateful day when her life changed course, Sita has not set foot in this part of the palace and it looks even more opulent, if possible. *The more I see of the palace, the more treasures it reveals.*

'You've upset many a princess and her scheming mother – they're all present today at the durbar, to assess you, determine what you have that they don't.' The woman squints up at Sita, her eyes sparkling speculatively.

'Is that why you're here too?' Sita asks coolly.

The woman laughs. 'Of course. I wouldn't miss it for the world.'

Sita smiles. She likes this woman. 'So is that the reason for the durbar? For everyone to ogle me, the usurper?'

This means the wedding is still taking place.

'I suspect so. The durbar is packed with the queen's cronies, the mothers of princesses who've not been chosen because *you* have. You do know you're entering the queen's domain?'

'Oh?'

'The east wing of the palace houses the queen's chambers, her durbar, staterooms and her kitchen. All the many rooms here are for the queen's personal and professional use.'

'I see.' They are more splendorous and eclectic than any Sita has seen so far in this extravagant palace, with the exception of the Throne Room. The queen may not have power, but anyone visiting her here wouldn't know it.

'All those thwarted mothers will now be setting their sights on the younger prince,' the woman says, panting from walking the long corridor, her face powder clotting.

'Well, good luck to them,' Sita says and the woman laughs.

'Here we are.'

The room is luxurious and endless, dazzling – antique armchairs jostle alongside embroidered screens, marble, carved columns, tapestries, exquisite mirrorwork, eye-catching paintings. Stained-glass windows line the length of the room, letting in kaleidoscopic light. Plush patterned carpets adorn the tiled floor. On an elevated dais at the centre dancers perform to a live ensemble. The soulful strains of the music mingle with the chatter of ladies, all elaborately dressed in their jewel-studded best.

On another, higher platform sits the queen, on a throne to rival the king's.

As Sita comes forward to pay her respects, the queen's gaze settles on her, holds. The ladies clustered around the queen follow her gaze, grim and evaluating. It is going to be an interrogation, Sita can see.

Sita's mother tenses beside her.

On the way here, she had said, patting Sita's knee, 'Try and be docile, Sita, think before you speak. Diplomacy is a skill you'll be needing a lot of, when you are queen.'

Sita had sat very still, unable to respond, blindsided by her mother's unexpected touch, coming after days of being aloof when not irritable – her default stance with Sita.

'You're very light-skinned,' the queen says, sniffing. It is not a compliment. 'I can see why my son is taken with you.' *You set out to trap him*, is what she means, and the women beside her all nod agreement.

'Those tawny eyes, very unusual.' Again said in such a way as to sound like a slur.

'Sita's grandfather on her father's side married an English baroness,' Sita's mother says. 'Sita takes after her.'

'Mixed blood.' The queen sniffs, still perusing Sita, her gaze piercing.

This woman, Sita understands, feels able to show her disapproval more obviously in the presence of her cronies. In the howdah, during the cheetah hunt, the queen was unpleasant and clearly unhappy to be there, complaining about everything, but she hadn't launched a direct attack on Sita.

'And you were a farm girl, I hear.' The queen turns on Sita's mother now.

Sita's mother blushes.

The anger is hot on Sita's lips. Her mother, reading her face, nudges her with her elbow, *Be quiet*, but Sita will not do so. Just because this woman is queen does not give her the right to insult her mother, especially in front of all these scrutinising women who are superior only by virtue of their husbands.

'What is a kingdom but a farm with some houses thrown in? In that respect, you and my mother are alike, Maharaniji. My mother comes from landowners and you have married into a landowning family yourself,' Sita says lightly.

A sharp, indrawn breath from the women collected around the queen; the hush spreading outward so in a matter of minutes, the room falls silent, only the plaintive notes of the playing ensemble, the thwack of the dancers' feet punctuating the shocked silence.

'Is that what you think of the kingdom?' The queen's voice deceptively sweet, dangerously low.

Sita's mother has gone rigid beside her.

'Yes.' Sita juts her chin out, meeting the queen's gaze.

'I see. Mixed blood on your father's side, farm blood on your mother's. Not a good idea to join such blood with ours. Which is what I told the king.'

Ah, there it is. She is openly admitting that Sita is not her choice.

Sita smiles serenely at the queen. 'But, despite that, here I am, soon to be your daughter-in-law.'

There is an audible gasp from the assembled women, for Sita has as good as stated that the queen does not have the ear of the king.

The queen sits very still, her lips pursing. 'The wedding date is not fixed yet. Things might change.'

'Or' – Sita smiles, trying for nonchalance, as her mother pales beside her – 'they might not.'

Sita's heart hammering in her ribs; perhaps this time she *has* gone too far. The knowledge reflected in her mother's eyes.

Food is served, elaborate and gourmet, delicate morsels of the choicest curries and different varieties of rice and rotis. Gold plates for the queen and her cronies, silver for Sita and her mother. Another way to subtly put them down.

The journey back to the house is quiet, both Sita and her mother subdued. For the next few weeks, the house is sombre, the mood suiting a home hosting a funeral rather than the abode of a girl set to marry the prince of the kingdom.

Sita's mother does not have the energy to shout at the servants and seems to have given up on her daughter completely, not even berating her when she skips all her many lessons on diplomacy, deportment, queenly behaviour.

Her father, more than a little unsteady on his feet in the evenings, has taken to locking himself in his study.

Every day, Sita waits by the pond, looking out for the car bearing the king's insignia, and, when it doesn't appear, formulating plans to run away again, create a new life for herself. But she can no longer garner the requisite enthusiasm. Every time she thinks of running away, she pictures the cheetahs, sleek and pulsing with reined-in energy, and she feels desperation take hold.

I don't want to run away, I want to be queen.

Eight weeks after the queen's durbar, a liveried messenger arrives with a gilded letter on a gold plate.

Sita's mother goes even paler than she's taken to looking lately, set to faint.

Sita, having run all the way up to the house from the pond upon seeing the car, is panting and breathless, but struck by a sudden paralysis. She wants to reach for the letter, tear it open. But she finds that she cannot lift a finger.

If it is another invitation to a hunt or a durbar, I will scream. And if it is to call off the betrothal, I will scream louder.

It is her father, summoned from his study, looking dishevelled and red-eyed, who opens the letter.

Sita and her mother wait, scanning his face.

Please, gods.

After what seems an age, her father looks up and at Sita, his face grave.

Time to recant all my dreams of becoming queen.

Then, her father smiles. Her mother joins her hands together, as if in prayer. It is hard to look at the naked hope dancing on her mother's face. Sita can taste it, anxious and anticipatory, in her mouth.

'Based on the horoscopes, the palace priests have decided on an auspicious date and time for the wedding,' her father says and Sita releases the breath she did not realise she was holding while her mother unclasps her hands, tears running down her cheeks. 'It is twenty weeks from now.'

'Not enough time,' her mother exclaims, galvanised into action. 'Not nearly enough. Sita, come, we have to—'

'Ma...'

Her mother leans forward and very gently cups Sita's cheek. 'If anybody can be queen, my girl, you can. I worried about you being too spirited. But a queen can never be too spirited. You'll be amazing, I can see.'

Her mother's touch, the way she said 'my girl', the first time she has ever said it, the pride in her voice, the throbbing heat of it, spread through Sita's whole being, setting it aglow, warming it from the inside.

I will be queen.

Chapter 31

Mary

Almost Perfect

1936

The main school building comprises three rooms, a reception room and two classrooms, each with a blackboard, a desk with chalk marks on it and mats upon which, presumably, the children sit during lessons.

Mary is introduced to Sister Theresa and Sister Hilda and after, Sister Catherine leads her into the annexe to the left of the building, where she meets Mother Ruth.

'You must be tired after your journey. Sister Catherine will show you to your room. Once you're suitably rested, do join us, my dear.' Mother Ruth's eyes twinkle kindly at Mary.

'Come.' Sister Catherine leads her into another annexe, all of these seemingly interconnected by corridors. And, opening a door, 'This is your room. The bathroom is at the end of the corridor and...'

But Mary is completely oblivious to what the nun is saying. She walks into the room, taking in the tiled roof, the wooden beams criss-crossing it, the bed in the corner, with its mosquito net cover, the desk and chair at the window and a door next to it, open, leading onto a veranda – her very own, private veranda, facing the garden and the orchard and beyond that, fields. She hears the chatter of the children, sees them, dashes of colour darting among the trees, playing hide-and-seek. She breathes in the scent of vegetation and fruit fermenting in the afternoon sun, tart green.

It is not at all like her home in England with its regimented lawns, its imposing facade. She feels very far removed from her life with her aunt and uncle and cousins, even as she misses it with a throbbing, all-consuming ache, all the more since discovering Vinay's perfidy. She cannot picture the proper English girl she has been, and still is, living here.

She closes her eyes. The tangy breeze caresses her face and she is a child again, with her parents, in their bungalow, the doors to the veranda open, everyday noises drifting in, a dog barking somewhere, her father's rumble of a laugh followed by her mother's wind-chime giggle, Cook humming under her breath as she dispenses lime sherbet and piping-hot onion bhajis…

Mary *can* picture the little girl she once was, with her dust-embroidered dresses, her dishevelled hair, playing in the garden with her ayah, walking the town with her friends Sita and Amin bookending her, one on either side – living here.

Life at the school is hot and humid, splashed with vivid brightness.

Mary tries very hard to embrace it but she desperately misses her life in England. She yearns for the companionship of her cousins, their easy banter. She wonders how their coming out went, whether their curtseys were up to scratch. She pictures them glowing and beautiful in their full-skirted, flattering white dresses and she experiences a burst of envy and regret. She imagines them at parties, being courted and feted, dancing waltzes with admiring beaus, their skirts swirling gracefully around them. She aches with desire and yearning and homesickness, wanting the cool green expanse of home, even as she tries to adjust to the persistent, demanding heat of this country where she finds herself. In the depth of night, when humidity and homesickness keep sleep at bay, she stares at the ceiling with bloodshot eyes and ponders what on earth possessed her to come here when she knew where her life was headed, when she was looking forward to it. And all the reasons for visiting India that she has so carefully prepared and parroted to herself recede behind a film of wavering, tear-studded grey as the ceiling pulses before her anguished eyes.

In the evenings, after she has finished for the day, once the children have gone home and the nuns are at prayer, Mary writes to her cousins. The nuns' evensong drifts up to her as she sits on the veranda, watching the sun set over the fields, heedless of the mosquitoes feasting on her flesh. Writing assuages her ache for them, for the easy comfort of life in England.

Every once in a while – if she is being completely honest, rather more often than that – her mind drifts to the ship and the different, bolder version of herself she had discovered there. But, just as she did with the memories of her childhood when she went to England, she resolutely pushes away the recollections of her conversations with an intelligent (untrustworthy) man, of sparkling cocoa eyes that looked at her as if she was the centre of his world, of dancing on a spray-washed deck in the glow of lamps, of laughter and daring and discovery…

One day, she is hunting for something in her wardrobe when her hand brushes a book and closes around a piece of paper.

Unthinkingly, she smooths it out, and when she sees the familiar handwriting, the words she knows by heart, she flinches, slapped by a tide of longing, the salt and seaweed swell of memories.

She knows she must not keep Vinay's note, and so, sitting on the veranda of her room in the glow of evening, the scent of dying day, the taste of ripe fruit and cooling dust and nostalgia, yearning and hurt, she tears it in two.

But even as she crumples the pieces in her fist, she cannot bear to throw them away.

She hunts in her desk for glue and very gently, with hands that shake and wobble, so it takes longer than it should, seals the note back together. When she is done, she runs a hand over it, a soft caress. The tear is virtually invisible. The note is nearly as before – almost perfect.

Her nose dripping, face wet, she tucks the note back in the recesses of her wardrobe, next to the book, and sets about the business of sealing her heart, gluing it back together so it too, is almost but not quite perfect.

Part 3

Wanting

Chapter 32

Sita

A Good Wife

1930

Sita's wedding to Prince Jaideep, everyone agrees, is the grandest the kingdom has ever witnessed.

The celebrations go on for several days.

Dignitaries and royals from all parts of India arrive at the palace with their entourages. There are hunts and soirées. Music, song and dance. Firework displays lasting well into the night, the palace and grounds lit up in an explosion of colour.

Jugglers and fire-eaters, holy men and fortune tellers, contortionists, snake charmers, performing falcons and dancing bears.

The glow of a thousand lamps transforming the palace into fairyland.

Cannon salutes.

For Sita, the days pass in a hazy dream. She is buffed and bedecked, ogled and admired, lavished with gifts. She hardly sets eyes on her husband-to-be – there are separate ceremonies for the womenfolk.

She sees far too much of his mother.

Her own mother basks in the glorious accomplishment of getting her only daughter married to the most eligible bachelor in the kingdom. Her face is lit up from the inside, a glow no number of barbs and snide remarks, whispers that her daughter is 'wayward', that she deliberately set out to trap the prince, can dim.

Both Sita and her mother know not to pay heed to the frustrated outpourings of defeated women; Sita does not bother to come up with ripostes to the queen's pointed vitriol, of which there is a steady supply. She has won. She is marrying this woman's son against her wishes. Nothing can trump that. If, in return, the queen wants to spew a few foul words, so be it.

But what does stop her in her tracks, douse her happiness just a little, is the gossip she overhears being whispered among the queen's cronies.

'The king doesn't look well,' they say. 'Is he not happy with the marriage?'

They're just making things up, she tells herself. But a part of her worries that, even at this late stage, something might go wrong.

She manages to corner her brother in a rare moment away from the deluge of women: a few well-wishers, like the woman who had warned her about the queen's cronies during the queen's durbar, but mostly women who side with the queen, who flash cold smiles when she is looking and calculating glances when they think she is not.

I will not stand for this, she assures them in her head, *when I am queen*.

Kishan looks flushed with too much partying. 'Sita, in addition to being heir to the throne, Jaideep seems a genuinely good man. Who'd have thought that you, we—'

'*I* did,' Sita says, sharply. 'I knew I was destined for great things. I was just waiting for the world to see it too.'

He laughs. 'Yes, that you did.'

'What do you think of the king?'

'What do you mean?'

'People are saying he looks pale, washed out. That he's upset by the alliance.'

'I don't think so.' Then, staring speculatively at her, 'Since when did you start worrying about what people think? The girl I know doesn't care a whit what anyone thinks, even if that someone is the king. That's what's so amazing about you. Don't tell me you've changed.'

Sita smiles brightly at a point above her brother's head, not meeting his gaze. How to tell him that she is so thrilled and excited that sometimes this in itself worries her. That she lies awake at night worrying something might go wrong; that all this good luck will come at a price.

She recalls her ayah saying, 'The priest at your naming ceremony decreed that a cost would be extracted for any good fortune where you were concerned.'

Mary blaming her for her parents' accident, her father saying she brought bad luck, her mother reiterating that Sita had the kind of character that heralded trouble...

Although she shouldn't set store by such things, apprehension hounds Sita in the dark of night, as she lies in this household of celebration. But now her brother is looking at her with such faith that, bolstered by his gaze, her anxieties seem insignificant.

'Sita, you'll be the best queen this kingdom has ever seen, and I'm not just saying so because I'm your brother. I *know* so.' Kishan, her ally once more. Will she be able to rely on him? Will he always be on her side? Why is she thinking like this? About enemies and allies? Why, when she should be ecstatic? When she has achieved what other girls would give anything to get?

'Eligible princesses and their mothers are peeved that the crown prince of one of the best kingdoms around is taken. They were all groomed for this and he has asked for *your* hand,' her mother had crowed, beaming at Sita, her smile looking more like a grimace as her hair was pulled back and manipulated into a complicated bun by one of the bevy of servants who were getting them both ready for one of the many ritual pre-wedding ceremonies.

'You're more beautiful than all of them, and far more intelligent and shrewd than them too.' Her mother surprised Sita with her unexpected compliment. Then, gently, while the maids tried to create perfect pleats in the skirts of their ornate saris, 'I've had to rein you in, your fierce intellect, your indomitable spirit. You are like me. We are bright, we want more. I was a farm girl and did well by marrying your father and you, you've done even better than I dared hope for you.'

Her mother's astonishing speech had brought tears to Sita's eyes. For once, she, who always had a riposte ready, found she had no words.

If anyone had told her younger self that, when Sita was about to become the most powerful woman in the kingdom, barring the queen of course, she would be anxious, nervous, she would have laughed in their face.

But now that she is on the cusp of achieving everything she has longed for and dreamed about, she is edgy, doubts whirling like swallows across a twilight sky in her head.

What Sita worries about most is her betrothed. He chose her, going against his mother's wishes, based on that one conversation she had with him, standing in the palace grounds, hot air spiced with sweetmeats and celebration fanning their faces, cheetahs standing docile beside them, monkeys watching curiously from the trees.

And that is when her most secret worry unfurls, becomes a snake, fangs bared, ready to strike. For all her cheek, she is really quite naive. Once they are married, once the prince gets to know the real Sita, will he be disappointed?

Sita is feisty and ambitious. But she is also innocent. She knows how to sing, to play an instrument, to run a household. But how to please a man?

Her governess certainly never told her, but then she was never married herself.

Sita cannot ask her mother, who has reiterated, for as long as she can remember, 'Be a good wife, a dutiful wife to your husband.' And added the slogan, 'Be a good queen,' once the marriage proposal from the prince arrived.

Sita has rehearsed the words often: 'How exactly does one be a good wife, Ma?'

But although she is fearless when delivering retorts, these particular words die on her tongue, they are swallowed up along with saliva before they leave the confines of her mouth.

She doesn't have any female friends she can ask, not any more. A pang as she thinks of Mary. Sweet, gentle, generous, admiring Mary, who would without doubt be so pleased for Sita, if she were to see her now...

Her ayah, whom she could have asked, has passed away.

And so, she worries. She is upset by this insecurity she is discovering within herself, this vulnerability.

'Stop worrying, it will all sort itself out,' Kishan says, as if reading her mind. 'The king has had too much to drink and eat. This level of celebration has never been seen by the palace and it's taken its toll on him, that's all. Once things get back to normal, he will be fine.'

And finally it is the actual wedding, when Sita will officially become princess.

Wedding gifts of all kinds are paraded in procession through streets lined with cheering subjects, musicians leading the way, celebratory trumpets and tablas and conch shells; cows and bullocks elaborately draped and decorated following and, behind them, men on horseback.

Distinguished guests on bejewelled elephants, the British Resident, English dignitaries and Indian royalty among them. English ladies outfitted in luxurious gowns, elaborate hats and wielding parasols, the gentlemen wiping sweat from their foreheads with voluminous handkerchiefs. Indian kings dripping jewels, each one trying to outdo the other. Their wives the maharanis veiled and hidden away in the howdahs, the openings to which are also veiled with beautiful gold cloth matching the howdahs' domed coverings.

A cheer goes through the crowd as the bridegroom arrives on the most ostentatious elephant.

Once he enters the palace gates, to a fusillade of cannons, the anthem of the kingdom playing, fireworks booming, the palace gates are closed to the crowds, who gather at the gates to sneak a glimpse of the festivities taking place inside.

All this is relayed to Sita later, in a letter from Kishan, who is in the howdah with their father, the king and Prince Praveen, Jaideep's twin – 'The king was all right, but Prince Praveen was most unpleasant.'

Now, Sita waits for the prince to enter the holy mandap where the sacred rites are to be held. All morning she has been bedecked and adorned with jewels and flowers, her hair elaborately fashioned and, along with every inch of her body, studded with gold and pearls and diamonds. When the prince is seated, Sita, clothed in a resplendent sari handspun with gold thread, is carried to the mandap on an ornamented, veiled throne and the priest performs the rites of marriage.

The prince, donned in regal attire and turban, rubies catching the light, sapphires winking, takes Sita's breath away when she sneaks a glance at him from beneath her veil. He looks like someone out of a fairy tale.

This is actually happening!

Then she and the prince are walking round the holy fire. Through her veil, Sita watches the queen avert her eyes, notes the scowl on the face of the younger prince – her brother-in-law now.

There are many people who want me to fail, Sita thinks, as each circuit round the holy fire binds her to the crown prince for life.

And this makes her even more determined not to. She will prevail. She will be the best queen the kingdom has ever seen.

Chapter 33

Priya

A Stranger

2000

At 7 p.m., Priya is seated at the kitchen table sipping wine when the doorbell rings.

Jacob is nothing if not punctual.

And yet, why doesn't he let himself in?

Why ring the doorbell like a stranger?

Will it not go the way she imagined, with Jacob grovelling and Priya reluctant until at last she says, 'Okay then. You can stay'?

She opens the door and asks, an edge to her voice, 'Why didn't you use your key?' even as she breathes him in, every familiar much-loved feature, his body that has given her so much pleasure, his profile that she can trace in her dreams. No nubile nymphet in sight. He is hers again.

And then she takes in his flushed face, watches the words evaporate in his lying, cheating mouth. 'I...'

Her gaze going to his ring finger. Bare now but for a small tan mark.

She fingers her own, her hand going automatically to it.

She wants to pull it off, fling it in his face. She wants him to break down and cry, 'Forgive me.' She wants to plead with him to stay with her.

She wants... Oh, how she wants it all to go back to before. When she was innocent of this knowledge that chokes her, taints her heart, her mouth, her body with bitterness. That makes her feel used, unwanted, wanting, old.

Her husband stands in their doorway, like a stranger.

He has barely looked at her, the hours that went into doing her face, choosing her dress, beautifying her body futile.

And then he utters the words that she has refused to consider. Words that cause a crater to erupt in her already broken heart. 'Priya, I… I want a divorce.'

Chapter 34

Sita

Surprise

1930

'So,' Sita's husband – her husband! – says, beaming at her as they set off on their honeymoon. 'Did you enjoy the wedding festivities?'

Should she be honest with him? Why not? It is, after all, why she is here, sitting beside him, his wife! The thought sparks a thrill of trepidation at what is to come. That weird feeling of uncertainty, of insecurity, that has crept in since her marriage to him was arranged.

'I did.' She adds, 'Although I'm quite relieved to actually be spending time with you. I've seen more of your mother and your various aunts – how can one person have so many? – than you, my husband.'

He laughs, his face alight. That admiring look in his eyes, mingling with something else, softer. Affection, she identifies, her heart somersaulting.

He takes her hand in his. She looks at their entwined palms and feels a thrill as he moves closer and casually puts his other arm round the back of her seat. They sit companionably as the car weaves along tiny winding roads, bullock carts topped with hay, horse-drawn tongas, small villages, mud huts, beggar children, then forest and hills, shimmering lakes, giant trees, wild animals lurking within.

She falls asleep and when a jolt of the car wakes her, her head is resting on his shoulder, his head against hers. The smell of sweat and comfort. Their intertwined hands slick with perspiration.

She realises his eyes are open and he is looking at her, tenderness in his gaze.

Dusk outside, their car moving through darkness, under a violet awning pinpricked with stars. It feels like they are the only people in the world. The two of them in the back seat and the driver in the front.

'Are you hungry?' he asks.

'I think we ate a month's worth of food these past few days, don't you?' she says and he smiles.

'In any case, we'll be there soon.'

'Where're we going?'

'It's a surprise.' He grins widely.

'I love surprises,' she says, adding, 'as long as they're good ones.'

He chuckles. 'This *is* a good one.' And, after a bit, 'What're you thinking?' His voice gentle as the darkness softly rushing past their window. Every so often a lamp flickers in a passing cottage. Otherwise only the gently descending night. After the busyness of the past days, it is calming, restful.

Should she spoil it by telling him what she's thinking? The truth has worked for her thus far, so why not?

'Your mother doesn't like me.'

His eyes soften even more, if possible. 'She'll come round in time. She cannot stay immune to your charms for long.'

Sita thinks of her mother-in-law. That set face, those glittering hard eyes. 'Somehow I don't think so. I've a feeling I'm not the daughter-in-law she had in mind.'

He laughs, a long, low chuckle from deep within him that explodes in a satisfying rumble. 'Perhaps not. But you're exactly the wife *I* had in mind. I haven't been able to get you out of my mind since I saw you that day standing up to my brother.'

'Your brother—' she begins. But whatever else she was going to say is silenced by his lips on hers. The shock of it and then the pleasure. She closes her eyes, gives herself over to this man, her husband, his lips, his body against hers in the car as it moves through darkness.

Chapter 35

Mary

Talk

1936

The scream that rends the air is sharp with panic and pain, unlike the happy squeals of the children just a minute ago.

Mary rushes to the girl who has screamed. She is lying on the grass, clutching her leg, which is gushing blood at the knee, tears coursing down her face.

'Snake,' the other girls yell, pointing at the marigold bushes, and Mary glances over just in time to see a sinuous tail flicker and slither on the grass, then, undulating, disappear into the undergrowth.

'Fetch the doctor,' she yells to Sister Catherine, who has come running out to see what all the commotion is about.

While the cook's boy is dispatched to town to get the doctor, Mary manages to determine that the girl was not bitten by the snake, just scared enough by its bared fangs to fall off the tree where she was hiding, banging her knee in the process.

The doctor is an older man, wiry grey hair, gentle eyes. He competently bandages the girl's knee, while telling her jokes to take her mind away from what he is doing.

Mary watches him and tries, and fails, not to think of Vinay. *Have you set up practice in your town? How is it going with your wife whom you failed to mention during any of our conversations? Do you think of me at all?*

Afterwards, Mary sits with the doctor as he partakes of the tea and pakoras the nuns have plied him with.

'I'm sorry, I thought it was snakebite and thus we sent for you.'

'Don't worry, it's always good to get these things checked out.' And, after a bit, 'You're the new teacher. Have heard talk of you in town.'

There's been talk, Mrs Alden's voice in her head. 'All good, I hope.'

The doctor, Dr Kumar, smiles kindly at her. 'Of course. The girls love you and their parents are grateful.'

Mary wonders if the doctor can see through her to her home-sickness, the second thoughts she is having about her decision to come here, and is therefore trying to make her feel better. She's been here a week and it feels as if she's stumbling through her days, counting down the time before she can go back home. She does not imagine that she will ever really feel comfortable in this country, like her parents were. But now that she is here, Mary wants to do what she came for and, in time, visit the town where she had spent her childhood, which, being directly under British rule, is not part of the kingdom of Hawaldar, but not far from this town either, she has divined, from asking the nuns.

While in England Mary had unquestioningly done what her aunt and uncle thought best for her. Here, she is responsible for the children and for herself and it is novel while also challenging. Her confidence in her decision-making, never strong, has received a knock since discovering Vinay's deceit and every day, she wonders if she's doing the right thing, guiding these children when she cannot even guide herself properly.

'So what do you think of our town?' the doctor is saying.

'I haven't really seen it yet.'

'We must rectify that at once,' he says, setting down his teacup.

*

Two days later, an invitation arrives for Mary from Dr Kumar.

'My wife and I would be honoured to have you join us for tea at our home this Saturday. The date coincides with the king's birthday, and to mark the occasion the king and queen parade through town. A royal procession is always a grand affair.'

The nuns are delighted. 'About time you had some fun.'

Chapter 36

Sita

A Full Moon

1930

'Here we are.'

The car has come to a stop while they were kissing, Sita lost to the world and only aware of the man beside her, the feelings he was evoking in her.

She opens her eyes and blinks, taking in the shimmering expanse spread out before her. It takes her a minute, as the shadows adjust, to understand what she is seeing.

A vast glimmering mirror and in the midst of it, floating serenely, a palace, its illuminated likeness reflected in the dark depths of the lake. Moonlight playing peekaboo with the stars, replicated on the placid, glowing water, which carries a sheen of starlight and a mystery all its own, hiding secrets within its soft, inviting depths.

'Welcome to the Lake Palace, your hideaway on Lake Samovar, Princess Sita,' her husband whispers.

She stares up at him, awed.

'Glad I've rendered you speechless,' he whispers in her ear, warm breath tickling.

'I love your surprise!' she whispers back and he smiles, his teeth bright white in the mystical, secretive dark.

A luxurious covered boat with gilded seats is moored to the bank. The boatman bows deeply and helps them on.

They sail to the palace, the boat rocking on the waves, a full moon shining blessings down on them, stars twinkling, the soft murmur of water wafting on the cool night breeze, jasmine and excitement.

The palace gleams, lit up, welcoming.

Sita trails a hand in the silvery, shadow-kissed water. She pictures the fish floating below the gently rippling expanse bisected by their boat. Just like in the car, it is as if she and her husband and the boatman are the only people in the world. She wants this dreamy, enchantment-tipped boat ride to go on for ever.

'I feel like I'm in the midst of a fairy tale,' she says and her husband smiles warmly at her.

The boat pulls up to shore, anchoring on the island, and they are escorted up the drive and, once inside, plied with delicacies, a gourmet feast.

While they eat, the water is heated for their wash.

Afterwards, warm and clean and perfumed, Sita is led to the opulent bedchamber, the enormous bedposts decorated with garlands, the bed strewn with rose petals. Her husband waiting there for her, gathering her in his arms.

All her anxieties, the fear that has plagued her recently, returns and, since being truthful has served her in the past, she admits, 'I'm scared I'll let you down.'

'You can never do so, Sita.' His voice, the conviction in it, calms her.

He kisses her and her body responds of its own accord, all her doubts dispersing as his lips find hers. The fragrance of crushed roses and love.

Chapter 37

Priya

Apology

2000

In the stunned silence after her husband says he wants a divorce, Priya tries to gather words on her tongue, sitting at the table where she sat just a few hours ago, painting a different ending as she painted on her face.

She is not proud of what she finally manages: 'I-I don't understand.'

In the years to come, she will go over it again and again, changing what she said, redoing it in her head. But now, she is so completely taken aback that she sounds very small, defeated. In all the various scenarios she concocted, she refused to imagine this.

Jacob looks close to tears, his eyes raw with emotion. 'I'm so sorry.'

Now it comes. The long-awaited apology. But there is no triumph. No making him grovel. His gaze is remorseful but it is because of what he has said, the impact his words are having on her. Devastating her, breaking her even more than the image of his disastrous birthday evening seared behind her eyelids.

She cannot speak, her mouth salty, bitter with shock.

'I… I was waiting for the right time. I didn't mean for you to find out like this.'

She is not his soulmate. His love for her came with an end date. What she witnessed, along with their friends the night of his birthday, is not a one-time weakness.

She waits for the news to percolate, but it doesn't. It just sits there, an impenetrable lump in her throat.

Her husband sounds distraught. 'Your breakdown… It took its toll on me, Priya. I had to be strong for you and I-I found it wearing.'

She wants to wipe off her make-up, throw away her dress and the person she has carefully painted on, the unflappable, irrepressible Priya he fell in love with. She wants to bawl, holding on to him. 'Please,' she wants to beg, 'you're my anchor. I don't know myself without you any more. Don't leave me.'

'I couldn't leave when you were down. I couldn't leave you at your worst. But now you're back to your normal self…'

She stares at him. And when she sees the tears in his eyes, she looks down instead at the table they picked from that antiques shop down the road, this table that must have witnessed such drama during its time with different families over the years, so many lives made and broken, devastated and patched together and undone.

'You're telling me that you stood by me, cajoled me to get better, just so you could leave?' she asks the table, betrayal, sharp and acidic, making her want to heave. There is a mark on the table, she notes absently, a bruise stabbed into the wood. Is it from her or Jacob dropping something heavy and sharp-edged on it? Or was it already there, the blemish lending it character, a scar wrought by another family, someone who owned it earlier? No, for if it was, she would have noticed – she had polished it lovingly with beeswax when they brought it home, until it shone like new.

'No!' Jacob is saying.

She touches the contusion etched into the wood. It can never be repaired. Did she do it, or did Jacob?

'Priya, please, you must believe me.' Jacob's voice urgent.

And now she remembers. It was when she lost her most recent baby. Jacob saying, anguished, 'It's okay…' She had chucked the first thing to hand – a great big tin of mango pulp – at him, channelling all the outrage, the pain, the sorrow she was feeling. He had ducked – thank goodness – and it had fallen onto the table with a resounding thwack. Was that when their marriage started to unravel? Or was it before, when she went to pieces after she lost her first baby?

'I…' Jacob sounds crushed. 'She… she's pregnant.'

Priya can't be hearing right. She cannot.

He wouldn't do it to her, surely? Jacob, who knows how much this means to her, how much it hurts her. The only one to know.

'I'm sorry, Priya. I…'

Priya reminds herself to breathe in and out, in and out. She sits there, very carefully holding herself upright, her face together, knowing that even if she moves an inch, she will collapse.

'Priya?'

From somewhere within the shattered depths of her, she finds a smidgen of her voice. It feels like knives tearing at her throat, but she manages to say, 'Leave.'

'Priya…'

She sets her head down on the cradle of her arms, her finger touching the gouge on the table.

Irreparable.

Chapter 38

Sita

Drums

1930

Drums, persistent, pounding in Sita's brain. She wraps her arms around her head, trying to squeeze out the sound, but they won't stop.

She gives up. Opens her eyes. She is in a man's arms. Sweat and salt and bruised blooms. He is snoring gently. Sunlight angles in through a chink in the elaborate brocade curtains, showing up crushed rose petals and flower garlands strewn on the lush, patterned carpet. Jasmine and marigold wreaths dangling from the bedposts. A vast room with ample, ornate furnishings.

Someone knocking on the door.

Bang. Bang. Bang. It reverberates right through her skull.

She wants to go back to sleep, ensconced in her husband's arms. She watches him, blushing a little as she recalls the previous night.

Is this what her mother meant when she intoned, 'Be dutiful'?

It's not a great hardship, is it, Ma?

The pounding on the door continues.

Surely the servants should be allowing them to sleep? Especially on their first morning as a married couple? Why are they beating the door quite so insistently? How dare they?

And then, a trickle of panic drizzling over her sunshiny feeling of sated contentment…

What if something has happened?

Her ayah's voice in her head: 'The priest at your naming ceremony decreed that a cost would be extracted for any good fortune where you were concerned.'

She sits up, her husband still sleeping peacefully beside her. He complains as she gently extracts her arm out from under him, murmuring his unhappiness, and then rolls over and is deeply asleep again.

She goes to the adjoining bathroom, splashes water on her face. She recalls the lake the previous night. She would love to see it this morning, in daylight.

But first... She will see what is so urgent that it cannot wait another hour or so.

Three servants stand outside the bedroom, all looking grave, one with his hand raised to knock again.

In the bed behind her, her husband stirs.

She steps out of the room and closes the door, to allow him to sleep.

'What is it that couldn't wait?' Her voice sharp.

'We're sorry,' the oldest of the servants says, 'but we've just received word from the palace...' The man's voice tails off and he looks, if possible, even more solemn.

'The palace?' For a minute, her sleep-deprived mind fails to make the connection. They are in a palace, aren't they?

Then, even as the man speaks, she understands.

'The queen sent word with one of the servants. The boat arrived half an hour ago.'

The servant must have been travelling through the night. What could have been so important as to...

Even as her heart seizes with fear, the man says, 'The king collapsed yesterday evening. He is dead. You are to leave for the palace at once.'

Sita rests her head against the door behind which her husband sleeps, oblivious. She thinks of the king, whom she has barely seen.

A plump man, kind eyes that he has bequeathed to his older son. He had looked so tired the last few days.

She remembers the whispers making the rounds that had her so worried. 'Is he not happy with the marriage?'

It wasn't that. He just wasn't feeling well.

Perhaps the festivities of the wedding were too much for his heart and it gave way.

And then, as the news gradually sinks in: the king is dead. Her husband is being summoned so precipitately because he is the king's eldest son, next in line to the throne.

Sita wanted to be queen, she dreamed of it. But she never imagined it would happen this fast, like this, she thinks as she goes inside, her whole being wobbly like the custard her ayah used to give her as treat for good behaviour, as she wakes her husband, watches his sleep-befuddled eyes light up when he sees her, sees the light go out of them again as she tells him, sees the incomprehension and then the pain that haunts them wiping away all trace of the twinkle that seems to almost permanently reside there when he looks at her.

He stands up and it is the weary stance of a much older man, one who carries the weight of a kingdom on his shoulders.

She wants to ease his ache, fold him in her arms. But now is not the time. She takes his hand in hers, and he flashes her a brief, grateful smile before he informs the servants that he will be ready in half an hour and to get the boat around.

Sita wanders onto the vast veranda encircling the palace, staring at the lake, serene and shimmering blue, like the guileless conscience of a less grasping woman. She is angry with herself for the trickle of excitement that shivers down her spine as the palace basks in the sunshine, as she traces its reflection in the water.

This is mine now.

Chapter 39

Priya

Announcement

2000

It's been a week since Jacob's announcement. Priya has ignored all the phone calls, the repeated knocking on the door.

He doesn't have a key. Furious and smarting from his betrayal, she'd asked for it back. He had posted it when he left and seeing it on the doormat, Jacob's key, with the Hawaii keychain that she had brought back for him from a research trip for one of her documentaries, the finality of what had happened had hit her.

He's having a child with another woman. Starting a family with her. The family I was meant to have.

Jacob is the only person in the world, other than the counsellor, who knows about her breakdown after she lost her babies. He was the reason she clawed herself back out of it.

When she found him out the day of his birthday, when he left her that evening to her doubts and her devastation at his betrayal, she had not succumbed to the blackness pulling at the edges she held so carefully together, wanting to unravel her. She had channelled rage instead, righteous anger.

She was able to fight off the darkness because she chose to assume that what she had seen was a one-off manifestation of midlife crisis by her husband. He loved her. True, she had not been a great wife lately, morose and down. He wasn't a saint; he had slipped. It was understandable. Even as she raged, she made excuses for him. Even as she was angry with him, she was also forgiving him, looking ahead, refusing to consider the worst-case scenario – that he was done with her.

But now she has no choice but to accept it. There is no future for them together. The future is the child Jacob has made with such ease with another woman.

The pain is unbearable, all-consuming. She lies on the bed, bereft of her husband, cheat and traitor, and she won't get up. She has no reason to any more.

'Look at the positives.' Her counsellor's voice in her head.

What positives? Priya cannot fool herself. This is the truth: she is a non-starter as a mother, a failure as a wife and in her professional life. Her last three projects have bombed. She was not able to sell them to any network, even the local ones. Her husband has left her for a bimbo who is pregnant, the child she, Priya, hasn't been able to give him.

'Think of a happy place,' the counsellor had said, during one of their early sessions.

'I don't have a happy place,' Priya had cried.

'When you were growing up, wasn't there some place that made you happy to look at it?'

Now, in her darkened room, which reeks of her grief, she shuts her eyes and pictures the garden just outside the gates of her childhood home, that wild profusion of flowers, a cornucopia of abundant, dancing hope…

Chapter 40

Sita

Feminine Wiles

1930

When Sita and her husband, the crown prince, soon to be king, step out of the car at the palace, her husband's twin brother is waiting.

He looks pale, reduced. The swagger he carries is gone, so he appears young. His eyes raw.

He ignores Sita, his gaze on his brother.

'Ma wants to see you.'

'How is she?' Jaideep's voice thick with upset.

'Not good.' His brother's tone clipped, short.

They go through the long corridors, sombre-faced servants standing to attention. The many rooms, open and yawning, ornate and yet, now, without pomp, music, festivities, feeling empty. Echoing with, reverberating from, shock and loss.

The queen is in her chambers, where Sita has not been before, having only attended the durbar, which she sees now was held in a room at the very beginning of the east wing that, although extravagantly opulent, did not give a hint as to the size of the wing or the treasures it held within.

The queen's chambers are almost a palace in themselves, separated from the main building by a huge rectangular courtyard, replete with palm trees, parrots, mynahs and other exotic birds chittering from the branches, a garden profuse with kaleidoscopic blooms, peacocks roaming among them, a pool the size of a small lake, dotted with fountains and, in the midst, a small temple, reflected in the rippling water. This courtyard is different from the one Sita saw when she was exploring the palace that fateful day when she met both princes for the first time.

The queen's rooms are even more lavish than what Sita has seen of the palace so far. They brim to bursting with tapestries and sculptures, paintings and mirrored screens, statues and mermaids, fountains and bowers. The queen obviously likes to collect beautiful, expensive antiques and surround herself with them.

They come to a halt in one of the biggest rooms Sita has encountered in this palace of wonders, where no room is smaller in size than a tennis court. More tapestries and wall hangings here, divans and armchairs as elaborate as thrones, cubbyholes with writing desks. A swing seat. A hammock. Huge columns of sculpted marble. Stained-glass windows. And behind a painted screen, a magnificent bed, swathed in silk.

The queen is reclining on a divan, propped up by cushions, looking alarmingly pale. Servants attend to her, one massaging her legs, another fanning her face with a fan made entirely of peacock feathers, the turquoise and navy eyes glinting knowingly.

Her eyes are closed but she opens them as they approach. Her lower lip trembles when she sees her sons, her eyes raw and bejewelled with tears, ringed with navy circles. Then her gaze lands on Sita and she recoils.

'What is she doing here?'

A trembling finger pointing at Sita, matching the tremor in her voice.

'You don't mean Sita?' Jaideep stares at his mother, appalled. After just a day, Sita's husband looks older, his features slack and tired, aged by loss and grief and weariness.

The servants avert their eyes.

'She is your daughter-in-law.'

'She brings nothing but bad luck.' The queen turns her anguished eyes on Sita and they are a snake's, small and hard, spitting venom.

'Ma, this is my wife you're speaking about.' Jaideep puts his arm round Sita, trying to shield her.

Every instinct in Sita wants to pull away. *I don't need protecting. I can defend myself well enough, thank you.*

'Her birth heralded destruction when a storm destroyed part of her house,' the queen says. 'I warned your father, but he wouldn't listen. He went ahead with the marriage and the moment she becomes part of our family, we lose him.' Then, softer, looking directly, mournfully at Jaideep, 'She's cursed, son. She needs to go.'

The servants are pretending they are deaf and dumb but her husband's twin is riveted. His wan face, just a few moments ago stripped of swagger, so Sita had almost been moved to feel sorry for him, is transformed. He appears to have come alive again, seemingly puffing up before her eyes.

'M... Ma, what on earth are you saying? Sita is my wife,' Jaideep says. 'Father blessed her, he was so happy to have her join our family.'

'He was taken in by her charms. Her beauty is poisonous, son. It warps the eyes, closes the mind to what is inside.'

'Ma!' Upset and anger inflating Jaideep's voice.

'It's not too late, son. You can—'

'Never. Your grief is making you say things you don't mean.' His grip on Sita tightening.

She means every word, Sita thinks.

You're going about this the wrong way, woman, she tells her mother-in-law in her head. *You think you'll win your son over by blaming me. But you are wrong. I can handle you, give as good as I get. But I'm keeping my mouth shut, for, by doing so, I'm the wronged party. You could have played this so much better, but instead, you are making your hatred of me known, making your son choose. He'll have to take sides and he'll not be happy. He'll resent you in time, if he doesn't already, for trying to break up our marriage.*

'She came into this house and we lost your father, too soon.' The queen closes her eyes, two fat tears squeezing out of the lids. 'Why is she here now? Intruding upon our sorrow. I want to be alone with my sons for a few minutes before the funeral rites commence.'

Jaideep looks at his mother and then at Sita, a plea in his eyes. He is torn, she can see. Her kind husband, not knowing what to do in the face of feminine wiles.

She squeezes his hand, the one that is slung round her shoulder. Then she slips out of his grasp. He smiles gratefully at her.

'I'll see you later,' she tells her husband.

Her mother-in-law, currently queen but not for much longer, opens her eyes, looks at Sita with a glint in them.

Sita meets her gaze steadily, hoping the queen can read the message in hers.

You think you are clever. But I am more so.

You don't want me here, you say. You want just your sons. What about the servants who are scattered about the room? Don't they intrude upon your grief?

I will give in now. I will go quietly. I will keep my mouth shut. For it wouldn't do for the new bride to hurt the grieving widow.

You want to play this game? Then let's.

But know this: I can play better.

And I will win.

You are losing already.

The queen must read it all in her gaze for she closes her eyes again, affecting weariness.

Prince Praveen ignores Sita, his attention on his prone mother.

Her husband's gaze lingers on Sita as she gives him a small smile and walks away, maidservants following to show her to her rooms.

Chapter 41

Priya

Out of Context

2000

There's an incessant banging somewhere at the edge of her consciousness. It goes on and on.

Priya pulls her husband's pillow down over her ears, burrowing deeper into sheets smelling of sweat and unwashed body and grief. She sniffs the pillow, but any lingering scent of her husband is long gone.

'Priya, open up. Please,' she hears, the voice familiar and yet jarringly out of context.

'If you don't, I'll break down the door.'

Her father. Isn't he supposed to be in New York?

'Priya? Sweetheart?'

She stands. At least she tries. Her head spins and she falls back down onto the bed again. How many days since she ate? She has been stumbling into the kitchen, drinking water straight from the tap. But she cannot remember eating.

'Priya?'

This time she is able to make it, with difficulty, to the front door and pull it open.

Her father stands there, immaculately clothed as always.

She has not dreamed him up. He is here, in the flesh.

'Baba?' she manages before her vision goes blurry.

She sways on her feet, a glimpse of her father's alarmed face, his arms reaching for her as she succumbs to the blackness that has been crowding the edges of her eyes, weighing down her body.

Chapter 42

Sita

Ephemeral

1932–1934

'I hear the girls' school you've started is up and running,' Sita's mother says.

Sita is visiting with her parents. They have been obsequious, her father sitting down to dine with her and her mother instead of taking meals in his study as he was wont to do before Sita left home. Kishan is away working.

'Yes, the school is well established.' Sita smiles. 'But of course, it was the king who…'

'Ha!' Her mother laughs. 'Being demure doesn't suit you.'

Sita grins widely. Just as she had always wished to, since her brother was sent away to school and she wasn't, she has started a girls' school in the kingdom. She knew her subjects would never send their girls to school if the teachers were male, and the only women teachers she was able to find were nuns. She had hired them on the condition that they educate the children but refrain from trying to convert them to Christianity. 'The school is more successful than even I envisioned. Girls attend from all parts of the kingdom. The nuns are looking for help – women teachers are proving hard to find. Let me know if you know of anyone.'

Her father looks up from his plate. 'I hear that if anybody needs anything, from running a policy by the British Resident to settling a dispute, they have to come to you, not the king.'

Her mother smiles fondly at her. 'You're doing so much good, Sita. You're providing for the poor; your subjects are happy, especially with the road construction. The roads are bringing together every corner of the kingdom! And in addition to starting the girls' school, you've affected improvements to the boys' one, I hear.'

'Aren't you going to mention the women's refuge?' Sita asks archly.

Sita has talked Jaideep, her husband the king, into starting a refuge for women (along with the girls' school, she is most proud of this) on the banks of the lake that harbours the Lake Palace, to house women in need, both unmarried and those abandoned by or wanting to escape from their husbands.

'It caused some controversy, I hear,' her father says mildly.

'I'm not fazed by that.'

'We know,' her mother says with feeling and Sita chuckles.

The refuge has caused a great furore, being the first of its kind in the kingdom, the advisory committee to the king (comprising entirely of men, of course) being against it. But Sita had stood firm and Jaideep, knowing how important this was to her, didn't back down despite an outcry from his committee. The refuge is up and running and hugely successful, managed, like the girls' school, by nuns, with funding from the palace.

'The kingdom is prospering under the new king, although everyone knows that the person running it is really the queen.' Her mother winks at her. 'So what's next on your agenda?'

'I'm planning to host a cheetah hunt just for womenfolk,' Sita says.

'It's a man's sport. Women are better off managing house—' Her father stops on seeing Sita's face, her set expression as she puts her glass down, pushes her plate away.

'Are you saying that what I, the queen, am organising, what the king has given his blessing for, is wrong?' she asks, her voice dangerously low.

Her father colours. Her mother has stopped eating. The servants, her mother's and her own who have accompanied her from the palace, hover, anxious.

'No, I... Of course not. Your mother is going, I presume?'

'I haven't invited her yet.'

Her father nods quietly. Her mother looks down at her plate. And Sita experiences, not for the first time, the heady effect of the power she wields. The hard-won triumph of her father giving in to her. This man who had dragged her up the steps of this very house and vowed to get her married at once when he thought she was swimming in the pond with Giri the cook's son.

'We're so proud of you. You're a worthy queen,' her mother says, smoothing ruffled feathers; her father nods agreement.

Sita smiles, sitting back and taking it, as is her due.

She returns to the palace on a high.

'You took your time,' the queen mother says.

Sita comes crashing down.

She will never fully feel like the queen at the palace when the queen mother is there at every turn, complaining, moaning. In mourning still, although it's been two years since her husband passed away, and milking privileges because of it.

It has gone on for long enough.

What is the point of Sita being queen when this woman acts as if she is answerable to her? It undermines her power, in front of the servants and dignitaries visiting the palace, especially when the queen mother is residing in the best apartments, the east wing.

The queen mother needs to be shown her place, and Sita must exercise her right as queen. The first thing she needs to do, what she should have done much earlier really, is move the woman away from the east wing, gradually ease her hold on the palace and on her son, Sita's husband.

Sita waits until Jaideep is falling asleep after being with her, that mellow time soft with love when he will promise her anything.

'I've been queen two years now,' she says, playing with the hair on his chest, 'don't you think it's time I moved into the east wing?'

He opens one eye and smiles at her. 'With my mother? You're effecting a truce?'

Sita has never let on just how much his mother and her barbed comments, her constant disapproval, affect her, make her question herself in that darkest time of night before dawn when the worries and insecurities she conceals from the world swamp and stab. And so her husband treats the distance between his wife and his mother, the fact that they insist on staying in separate apartments within the palace instead of together in the east wing, as a gentle disagreement that will disappear with time.

'Not quite yet,' she says and he chuckles.

She places her head on his chest, the better to hear the rumble of his laughter.

'I'm planning on hosting a weekly durbar for the kingdom's womenfolk so they can come to me with their problems – their men may not always champion their best interests and this way they have a voice. The east wing is best suited for that. Your mother could move into the suite of rooms at the back of the palace. They're not currently being used.'

Her husband's laughter dies and he pulls himself up, resting on his elbows to look at her. She smiles innocently at him.

'Does Ma have to move? The east wing is big enough that—'

'She has made it abundantly clear that she doesn't want to share with me.'

'But Sita… Ma's been in the east wing since she married my father.'

'Exactly. And it's been two years since I married you.'

His gaze in the flickering shadows cast by the lamps is troubled. 'I don't know, Sita, if it is wise… She's grieving.'

'And doing up her new rooms will take her mind away from it, give her some purpose!'

'I… I suppose.' He still appears anxious and so she leans in and kisses him deeply.

He gathers her in his arms and as he kisses her again, she asks, 'Will you speak to her tomorrow?'

'I will,' he promises just before his lips meet hers.

As expected, the queen mother creates quite a hubbub, using emotional blackmail and upping the grieving widow act.

'First I lose my husband and then you evict me from the rooms my husband brought me to as a new bride, filled with memories of him, treasures we collected on our trips together?' she cries, tears budding in her eyes.

'Ma…' Jaideep wavering.

'Sita has turned your mind. She caused all this bad luck to our family. She—' The queen mother stops, seeing his gaze harden.

But the damage is done.

'What bad luck are you referring to? The kingdom is prospering, my subjects are happy. Is there something I should know?' Jaideep's voice flinty.

'No, son, I… Your father—'

'He died two years ago, Ma. Since then, the kingdom has run smoothly, has it not?'

'It has. But Sita—'

'Enough, Ma. Will you share the east wing with my wife?'

'I will not.'

'Well, then…' Jaideep stands firm and the queen mother moves out, complaining all the way.

Sita has won.

And yet, when her husband comes to visit her in her rooms in the east wing, she detects a change in him. A slight hesitation. A holding back.

She wonders if she is imagining it.

But his eyes… those eyes that had been so easy to read before, and soft with love, now flash with something – doubt, uncertainty – when he looks at her.

Although Sita has evicted the queen mother, appropriated the east wing for herself, or perhaps because of it, the queen mother will not leave her alone.

Sita is in the library when, 'Ah, there you are. *Reading.*'

The queen mother invading her sanctuary feels like sacrilege. The word 'reading' sounds like an accusation. Derisive, thick with scorn.

'When I was queen I had no time…'

'But you are not queen now, *I* am.'

'For now.' The queen mother sniffs. 'But your womb is yet to be filled. If Praveen provides the kingdom with an heir and you don't…' She snorts and leaves, her sentence dangling in the air.

Sita bites her tongue, hard, as it dawns on her afresh that this position of power she revels in is ephemeral, subject to conditions.

Prince Praveen, her husband's twin, has married a princess, the kind of girl the queen mother wanted her eldest son to wed instead of Sita.

Praveen's wife, Latha, is sweet and kind and reminds Sita of Mary, and, instead of the dislike she was expecting to feel, she has warmed to her.

When Praveen married Latha, Sita had been worried for this naive girl. But she has watched with amazement how gentle and solicitous her prickly brother-in-law is with his wife, the sarcasm and hard-done-by veneer that he wears like armour disappearing in Latha's presence. And she in turn adores him, although she is awed by and more than a little afraid of his mother.

'You're amazing to stand up to her,' she's said more than once, referring to Sita's battles with the queen mother.

'You could too, easily. She's all bluster.'

Latha had shrunk visibly when Sita suggested this. 'I… She… I'm glad she lives with you.'

Sita had hoped that the queen mother would move in with her favourite son, Praveen having relocated to the sprawling palace at the base of the hills that marked one edge of the kingdom, gifted to him by Jaideep on the occasion of his marriage to Latha.

She had even manipulated Jaideep into suggesting it.

'I think living by the hills will be good for your mother's health. She's been beset by ailments lately.'

Illness – another of the queen mother's ploys to win her eldest son over.

Jaideep had mulled it over and agreed with Sita – as always.

'The air at the foot of the hills will be better for you, Ma,' he'd proposed gently.

'Are you trying to get rid of me?' his mother had barked. 'I arrived here as a young bride and I'm not going anywhere. This is my home. As it is I've been relegated to the back of the palace, a few poky rooms instead of the east wing that I've occupied from the time I was a bride.'

Try as she might Sita cannot concentrate on her book in the wake of the queen mother's interruption, the words swimming before her eyes, the iron taste of defeat in her mouth.

Despite now being able to read as much as she wants, as often as she wants, Sita cannot derive the same pleasure from books that she used to as a child. Reading doesn't calm her as it once did.

She walks out of the book-filled room that she had coveted when she first laid eyes on it, that fateful day when she met both princes and saw the cheetahs for the first time, her steps quickening, her strides lengthening. This palace, in spite of its extravagant trappings, does not feel like home. She cannot relax in here with the heckling presence of the queen mother casting a pall.

She is walking so fast that she practically sprints down the maze like corridors, wanting escape, fresh air. She runs down the vast gardens, the exotic flower beds, the trees, past the ambling, curious monkeys, until she comes to the cheetah enclosure.

One day, I will own a zoo, she had promised herself when she saw Mary's. And now she has one even better.

She looks at the palace silhouetted by the setting sun, the pristine grounds sloping down to the lake at the far end.

She has achieved everything she wanted. She has won, the queen mother and Prince Praveen have lost; but then why does her mouth taste bitter with defeat?

She looks at the beasts, wild, beautiful, their caged power exuding from their captive bodies.

I am like you, she thinks, not for the first time.

She has power, adulation – that of her parents and of a kingdom, of a loving husband. She has all the wealth in the world and yet, the palace feels like a gilded prison. She is trapped in there, trapped by duty, by what is expected of her.

Chapter 43

Mary

Milk and Honey

1936

'Miss Brigham, so delighted you could come.' Dr Kumar smiles warmly as he ushers Mary inside. 'This is my wife, Brinda.'

A plump woman, who blushes as she echoes her husband's words. 'Delighted you could come.'

'And this,' the doctor says, gesturing towards a tall, swarthy Englishman, 'is Dr Charles Soames. He has a practice in the city but is staying in town, in a cottage a few doors down from ours, for a few weeks. He's recently been ill and the fresh air will do him good, isn't that so, Dr Soames?'

'I've only been here a few days but I feel better already.' Dr Soames smiles.

The Kumars have conjured up quite the spread – cucumber and egg sandwiches, potato bondas and onion bhajis, rice pudding and a wide variety of cakes, kheer and laddoos and barfi, tea and coffee, fresh lime juice and mango lassi.

But it is in the unexpected company of Dr Soames that Mary feels at home for the first time since she arrived in India. His solicitousness, the attentive tilt to his head, reminds her of England, the men paying court to her and her cousins during their jaunts in the carriage around town or while accompanying her aunt on visits. After days of trying to fit in, find her place in this familiar yet strange country, it is a relief to follow the familiar script of polite conversation with someone who responds exactly as expected. It is like slipping into a pair of comfortable shoes after having spent a day wearing ones that pinched.

Afterwards, 'Are you up for seeing the king's birthday procession?' Dr Kumar asks.

'Very much so,' Mary replies, smiling.

The town buzzes with festivity. Vendors selling sweetmeats and wooden toys, embroidered scarves and bangles. Multicoloured bunting slung along wooden pillars by the side of the road fluttering in the saccharine breeze.

Dr Kumar buys cotton candy from a passing vendor.

'Children are not the only ones who love this,' he says, handing Mary a frothy pink stick and his wife another.

Sweet spun sugar, bright pink, melting in her mouth, transporting Mary back to childhood, that time her father had taken her to a fair and carried her high on the throne of his shoulders.

The roadside is crowded with people angling for a good spot from where to watch the procession. 'There's space over there,' Mary says, noticing a cordoned-off section where there are chairs laid out, some of them empty.

Dr Kumar and his wife hang back. 'It's only for English sahibs and memsahibs.'

'Then we'll stand here with you,' Mary says loyally and Dr Soames nods assent.

'You cannot see anything from here. We've been spectators at many of these processions over the years. In fact, we'd like to head home now,' Dr Kumar says. 'Dr Soames, once the procession is over, if you'd kindly walk Miss Brigham to our house, we'll arrange a carriage for her return home.'

'Please don't worry about me. I'd like to walk back. It isn't far at all and this way I get to see the town,' Mary insists.

'Please call me Charles,' Dr Soames says to Mary, once Dr Kumar and his wife have left.

She smiles. 'And I'm Mary.'

'Shall we…?' Charles nods towards the cordoned-off section.

Mary hangs back, embarrassed to be sitting while there are so many people crowding on the Indian side.

But then a cheer goes through the crowd, everyone pushing and surging as they try to catch a glimpse of the procession, and curiosity gets the better of her. She ducks under the rope, followed by Charles, and stands by the roadside – everyone is standing now, the chairs lying abandoned – looking up the hill towards the palace.

The gates of the palace open and men with drums emerge, followed by trumpeters and others wielding musical instruments Mary doesn't recognise. Behind them, men on horseback, the horses draped with glittering cloth, their riders wearing jewelled turbans. Bullock carts ornamented and garlanded and heaped with gifts, presumably the king's birthday presents, and behind them, earth thundering in their wake, elephants, once again sumptuously adorned, topped by bejewelled throne-like seats carrying royalty.

'Such riches on display. Too ostentatious, actually rather vulgar, I must say,' the woman next to Mary breathes, fanning herself with an intricately patterned fan. She is wearing an enormous hat that nudges Mary's cheek every time the woman moves her head.

'Rumour has it the queen bathes in milk and honey every morning,' Charles murmurs.

Mary swivels to face him. 'Does she?'

'Not really.' His eyes twinkle as he grins at her, wiping the sweat that has collected on his nose with a voluminous handkerchief.

She can't help but return his smile, and as she adjusts her hat and turns back round a hush descends on the crowd.

The mosquitoes biting, the press of humid heat – none of it matters as Mary takes in the king, dripping rubies and sapphires, pearls and gold, waving at his adoring public from a jewelled box set upon an elephant.

The queen, following in her own jewelled box, looks haughtily at the world from atop the elephant and from beneath her veil, her gaze hidden and yet encompassing.

Something about her – the way she holds herself, the tilt of her chin, the way she stares, imperiously and unashamedly at the crowd, her subjects…

It comes to Mary, a shocked gasp, an all-consuming thrill. *I know her.*

It is then that Mary faints, slick from heat and excitement, darkness swarming her, dense black wiping the brightness from her glittering, dazzled eyes.

When she comes to, head groggy and heavy, an angel with a dark curly halo is hovering over her.

She blinks. The sky endless and yawning above her. Sunny without a trace of a cloud. Hot white. She is in India. In a stranger's arms. The scent of musk and ginger.

'Here, drink this.'

A shiny receptacle placed at her lips. She sips the water in soft gulps. It tastes metallic, but is cool in her parched throat.

'You fainted just when the royal howdah bearing the queen went past.'

The queen…

Her childhood friend?

Sita, so focused and feisty and determined. 'I'm going to change the world,' she would declare. 'Make a difference. Be someone.'

Well, Sita, if it is you, you've become someone all right.

'The townspeople say your fainting is an omen of some sort.'
When he smiles, Charles Soames looks like a vision.

'I thought you were an angel.' She sits up, his strong arms
helping her.

He laughs. 'I hate to disappoint but I'm very human.'

All around them, people are leaving, the air rent with stamped-
ing feet, receding elephants, the smell of fading afternoon, dust
and dung and anticlimax, the taste of spices and milky tea.

'Do you feel able to stand?' Charles asks.

'Yes.' She stumbles to her feet, feeling dazed, unsteady.

He notices. 'I'll call a carriage for you.'

She feels too faint to protest.

When the carriage arrives, he says, 'I'd like to accompany you,
if I may, just to make sure you're all right.'

Once again, she is too spent to resist. 'Thank you.'

'What brought you to India?' Charles asks, once they're in the
carriage.

'I was born here and when my parents – when they died in an
accident – I was sent to England.'

It is easy to converse with Charles. Like another doctor who
she will *not* think about, Charles doesn't talk down to her. And
with Charles, polite and proper, there's the added comfort of that
flavour of England, home. By the time they arrive at the school,
they've become friends.

'What's the queen's name?' Mary asks Sister Catherine when she
comes in after bidding goodbye to Charles.

'Queen Sita.' Sister Catherine smiles. 'Why?'

'I knew her as a child.' Mary muses on it. 'She was visionary
and ambitious, even then.'

'Well, well! Will you write to her, requesting an audience?'

'Oh, I… I don't know.' Mary had come to India hoping to reunite with Sita and Amin at some point. But now that she has found Sita, misgivings take hold.

Sita was her best friend; she made Mary feel privileged and lucky to have the parents and upbringing she had. But Sita had outshone Mary in every way – Mary's parents had noticed and appreciated this, making Mary feel deficient, lacking. She loved Sita but was also just slightly jealous of her. And although her parents' accident had not been Sita's fault, a part of Mary can't help thinking, even now, that it would never have happened had Sita not come into her life…

A thought strikes her: 'Was this school built by the queen?'

'It was one of the first things the new king did, start a school for the girls of the kingdom. I'm not one to gossip, but they do say the queen is behind every one of the king's decisions.' Sister Catherine twinkles at her.

If it wasn't for Sita starting this school, I wouldn't be here.

Chapter 44

Sita

Stubbornly Empty

1935

Sita is hosting a celebratory durbar on the occasion of her birthday when the commotion takes place.

She is seated on her throne, dressed in a handspun sari threaded through with pure gold, sequinned with diamonds and studded with rubies, jewels in her hair, pearls crowding her neck alongside gold necklaces, gold bangles tinkling on her arms. Women come up to her to pay their respects and shower her with gifts and compliments, while in the centre of the vast hall, dancers entertain the guests who have already paid court to her.

Sita recalls mediating at the panchayat with Mary and her father, her first exhilarating taste of power. How Mary's father's eyes had lit up in admiration when he said, 'You're a better arbitrator than I am.'

If you could see me now, Mary, Sita muses, as she sips aam panna, spiced green mango juice, and watches the women in her durbar.

Sita's sister-in-law, Praveen's wife, Latha, was unable to attend, as she is visiting with her parents.

Sita's mother-in-law has no such excuse. She and her followers are conspicuous by their absence – the few cronies who have retained allegiance to the queen mother instead of switching over to Sita's camp, that is.

Sita has installed spies among the servants attending to the queen mother so she knows all that goes on: who visits her, what is being discussed in her chambers at the back of the palace.

'If only my younger son, younger by a minute, had been born first,' is the queen mother's latest lament. 'He's married a princess, a girl from the right family. A girl who listens to him, does as he asks. My older son on the other hand... Completely under his wife's thumb, ruled by her. That woman is the reason I'm here, relegated to a forgotten corner of the palace while she holds court in the rooms *I* decorated and furnished.'

Sita sighs. She's not going to let thoughts of her mother-in-law or other unhappy thoughts mar this, her birthday durbar. And yet they come relentless. They hover and prod. They hurt and sting.

Five years since her marriage. Five years she has enjoyed the privilege, the pomp and the power of being queen.

Her husband loves her. She knows this despite the watchfulness, the seed of uncertainty that has crept into bed with them since she insisted she move into the east wing and his mother move out. Jaideep gives her more freedom than other men do their women. And yet, she knows he yearns for a child. He waits, she understands, every time he comes into her chambers, for her to say he is to be a father. And when she is silent, something in his face congeals.

It scares her and haunts her, this hardness etched on her husband's kind visage, the set to his face as the months roll into years with no heir. In the depths of night, she traces his features and worries he might turn on her, that he will direct that hardness upon her, that he will blame her. And then where will she be? *He* is the reason she is queen.

Sita had assumed being queen would grant her freedom, but in fact it has meant she is bound even more by rules and regulations, by tradition and what is expected of her. She is answerable to *everyone*; she has all eyes on her.

It is wearing and sometimes she thinks with longing of the days before, when she was an ordinary girl, and the only cares she had were railing against the injustices done to girls and trying to outsmart her governess.

But... she has loved rising up to the challenge of appearing dutiful while also trying to do as she wants. She has loved gently manipulating her husband, nudging him towards the right decisions, the ones best for the kingdom. She has loved outsmarting her mother-in-law and her brother-in-law, having the ear of the king while they don't.

However, as the months pass and her womb doesn't quicken with child, it appears as if her mother-in-law and brother-in-law might win yet, the knowledge leaving a permanent bitter taste in her mouth even while she eats the sweetest of foods.

If her brother-in-law has a child and she doesn't, she has lost. It is imperative that she conceive.

Her husband is wearing lines on his face that weren't there before. Some of them can be credited to age, others to the pressures of kingship, yet others to having to constantly deal with his mother's vitriol and his brother's barely disguised dislike of his wife, the grievance his brother carries, wearing his burden of being hard done by on his face for all to see, his ambition to be king thwarted by the cruel whim of fate. But yet others... Those can be attributed to the lack of a child, an heir. What all those other women his mother lined up for him to marry would have given him. But not Sita.

'You *will* have a child,' her mother has assured her, giving her potions she has obtained from sanyasis and gurus. Tonics blessed by the gods.

But her mother's face looks drawn. The smile that has been a permanent fixture since her daughter became queen not quite reaching her eyes. The reassurance as much for her sake as for Sita's.

Sita's mother is a proud and happy grandmother to Kishan's children but what she is waiting for, Sita knows, is a grandchild destined to rule.

Five years now since Sita wedded the crown prince.

Her womb remains stubbornly empty.

Sita looks at her mother, sitting amidst her own adoring coven of ladies, basking in the advantage afforded her as mother of the queen. Every time Sita hosts a durbar, she sees in her mother's eyes the memory of the day the queen mother had insulted them – and the flicker of triumph when she takes the queen mother's place.

Sita's parents are proud of her, but they will be happier, breathe easier, once she bears an heir. A grandchild who will one day take over the throne.

'Maharani…'

With effort, she pushes the melancholy thoughts away as she is gently but persistently called to attention by her maidservants.

The queen mother stands at the back of the room, the few women still loyal to her grouped protectively around her.

All eyes turn towards her. The vast hall full of women, filled with noise and laughter, song and dance, of a minute ago, now silent.

This is the first time the queen mother has graced Sita's durbar.

Sita stiffens before drawing herself up to her full height so she is sitting grandly upon her throne, regarding her mother-in-law, unsmiling. What does she want?

'This woman came to me,' the queen mother calls down the hall, her voice clear and loud. She is holding the hand of an old woman. Unruly, matted hair, torn sari. Begging bowl in her hand and wildflower chains draped round her neck. Mad, rolling eyes.

Sita's eyes briefly meet her mother's, seated to her left. Her mother's face wary, her whole being tense.

'She has a message for you,' the queen mother says. 'A birthday present, if you like.'

Sita nods shortly at the woman. 'Let's hear it then.'

The woman raises her hand, pointing an accusing finger at Sita. Her voice when it comes is gravelly, like sea-battered pebbles, like age-tempered sand. 'You are cursed.'

A shocked gasp spreads through the crowd, their eyes wide, gossip-flavoured spittle blooming on their lips.

Sita laughs, her mirth echoing down the hall. 'Tell me something I don't know.'

She sees her guests looking confused at first, then laughing along, relieved.

'You might laugh,' the old woman says and her gruff voice floats above the amused crowd despite her not having raised it, choking their laughter. She sweeps her hands over the crowd, pointing, it seems, at each woman in turn, their mouths open, faces frozen mid-smile. 'But know this. Your queen's womb is empty as the river during the drought and just as barren. She will not provide this kingdom with an heir, a new king.'

The crowd falls silent and Sita sees questions blossom on everyone's lips. She looks at her mother and sees the panic, the raw hurt she herself is feeling reflected upon her face.

This is nonsense, conjured by your mother-in-law. You surely cannot allow her to get to you, her inner voice chides.

'A rather odd birthday present, but thank you all the same. Now, would you and your friends care to join us in the festivities?' she asks the queen mother, making sure to keep her voice light, amused.

The queen mother's face darkens, becoming stormy.

Without another word she turns and leaves, her few friends following, the old soothsayer bringing up the rear, grumbling quietly to herself.

Everyone still looks slightly stunned but Sita asks the musicians and dancers to resume their programme, servants to circulate with snacks, and gradually the hall returns to normal.

Sita, more shaken than she wants to admit, is not able to partake of even a morsel of the elaborate birthday feast and she notes that her mother can't either.

She remembers her ayah saying, 'The priest at your naming ceremony decreed that a cost would be extracted for any good fortune where you were concerned.'

Does she get to be queen only to relinquish the kingdom to Prince Praveen's child, when he has one?

She pictures the gossip about what took place today spreading to the remote ends of the kingdom, courtesy of all these women who are eating her food and thanking her so profusely and going home with a gift bag consisting of sweets, fruit, a sari, an embroidered shawl, bangles. She pictures her brother-in-law (who is sure to hear of this despite his wife not being present at the durbar) laughing, delighted.

He has been biding his time, waiting for her downfall. He cannot win. He cannot.

Chapter 45

Mary

Earnest

1936

A couple of days after the royal procession where Mary recognised Sita, Charles calls upon her. 'Dr Kumar tells me you aren't properly acquainted with this town. Will you permit me to rectify that?'

They take to meeting on alternate days, going for walks, discovering the town. They sit by the riverbank, the salt and silt aroma of the water, the coconut trees bordering the sandy bank, the caress of the warm, fruity breeze.

Charles is good company. He makes Mary laugh. He reminds her of England, at once intensifying her longing for her cousins, for the country where she was brought up and, strangely, at the same time also easing her homesickness.

'So, what do you make of this country, Mary?' Charles asks as they tour the market. He is helping her navigate piles of rotting vegetables, mounds of potent-smelling spices in all colours of the rainbow spilling from cane baskets, lurid yellow dough confections sizzling and sputtering in huge vats of oil. Cows and dogs weave in between people dressed in kaleidoscopic garb, a cacophony of noises and scents, inciting a silent scream from deep within Mary, a clamour for the peaceful order of England.

'I…' She feels her eyes flood with unexpected tears. *I miss England with all my being. I yearn to be back. I don't know why I came, giving up all I knew. I was happy. Then, I packed it all in to come here, to try to discover the person my parents saw in me. But now that I am here, I cannot rid myself of the conviction that I am not the person my parents wanted me to be, that I will never be. It scares and upsets me. I have let the memory of my parents down by enjoying and identifying too well with my life in England and now that I am here and not able to settle, I feel I am letting them down all over again. And it hurts.*

She cannot put it all into words so she says nothing at all.

And yet, Charles seems to understand. He leads her very gently away from the chaos of the market. He sits her down on a log by the riverside.

Men washing their mud-spattered buffaloes look curiously askance at them. Somewhere someone laughs. The clinking of bangles, the cheerful tune of anklets as a woman dips a pail into the water, lifts it up onto her veiled head and walks gracefully away.

'On Sunday, if you will permit me, I would like to take you to the city,' Charles says. 'I've been invited to a ball and I don't wish to go alone. Will you accompany me, my dear?'

Mary wears the yellow silk chiffon dress – 'It brings out the gold in your eyes,' Rose had said when they were selecting fabrics – that her aunt had had made for her season. When Mary decided to give up on that season and travel to India instead, she had packed the dress, unable to give it up too, along with the white coming-out gown that still waits in her trunk, unused, for a suitable occasion on which to wear it.

'Mary!' Charles's eyes gleam when he comes to collect her, taking her gloved hand in his and planting kisses on it. 'You are a vision of loveliness. You will be the most beautiful woman there by far.'

She blushes as he helps her into the carriage, even as she feels a pang. *This is how it would have been if I had stayed in England, come out as intended and had my season – attentive men lavishing extravagant compliments.*

It is a thought that resonates throughout the charmed evening, as she dances with Charles and myriad other partners in the grand hall filled with grander people. She is introduced to the cream of English colonial society in this part of the world, she is plied with drinks and feted and admired, by both men – who praise her looks – and women – who praise the cut of her dress and its exquisite design and ply her for news of England.

At the end of the evening, as Charles escorts her back to the school in the carriage, Mary having forgotten herself and her homesickness while also having missed England keenly, drunk on happiness and laughter, says, 'I had such fun.' Tasting the heady abandon of dancing her cares away, the sweet pleasure of the compliments bestowed on her.

The evening is cool, the heat of the day brushed away by night. The clip-clop of their horses cutting through the darkness. The air smelling of jasmine and intrigue, whispering secrets as it caresses her face.

'I'm glad.' Charles smiles. Then, 'I agreed with the townspeople when they said that you fainting in my arms during that royal procession was an omen.' He goes on, softly, 'We're meant to be together. Will you marry me, Mary?'

Mary looks up at him, taken aback, her mouth dry, words dying on her tongue.

One of the horses whinnies and the coachman murmurs reassurances. The air rushes past, loud in her ears, a sliver of moon visible in a stormy sky, punctured here and there by stars – creamy buttons on a navy pinafore. Charles's face is in darkness, only his eyes visible, bright, eager, earnest.

Mary has not thought of marriage at all, although she realises now that she has been naive. Why else would a handsome young man be so attentive to her? If her cousins were here, marriage would be the first thing they would think about. But since she has been too homesick and heartsick to give a thought to marriage – it is not why she came to India; she plans to marry and settle down in England – she did not think of Charles as anything other than a good friend, and blithely assumed he felt the same way about her.

Mrs Alden comes to mind. Mary has been gallivanting around town with a man, unchaperoned, with not a thought to her reputation. Living in this small town, in the company of nuns, reputation has been the last thing on her mind, although by rights it should have been the first, given how much she tells herself propriety means to her.

Those people at the ball just now, she understands, must have assumed she and Charles were together. *Why didn't I think of it?*

You didn't much care for propriety when on board the ship, her conscience chides.

And this is the other reason, the *real* reason she hasn't considered Charles as a suitor. Her traitorous heart, disregarding her stern decree to it to move on, to look forward, to set aside what happened, pines for Vinay, despite his deceit. She has tried telling herself it was a brief dalliance that meant nothing – which, for Vinay, it was. She's tried to convince herself that it was just her trying on a different persona, being a more daring, less timid girl. But it hasn't worked. The only thing that does is the unflinching truth: *He is married. He is the past. He is never going to be your future.*

Charles is looking at her, his face in shadow, his vivid brown gaze hopeful.

Spending time with Charles has helped dull the ache of hopelessly loving Vinay while simultaneously trying to hate him and forget him. Charles has eased her homesickness. He has been a good friend, the best.

'He's quite the catch.' She hears her cousins' voices in her head. 'Good-looking, a doctor, from a good family, a man of means.'

She knows all this for Charles has told her about his parents, his family, his background. Now she realises that by opening up to her, he was laying the ground for his proposal.

'There's one skeleton in my family closet,' he had said during one of their walks, colour flooding his darkly handsome face.

'What's that then?' she'd asked, smiling.

'My grandmother on my father's side was Indian.'

That explained Charles's swarthy colouring. 'How curious!' she'd gasped. 'My grandmother on my mother's side was Indian too.'

He had laughed, sounding relieved, and now she understands why.

'Mary, being with you feels right.' Charles is looking ardently at her. 'I've known since the first time I saw you that I'd like to spend the rest of my life with you.'

Do I want to spend the rest of my life with Charles?
He's eminently suitable.
He's not the man I want.

Charles is kind, gentle, caring. His friendship has helped her navigate her initial days in India. He is comfort, someone *known*, in a new, and yet strangely familiar, confusing world.

But… she doesn't love him.

Her father loved her mother so much that he was willing to be disowned by his family – he never saw them again.

Frances, her travelling companion aboard the ship, loved her Alfie and, in her own words, 'spent the best years of my life missing him, grieving for him.'

Mary doesn't love Charles in this way. If she did, she'd feel something now other than blindsided, stunned, numb.

'I-I'm sorry, Charles.'

In the sighing, whispering darkness, she sees his face fall.

'It's sudden, I know. I've sprung it upon you without warning—'

'Charles, I… I don't—'

'Please. Think about it,' Charles says, taking her hand in his, his gaze bright in the darkness, sincere. 'I shall wait for your answer.'

It is all she can do to nod.

Chapter 46

Sita

Naming Gift

1936

'I was thinking of giving Praveen's firstborn the Lake Palace as a naming gift.'

Sita's hand stills on her husband's chest. They are in her chamber, dawn stroking the edges of night, gently wiping darkness away with silvery grey brushstrokes. Jaideep always wakes early, the cares of running a kingdom, being responsible for the welfare of his people, weighing heavily on him. Even though the British Resident handles much of the administration and weighs in on all major decisions concerning the kingdom, their subjects still come to Jaideep, their king, with their problems. He is the one they look up to and he takes this responsibility very seriously.

In the early days of their marriage, she would wake to find him leaning on his elbow, gazing at her. 'I love watching you sleep,' he'd say. 'You conduct whole conversations behind those closed lids. You fidget and thrash and innumerable expressions flit across your beautiful face.'

She had laughed. 'I don't recall any of it.'

'A shame. I'd like to know what goes on inside that lovely head.'

You wouldn't like it at all, my kind, naive husband, she had thought.

She learned to wake when he kissed her softly in preparation for getting up, and they would lie talking, enjoying those few precious moments of privacy and intimacy before they donned public personas and rose to greet the day.

She experiences a pang for the days when he was so totally in love with her, when he believed the best of her. Now, as she traces the new lines that have drawn themselves, seemingly overnight, upon his face, she feels a rush of affection for this man who, although he doesn't completely trust her any more, is still with her. Who saw her with the cheetahs and loved her, and has not stopped loving her since. Even though he is forever keeping the peace between the wife he chose and the mother he loves but who doesn't love him enough to accept his wife. Even though his mother, since she gatecrashed Sita's birthday durbar, has upped her campaign for him to get a new wife, 'one who is not barren', bringing priests and holy men to underline her conviction that Sita is cursed, that she will continue to rain bad luck upon them all.

Marrying Jaideep has given Sita everything she craved growing up – status, power, respect, her parents' approval. And so, she desperately wants to give him the one thing that he wants. A child. An heir.

You want it just as much, if not more, her conscience chides.

And now, what she has feared, dreaded, has happened. Her brother-in-law, who has never bothered to conceal his dislike of her, has a son – the heir to this throne, if Sita doesn't bear a child.

Just as the queen mother had to give way to Sita, Sita will have to give way to Praveen's son if she doesn't have a child of her own.

'My father stipulated that the palace on the lake go to the firstborn son and heir,' her husband says, gently.

The palace on the lake where Sita and Jaideep had their aborted honeymoon, where they go every so often for a couple of days, to get away. Sitting on the veranda watching the fireflies dance on the water, pinpricks of light performing just for them. The susurrating darkness thick and scented with jasmine. Her husband's hand in hers. Just the two of them in a quiet world, the gentle whispering water, the stars shimmering above and the fireflies frolicking. The taste of her husband's lips, his dreams, in her mouth. Boat rides on the lake, trailing her hands in the glimmering water, fish dancing beneath. Her husband letting go of the cares that come with kingship.

It is *their* magical getaway, a place she associates with just the two of them. She cannot countenance it going to the man who loathes her, and his son.

'*You* are the firstborn son.'

'Yes. But…' Her husband's eyes clouding over. His shoulders defeated.

The words bloom on her lips before she can stop them; they flow out of her mouth before she can rein them back. For the first time since her betrothal to Jaideep was fixed and she started taking lessons in diplomacy and decorum, she speaks without thinking it through first, uttering the first words that come into her head.

'I was going to wait a bit longer, until I was absolutely sure, to tell you…'

Hope blossoms on her husband's face, chasing away the shadows that have etched gloom and added years to him, his eyes alert with love and anticipation. 'Tell me what?'

Too late now to backtrack, isn't it? She swallows, then in a rush, 'You're going to be a father.'

'Oh, Sita!' His eyes shining. 'I've longed to hear this.' His words muffled as he gathers her in his arms, kissing her.

'I'd hold back from telling people for the next few weeks at least,' she says when she can speak.

'Of course.' Her beaming husband looking so much younger, all the many worry lines having briefly disappeared. 'We'll tell everyone in three weeks, at the naming ceremony for Praveen's son.'

'It might be a boy. Why don't we wait and see before you give the palace to your nephew?'

Her husband grins. 'I'll give him a gold crown and jewels instead.'

She smiles along with her husband, returning his ardent kisses, tasting his joy, his excitement, even as her heart beats so loudly in her chest at her audacity that she thinks it will explode out of it.

Chapter 47

Mary

Knowing

1936

The night of Charles's proposal, when he chooses to misunderstand Mary's refusal, preferring to assume she had been caught off guard, she has vivid dreams. Of her parents, cousins, her aunt and uncle, the house in England. Mrs Alden. Frances. Amin, Sita as a child, bossy, ambitious. A procession of elephants. An imperious veiled gaze upon her. A gaze she recognises. And then darkness...

The ship. Dancing on deck, under a canopy of glittering stars, in a pool of yellow light, with a dark-haired man, the navy sea surging around them...

She wakes knowing something is different. Knowing something fundamental has changed, is changing within her. Knowing...

She counts back the days, panic growing and settling in her stomach.

You were warned, her conscience chides.

Vinay. His piercing eyes. His sharp intellect. His lies.

His child.

She is all alone here. She has only recently arrived. She cannot turn to the nuns. Kind though they may be, what she has done goes against what they believe. Furthermore, they are her employers. She might lose this job. Then what is she to do?

Mrs Alden's words come to her: 'A woman's reputation is a precious thing, my dear. I understand you want to get married at some point.'

She has scorned Mrs Alden, scoffed at propriety, and now she has to bear the consequences of her impulsive actions.

She cannot return to England, not like this. The thought stabs her, incites tears, causes a fissure in her heart, even as she acknowledges the truth of it. If her aunt and uncle, for whom reputation, standing in society, is everything, find out she is carrying the child of an Indian man – and, worse, a man who is married already and cannot marry her and give the child legitimacy – they will disown her. Her father was disowned for marrying outside of his social class, a woman who was half-Indian, and here she is, a mother before she is to be wed, bearing the child of an Indian married man.

She has the addresses of her father's old friends, the ones her aunt wrote to when Mary was coming here, but she doesn't *know* them. She cannot turn up at their doorstep, an unwed mother trailing scandal.

She will not turn to Vinay.

She does not know anyone else here in India. Except… Charles.

Charles, from a good family, a man of means, a man her aunt and uncle would approve of.

Charles looking ardently at her. 'Being with you feels right.'

Charles, dark, swarthy, with Indian blood in him.

His refusal to acknowledge her rejection of his suit could now work in her favour.

She hates the direction her mind is going, but she is desperate, trapped. She has nowhere else to turn. Charles's proposal appears fortunate, timely, *meant*.

She washes her face, battles with her conscience. She waits.

'Have you thought about… us?' Charles is apprehensive, his nervous gaze upon her.

Should she do this? Can she?

They are at their favourite spot by the river. A bird calls, plaintive, somewhere among the trees. A hawker walks past, his wares, vegetables wilting in the unrelenting sunshine, displayed in a basket jutting from his stomach, held there by a rope that is tied to the ends of the basket and slung across his neck.

Accepting Charles's proposal is the only way she can see out of her bind. There is not much time – that is the one thing she doesn't have.

She will not have a season on her return to England, as she had hoped. In fact, if she accepts Charles's proposal – even if not – her being with child means she will not be going back to England after her year here, as planned. It makes her want to bawl, scream and not stop until the ache in her heart, the longing for her cousins, the yearning for the comfortable, ordered life that she had taken for granted in England, eases.

One impulsive action, one thoughtless decision and the course of her life has changed, once again.

How naive she had been, to think that coming to India would resolve the conflict she was experiencing since her memories returned, between the expectations her parents had for her and those of her guardians. How foolish to think that coming here would absolve her of guilt for her choices. How immature to consider, even for a moment, that the freedom her parents had wanted for her meant sleeping with Vinay…

And now she plans to compound her mistakes by involving Charles, adding another load of guilt to the burden she already harbours.

Charles, who waits patiently for her answer.

More than anything, she wishes she could turn the clock back, to the innocent time before Major Digby and the assault of her memories, when she knew exactly where her life was headed, when she was happy and assured of her place in the world.

Her father gave up his home and country for love. She will be marrying not for love, but for convenience, tricking a good man, taking advantage of his guilelessness, his love of her.

She will have to pass off this baby as Charles's. And, serendipitously, because of his Indian ancestor and hers, she will be able to.

She will have to lie to him every single day.

She looks down, away from Charles's gaze, and says shyly, demurely, an actress performing a role, 'Yes.'

What a person I have become, so deceitful and unworthy.

'Yes, you have thought about it or yes, you will marry me?'

'I will marry you,' she says, thinking again of her father, who was willing to be disowned so he could wed the love of his life.

The river water swells in outraged ripples, it rebukes and scolds: *What are you doing?*

Charles beams, taking her in his arms.

She holds on to him for dear life.

Chapter 48

Sita

Pomp and Bluster

1936

The naming ceremony for Prince Praveen's son is extremely grand. True to form, Praveen has gone to a lot of expense to trump any celebration hosted by Sita and Jaideep.

Praveen's palace at the base of the hills is lit up and festooned with banners. There are snake charmers and fire-eaters, magicians and holy men with snakes wrapped round their bodies, fortune tellers and conjurors walking on beds of nails and flaming pyres. There are fireworks and musical fountains, performing falcons, parrot shows. There are monkeys stealing food, causing havoc. There's even a zoo with a leopard, a tiger and two growling, pacing lions.

Children mill, shrieking with laughter and fear. Guests partake of food and gossip, their every whim tended to by the many servants.

The ceremony itself is conducted with pomp and bluster, three priests blessing the child.

'The firstborn grandson of the late king, my husband,' the queen mother declares proudly, sitting amidst her coven of cronies, her eyes seeking out Sita to rub the hurt in. 'Destined to be king.'

The women surrounding her smile along with her, but their gazes rest worriedly upon Sita.

Sita smiles sweetly at her mother-in-law and says nothing.

'Pity my older son couldn't produce a child. It's been long enough.'

This time the other women do not smile, instead looking warily at Sita. She is the queen, after all. Their fate is in her hands.

Only the queen mother titters joyfully, biting into a laddoo. 'What use being king if you have no heir to pass the kingdom on to? I gave my husband two strapping sons. And at least one of them has now produced a son himself.'

Again, silence in the women's durbar. No sound, of munching even, as the women wait, spellbound, to see what happens next.

You've all been thinking it and yet only the queen mother is brave enough to say it. Sita smiles, caressing her stomach. Savouring this moment. She will unpick it later to replay over and over. It will make the lie she is living worth it. The only cloud marring her triumph is that Jaideep has insisted he tell Praveen privately – she would have liked to watch her brother-in-law receive the news.

But the look on her mother-in-law's face as she observes Sita, who stands unruffled, stroking her stomach for a long moment before declaring calmly, 'You don't need to worry on your older son's account. He is to be a father,' is worth everything she has done to get to this point.

A gasp from the assembled ladies and then cheering.

Praveen's wife, Latha, envelops Sita in a hug, tears running down her face. 'I'm so happy for you and the king.'

She is too, Sita can see.

The queen mother opens her mouth, wanting to say something, anything, to refute Sita's statement.

I think you're lying, she's musing, Sita knows, as she stares at Sita's stomach, assessing, having set too much store by the prophecy of the wise woman she brought to her daughter-in-law's birthday durbar.

In the end she settles for a cool, 'Let's hope it's a boy,' before pointedly turning to the ladies beside her and blanking Sita.

Sita smiles. She's got the reaction she wanted. The other women applaud and congratulate her, but she watches the queen mother, her mouth small, eyes narrowed, her big day, her chance to gloat over Sita, ruined.

Part 4

Too Much to Lose

Chapter 49

Mary

Secrets

1936

'Go back a few years, and that would be myself, Amin and Sita,' Mary says as she and Charles walk beside the river, pointing to the children who skim stones in the water some distance away.

'Sita, as in the queen whom you recognised the day we met?' Charles smiles at her.

'The very one.'

'Have you written to her, like you said you would?'

'Not yet.'

He looks at her, curious. 'Why?'

'I… I don't know. It's been a while. We're two very different people.'

'Are you worried she might have forgotten you?'

'I'm sure she has more important things to do running a kingdom than trying to recall an old friend. She must get many letters from people.'

Charles takes her hand then, on the road. It's deserted now, the children skimming stones having disappeared, no doubt heeding the calls of their empty stomachs.

'I don't think anyone is likely to forget you once they've met you, Mary. You don't realise how special you are.'

She is shamed by his earnest gaze, eyes shining with love, and so she looks straight ahead, concentrating on the dust cloud rising above the mud road, the cows grazing in the fields, the birds pecking at the ripe cashews and flustering about in an intoxicated daze, the smell of heat and fermented fruit, the taste of the spiced guava they'd bought from a persistent vendor – and remorse.

Why can't I love him?

An image of another pair of deep brown eyes, desire shading them ebony-gold. She blinks it away. *Not now. Not here. Not ever.*

Charles gathers her in his arms. 'All I am, everything, is yours, Mary,' he whispers.

They sit in the shade of the mango, cashew and jackfruit trees at the edge of the fields, the grazing cows regarding them placidly, flicking away with their swishing tails the flies that dare to alight on their backs. A stream gushes gleefully as it feeds into the river and the sound of burbling water brings back memories of dancing on the deck of a ship with a man, intelligent eyes and a glowing smile, whose legacy she carries. She bites her lower lip, once again pushing the memories, the man, away.

'I… I haven't been completely honest with you,' Charles says, holding her close.

She looks up at him. It never occurred to her that this man might be keeping secrets from her as she is from him.

A bird startles out of the branches above them and she flinches, shivering although it is hot, a slick, sticky heat.

'My father, he…' Charles takes a deep breath. '…repeatedly cheated on my mother. My mother took to drink and died when I was fifteen.'

'I'm sorry, Charles,' Mary says softly. 'Losing your mother like that…'

'I despised my father, blamed him. When he died, I hadn't talked to him for years.' He sniffs, swallows. 'If there's one thing I hate,' his voice fierce, 'it is spouses keeping the truth from each other, cheating on each other.'

She stills within his embrace. Should she tell him?

You can't. No man would agree to marry a woman carrying another man's child. Charles would break off the engagement in a flash. And then where would you be?

Her aunt, uncle, cousins… Mary yearns for them and for her life in England. She hopes that, once her child is born under the mantle of legitimacy marriage to Charles will bring, they *will* return, even if just to visit. It is better than not returning at all, being disowned, which is what would happen if her guardians discovered the truth.

'My mother is the reason I decided to become a doctor. I couldn't save her, I was too young, but perhaps I could save someone else. My father was against it – he thought my profession common and that made me all the more determined.' He plants a soft kiss on her head. 'Mary, the reason I feel so at ease with you, I think, is because, with losing your parents so young, you too have tasted sorrow, survived loss. You *understand*.'

He kisses her. She tastes his tears and hers. His: raw emotion and love and catharsis; hers: guilt and betrayal.

He cups her face in his palm. 'With you, I've found a soulmate. We will have no secrets from each other. You know all about me now. Tell me about you?'

She does. Everything except the one thing that has made her marry him.

The truth, but for one lie.

My aunt and uncle lied to me by keeping the truth from me, as did Vinay. I was devastated when I found out. I will do everything I can to make sure Charles never discovers what I am keeping from him.

'I knew when I met you that we were meant to be together.'

He deserves better than her. But… She is not strong enough to tell him so, to release him from their engagement.

Although I cannot be honest with you, I'll be a good wife to you. I will love you as much as it is possible to love someone I am deceiving and lying to every moment of every day.

Chapter 50

Sita

Only the Best

1936

'My mother relied on midwives during her pregnancy, not wanting a man examining her. But times have changed,' Jaideep says. 'I'll ask the royal physician to recommend an expert in childbirth. Only the best will do for you, my queen.'

'I don't agree with many of your mother's ways, but in this I'm with her.' Sita smiles.

'I'll try and find a lady doctor, there must be one somewhere in India.'

'I'm happy with a midwife. They have all the experience,' Sita insists.

'I'll find the best midwife in the kingdom…'

'Please.' She squeezes her husband's hand, smiling gently at him. 'Leave it to me. I'll find a midwife I'm comfortable with.'

Sita summons her governess, whom she had led on a merry dance and who had despaired of her. The woman hasn't aged well – she looks frail and much older than her years.

'I know of your affair with my uncle,' Sita says without preamble once she has dismissed the servants and they are alone.

At Sita's words, her governess looks fit to faint. A weak, 'How?' is all she manages.

'All those afternoons while you slept and I was bored out of my mind, because you denied me books. I rifled through your belongings to find something worth reading.'

'It… was a long time ago.' The woman's voice trembles as much as her hands.

'I know of the baby.'

'Oh, oh, oh…' This time the woman does faint.

Sita is surprised by a shaft of tenderness as she rings the bell to summon her maidservants to try to revive her.

Her old governess comes to slowly, looking groggy and bleary-eyed, greedily slurping the water the servants offer.

When Sita is, once again, alone with the governess, the woman prostrates herself at her feet. 'Please. Have mercy. My child is with parents who love and care for her. She doesn't know about me and your uncle. If she finds out, it will destroy her.'

'Get up. You're embarrassing both of us. I've no intention of telling your daughter anything.'

The woman looks at Sita, wild-eyed. 'Then what do you want?'

'Find me a midwife I can trust. One with impeccable credentials but who is willing to bend the rules.' Sita hands her governess money, boxes of freshly prepared carrot halwa and doodh peda (having remembered that these were the woman's favourites), a couple of saris and a gold bangle. 'And if word of what I've asked of you leaves this chamber, your daughter will know the truth.'

'It won't, I promise.'

The governess keeps her word, sending Sita a midwife with a long list of references but no morals. Presumably even her credentials have been bought, just as Sita is now buying her silence. God help her patients.

Chapter 51

Mary

Intimate

1936

The wedding is small, intimate.

A few friends of Charles's.

The nuns.

When Mary had imagined her wedding, she had always pictured it taking place in the grand old church that she had attended every Sunday with her aunt, uncle and cousins, dressed in their best, the church where her father's parents are buried alongside countless Brigham ancestors. She had pictured her uncle walking her up the aisle, giving her away.

On her wedding day, the sun shines, as it does every day here in India. Mary wears the white lace and chiffon flowing dress whose design she had chosen after intense discussion with her cousins, seasoned with much laughter. The dress she had fondly imagined she would wear for her coming out. She lifts the dress out of the trunk where it has been waiting all this while for a suitable occasion, and slips it on, grinding the dust of the dreams she had spun onto the shimmering cloth beneath her feet, her reflection wavering in the mirror, viewed through a haze of remorse and homesickness and heartache.

Charles looks ecstatic and Mary smiles as hard as she can to bury, alongside the secret nestling in her stomach, her regret, her qualms, her yearning for the family who took her in when she was lost and broken.

How far from my dreams I have come.

'I do,' Mary says out loud, while inside she whispers, *I am sorry.*

Even as she misses them, longs for them, a part of her is glad her cousins, her uncle and aunt are not here to witness this mockery of a marriage.

We never expected you to be married within a few weeks of travelling to India, Mary! her cousins had written. *What magic that country must weave upon you! Do come for a visit soon, cousin, with your husband. We'd love to meet the man who has won your heart. He must love books quite as much as you!*

'I'm the happiest man alive, Mrs Soames,' Charles says, beaming, when they are pronounced man and wife.

The guilt she is harbouring overflows into her eyes. He gathers her in his arms and kisses her, his eyes shining.

'I love you, Mrs Soames.' He waits, his smile faltering ever so slightly. And so, she whispers, 'I love you too.'

The lie bitter in her mouth, soft with his heartfelt kisses.

I might have started off this marriage on a lie, but you'll never know any different. I'll make it my aim to keep you happy, Charles. I'll be a dutiful wife, a good wife. And one day I'll say these three words, I love you, to you and I will mean them, I promise.

What she is doing, marrying him for convenience, while he looks at her with his eyes glowing, is wrong. But, a small consolation, she is not coming into this union penniless, her aunt and uncle having settled her dowry – the inheritance her father's parents left for him – in Charles's name.

Their wedding night.

Mary tries to shut out memories of Vinay and that night, stolen from fate, drunk with the heady independence of spurning Mrs Alden, doing what *she, Mary,* wanted.

'You are so beautiful,' Vinay had whispered, his voice thick with awe.

She had trembled, trepidation, anticipation, desire, as he fumbled with her stays, as she helped him undo her corset. As she stood before him naked. Shy. Cold. As he warmed her with himself.

Now she is in a room with a man she has married out of necessity. That one impulsive night spurring this one.

She has examined her body carefully. There is no evidence, physically, of the child growing within.

Tenderly Charles kisses her. She tries to reciprocate, resolutely pushing away the taste of another man's kisses, deliciously forbidden, tantalising, welcome in a way her husband's are not.

She shivers in Charles's arms as he carefully undresses her.

'You are so beautiful,' he says, unconsciously mirroring Vinay's words.

She examines his voice, his gaze. Can he detect that she is not the perfect, pure woman he thinks her to be?

But his attitude doesn't change. If anything he gets more passionate, his kisses more urgent as they travel down her body, his eyes dark with the passion she cannot reciprocate, hooded with desire she does not feel.

Gently he enters her. She tries not to shudder, to flinch, to pull away.

She moves with him, guilt and regret mingling, causing a hard lump in her throat, colouring her cheeks the blush pink of a virgin bride.

Afterwards, he holds her close. 'I'm the luckiest man alive,' he whispers.

She stays taut in his embrace until his breathing evens out and he falls asleep.

Then carefully, she turns in his arms – he stirs for a beat and then is asleep again – and looks at him, this man she has married under false pretence, to give legitimacy to her child. She memorises his features, the insanely long lashes fanning the cinnamon-gold stubble on his cheeks, his regal nose, his dimpled chin.

I will *learn to love you.*

Unbidden, Vinay's face dances before her eyes. His intelligent eyes, that intense gaze, pinned within which she felt warm, known, seen, alive.

Bad enough you conned your husband into marriage because you can't take responsibility for your actions. Now, you dare bring the father of your child into your conjugal bed on your wedding night?

She bites her lip hard, until she tastes blood, pushing away the tears that threaten, salty blue.

You've landed on your feet. What have you got to cry about?

Chapter 52

Sita

Out of the Ordinary

1936

With each advancing month Sita continues to pass her pregnancy off impressively.

If the queen mother gives her the odd glance when their paths cross, not quite believing her despite her expanding stomach, Sita ignores her, smiling coolly and rising serenely above it all. She models herself on the cheetahs she loves – she has given them names and visits them almost daily. They ground her.

'Nobody really knows me,' she tells the sleek animals, 'this person I've become.'

The right thing would be to set the cheetahs free, to let them be true to their nature, wanderers of the wild, swift beasts who will outrun anyone.

In this way, too, she would emulate them, run fast and far, outrun this bind she finds herself in.

Perhaps this desire of mine to stop at nothing to get my way is what my mother was so afraid of.

Her mother knows her, *all* of her. Or did. But now, she has been so blinded by the need to be the future king or queen's grandmother that she has happily swallowed Sita's charade and will not see past it.

Sita wishes she would. As much as she rebelled against it when she was younger, now she wants her mother to take her in hand, try to fix this mess she finds herself in. She wants rid of the responsibility, the worry that gnaws at her stomach, the panic that swells in place of a child.

She wishes the queen mother was not the only one who vaguely suspected that all was not right. She understands that since only she has a mind as twisted as hers, it stands to reason that she'd be the one to suspect something out of the ordinary.

Sita stands watching the cheetahs. She will not set them free; she loves them too much.

And likewise, she will not set herself free, out of desire for the very ties that are wound so tightly round her: her queenship, this palace and everything it represents, choking her of who she once was, leaving behind a person she does not recognise: hard, unprincipled, ruthless, a liar.

Chapter 53

Mary

Lies

1936

'The riots in Bombay have escalated,' Charles says, looking up from the newspaper, his forehead scrunched in worry. 'I hope they won't spread here.'

He looks tired, Mary notes. Should she tell him now, or wait another week?

It is tempting to wait, but she doesn't have time. It is already verging on too late. Best to get it over with.

She takes a deep breath.

'Charles?'

He stops in the act of buttering his toast, smiling absent-mindedly at her, his attention on the newspaper spread out before him. 'Yes, my dear?'

'I'm pregnant.'

She is terrified and relieved in equal measure that the secret she has been harbouring is out in the open. Charles has never been anything but loving towards her during their weeks of marriage, but nevertheless, she is apprehensive, afraid to look at him, this kind sweet man whom she is cuckolding. If he *does* suspect anything, if he is aware of the deception she has indulged in, she will know now.

'Is married life as wonderful as we imagined growing up?' her cousins had written. 'Tell us all.'

How to tell them that she wanted for nothing, that Charles was the perfect husband and yet she wasn't happy?

How to tell them that fooling a good man, lying to him every day, was harder than she had imagined?

How to tell them that it amazed her and dismayed her, her ability to fool everyone around her and, especially, herself?

She and Charles had very quickly fallen into a routine after marriage, her husband staying at his practice in the city during the week, returning at the weekends.

'I need to start up my practice again, attend to my patients,' he had said, sounding hesitant, a few days after the wedding.

'Of course you must,' Mary had replied, trying not to show the relief she felt – she was finding it harder than expected to keep at bay the guilt that stabbed her when Charles was around, being solicitous and caring.

'I… I'd have to stay at Winey Gardens during the week.' He looked apologetic.

Even better.

Winey Gardens was Charles's residence in the city – they had stayed there while they took in the city sights and attended tea parties and flamboyant suppers with his friends, right after their wedding.

Horrid woman. You vowed to be dutiful to make up for your lies and now you're glad he is away during the week?

'Would you like to join me?' Charles asked, eyes hopeful.

I would love, more than anything, to reside in the city, attending balls and card parties, recreating a little slice of home here in India, up until the time I can return to England. But if it means maintaining the charade of being a good wife, a dutiful wife, then I cannot. Being denied the company of people who remind me of home, make me feel at home, is fitting punishment for lying to you when you're so good to me.

'Charles, I... The nuns and children are expecting me at the school.'

His face dimmed for a brief second, but then he smiled. 'Of course. I'll look forward to the weekends, when I can see you again.'

Charles had left for the city the following week and Mary, eschewing the carriage he had insisted she use, had walked to the school, the fields glowing in the honeyed, dew-kissed light of morning, the heat of the day yet to come, the earth soft and powdery beneath her feet.

The nuns and children welcomed her back enthusiastically from the few days off she had taken after her wedding, and as she went about her work, for the first time since she had decided to marry Charles, Mary experienced some respite from the guilt and remorse plaguing her.

She spent the evening pottering around the cottage she shared with Charles, revelling in the solitude, her husband's absence, even as her conscience worked overtime: *He loves you and you – you want rid of him.*

'It's small,' Charles had said of the cottage when first showing her round. 'But until we decide what to do, whether I move my practice nearby or work in the city, it will have to do.'

'It's perfect,' she had said.

And it is. A beautiful haven, set away from the road, in a compound overlooking fields. A hammock slung between coconut trees. The scent of lime and guava, ripe mangoes and jackfruit.

'There's a maid who does the cooking and the cleaning. She stays in town but arrives here at dawn, staying until all her chores are done,' Charles had said. 'You can hire more staff as you see fit.'

Just the two of them in this paradise. *What will we talk about?* she had wondered, nervous.

That first evening without him, she rooted among his books.

Perhaps by seeing what he read, learning who he was, she would learn to love him.

The maid shyly fetched tea and a snack – a confection made with puffed rice that Mary recalled from her childhood. This is what India had brought back, the tastes and experiences of her youth. Spices and flavours of long-forgotten dishes that had been her staple as a child, whose names she did not know but which her taste buds recognised. It was like being reacquainted with a friend she had lost touch with and now all their mannerisms, their ways, were coming back, familiar and beloved.

After the maid left, Mary tried reading one of Charles's books, lying in the hammock, the taste of fruit and evening, the gentle caress of the breeze carrying the scent of waning day. But her mind couldn't make sense of the words. She touched her stomach. Just slightly rounded. Growing another man's child.

When it was dark, she went to bed – the bed she and Charles had shared since their marriage, where Charles slept but she lay awake – now hers alone for the rest of the week. But once again, she could not sleep.

What if Charles is somehow able to read the truth written in my body?

And if he doesn't, can I carry out this subterfuge for the rest of my life?

'Oh my darling!' Charles says now, gathering her in his arms, kissing her, his eyes shining.

It hurts to smile, to laugh, to partake in his joy.

It is torture listening to him concocting a thousand blissful plans for the future, for their child.

And yet she does.

How effortlessly she lies now, the falsehoods falling from her lips like offerings.

That night after an ecstatic Charles is finally asleep, she stares, bleary-eyed, heavenward.

Lizards dart across the bubbled, cracked ceiling and a memory comes to her, long forgotten, suddenly vivid: Amin had once caught a lizard, the tail coming off in his hand, and Mary and Sita had stared, fascinated, Sita going so far as to touch it.

'It's scaly,' she had declared, repulsion and interest warring on her face.

Sita... Mary has still not written to her.

Remember when we were children and carefree, roaming the streets of town, devising plans for our futures?

If only life were so easy, so effortless, again.

Are you happy, Sita, now that you've realised your childhood dreams, become someone who makes a difference, someone nobody can ignore?

I have everything I dreamed of: a suitable husband, respectability, a child on the way.

And yet, I'm not happy. In fact I've never felt so defeated in my life.

Chapter 54

Sita

Burden

1936

'Sita.'

Something in her husband's tone of voice makes Sita open her eyes and look at him.

They are in bed, Sita pretending to sleep. Once Jaideep is asleep, she will pace her rooms. She prefers the nights he does not come to her chamber, for then she doesn't have to pretend. She can dismantle the burden of her lie, put it away for a brief while, alongside the cushion tucked into her sari skirt – at least that is the hope, although it never quite works that way. Her lie is always there, growing like her pretend child, demanding action, making her paranoid, suspicious about everything and everyone. Even her husband, right now…

'My mother asked to see me today.'

Sita's nostrils flare and she bites her tongue, hard, so she will not say anything out of turn. What is that woman up to now?

'She… she'd like to make her peace with you now her grand-child is on the way.'

'Has she accepted that I'm not barren then, has she taken my word over the wise woman's, who declared me cursed and my womb dry?'

Her husband flinches from the bitterness in her voice. But he says, gently enough, 'I know you're very hurt. But—'

'Why come to you and not me?'

There was a time when her husband had liked her outspokenness. Now, he closes his eyes, looking immensely weary. 'She worries you may not be receptive to her—'

'With good reason,' Sita snaps.

She hates being like this, but cannot seem to help it. Since she told that first lie, it has ballooned, as her stomach should have with child, spawning other lies to perpetrate it.

Some days she longs to run away. But she has too much to lose. Her lie would be found out. Her mother-in-law would gloat, her brother-in-law's son would be king. Her parents would be ashamed, disgusted with her again. Her husband would be disillusioned, broken by the truth that the wife he chose is a fabricator, a cheat who will stop at nothing to get her way, who will manipulate her loved one's feelings to get what she wants.

Some weeks ago, during the weekly durbar Sita held for ladies of the kingdom to come to her with worries, pleas, problems, the solution to her own dilemma presented itself.

She was sorting out a dispute between two women from wealthy families when the Lake House refuge, which Sita had established despite opposition from the king's advisory committee, was mentioned as being the place where one of the women had given birth to her illegitimate child; the nuns there had then arranged for the baby to be given up for adoption.

And it was then that something clicked in Sita's head. She knew just what she would do.

The next night in bed, she'd said to Jaideep, 'Since getting pregnant, I've decided I should give something back, do charity work with orphans and women who've fallen upon hard times.'

Her husband had smiled. 'Instead of cutting back on your duties now that you're pregnant, you want to do more. Please try not to exert yourself too much, my love.'

Since then, Sita has toured all the orphanages in the kingdom in the guise of doing charity work. She plans to visit the Lake House refuge soon, where she will identify women who are due to give birth around the same time as she herself is supposed to. She will vet them, making sure they are from good families. These women are desperate – they're giving up their babies anyway, so why not give them up to the queen?

If in the event she does not find any such women, she'll have to adopt a baby from one of the orphanages, which is why she has visited them all – to determine what kind and class of women the babies are born to. But that is a last resort: she'll not be able to vet a baby from an orphanage as thoroughly – there wouldn't be enough time, as she'd have to wait until her ninth month of pregnancy to choose a newborn from one of the orphanages in order to pass it off as her own.

Now, her husband says, 'My mother would like to help. There's a woman she knows who can determine if you're carrying a boy or a girl just by touching your stomach. She's ancient – she blessed my mother when she was pregnant with myself and Praveen. In fact, she predicted that my mother was carrying twins!' His eyes shining. 'Just imagine, you might be too!'

'I don't want some old woman touching my stomach,' Sita says shortly.

Her husband's open expression closes, hurt taking over his face. 'She's not just any old woman...'

'Jaideep,' she says softly, appealing to the love her husband still carries for her, 'you must understand that I don't have cause to trust your mother or any woman she might recommend, especially after what she did on my birthday last year.'

He nods, his face shut right down now.

She leans towards him, wanting to close the gap, this distance that has sprung between them.

But he turns away.

Chapter 55

Mary

Silence

1936

After a day teaching at the school Mary takes long walks in the evenings, loath to go home to the cottage she shares with Charles; it is empty and soulless without him, the silence shouting recriminations in the voice of her conscience.

You should tell him that the child he's looking forward to, that he's so excited about, is not his.

It is harder at the weekend, when Charles comes home, bearing gifts and showering her with compliments, beaming and solicitous, making plans for the baby, for their future as a family.

Stop, she wants to yell. *I cannot bear it. Please. Stop.*

It is only while she is teaching that she gets a respite from her guilt.

Each morning when she enters the classroom and her students greet her with genuine and happy enthusiasm, for a brief while she forgets her troubles, the charade she is living, her lies.

The weekend after she told Charles she was pregnant, he had said, his voice tentative, 'I know you love working at the school, but if it gets too much, you could come and stay in the city? There'll be plenty to do...'

He paused when he read the dismay she couldn't hide.

'If ever you change your mind, promise me you'll...'

'I promise,' she said. Another lie to add to the many she'd uttered since agreeing to marry Charles.

She wanted him gone and yet, after he left, she paced the cottage, unable to settle, to sleep when it got dark, unable even to read, guilt haranguing, remorse choking her.

And so, in the evenings after school, rather than return to the cottage, she walks the paths she took with Charles, when he was showing her the town.

She still misses her cousins, her home in England, her aunt and uncle sorely. It is a constant, stabbing, painful wound. But, as she walks the town, seeking respite from her guilt, the air vinegary with overripe fruit hosting a buzzing coven of flies; as she watches the cows grazing placidly in the fields, the farmers washing their buffaloes in the river, birds flying in a wide graceful arc above the banyan trees, she's starting to rediscover the love she had for India, back when she was a child. She's beginning to see what fascinated her parents about this beautiful land.

She likes sitting by the river, the ripples and susurrations of the gently burbling water, chickens pecking at the riverbank, women coming to fill their pails and wash their clothes looking at her archly from beneath their veils and then away again.

She remembers the games she, Amin and Sita used to play by the riverbank in a town not far from here, and yet a lifetime away, how Amin would keep watch by the cloth door of his hut and skip to join Sita and Mary when they arrived, grinning widely.

One day, she means to go back to that town, find Amin. One day, she means to write to Sita. But not now, when she should be happy but is torn. What is she doing, bringing a child into the world based on a lie?

Oh, the mistakes she has made, trapping Charles, using his love for her in this way! It dismays her, her ability to keep on going, doggedly, even when she is almost convinced she is going the wrong way.

Sometimes children come to play in the river, making the most of the waning light before the sun drowns in the water. She caresses her stomach and wonders, will her child look like them, sun-browned almond?

It is by the river one day that Mary feels it. A fluttering in her stomach. Like bubbles being blown by a minuscule mouth.

She caresses her stomach, awed.

'Hello,' she whispers to her child and she feels it again, the fluttering.

She pushes her hair, dislodged by the perfumed breeze, away from her face and her hand comes away wet.

Perched on the fallen coconut trunk that she has been using as a bench, in the shadow of the mango trees, the silvery blue water glinting in the glow of sundown, she talks to her child.

Mary walks back to the cottage resolute. She knows what she must do. After the deliberation, the upset, the guilt of every single day of her married life, when she should have been happy but has instead been in turmoil, finally, she feels – despite the uncertainty awaiting her, the heartbreak and pain she must inflict – if not relieved, then calm.

Growing up, she was distressed that her parents' idea of her and her notion of herself were so dissimilar, that her parents always encouraged her to be someone she was not. In fact, right until now, Mary has been convinced that what she wanted and what her parents had wanted for her were two different things.

But now she is not so sure.

Mary has always felt safe within boundaries; she has felt sheltered by rules. Which was why she married Charles, to stay within the bounds of propriety, because she was not brave enough to countenance the alternative: shame and ostracism.

Not any more.

'You are a gift more precious than my reputation. More valuable than propriety,' she assures her child. 'I'll do right by you.'

Chapter 56

Priya

Cocoon

2000

Priya dreams that her father is beside her, watching over her as she sleeps in the bed she shares with Jacob. Where *is* Jacob? He must be away on one of his trips for work.

No.

No, he is… Jacob is…

She wakes, tears swamping her face, a lump choking her throat so she finds it hard to breathe, to swallow, the sobs congealing, briny violet in her chest.

'Priya?'

She blinks. She was not dreaming. Her father really is here.

That tiny portion of Priya's heart not deadened by Jacob's leaving is warmed by affection for her father. He has been there for her, always. When she was seventeen he guided her across the chasm of losing her mother to a sudden, unexpected heart attack even though he was grieving himself, making sure her life didn't derail because of it. Urging her to do the film-making course she had set her heart on, even though it was in England. Visiting her often during her early days here as she tried to find her feet.

And he is there for her now.

'Jacob called me. Left a message saying he was worried about you.'

The anger that overcomes her has the fiery potency of a thousand raw chillies. 'He's worried about me? Ha!'

'The bastard,' her father says quietly and yet there is such rage and venom in his voice.

'Did Jacob tell you what he's done?' she asks, her voice a squeak of humiliation and upset.

Why is *she* humiliated when it is Jacob who should be?

'I couldn't get hold of him when I called him back. Good job too. I've a mind to go over there and—'

'Baba...'

Her father's face softens as he looks at her. 'I tried calling you, but when you didn't pick up, I called your production company and they... They told me.' His voice pulsing with fury.

Heat, blush red, ambushes her face. The party. All those people. All of her crew. What possessed her to organise that surprise? If she hadn't, then she'd still be in a blissful cocoon of not knowing.

But now, it seems the world knows, including her family.

'Does Dadima know?' Priya asks, hoping her father hasn't told his mother. Why would he? They're not close. But in the unlikely event that he has, she needs to prepare herself.

She closes her eyes, weary. She cannot deal with her grandmother's opinion, her judgement, on top of everything else.

'Your grandmother doesn't know about Jacob. She's ill,' her father is saying. 'Her doctor called, asking me to return to India as soon as possible.' He has been in New York on business these last few months.

She opens her eyes, stares at her father as what he's saying sinks in. 'It's bad then.'

He nods. 'She doesn't have long. I was going to call you and then when I found out about Jacob...'

Priya sinks back onto the nest of pillows, carrying the briny tang of her grief, the spicy mauve flavour of loss.

She cannot begin to process what she feels about her grandmother. The devastation of Jacob's betrayal trumps everything.

'Would you come with me? Your dadima would like it, I think, if we visited her together.'

She craves the emptiness of dreamless sleep. She wants to forget.

But the world intrudes, regardless.

Her grandmother is dying. Despite Priya's rocky relationship with her, she has been a constant in her life. Like Jacob was. Both are shifting now, proving themselves to be ephemeral, mortal, and it is unnerving, overwhelming.

The day her mother had her fatal heart attack, Priya was in college. She had been called out of class, told her mother was dead. All she had thought, over and over as she tried to make sense of what she was hearing, was that she could not even remember if she'd said goodbye to her that morning.

I'll never forgive myself if I don't see Dadima before she dies...

'Come to India with me,' her father is saying. 'You can lie low over there, recover from what has happened. And you can bid goodbye to your grandmother too, while you're at it.'

His proposal is tempting.

She cannot live like this, hiding from everyone, punishing herself for Jacob's indiscretion.

Sorrow bites. Before it can reduce her, run roughshod over her, she says, 'Yes, I'll come.'

Chapter 57

Mary

Bind

1936

Sunday morning.

They are at breakfast, Charles shovelling scrambled eggs into his mouth while reading the paper, Mary picking at hers.

'Charles?'

'Yes, my dear?' He smiles absently at her, his attention still on his newspaper.

I am so sorry, Charles.

'I...'

He stops eating. Looks at her properly now, the smile replaced by worry.

I vowed when we married that I'd make sure you were happy, always. I did not realise then that by marrying you when I didn't love you, marrying you while carrying another man's child, I was guaranteeing your unhappiness. I was only thinking of how to save myself. I did not spare a thought for you.

'Is it the baby?'

You've been nothing but kind. You don't deserve this. I am so sorry.

'Mary?' Anxiety pulsing through his voice.

He reaches for her.

'Don't, Charles, I couldn't bear it.'

'Mary? What *is* the matter, my dear? Are you unwell?' His face crumpled with concern. His breakfast half-eaten. Newspaper dropped, open, beside his plate.

I'm interrupting his ordinary, happy Sunday morning with his wife and soon-to-be family to devastate him.

Blood loud in her ears. Cheeks flushing the crimson of remorse. Her guilty, horrid heart thrumming in her chest.

She could lie. Say that she's ill. Continue as before.

She touches her stomach and her baby flutters against her hand.

'I'm so sorry, Charles. I can't go on like this.'

'What do you mean, Mary? My dear, is it the baby?' he asks again, his gaze piercing, raw, his voice bubbling with care.

She alone has got herself into this bind. Nobody forced her into doing what she did with Vinay; in fact she was warned against it. Nobody forced her into compounding that mistake by involving another man, lying to him, marrying him.

Now it is up to her to right it the best she can. Although it will mean breaking this man.

She feels weak all over. She opens her mouth. Nothing comes.

Again, he reaches for her. This man who loves her, whom she has cheated and trapped.

She leans backward, away from him, and sees his face fall, his gaze wounded.

What I'm about to inflict is so much worse.

She closes her eyes.

Coward. Look at him, face what you've done, everything you've done.

Look at him while breaking his heart.

'This baby, Charles…'

'The baby?' Fear written across his face.

She can't do this.

She has to.

'It… it's not yours.'

Incomprehension. Bemusement.

Look at him. Meet his gaze, traitor.

And as what she is saying sinks in, his face crumples, fragments. 'Wh… what are you…? You can't be…' His shattered words reflecting his upset, surprise, puzzlement, panic, pain.

'I'm so sorry, Charles.'

Injury. Devastation. His mouth opening. A tremulous, fragile word splintering from his throat. 'No.'

I was upset because Vinay kept the truth of his marriage from me, my aunt and uncle kept the truth of my past from me. What I'm doing to Charles, who has been nothing but good to me, is far worse.

He pushes his plate away, rests his head in his hands.

After a second, an age, he runs a hand across his eyes, looks at her, his face a ruin.

Agony, torment and, finally, anger, bright and hot in his eyes.

She sees herself through his eyes. A liar. Like his father.

He was honest with her, bared himself to her, and she… She had so many chances to do the same and yet she kept her truth from him.

She duped him for her own means. To be able to get away with what she had done. She did not think of him. She refused to consider the eventuality that he might find out. She did not want to dwell on what finding out might do to him.

He looks crushed. Shadows stalking his eyes, shimmering with hurt, even as they rage.

'You've been with someone else,' he says. Each word choked out, sounding strangled. 'Who is he? Do you love him?'

She cannot bear the agony throbbing in his voice. 'No.' She manages to get the word, the lie, out.

'How can I believe you? How can I believe anything you say? If you'd been honest with me… Are you being honest now? Look at me.'

She meets her husband's tormented gaze, upset leaking out of hers.

I'm still lying to him.

'Is there a possibility this child could be mine?'

She flinches from the hope threading his voice.

She wants to say yes. Even now, the instinct to save herself is strong, but the word sticks in her throat.

'As I thought.' He is broken. 'Why tell me now?'

'I couldn't bear to bring this child into the world based on a lie.'

'And yet, you have lied to me. You've lied to me, Mary. I love you so much, and you deliberately and purposefully tricked me. How could I have got you so wrong?' He takes a shuddering breath. 'You dared to trap me into believing another man's child was my own. How could you? Who is he? At the very least, I deserve the truth.'

'He... I...'

'Tell me.'

'I...'

He jumps to his feet, strides into their bedroom, pulling out Mary's things from her wardrobe, flinging them onto the floor.

'No, Charles. Please...' Mary, having followed him into their bedroom, pleads.

She has never seen him like this, so out of control, as if someone else has taken him over.

He ignores her, charging back into the dining room, pulling out a chair and dropping onto it, spent. 'The fool that I am.' His words a lament. His head in his hands. Then he looks up, resolve bruising his wretched eyes, right at Mary, slumped in the dining room doorway.

'Leave,' he says.

'I'm sorry,' she manages. 'I didn't mean—'

'Leave,' he thunders, bringing his fist down hard on the table. 'I can't bear to look at you.'

'I—'

'You're no better than my father.'

'Charles, I—'

'Don't you dare!' His eyes flashing. 'I waited a long time for the right woman, someone as different from my father as it was possible to be. I saw how my mother suffered...'

'I have been faithful within this marriage.'

'You lied to me. I wanted someone who would share their life with me, love me. Not someone who would betray me. I told you who I was, told you everything. I asked you not to keep secrets from me. If you had told me...'

She looks up at him then. 'Would you have married me if I had told you?'

He turns away, resting his head in the cradle of his arms. 'Leave,' he whispers.

And she does.

Chapter 58

Priya

Microwave Meals

2000

Even after she has agreed to return to India with her father, Priya dithers, changing her mind a thousand times. She burrows into the comfort of her bed, only her father's coaxing her to share some of the microwave meals that he has heated up – 'I hate to eat alone, please, Priya,' – getting her up.

She takes a bite of the meal her father has placed in front of her and tastes sorrow. The realisation that she will never again sit at this table with Jacob slaps her. But her father is there, sitting at the scarred table, and so she fixes her eyes on the savagely gouged wood and she shovels the food into her mouth, each mouthful tasting of the unsalvageable dregs of her relationship.

'Priya, the taxi's arriving in an hour,' her father urges, the day they are to leave.

Her stomach dips and she feels nauseous. 'I can't,' she whispers, shutting her eyes tight, burrowing into Jacob's pillow, which no longer contains any trace of him. 'You go.'

Getting up and about means facing the world without Jacob in hers, accepting what has happened, the hateful truth that her husband is creating the family she yearned for with another woman. She doesn't know if she can.

Here, she can shut her eyes and pretend all is well, that Jacob is away on business and will be coming home to her soon. And what if he *does* come back and she is not here?

You're pathetic, a voice whispers, a remnant of the old Priya, feisty and spirited. *Where's your backbone? You're someone in your own right, you don't need Jacob to validate who you are.*

'Your grandmother is dying, Priya,' her father is saying. 'Come home with me. You know I don't really talk to your grandmother. I need you there. Please.'

It is her father's plea that does it. He has always stood by her, been there for her when she needed him. Now, *he* needs *her*, and truth be told, Priya needs to see her grandmother before she dies.

Gathering every ounce of will, she shoves clothes into a bag, calls her crew members, informing them she is going to India for a while – a family emergency. If there is a telling pause when she says so – they were at the party after all – she ignores it.

She leaves without looking back at the home that she had hoped would one day house her children, hers and Jacob's. A chapter of her life, fifteen years with Jacob, ended just like that, a shut door and the clatter of her shoes on the stairs.

Chapter 59

Mary

Black Nothingness

1936

'I… Can I stay here?'

The nuns peruse Mary's face, their peaceful eyes worried. 'Of course, child.'

She is back where she started, in her room at the school, but now she has a failed marriage and a child growing within her. A child who does not belong to her husband.

The nuns treat her gently, but she can see the worry etched into their faces, read the questions they will not ask.

Their kindness hurts.

I don't deserve it.

She cannot impose on their hospitality for long. Keeping the truth from her husband has caused this bind. She cannot afford to do the same with the nuns, lose their trust. Although she runs the risk that, when she does come clean, she might do just that.

She slips into the small chapel where the nuns pray, pews bare, Jesus looking at her, benignly, from the cross.

Help me, Lord, she prays, her head bowed, knees digging into the cool cement floor.

But the Lord is impassive. Why would He help her, when she has made so many mistakes?

And after all, her prayers are mere words. She doesn't have all-encompassing faith like the nuns.

It is break time and Mary is preparing a lesson plan based on *The Jungle Book* when there is a knock on the door.

Sister Catherine. 'A letter arrived for you. Here.'

Mary recognises the handwriting at once. Her fingers shaking, she opens it. She has been expecting this, but it is still a shock.

She must make a sound, for Sister Catherine, who has gone back towards the door, turns, her face alarmed, as the letter floats from Mary's trembling fingers to the ground.

Sister Catherine holds her with one hand and picks up the letter with the other.

'Your husband?'

'Yes.'

'I don't mean to pry but this is not just a tiff, is it?'

His ugly words. Calling her names that she deserves but would, even a few weeks ago, not have thought applied to her. And at the end, *I want a divorce.*

'We didn't like to ask. Your marriage is your matter, but we've wondered…'

'It's not just a tiff.'

'It's not common for couples to stay apart so soon after marriage, but we hoped it would blow over. We've been praying for you.'

No amount of prayer can fix this.

She looks about the familiar classroom, the scent of chalk dust and worn pages, musty yellow. Being here, sharing her love of books with the children in her care, has seen her through one of the most difficult periods of her life. Will the nuns let her stay here after she confesses? She doubts it.

'Child, is there any hope of reconciliation with your husband?'

She wants to throw herself on this nun's mercy. She wants to cry her eyes out. She wants her family: her aunt and uncle, her cousins. But she knows that after what she has done, she cannot turn to them – she will not be welcome.

'Mary? Child?' The nun's voice spiked with panic as Mary's body loses its battle with upset, giving in to the exquisite pull of black nothingness.

Once again, when she comes to she sees angels.

Several worried faces, bobbing heads haloed by wimples.

'Mary?'

She sits up. Sips the water they offer. Her head is spinning, but she knows that the nuns are owed an explanation.

'On the ship here I…'

How to say it, put into words what she has done? She bites her lower lip, tastes the hot, sweet tang of blood. 'I'm pregnant.'

The nuns don't say anything for a moment. Then Mother Ruth: 'It's not your husband's.'

A question couched as a statement.

She closes her eyes, her reply a weary exhalation. 'No.'

'Your husband knows?'

'He wants a divorce.'

The nuns sigh as one.

Then Mother Ruth, gentle. 'And you? What do you want?'

She thinks of England, her life there – ease and comfort, order, the companionship of her cousins, laughter, sisterhood, love – now denied her as she has flouted all the rules.

She thinks of her room here, its small veranda with its view of the fruit orchard. The children, listening rapt as she reads from *The Jungle Book*. Discovering, just as she had, the power and magic of stories. 'I… I'd like to continue to work here.'

'What about your family in England?'

Her aunt and uncle, with their regard for family name, for whom appearances matter. Who had shuddered when they said, of Mary's mother, 'She was half-Indian.' They will not want a niece who is divorced and pregnant, carrying not the child of her estranged husband but that of a married Indian doctor who will not be able to claim responsibility for the child.

'They won't take me back.' Her voice shudders and breaks.

The home she had in England, the simple ease of following rules, doing as she was told, now surely denied her. The camaraderie of her cousins, the luxury she had taken for granted... She will not dwell on it, for if she does, she will break. She needs to be strong for the baby growing within her.

'You will have to give up your child.'

Her hand goes to her stomach where the child she created in a moment of abandon resides. She married Charles so she could protect this baby, wrap it in a cloak of respectability. It is also why she left the safety of her marriage – so her child, already so loved, wouldn't come into the world based on a lie. 'I want to keep it.'

Mother Ruth's gaze piercing. 'It won't be easy. Either for you or for the child.'

And especially hard for a child who is half-Indian. I will have no dowry either, no cushion of wealth to ease the way; my inheritance from my grandparents is in my husband's name and after all I put Charles through, I cannot in all decency ask for it back.

'I want to keep my child,' she repeats. Then, 'I... I also want to do my job, stay here, if you will let me.'

Mother Ruth sighs. 'You can't keep the child and stay here, Mary.'

The other nuns look away. Sister Catherine wrings her hands.

'We cannot condone what you plan on doing, raising a child born out of wedlock. I am sorry.'

'So, if I want to stay here...'

'You'll have to give your child away,' Mother Ruth says softly. 'Think about it. I'll ask you again in a few weeks.'

She doesn't realise she is crying until wet drops fall on the hand that cradles her stomach.

True to her word, some weeks later Mother Ruth asks, 'Mary, have you decided what to do?'

They are in the garden, walking among the fruit trees, birdsong and ripening mango and settling dust and burgeoning life and receding light – the sky streaked with colour, varying shades of red fading to pink to navy grey.

Mary caresses her stomach and the baby somersaults, responding to her touch. She doesn't know what she will do, where she will go, what is in store for her next. But she does know one thing: she will not part with her child.

'I want to keep my baby,' she tells Mother Ruth.

Mother Ruth nods. 'I was hoping for our sakes that you had changed your mind. But I admire you for what you're doing, Mary. It takes great strength to go against convention.'

Tears spring up in her eyes at the unexpected compliment. She had thought the nuns were disappointed in her.

Mother Ruth says, gently, 'For the last few weeks of your confinement, I think it's best if you go to our sister charity at the edge of the kingdom, by Lake Samovar.'

Their sister charity by the lake. Mary has heard of it. It's where women in trouble go to have their babies. At the end of their confinement, they come back to their lives, their children having been given up for adoption.

Mary's feeling of warmth at Mother Ruth's compliment dissipates. 'I'm not giving up my child,' she says again, eyes flashing, one hand protectively on her stomach.

'I know that, Mary.' Mother Ruth's voice soft. 'But there are trained nurses and midwives there, who'll take good care of you and help with the delivery.'

Once again Mary pushes away tears, touched by the nun's concern and by what she is really saying. This is goodbye. Mary will go to their sister charity and after she gives birth, if she insists upon keeping her child, she's on her own.

She will miss teaching the children who have come up to her, wide-eyed, asking questions about the baby, innocent and yet curiously knowledgeable, giving her advice gleaned from their mothers, the older girls telling her proudly that they take care of their siblings and that it is easy, nothing to worry about.

'Where's your husband?' the younger girls ask.

'He… I'll bring up the baby alone.'

They nod, accepting, one of them saying, 'My father died and my mother is bringing me and my brothers up alone.'

'My father left because he was angry with my mother for only having girls,' another says. 'He wanted a son.'

Working with the children has given her the strength to cope with the aftermath of her separation from Charles, the far-reaching consequences of her actions.

'How could you bring disgrace upon our family like your father before you, Mary?' her aunt had written. 'Charles wrote to us, told us all.'

Her aunt taking Charles's word over her own had hurt almost more than she could bear.

'Please don't contact us again. I don't want the scandal attaching itself to my daughters. I was upset when you insisted on going to India but the one saving grace now is that you're far away.'

Her aunt's harsh words caused a crater to erupt in Mary's homesick, bruised heart. A huge part of her had held out hope that the affection her aunt had revealed when Mary announced she wanted to travel to India would prevail, that it would trump her guardians' love of status, family name, their desire to uphold appearances. She had dared to wish that they would forgive and forget, welcome their prodigal niece – and her illegitimate child – with open arms. Her aunt's brutal letter crushed that hope: England, home, was no longer so.

It made her want to give up, to go back in time to before Major Digby's arrival and the return of her memories. But then her child moved within her, reminding her that it depended upon her – it had no one else. Her child moved within her and she knew, without a doubt, that if given a choice to go back to her life before Major Digby, wiping out all that had come after, she would not take it. For then she wouldn't have this child, whom she loved more than she had ever loved anything or anyone. No matter how heartbroken and devastated she felt at her banishment from her family in England, she would not shirk her responsibility towards her child. She had created it, she had caused all this furore, so she would do right by it. She would not let it down. She would give it what she herself ached for: love, belonging. She would put it first, before status, society, before everything and everyone else.

Returning to England is not an option. Disowned, with most likely a dark-skinned child and no husband, she will be shunned, derided... How will she go about getting a job?

At least if she stays here, she hopes, by virtue of being English, she might get a job as a governess. She knows, from conversations overheard on board the ship, that wealthy Indian families employ white governesses so their children can learn to speak the queen's English.

In the weeks since she left Charles, devastating him, she has worried about how she will provide for her child but she hasn't been torn apart by the guilt she felt when she was married. Now she is resolute. She's disowned by her guardians, and, although she will miss her family for the rest of her life, having broken all the rules is, in a strange way, a relief. She's able to do what she wants – she is not bound by what people will say, how society will judge her. For they, her loved ones included, have judged her already, found her wanting. She cannot sink any lower. And curiously, that is liberating.

Finally she understands that *this* is the freedom her parents talked about. This was what they meant when they urged, 'Live your life your way.'

Like them, she does not have anyone or anything to fall back on – no cushion of family or wealth. Her child's future and her own are entirely in her hands. It is scary but also freeing.

Her parents rebuffed the decrees placed by society and lived their short lives *their* way.

It was what they wanted for her, *all* they wanted for her: the freedom of doing what felt right to her as opposed to what society deemed was right.

I understand now, Mama and Papa. I do.

Part 5

Different Versions

Chapter 60

Mary

Haven

1937

The Lake House refuge is beautiful, a haven. It is situated right beside the lake, overlooking the sumptuous palace, which appears to float serenely on the water.

Her first day there, Mary wanders into the garden, vast and profuse, which surrounds the buildings that constitute the refuge: two houses, one for English and the other for Indian women, and a library, which is a small, tiled cottage equidistant from both houses.

The gardener, an aging Indian man who reminds Mary of Khan – too old to garden but whom her mother did not have the heart to let go – is trying, and failing, to pull out a giant weed.

'Let me help,' she says, squatting beside him.

He blushes. 'No, memsahib.'

But Mary pays no heed and, together, they manage to pull out the weed, almost falling over backwards into the squelchy, just-watered mud in the process.

Mary laughs, and is surprised by the sound. It feels like the first time she has properly laughed since her marriage to Charles and its subsequent disintegration.

Mary takes to helping the gardener, Bilal.

He is reluctant at first. 'You shouldn't be doing this work, memsahib.'

'The nuns are happy for me to help you.'

'You speak our language very fluently,' he says, as they dig out weeds in a patch where he's decided to grow pineapples.

'I grew up not far from here. We had a gardener named Khan…' It is liberating to share her memories with someone, talk about her parents. Bilal is tactful and does not ask questions, instead listening intently to the stories she is willing to share.

In growing plants, tending to them, Mary finds the solace that evaded her while praying in the chapel at the school, which she had taken to doing. The plants thrive under her care and it is so simple – she looks after them and they reward her with beauteous blooms, bountiful produce. When she is nurturing the plants, the worry about the baby (Is she doing the right thing by her child in wanting to keep it? Is she doing it for the baby or herself?), the breakup of her marriage and the rejection of her family in England are left behind. She buries her hands in rich soil, pungent and fertile, and she can calm her mind, clear it.

She works in the garden, the fresh, red perfume of earth and burgeoning vegetation, the flowers nodding in the breeze, bees hovering around the lush fruit, the heady scent of ripe guavas and fermenting jackfruit, the lake shimmering beyond and the palace magnificent at the centre of it: Sita's palace. Mary never got round to contacting Sita and doesn't have the heart to now. Although, perhaps due to the proximity of the Lake Palace, she wonders about Sita more than she has since she saw her atop the elephant, regally surveying her subjects. Queen Sita. Has she changed much? What would she make of Mary's actions, Sita who was, even as a child, so vehement about the rights of girls?

It is a shame that Sita's Lake Palace, such an impressive building, is occupied by the royals only every few months, if that. In the evening, lights twinkle from it, reflected in the water. A festive celebration of lamps, heralding a residence waiting for its owners.

'Fifty-odd staff live in cottages on the palace grounds all year round,' Bilal informs Mary. 'They look after the palace, keep the rooms in order for when the royals visit.'

Every morning, the boatman ferries over the palace servants' children, chattering and giggling and skimming stones, an explosion of happy noise cascading over the lake, fish darting and water rippling joyfully in their wake. The children, their uniforms tidy, the girls' hair oiled and plaited, spill out of the boat as it anchors on shore and, boisterously pushing each other, messing about, walk to school.

In the evening comes another eruption of gleeful clamour as the children return, grumbling about homework, gossiping about their school day, their plaits undone, uniforms awry, ribbons unravelled.

The children's laughter rings out, striking pain and accusation in the hearts of would-be mothers at the refuge. Mothers who will not be allowed to be mothers, who'll be scorned and shunned if they insist on keeping these children labelled 'mistakes' and worse. Mothers who will become mothers later, to other children, created 'properly', via the right channels.

Apart from the garden, the other place where Mary finds solace is in the small library. It is usually occupied by her alone – the other women at the refuge are not readers.

When it gets too hot to garden, Mary sits reading by the library window with its view of the garden and the lake beyond. Reading, as it has always done, gives her unquestioning succour, transporting her to other lands. When she has read all the books in the library, she reads the book Vinay gave her – she has been unable and unwilling to part with it – and her father's books too.

After what Mary did to Charles, she has come to, if not forgive Vinay for keeping the truth of his marriage from her, then at least understand him. She understands now that no person is all good, that everyone has secrets and practises small deceits, that they are driven to lie, by fear, by attraction, by love.

One morning, there is great excitement at the refuge.

'The queen is visiting the Lake Palace and she wants to tour the refuge,' the maid doing Mary's room tells her.

I'm to meet Sita at last!

'The nuns are most flustered,' the maid adds, plumping the pillows vigorously. 'The queen is rumoured to be a difficult woman. All the times she's stayed at the Lake Palace she's never visited here, although it seems starting this refuge was her idea. I wonder why now?'

'I heard the queen has started doing charitable work recently. Perhaps that's why she's coming here,' Bilal tells Mary as they water the plants.

'Is the king accompanying her?' Mary asks. She hasn't told Bilal that she knew the queen as a child.

'No, it's just the queen staying. I heard the servants are very nervous. Especially as she's pregnant, carrying the heir to the throne.'

How curious, Mary muses, caressing her bump, *that Sita and I are having children at the same time. Wouldn't it be fantastic if our children were to be friends?*

It would indeed be fantasy! her conscience chimes. *Why would the heir apparent to the throne want to associate with the child of a disgraced woman?*

*

The morning Sita is to arrive, Mary is in the garden, giving it a tidy, when she sees the boat. Both it and the boatman have been spruced up in honour of the queen's visit, the boatman wearing livery for the first time since Mary arrived. The boat has been washed and cleaned, the coat of arms on it brightened with a lick of paint. It sports a U-shaped umbrella shade, glittering with jewels and gold cloth. The queen reclines upon embroidered plush-velvet cushions, one elegant hand trailing the water.

A stately car emblazoned with the royal arms is waiting at the shore, to drive the queen the few short paces to the refuge.

Surely it would be faster to walk – but I don't suppose it's something a queen does, arriving on foot, Mary thinks as she washes her hands and goes to the library, settling down in her favourite armchair by the open window with Vinay's book. How was she to know that it was not the only thing he would gift her to remember him by?

She sees Sita alight from the car, nodding graciously at the nuns. Her head is covered by a veil but her face is visible, unlike at the procession when Mary only caught a glimpse of her proud smile. She is beautiful, glowing, her skin a very light brown, almost but not quite white. Adulthood has honed and sharpened the beauty that was very evident even as a child.

Sita turns to follow the nuns into the house for Indian women and as she does so, she looks up and through the open window of the library, her startling amber gaze, which had mesmerised Mary when she first laid eyes on Sita all those years ago, meeting Mary's inquisitive one.

Sita flashes an automatic haughty smile, the kind reserved for subjects. But then her smile falters and her eyebrows scrunch and then rise up almost to her hairline. She stops, swivelling towards the window.

She recognises me.

'Mary?' Sita mouths and her face lights up in one of those glorious, heart-stopping smiles that she always reserved for those closest to her, that charmed everyone who was the recipient of them, so that they forgave her anything. This smile has not changed. Even as a child she had a way of smiling that made one feel special, honoured to have been singled out by her.

Mary, trapped in that feline gaze, feels light-headed as she did on the day of the procession when she fainted in Charles's arms.

She lifts her lips in an answering smile but Sita is gone.

'The townspeople say your fainting is an omen of some sort,' Mary hears Charles say in her head.

Why, when she sees Sita, does Mary feel queasy? Why has she never felt able to write to Sita, even as she's wondered about the path her childhood friend took that has led her to becoming queen?

Get a hold of yourself, the sensible part of her chides.

And yet… There's a dip in her stomach. Like nerves.

She has no time to dwell on it, for Sita suddenly appears in the library, her voice as musical as it is commanding. 'Mary, is it really you, after all this time?'

Chapter 61

Sita

Artifice

1937

'Mary, is it really you, after all this time?'

Sita cannot believe it. She has wondered so many times about her childhood friend, the girl who had admired her and made her feel special, the first person to have seen who Sita was inside, and the first to have wholeheartedly believed in her. The girl whom she had loved and envied and whose freedom she had coveted. The girl whom she had missed tremendously when she left for England after her parents died.

The girl who accused Sita of causing her parents' deaths.

Several times over the years Sita has wondered if things would have been different, if the arc of her life would have changed, had Mary's parents not died that day. What if they had convinced Sita's parents to allow her to study? Would she be in this predicament now?

'If I had what Mary had,' Sita had often thought, 'I'd be a doctor, a teacher, a scientist.'

All that freedom, all those books, and Mary is here, at this refuge Sita has built for women in need, unmistakably pregnant, presumably with someone highly unsuitable.

Given the situation Sita herself is in, the farce she is conducting, it is something of a relief to see Mary in just as desperate a situation as herself, if not a worse one.

At least nobody knows of Sita's charade. And after all, she *is* queen. She has the safety net of wealth, respectability, honour to fall back on. Which is why she'll do anything within her power to maintain it…

Mary hasn't changed. Her face is less angular, more rounded from pregnancy, but her eyes, huge, brown and vulnerable with tawny orange cores that hint at hidden depths, are the same.

She is smiling at Sita, and her smile hasn't changed either, warm and slightly unsure.

'Queen Sita!' She holds out her hand. 'Or should I bow? Curtsey?'

Sita chuckles, taking Mary's hand. 'You don't need to stand on ceremony with me, Mary, when we used to fly kites and race boats and get into trouble together.'

'If my memory serves me right, it was you leading myself and Amin into trouble,' Mary says and Sita feels all the worries of recent weeks dissipate slightly as she laughs, heartily, for the first time in months.

A few days earlier, Jaideep had arrived at her chambers laden with gifts, looking apologetic. He was still distant with her, a distance spawned when she refused his mother's overture. Yet still, Sita knew he loved her. And nothing at all could dull his enthusiasm, his eager joy regarding his child.

'I hate to leave you when you're pregnant, Sita,' he'd said. 'But I have to travel to the kingdom of Nawar for a few days – the king has issued an invitation I cannot refuse. We're going to discuss, among other things, the possibility of the British leaving India. If they do, we kings have to stay united. Wives are not invited; you know how traditional the king of Nawar is.'

'Go,' she said, gently, thinking, *this is perfect!* She'd been planning a visit to the Lake House refuge for some time to scout pregnant women who might provide her with the child she needed.

'I'll be back in a fortnight.'

'Actually…'

'Yes?'

'While you're away, I might stay at the Lake Palace. That'll make your absence more bearable. Perhaps you can join me there on your way back from Nawar?'

He smiled at her. 'Perfect. I feel better knowing you'll be at the Lake Palace, taking a well-deserved rest.'

And now here she is, in the library at the refuge, wide-open windows letting in air tasting of a fruity feast, the ink-and-knowledge fragrance of books, reunited with Mary, her childhood friend.

It is, Sita finds, a relief to be with this woman who knew her before she was queen, to look into Mary's eyes and be reminded of the girl she once used to be: feisty and fearless, ambitious and daring. The girl before all the lies and obfuscations, the girl hidden under the layers of subterfuge, the girl Sita has forgotten she once was.

And it is rewarding, also, to see herself through Mary's eyes now: Queen.

But if she had a chance to go back to before, would she choose to be queen, bound by chains of tradition and duty, by what is expected of her? Would she pick this life, where she's trapped in the lie she had uttered in order to hold on to what she's won, in order to keep her brother-in-law and mother-in-law from laying claim to the throne, this lie that has swollen inside her stomach in place of a child, taking her over?

The girl she used to be – the girl who had said out loud anything that popped into her head, even with Jaideep, which was what made him fall in love with her – where has that devil-may-care girl gone? Is she still there, hidden beneath the skin of artifice Sita has grown, the persona she has so carefully crafted?

If she had the chance to live her life again, she would run away as she had planned to do, into a new life of her own choosing, a destiny *she* would create and control, instead of marrying Jaideep and becoming queen.

Wouldn't she?

'Thank you for showing me round,' Sita says to the nun who has accompanied her. 'I'd like to spend some time here.'

The nun executes a curtsey. 'I'll be in the chapel, your majesty. A maid will wait outside the library and escort you there.'

'Isn't it fitting,' Sita says to Mary once the nun has left, 'that we meet in the library of all places, surrounded by books? It reminds me of your room in your childhood home.'

A shadow crosses Mary's face briefly, before she manages a small smile that wavers at the corners.

You still wear your emotions on your face, Mary. You haven't changed at all, except for being pregnant and being here.

'I saw you curled up in your armchair reading and, just before I recognised you, I thought, that looks comfortable.'

Mary laughs, music and waterfalls. 'Do you still love to read?'

'I don't read quite as much as I used to; not enough time any more.' *I don't read at all. I cannot concentrate. I wish I could go back to the blissful days when I could open the pages of a book and be lost in it.*

'I can imagine,' Mary says. 'I saw you a while back, when you were parading through town on the occasion of the king's birthday.'

'Why didn't you get in touch?'

'I meant to. But... You're queen now, you have realised your childhood dreams.'

If only you knew. Being queen, achieving dreams, is not all it is cracked up to be.

'Have you… do you know where Amin is now?' Mary asks.

'No, I lost touch with him after you left for England.'

'I wonder whether he too achieved his dreams?' Mary's voice wistful.

'What about you?' Sita asks, to move the conversation away from Amin and nostalgia – what's the point? They've all moved on. She wants to take the question back almost as soon as it's out, she who has become well-versed in diplomacy displaying a graceless lack of tact. How could Mary have achieved her dreams – Sita cannot remember what they were – if she's here?

'I… I was working at the school you started for girls.' Another shadow populating Mary's face, stealing her smile, the lightness, the laughter.

'You're the new teacher? The one who's had to leave because of personal circumstances?'

Mary smiles but the joy is gone. 'Yes.' She cradles her stomach, and her eyes shine with emotion.

Surely she's here to give her child up? That's what all the women come here for. So then why can't Mary go back to her job? The reports that arrived from the school with the quarterly accounts had been very flattering about the new teacher and it appeared she was enjoying her job. So why give up? Is Mary planning on returning to England? If so, then why isn't she in England already?

'You're not returning to work after the child…?'

'No.' Short, sharp. Not inviting question.

Mary could be like this, Sita recalls, even as a child. If she didn't want to talk about something, she wouldn't and nothing could make her budge. It had frustrated Sita no end. But it meant she was very good at keeping secrets and Sita had learned quickly that if she wanted to talk something out, she could tell Mary, ask her not to tell anyone and she wouldn't, no matter what.

'Isn't it wonderful that we're both expecting children at the same time? That our lives diverged so suddenly and now they've converged just as abruptly and we're almost at the same juncture of our lives, about to bring new lives into the world?' Mary smiles, but Sita can see the effort it takes for her to do so.

'Yes,' Sita says, shortly. If Mary can be abrupt, so can she.

There's an awkward silence. It stretches, taut, until Mary breaks it.

'You've come to see the refuge and I'm keeping you.' She waves her hand around the library. 'As you know, this is the library and you're welcome to borrow any book you want as long as you bring it back.'

The tension is broken as Sita, once again in the space of a few minutes, laughs out loud. 'Thank you. But I've quite enough books at my palaces now.' Then, 'You loved fairy tales as a child. What do you like to read now?'

'Oh, I read anything at all as long as it engages me.'

'And the book you're reading just now?'

'It's one of my own: *An Essay Concerning Human Understanding* by John Locke. I learn something new each time I read this book. It's fascinating.'

'Can I...?' Sita takes the book from Mary, leafs through it. '"We have our understandings no less different than our palates; and he that thinks the same truth shall be equally relished by everyone in the same dress, may as well hope to feast every one with the same sort of cookery..."' Sita quotes from the book, thinking of her husband, his brother, his mother and herself: One kingdom, four different versions, four different kinds of understanding.

'Food for thought, isn't it?' Mary says, eyes twinkling. She's beautiful when she smiles, her face lighting up.

'Why are you here, Mary?' Sita asks, having had enough of dithering.

Mary takes a deep breath as if deliberating. And then, she tells her.

'It's a relief, I admit,' she says when she's finished, 'to tell someone. Thank you for listening, for your time. I know you have far more pressing—'

'Oh, don't be like that,' Sita says. 'You won't give up the baby?'

'No.'

'So what's your plan?'

Mary juts her chin out. 'I don't know yet. But I'll think of something.'

'It won't be easy, given the circumstances.'

'I know.' Her eyes shine with determination, a hard, steely core that wasn't there as a child.

And a thought comes to Sita, unbidden. *I admire you. You have the strength to go against convention, do what you think is right. You have the courage to break off your marriage, accept banishment from the family you yearn for, turn your back on a comfortable life, in order not to bring your child up based on a lie.*

Whereas I… I am living a lie. I wanted freedom and instead I've tied myself in bonds of tradition, duty, parental approval, greed and falsehood.

'I don't know what the future holds, but I feel stronger than I did when I was married. At least now, I'm being honest with myself, true to myself and my child,' Mary says, caressing her bump.

Honest. True. Sita blinks back sudden, hot, surprised tears. This woman has made her laugh, wholeheartedly, and now reduced her to tears.

Mary was always the wimpy one, afraid of change, afraid to take risks. And yet, she is now taking the biggest risk of all. Standing up for what she believes in, being true to herself.

When she first saw Mary here, Sita had pitied her friend who was in, she thought, a situation even worse than the one in which she found herself. She had felt disdain that, despite all the opportunities afforded Mary, she had ended up here. And it had made Sita magnanimous. She could be generous in her feelings towards Mary, for Mary had sunk low.

But now…

Now her feelings have done an about-turn. She is experiencing the same inadequacies and jealousies she felt towards Mary during their childhood. She is back to feeling hard-done-by, back to coveting what Mary has.

As a child she had bossed Mary about, in this way trying to feel superior.

Nothing has changed.

Sita is still the posturing one, acting as though she is the bigger, when all the while it is in fact Mary. Mary has always had what Sita had desperately wanted. And it is the same again.

Mary is having a child.

Mary values being true to herself over disrepute, dishonour. She has the courage to stand up to society, convention, while Sita is mired in it. Sita is even more bound by duty than she was as a child.

I have underestimated you, Mary.

I thought I was the strong one, the brave one. But it is you.

'Your majesty…?' One of the nuns sweeps into the room.

'Take care, Mary. And write to me, keep in touch.'

With that, Sita turns away, her mind in turmoil, as envious of her friend now as she had been as a child.

And despite owning the refuge where Mary currently resides, despite her fawning subjects, the wealth she takes for granted, her many palaces, her elevated stature as queen, feeling deprived, short-changed.

Small.

Chapter 62

Priya

Dreamless Sleep

2000

In the taxi on the way to the airport, Priya says, 'You're not to tell Dadima about Jacob.'

Her father smiles wryly. 'We don't talk, Priya, your dadima and I, in case you hadn't noticed.'

She looks at her father, the tired lines etched on his face. 'Baba, you and Ma have always been so loving with me. How come you're so different to your mother?'

'When you were born,' he says, smiling tenderly at her, 'your mother extracted a promise from me to never allow my relationship with you to disintegrate to the level that mine has with my mother, no matter how hard things got between us. But Priya, I didn't need to make that promise. I held you in my arms and I knew I would move the world if I had to, to protect you, keep you happy. That is why now... Jacob...' Her father's voice tight with anger, his hands fisted at his sides.

Jacob. Rage and pain. Desperation and ache. She takes a deep breath and, gathering every ounce of strength, pushes Jacob away, changes the topic. 'Why don't you and Dadima talk?' It's a wonder she's never asked this of her father before. She's just accepted the status quo: her father and grandmother silent with each other, morose.

Her father rubs a hand across his face, sighs. 'She... she wasn't a very hands-on mother. It was just easier to avoid speaking to her as then she wouldn't cut me down. And gradually, I… fell out of the habit.' He sighs again, deeply. 'Your mother, bless her, she urged me to repair the relationship. But by then it was too far gone.'

Too far gone. Like with her and Jacob.

The wait for their flight to be called is interminable, the airport too loud. Priya wants to run out of the terminal – the excited chatter of children, the wailing babies, the harassed parents, the smartly dressed flight attendants, the creaking wheels of overstuffed suitcases, the hiss of coffee machines, the noise of the tannoy – until she runs clean out of her disastrous life and into a happier one.

But when they're finally on the plane, Priya beside the window, her father in the aisle seat, she's unexpectedly able to achieve the dreamless sleep she has been craving.

She wakes to find her head resting on her father's shoulder, him sitting stiff and to attention so she can rest her head comfortably in the crook of his neck. Watching him hold himself so rigidly while also attempting to read the newspaper makes her smile for the first time in days.

'Baba, you can relax. I'll still be comfortable,' she says and he grins, sheepish.

When they land and she breathes in the gritty, spiced air of home, Priya feels ever so slightly better.

Chapter 63

Sita

Inkling

1937

'The baby Mary Memsahib is having is that of an Indian man.'

'Mary's baby's father is Indian?' Sita sits up on her divan, her voice spiking in surprise.

She has asked this trusted maidservant to find out some details about her old friend. Sita knows she will not breathe a word about what she's doing to anyone, either now or in the future, for she has seen what happens when Sita is displeased or angered. The woman nods. 'A married man, a doctor. Comes from a wealthy family. Related to the queen mother.'

When, during their meeting at the refuge, Mary had mentioned her brief liaison on board the ship, Sita had had an inkling, judging from the haunted look in Mary's eyes, the pain she was unable to hide, that there was more to it than she was letting on. When Sita had returned from the Lake Palace to resume her duties as queen, she had been unable to get Mary's confession, how Mary had made her feel, out of her mind. She had asked the maidservant – who was looking into the pasts of the pregnant women Sita had identified as possible donors of her child – to find out more about Mary's mysterious beau.

Mary, since when did you become so brave? Sita thinks now, feeling that stab of jealousy bite again. *You're carrying the child of a married Indian man and you insist on keeping it, despite knowing the future won't be easy, either for you or your child.*

There was a time when Sita was the one who didn't care about society, consequences, only about doing what was right.

Meeting Mary has made her confront the younger, truer self she used to be and she cannot bear it.

What had Mary seen when she looked at Sita? Had she been impressed, envious, as Sita was by Mary? Sita doubts it and that upsets her more than she will admit. She is queen, she has power, wealth, adulation – and yet, the freedom she had longed for so badly is as out of reach now as it has ever been.

Sita has become queen but she has lost herself along the way.

Mary, on the other hand, has emerged stronger. Someone with convictions, principles. Someone who can live with herself and be proud of who she is.

An irrational and all-consuming anger swamps Sita, and she swells with fury directed at her childhood friend.

A small part of her – which she instantly quiets – knows that her ire should rightly be directed at herself for not being stronger, for not having the guts to denounce her queenhood, for lying to herself as well as everyone else, culminating in this horrible charade of pregnancy. She cares for what people think, very much so, and Mary does not. Once upon a time it would have been the other way round.

But her queenship, her kingdom, is all Sita has and she will do everything in her power to safeguard it.

Nevertheless, her thoughts keep returning to Mary as they have done since Sita met her again.

Mary, blessed with a baby that Sita would give anything to have…

And that is when the thought that has been brewing in her head since she saw Mary crystallises.

The plan is there, in her head, fully formed and she is surprised and delighted with the ease of it.

Sita is light-skinned, taking after her paternal grandmother, who was English. Jaideep is very pale himself, only a shade darker than Sita.

It will work – it has to.

I'll be doing Mary and her child a favour. It will be my way of thanking her for lending me books so generously and allowing me to share her life, giving me respite from my own, all those years ago.

Mary's face when she said, 'I don't know what the future holds, but I feel stronger than I did when I was married. At least now, I'm being honest with myself, true to myself and my child', rises before Sita's eyes.

She quashes the image, wills it away, even as a small voice in her head whispers, *This is your way of punishing Mary for having principles, for not caring about what people say or think when that is all you care for, for being true to herself when you are not true to anyone, least of all yourself. Having met her, you look up to her, admire her, envy her and you don't like it. You want to reduce her like you yourself are reduced. You want to take the one thing she's willing to give everything up for, the one thing she cares for and loves, for you don't want her to have the one thing you yourself have been denied.*

Impatiently, angrily, she shushes the voice of truth in her head, chanting instead the lie she has prepared. She lies so many times that it feels like the truth although her mouth is bitter with it: *This is the best option all round. Mary will be well provided for, as will her child.*

Chapter 64

Mary

A Better Life

1937

Mary wakes to someone wrenching her stomach, ripping her in two. Whoever it is means to break her, tear her soul out of her in the most painful way imaginable.

She wakes screaming. Monsters from the vivid dreams she's been having the past few days, monsters wearing her own face while Charles cowers in the corner, plague her. She is wet. Her whole body. Between her legs. And she is dying. Someone means to kill her.

She flails, hitting out blindly, screaming all the while.

The door to her room is flung open and the nuns and nurses are there, soothing, comforting. One holds her hand. Another applies a cool cloth to her sweaty forehead.

'Push,' they say.

Push? She squints up at them, in the weird half-light cast by her dreams as her eyes adjust to reality. What do they mean? Push the assailant away? Why should she? Why don't they?

'The baby is coming.'

The baby. *Her* baby. The child created in one impulsive moment of love and madness. The child she loves more than anything in the world.

Can she give this baby the life it deserves? A better life than her own?

All of these weeks as her baby has thrived, as she has worked the soil in the garden of the refuge, she has argued with herself.

For whose benefit am I doing this? Mine or my child's? Is it selfish to want to keep my child, bring him or her up in the miasma of disgrace that trails me? Wouldn't it be best if I gave my child away, like the other mothers here, with their haunted eyes that speak of the stories they guard fiercely, the paths they have taken that have brought them here, the paths deemed wrong, their children labelled mistakes?

'It would be best all round.' The nuns here have tried to convince her to change her mind. 'If you insist on keeping it, your child will grow up without a father.'

But it will have a mother. Will anyone else love it as much as I do already?

These thoughts have plagued her late at night, dancing in her head like the fireflies on the lake, as the wind sighs among the fruit trees and the plants she has lovingly nurtured. The child kicks, making its presence felt, talking to her in that secret time so it feels like it is just the two of them in the world. This child that is her flesh and blood. The only person completely hers in this world. She talks to it and she loves it in the clandestine soughing dark. But then a voice whispers, mocking, *What can you offer your child, you who cannot even guarantee that it will be happy like the children of the servants at the Lake Palace who arrive by boat at school? Your child will be ridiculed because of who they are. They will be made to feel ashamed. Of themselves and of you.*

You say you love your child. Surely loving means wanting the best for it? Surely loving your child means giving it away so it grows up in a loving, two-parent home, far removed from its divorced, disgraced birth mother and her scandalous past?

She pushes against the pain. It comes in waves and she tries to ride them, endure them. She pushes and pushes until at last...

A gush, a release.

A mewling cry from her newborn child.

But from the nuns and nurses helping her, silence. It is a silence that is different from their calm, efficient one. This silence is thick. Accusing.

'What's the matter? Is it my baby?'

Into the silence that no adult breaks, her child wails.

Instinct takes over and Mary sits up, with difficulty, and gathers her child into her arms.

A boy, a slippery, scrawny bundle of perfection, with a scrunched-up face and a kittenish wail. His mouth is open, minuscule pink gums showing. Wisps of black hair frame a face that is brown as a shaved coconut. She gathers her exquisite baby to her and he roots about, blindly, arching for her breast.

She settles him on it and as he draws succour from her, his miniature gums closing around her nipple, she knows she can never part with him: he is hers, of her. She will protect him, look after him with her life, if need be.

As if following her train of thought, the nuns come to life.

'You can't keep him. Not looking like that,' one of the nuns says.

'What's wrong with him?' Is there something she's missed? She counts his fingers, his toes. They're all accounted for. Puzzled, she looks at the nuns' faces and it dawns on her: she has not told them, not the nuns at the school nor the nuns here, that her child is half-Indian. She has kept the secret of his parentage close, held it in her heart, something only hers.

'I'll not give him up.' She is fiercely assured.

'Be free,' her parents had urged. 'Live your life your way.'

'How will you bring him up? You don't have money. You're estranged from your family, a divorcee. And with a child, especially a child such as this, you'll be hard-pressed to find a husband,' one of the nuns says.

'We'll find a good family where he'll fit in well,' another urges. 'An Indian family as he's so dark. No white couple will accept him. Indians like light-skinned children and he's suitably light-skinned for an Indian to be highly prized.'

'I want to keep him,' she repeats, holding her child, *her* child, close.

'It is selfish to...'

That word.

It is *not* selfish. It is the right thing, the *only* thing to do. This child is hers, the one person in the world completely of her. She cannot part with him.

One of the nuns reaches for him, and Mary surprises herself by the ferocity with which she says, 'No.'

Her baby's eyes flutter but he continues to calmly suck from her breast.

Mary knows that the other mothers here do not hold their children – this is kindness, not cruelty. It is so they do not bond, so it is easier to stick to the plan of giving the children away, the nuns have said.

But Mary's son is holding on to her for dear life, or perhaps she is holding on to him.

Chapter 65

Sita

Opportunity

1937

As Sita approaches her ninth month of pregnancy, her husband says, 'You're doing too much. You need to slow down, cut back. Stop the charity work, at least.'

'What I will do is go to the Lake Palace, use that as my base these last few weeks – being there relaxes me.'

She has been meaning to suggest this to her husband for a while, as this way she'll be close to Mary. And now, he's afforded her the perfect opportunity to do so.

'That's good.' Then, his face creasing with worry, 'I'll visit when I can, every week if possible, but I can't stay there with you. What if you go into labour early?'

'The midwife is coming with me.'

'But—'

'As soon as labour starts, I'll send for you.'

'What if there are complications? I don't – God forbid I…'

'Please don't worry. I'll have the midwife with me at all times and I'll make sure a boat is on standby at the palace and a car waiting at the shore, always,' she says, leaning over to kiss him.

In the ninth month of her fake pregnancy, as Sita is sitting down to breakfast, the maidservant she is bribing at the Lake House seeks an audience.

The maidservant is breathless, looks worried. She is trustworthy – she knows that if word gets out about the queen's interest in the women of the refuge, Sita will stop all payment and make sure she never finds another job.

Sita asks all of the servants attending to her to leave.

When they are alone, she turns to the panting, anxious woman. 'What is it?'

'Mary Memsahib went into labour during the night.'

'And you're telling me now?' Sita's voice sharp with nerves.

'I-I'm sorry, Maharaniji. I didn't want to disturb you in the middle of the night.'

'I said, *any time*, day *or night*. Which part of this didn't you understand?' Despite Sita trying hard to keep her voice under control, it rises in ire, even as her mind works frantically, concocting a plan.

She'll need to sequester herself for a couple of days, get the midwife to say it happened too quickly to send word to Jaideep, that Sita lost a lot of blood and needs complete, undisturbed bed rest, and arrange for the baby – if it is healthy and suitably dark-skinned – to be brought here.

If the child is not suitable, she'll have to take her chances from among the other pregnant women in the refuge who are due to give birth around now, or the newborns at the orphanages she has deemed acceptable.

'She gave birth early this morning. A healthy little boy. Dark-skinned. Caused quite a furore.'

Thank you, gods.

'The nuns were understandably shocked. But the mother...'

I *am going to be the mother.*

'She's adamant she'll keep him.'

An image of Mary as a child, eyes shut tight as she climbed tentatively up the rope bridge, one hand in Amin's, the other gripping the rope so hard that her knuckles were in danger of piercing fragile white skin. Sita commanding, 'Mary, how will you cheer your boat on if your eyes are closed?' And the wonder in Mary's eyes when she opened them! The joy, the sense of accomplishment, her delighted laughter. So infectious that it had started Sita and Amin off.

She shakes her head to wipe the image away, the sudden qualm that assails her: *Can I do this?*

I have *to do this. It's for the best. She'll understand in due course.*

'You should really have come to me when she went into labour,' Sita says to the woman standing penitent in front of her.

'Sorry, Maharaniji, I didn't want to disturb you.'

'You would have been following my orders, what I *asked* you to do. I wouldn't have asked if I had not meant it.' Her voice cutting.

She sees the woman wince.

Good.

'I'll not be needing your services any more.'

'I'm sorry, Maha—'

'And if you repeat one word of this to anyone, at any time...'

'I won't, Maharaniji. I swear on my life.'

'Not even to your loved ones. You'll take this to your grave.' She inserts a threat into her voice.

'I promise.'

'Leave. This is over. Don't speak of it again.'

Chapter 66

Mary

Something Odd

1937

Mary is summoned to the Lake Palace via a gold-embossed, ostentatious invitation delivered by an obsequious maid. 'You are granted an audience with the queen. She knows of your situation and would like to help. The boat will arrive at 4 p.m. Please come alone.'

Mary looks at it for a long time. Why hasn't Sita written a personal note? Perhaps she is too grand for that – after all, she *is* queen. And yet, the woman Mary met here, who for the most part laughed and joked with her – apart from a few awkward moments, to be expected since this was their first meeting after many years – that woman had seemed approachable. Haughty and regal, yes, but also down-to-earth, human. Mary had been left with the impression that Sita had seamlessly made the transition from ordinary young girl to queen with not much change to her character.

She knows the rumours of course, has heard from Bilal and the maids, and even a couple of the less discreet nuns, that Sita is formidable, ruthless.

'She rarely even smiles, they say. Her servants are terrified of her,' Bilal has said as they water the plants together.

Mary takes his, and the others', pronouncements with a pinch of salt.

Sita had been formidable as a child too, but she was also kind – when Mary had fallen and split open her knee, it was Sita who had soothed her and commandeered Amin's help to carry her home – and vulnerable, hiding it behind a sharp, bossy exterior. Mary saw evidence of it once when she and Amin had had enough of Sita's high-handedness and, in a rare show of solidarity and bravery, united against her: 'We don't want to play with you any more.'

Sita's eyes had filled with tears then become wide and raw with shocked hurt, and that look had pierced Mary's heart even though Sita had immediately regained her composure, folded her arms across her chest and huffed, 'That's fine. I don't want to play with sissies anyway. I'm going home,' and stormed off.

Mary had run after Sita, who had made them grovel and plead (Amin, fed up with Mary but, as always, giving in and joining her in asking Sita to stay). And just as Mary and Amin were getting annoyed again, Sita had smiled and thrown her arms round Mary, her hot sweet breath in Mary's ear: 'I'm sorry, I didn't mean what I said. You're my very best friend, and not a sissy at all.'

The woman Mary met in the library, while looking grand, her pregnant stomach protruding out of her sari, bejewelled and decked to the nines, was also the girl she remembered, albeit more brittle; although when she had laughed, even that brittleness had disappeared. There was a wariness about Sita's eyes now, a distance. But otherwise she had been the Sita Mary remembered.

Her best friend.

This was why she had opened up to Sita, told her everything, only holding back about Vinay. Knowing that, queen or not, if there was one person who would not judge, one person who had always championed the rights of women to do as they wished, it was Sita.

And her instincts were right.

Sita's expression had not changed when Mary briefly mentioned her liaison on the ship, and she hadn't blinked when Mary confessed her remorse, the guilt that stabbed at her for her treatment of Charles. Sita had only nodded when Mary said she was keeping her baby, thoughtfully caressing her own belly, full with child.

Perhaps this is why Sita is summoning Mary now. Sita is at the Lake Palace, waiting out her last few weeks of pregnancy, she knows. Although Sita did not contact her again and Mary had not got in touch either, not wishing to seem as if she wanted something from the queen, Sita must have been keeping tabs on her. Having found out that Mary gave birth early this morning, she has wanted to get in touch.

And yet, why via this impersonal note? What message is she trying to convey?

Once again, Mary feels that unease that stabs where Sita is concerned.

But… She looks at the sentence again: *The queen knows of your situation and would like to help.*

Mary is desperate. She is keeping her child (she's named him Richard, after her father), but she knows the road ahead won't be easy. And when Sita is offering help, it would be remiss of her not to go. For her child's sake she cannot decline this invitation from the queen, no matter the tingle of disquiet she feels, not least because Sita has specifically requested that she come alone. Mary doesn't want to part with her son. But… she *will* go, leaving her baby in the nuns' care, although it's a wrench to be away from him.

Mary wears her best dress, the one meant for her coming out that she had instead got married in, unpicking the seams so it fits around her pregnancy-swollen body. It is strangely fitting, she thinks, as she gets off the boat, that she is wearing the dress fashioned for her presentation to the king of England for her audience with a queen in a palace in the middle of a lake in India.

Impeccable lawns and perfectly maintained beds singing with exotic flowers, which make the garden of the women's refuge look like a haphazard mini-jungle in comparison, lead to the palace ensconced within a marble-columned veranda. A pool shimmers in the sunshine, replete with fountains and sculptures. Peacocks strut on the lawns.

The inside of the palace is even more breathtaking, rendering Mary speechless. Art on the walls and on the domed ceilings, paintings and tapestries, mirrored screens. Antique furniture. Stuffed animals. Ornate chess sets. Mosaic tiles. Innumerable rooms, all offering glimpses of more treasures. Myriad servants, cleaning, dusting, sweeping, polishing.

The queen's chamber – luxury on a different scale, all the rooms Mary has seen on her way here paling in comparison.

Sita is lounging on a divan. She has covered her heavily pregnant body with an intricately patterned shawl, so Mary cannot make out her protruding stomach.

There's something odd about the setting. At first Mary doesn't understand. And then she does.

No servants in here, despite the hordes she saw milling in the other rooms. She's alone with Sita, just the two of them.

Sita's amber eyes on her.

Mary is once again gripped by a strange unrest.

Sita's gaze speculative, relaxing into a smile when Mary curtseys.

'You don't have to do that, Mary.' Her face softens and Mary relaxes, shrugging away her disquiet. This is her childhood friend.

'Congratulations on the birth of your son. I hear he's a beautiful child.'

Mary beams, even as her arms ache to hold him. 'He is that. I was surprised by your invitation – didn't think you'd hear so quickly.'

'I have my ways.' Sita's smile is calculating and once again, Mary experiences a tug of agitation.

'Thank you for inviting me here.'

Sita waves her words away, saying languidly, 'Since I spoke with you, I've been thinking.'

Here it comes, her friend's offer of help. So why is Mary so apprehensive? Why does she feel the urge to run away, back to her boy? 'Yes?'

'I've found the perfect solution to your dilemma.'

'I… I'm not in any dilemma.' When she held her baby, all her worries had disappeared and she had known, without a doubt, that the best course of action, the *only one* course of action, was to bring up her child to the best of her ability. Nobody would part them.

'You are.' Sita's voice suddenly sharp, even as she relaxes lazily on her divan.

This, Mary recalls, feeling irritation chafe, pushing away the apprehension, is typical of Sita. To tell you what you're thinking, what you must feel. To feed her ideas as your truth.

'Your baby looks Indian. You're divorced, currently jobless, with no money to your name but plenty of disgrace. How will you bring your child up?'

'That's my concern,' Mary says, shortly, thinking, *This was a waste of time. She has brought me here to lecture me. To highlight the differences between us, the way our lives have diverged. What a fool I was to come…*

Mary had naively hoped Sita would offer her a job. But evidently, this is not to be.

She's about say her goodbyes, get back to her child, when Sita speaks. 'I'd like to adopt your son.'

All thought, everything she has experienced since coming here to the palace – to this country – leaves Mary's mind. 'I-I'm sorry?'

'You heard me. I'd like to adopt your son. He'll be brought up as my child, mine and the king's. The heir to the throne. In time, he'll inherit all this. But for this, you need to relinquish all claim on him, return to England.'

Stunned, Mary can only stare at Sita, thinking of the way her son feels in her arms, his perfect unformed features. The emotion he has aroused in her.

'But you're pregnant yourself…'

In response Sita removes the shawl covering her body.

Mary blinks, unable at first to comprehend what she's seeing. She knows that Sita is pregnant – heavily so. But she cannot see any signs of it. Her stomach flat. Beside her, a pillow, folded up. Mary's gaze snags on it.

'You… you're not pregnant?'

Now it makes sense, the absence of servants.

'No.'

'But… Why?'

'That's none of your concern. And what you know, what I have revealed to you, stays in this chamber. If word gets out…'

This is the queen Bilal was talking about. The queen everyone is afraid of.

'Mary?' That hard tawny gaze.

The unease in her stomach solidifying into an ache, so she feels faint. She swallows. 'I-I can keep a secret.'

Sita smiles, a brief lifting of the lips. 'I know you can. You've kept my childhood secrets and now I'm sharing my biggest secret with you.'

'How? Why?'

'I do not like to be interrupted when I'm speaking.' Sita is regal. Cool. A curve to her lips as if she finds Mary slightly amusing.

That haughty indifference... Mary is repelled by it. It is her childhood friend and yet not. This woman, brittle and mirthless, the laughter of the other day not in evidence, her gaze hard and narrowed, is quite mad.

Why, Sita? Why, when you are queen, would you fake a pregnancy?

And, realisation dawning. *Ah, perhaps* because *you are queen. You've always been single-minded in your determination to get what you want.*

A memory, long forgotten. A book, *The Wind in the Willows*, that Mary received for her birthday and which both she and Sita had loved.

'Can I take it home and bring it back next week?' Sita had asked.

'I haven't finished reading it. You can borrow one of my other books. I'll finish it and give it to you next week.'

Sita's face had fallen, but she had agreed.

That evening, Mary asked Papa to read to her from *The Wind in the Willows*, but they couldn't find the book. They had looked everywhere, but it never turned up, and Papa had given her another copy.

The next week, when Sita visited, Mary asked, 'Did you take *The Wind in the Willows* home with you?'

'Are you calling me a thief?' Sita screamed.

'No! I wanted to know if you took it by mistake.'

'I did not.'

'What is this book about?' Amin asked.

As Mary recounted the story to him, Sita had pitched in.

'How do you know the story? I thought you hadn't finished it yet,' Mary asked.

'I did finish it, last week,' Sita had insisted, colouring.

'So why did you want the book to take home then?'

'I liked the story so much, I wanted to read it again.'

Mary did not offer Sita her new copy of *The Wind in the Willows* and she did not ask for it. In time, Mary had forgotten about it.

Until now.

Now she stares at Sita, who wants something else of hers, far more precious. This woman she thought she recognised but doesn't at all.

Or perhaps she does – which is why she was uneasy every time she looked at her. Perhaps this was why she didn't write to Sita after she saw her during that procession, something holding her back every time she thought of contacting her childhood friend.

'Mary,' Sita is saying. 'I'm offering your son the chance to be king.'

Mary pictures her son at the refuge. She wants to run back there, hold him, not let go. The dusky skin. The plum lips. The wispy black curls.

You stole my book. You stole my parents' admiration. You stole my parents – *they died in an accident on their way to speak to your parents on your behalf. You will* not *have my son.*

'No,' she says. She doesn't know why her voice is a whisper, why she feels tears threaten. She does know that it is not good to make an enemy of the queen. She has heard enough stories bandied about in the refuge. She has seen it in the panic of the usually unruffled nuns when the queen's visit was imminent, how they rushed about making sure everything was just so, how they courted her approval.

'The queen is generous to those who please her and ruthless to those who don't. This refuge seems to be in favour at the moment and the nuns want to keep it that way,' Bilal had said.

She sees Sita's face harden almost imperceptibly, the flinty, snake-like eyes flash sparks. Yet her lips remain as they are, tilted upwards just slightly, as if she finds Mary's reluctance to part with her child funny. Laughable.

'You've loved working at the girls' school, I know. Well, I'll give you ample money – enough to start your own school, if that takes your fancy.'

'How can I teach other children when I'm abandoning my own baby? I will not be bribed into giving him up.'

'You'll not be *abandoning* your child, you'll be bequeathing him a life of luxury, a life where he's destined to be king,' Sita snaps.

For a brief moment, Mary considers it. But then she thinks of the warm weight of her son in her arms.

'Let's say you don't take up my offer. How will you look after him? You have no money. You are a single mother, an English divorcee with an Indian child.'

'I'll find a way.'

Sita smiles benignly, although her words are anything but. 'I'll make sure that you don't. My reach is wider than you might think.'

'Why *my* child?' Mary swallows the tremor in her voice, the panic that has taken her over.

'Because he's a boy. Because you're intelligent and well educated and so is his father. Because he's dark-skinned enough that I can pass him off as mine.'

'I don't want to give him away.' Her eyes prick with tears. Fiercely, she pushes them away.

'You're a mother now. You have to think of your child and not of yourself. I can see why you might want this child – you don't have anyone else to call yours. I ask again, what life can you give him?'

Mary pushes her shoulders back, defiant. 'I will think of something.'

'Your son will be king. He will have all this.' Sita waves her hand around to indicate the palace.

He'll have you for a mother. A possibly unhinged liar who fakes a pregnancy. She does not say this out loud – she is defiant but not suicidal, she does not want to see the queen's rumoured bad side.

'He'll want for nothing.'

'But he'll not have his mother.' Mary shifts impatiently from foot to foot, not wanting to engage in this pointless discourse with her childhood friend who has morphed into this crazy woman she is afraid of, not sure what she might do if she is angered – which is why Mary cannot leave until she is dismissed, although all she wants is to be back at the refuge with her son.

'He'll have two parents. He'll have the adoration of thousands. The acclaim, respect and devotion of a kingdom. With you, he'll have an uncertain life. You don't have money. How will you work with a child to look after? If you decide to go back to England, how will you do it with no money? And will you be welcome there with a child of questionable parentage? He will be maligned and so will you. Don't be selfish, Mary. Be the bigger person. Think of your child.'

She has heard enough. 'I may not be queen, I may only be a woman who has fallen on hard times, but I'm still his mother.'

Sita laughs, a short, joyless bark. 'Love is blinding you to doing what is right. I understand that.'

Mary wants to wipe the smile off the queen's face – she cannot now think of her as Sita, it is too personal for this monstrous woman. She wants to slap the patronising liar, crush her smug smile. She bunches her palms into fists.

'And that is why I'm going to help. Intervene. This is a new mother speaking, I know. Your hormones, the emotions released by motherhood, have hijacked sense. You're being incredibly selfish, wanting to keep the boy when even a fool can see that he'll have a better life with me. Hence I'm going to do you a favour. You're lucky I've singled you out.'

Anger is replaced by incomprehension. What is she saying? Has she gone quite mad?

'Look—' Mary begins, but is unceremoniously cut off.

'I only summoned you here to tell you of my plans for your son – well, he's not yours any longer. You may go now. I do not want to see you again.'

The anger, the incomprehension, is displaced by dread as the queen's words sink in. Mary's legs give way, unable to hold her up, and she sinks to the floor, so she is at the queen's feet. The queen, sprawled on the divan, nonchalant, that smirk still playing on her lips.

'What… what're you saying?' Her voice a gasp.

'I have recompensed you very generously, you will find. Take the money and go back to England. There's talk of war in Europe. Perhaps you can do some good there.'

Her son, whom she had left with the nuns… What is this woman—? No, no, no, no…

She's not aware of screaming, but she must do, for…

'Stop that racket at once! I thought you'd be more dignified, not resort to making a scene like a fisherwoman.'

The queen tucks the pillow under her clothes, drapes the shawl over her body and rings a bell. Immediately, servants appear.

'She's gone crazy because I refused the help she wanted. Take her away,' she says, lazily, pointing at Mary.

Mary wants to claw at the queen's face, hit her, pull her apart, until she is reunited with her son. *Please, no.*

Her body crawling with terror. Instead of shouting at the queen, she begs.

'Please don't take my child. He's all I have. Please.'

She is still begging as she is led away, gently but firmly, by the servants. This time she does not see the palace's splendour, her eyes blurred by tears, her body jellied by horror. She is ferried across the lake and taken to the refuge, where she finds a lump sum of money under the pillow but no son.

No child.

Part 6

One Decision

Chapter 67

Mary

Drowning

1937

All it takes is one decision, one moment of madness, of curiosity winning over sense, for your life to change for ever.

One decision: Mary becoming friends with Sita, guilelessly inviting her into her life.

One decision: Mary's parents deciding to visit Sita's parents, and having that accident.

One decision: Mary deciding to return to India, giving up her coming out, her season.

One decision: Mary choosing to sleep with Vinay that magic- and yearning-sprinkled evening.

One decision: Mary going to see Sita, believing she would help.

And now, her arms empty. Aching for her child.

The nuns try to comfort her and she turns on them. 'I thought my child was safe here.'

'We're sorry.' They're almost as distraught as she is. 'That maidservant *is* trustworthy, or she was, up until she ran away with your son. She's been with us for ever. She's a trained midwife.'

'Sita— the queen has my child,' she cries. 'She has Richard.'

Richard, her son, named for her father. This pain, the ache of missing him, losing him, is worse, if possible, than the grief she experienced when she lost her parents.

The nuns look at her as if she is mad. They console her as if she is a child.

'Shhh… It's the grief speaking.'

She flings their soothing arms away, the anger and frustration she feels, the upset, transforming itself into rage at these women who stand about doing nothing. 'Don't you understand? The queen has him.'

'Why would the queen take your child? She is pregnant herself. There are people looking for the maidservant who took your child. Hush now.'

'Hush? How can I, why would I hush when you don't see—' Her voice breaks as sobs tumble out of her. Her dress – her coming-out dress that she wore for her audience with her childhood friend, queen, traitor, thief – is wet with milk.

'There now.'

She throws off their arms. But they are holding her, restraining her, and then a prick on her arm and she is floating, drowning…

'It's because she saw the queen just now that she's got this insane notion in her head that Her Majesty has her child. Shame! The queen wanted to help her. She took a fancy to her. She'd have placed the child. But now…'

The nuns' whispers are the last thing she hears before she's lost to the world, drowning in grief, wading through a sea of loss, towards her child. Her baby, her Richard, who drifts further away from her the more she tries to reach him. It's like when she was on the ship, heading west as an orphaned child, and then again as a young woman heading east, and the shore, holding all that was beloved to her, was floating further and further away, as she was ferried to a new life.

Chapter 68

Sita

Auspicious

1937

Sita is back at the main palace now, having left as soon as the palace priest declared it auspicious for her and the baby to return, wanting to be as far away from Mary as possible. The palace is ablaze with celebration, alive with festivities. Song and dance, performers and soothsayers. Fireworks and feasts.

A three-day holiday is declared, in celebration of the birth of the longed-for son and heir to the throne.

Dignitaries come from all over, bestowing gifts upon the newborn and heaping congratulations upon his proud parents. The subjects of the kingdom flock into the palace grounds. There's a petting zoo for children to get up close to cheetahs and tigers, lions and dancing bears. Elephants fill their trunks with water and splash the squealing youngsters. There are boat rides across the lake at the bottom of the grounds. There are fire-eaters and jugglers, sorcerers and snake charmers, contortionists and dwarves and all manner of food vendors.

Sita summons her trusted aide. 'While I was leaving the Lake Palace, an English memsahib followed our car, screaming obscenities, claiming my son was her own.'

'Oh!'

'It's sad really. I heard that she recently lost her child and that has driven her mad with grief. She's convinced the prince is her son. She's most likely harmless. Nevertheless, I don't want to take any chances. Make sure she does not enter the palace grounds.'

The aide requests an audience with Sita a couple of days later.

'The woman you warned us about is here, insisting you stole her son and begging to be allowed in.'

Sita looks at her son being fed by the wet nurse. 'The poor woman. Much as I feel for her – I cannot imagine a fate worse than losing your child – I'd rather not allow her inside.'

'Of course, Maharaniji.'

'Whatever she says, she's not to be allowed in.' Her voice sharp.

The aide nods gravely and leaves to relay Sita's orders to the gatekeepers.

Chapter 69

Mary

Permission

1937

'I want to see the queen.'

'You need permission, memsahib. A royal invitation.' The guards at the gates hold Mary back.

'She has my child.'

They stare at her as if she is crazy. Just as the nuns at the refuge have been doing. Why will no one believe her? Why will nobody see the truth?

'We have people searching for your child. We'll find him,' the nuns assured her, whenever she came out of the sea of sedatives enough to be able to scream for her child.

'I know where he is,' she had yelled. 'He's with the queen,' she had cried.

'Now, Mary…'

She fought them as best she could, but they were stronger. The sedatives at least left her numb, but they made her dream. In those dreams she was with her child and it was perfect. Then he was wrenched from her and it was devastation. This was when she woke gasping and the nuns tried soothing her and, when she would not be soothed, gave her more of the deadening sedatives.

Until the previous day when, just as she was gasping awake on a wave of sorrow, yearning and loss and anger bitter in her throat, she had heard the maids who were assigned to watch her whispering, 'The queen has left for the palace in town. The royals are having a grand naming ceremony for their son.'

My son. Mine. And he has *a name: Richard.*

That was when the anger, the hatred channelled itself into resolve. Instead of screaming out her pain, her outrage, she had lain quiet. She had shut her eyes and pretended she was still asleep, and made plans. Then just before dawn, when the maids guarding her room were asleep, she had packed her clothes and the money that had been left under her pillow in lieu of her child and left the refuge.

The lake shimmered in the darkness, the Lake Palace lit up and reflected in the whispering water, a giant floating monstrosity, mocking her.

The garden she had tended and loved, the plants she had nurtured waved softly goodbye.

She brushed away her tears, fiercely. No time for grief now.

So many mistakes. So many wrong choices. But no more.

Now, she would act.

She had walked to the palace. It took her the whole day. But she did it – she had to. Her baby was there. No more sedatives. No more wallowing. Mary was going to get her child back. Sita was not going to get away with what she had done.

On her way she watched the villagers, some living in mud huts, others in cloth tents cobbled together by slinging holey saris across posts made from tree branches. Their sunken eyes and stomachs. Scrawny children sitting in the dust, watching her, huge eyes curious.

She was desperate but she wasn't destitute. She was suffering, but there were many different kinds of suffering and hers was not the worst. Although it felt like it.

As she neared the outskirts of town, she saw signs of celebration, the town decked out as it had been for the procession when she first set eyes on the queen, only grander. Bunting and balloons. Celebratory banners flying. A parade of grand carriages and grander cars churning up dust as they climbed the hill to the palace. Dignitaries gathering to celebrate the naming ceremony of a child who was already named. The child Sita had stolen from *her*.

And now, she is at the gates to the palace, a few paces separating her from her son. The palace grounds transformed into a fairground. Music and pomp; people milling, drinking, eating, laughing. Monkeys chattering with carefree abandon even as they look for unattended food they can steal. Luminaries welcomed into the palace while the common people camp on the grounds.

'I thought everyone was invited to the celebration,' Mary says to the gatekeepers.

'They are, memsahib. But you need an invitation from the king. Every house in town got one. Where's yours?'

The gatekeepers are not unkind, just brusque. Doing their jobs.

'Do you have children?' she asks.

The gatekeepers look startled. It is the older man who answers: 'Yes. Two.'

She looks right at him. 'Then as a father you understand. Please. The queen has my child. I want to see him, just once.'

She can see pity in the man's eyes, keeping pace with distaste. They think she is crazy.

'Memsahib, why would the queen have your child?'

'Because she cannot have any of her own!'

'Beware, memsahib, you're committing treason, making these accusations.'

The younger man is opening the gates to allow a decorated carriage in. Mary tries to slink inside in its wake, but the guards are too quick for her, blocking her just in time. She catches a glimpse of a heavily made-up face, arms and neck hidden by jewellery.

'Please,' she begs, but they are gone.

She waits in the sweltering heat, her milk leaking, dress stained, body coated with the dust and angst of her journey here, feet sore and bruised, alert to every opportunity to sneak inside. But the guards have their eye on her and so she camps outside, setting her bag down and sitting on it, watching people arrive and leave, the taste of desperation and dust and ache in her mouth as she inhales the smells and sounds of celebration: perfume and excitement, smoked meat and candyfloss, syrup, spices, music drifting from the palace.

She sits there until dark, when the guards change and the new guards watch her just as warily and beady-eyed as the others.

'Please,' she begs. 'Let me in.'

They ignore her.

She wakes in the night to find she is lying on the pebble-littered earth. The palace resplendent, bathed in a golden glow. Somewhere inside is her son, being attended to and looked after by someone else, while her milk for him soaks into the hard, unforgiving ground.

Chapter 70

Sita

To Forget

1937

'I want my son,' Mary screams, Sita is told.

Mary stands outside the palace gates from morning till night, the blouse of her dress soiled by milk, her skirt torn, hair dishevelled, tears running down her dirty face.

The English dignitaries invited to the palace turn their gazes away, their faces impassive, from one of their own making a spectacle of herself, pretending Mary isn't there, Sita is told.

Townspeople coming to the palace to partake of the festivities gather around Mary, awed that a memsahib could be reduced to this.

'I thought sahibs and memsahibs didn't make scenes,' they whisper, Sita is told. 'They don't even cry at funerals, standing ramrod straight, not a tremble to their lips!'

'But this woman is different. Her grief, I can understand. Her madness, I can sympathise with. When my babu had that fever that would not go down for two whole days, I nearly went crazy,' they say.

The townspeople gawp at Mary, Sita is told, until the sounds from the palace grounds, the squeals of happy children, the shouts of the hawkers and the smells of fried food and sweetmeats are too much to resist and they slip inside the gates.

Mary follows.

'Please,' she begs, clutching at their hands, Sita is told. 'Take me with you. I just want to see my child.'

The gatekeepers intervene, one of them allowing the embarrassed and pitying family group in, another standing between Mary and the gates.

Sita has asked her maid to relay everything Mary is doing, needing to be appraised of her every move in order to determine how much of a threat she is.

Once she has determined that no one is taking Mary seriously, not her fellow Englishmen (Sita has made sure they know about Mary's past – the right whispers in the right ears – ensuring they want nothing to do with a disgraced, divorced woman whose grief has turned her head), nor the townspeople, nor the Indian dignitaries invited, she resolves to lock Mary away in that secret part of her mind where she also locks her guilt at the deception she's carrying out, the pang she feels when her husband coos tenderly at the boy he thinks of as his son.

Jaideep has taken to fatherhood effortlessly, cuddling his son and talking to him, much to the delight of the child's many ayahs.

'He's perfect. The image of you,' Jaideep says, holding the baby out to her.

But Sita turns away, unable to look at the child, unwilling to find Mary in his features. That look on Mary's face – incredulity solidifying into horror, desperation and rage, anguish and pleading, as what Sita was saying sank in – hounding her.

A question forms in Jaideep's eyes as one of the ayahs takes the child from him, expertly rocking him, humming lullabies.

'I'm tired,' Sita says shortly, turning away from the confusion and disappointment gracing her husband's face.

'I'll let you rest,' he says and she nods, while inside she is screaming, railing at the gods who did not give her the one thing she wanted, a child, so that she had to resort to this.

Why can't I hold him? Why can't I love him?
The love will come when I forget that he is Mary's. I need to forget.
He's better off with me. I *am his mother now.*

Chapter 71

Mary

Lone Hibiscus

1937

In the morning, the guards change again.

Scents of breakfast: cardamom and ginger, stewed milk, raisins and cashew nuts roasting in ghee, waft on the cool jasmine and marigold breeze. Mary tries, in vain, to trail the milk cart into the palace – the guards, once again, too quick for her.

She sits on her bag and watches the palace come to life.

The guards bring her tea and a chapathi.

'Eat this and leave, memsahib.'

'I have to see my son,' she begs.

'Please, memsahib, don't you have family you can go to?'

Family. Tears threaten but she pushes them away, choking on a piece of chapathi, brine-soaked dough. 'My family is my son and he's inside,' she pleads when she can talk.

Their pity is hard to bear. But she will take it. She will take anything as long as she is reunited with her son again.

She sits there in the sweltering heat of mid-morning and as she waits, she casts her eyes around her.

Among the mud and rocks of the untended land just outside the palace gates is a hibiscus plant, wilting in the sun. Perhaps this lone hibiscus is the product of a stray seed that fluttered over the palace walls and despite no care being bestowed on it, despite the hard conditions, thrived. As she waits, in those long hours of inactivity when nobody enters or leaves the gates and the palace slumbers in the sunshine, she tends to the plant, begging water from the guards. She smothers it with water and love, the love she aches to give her child. She is rewarded by its drooping leaves glowing and singing in the sunshine.

As the hours pass, as she looks at the gates of the palace, shut to her, it dawns on her that getting her son back might take longer than she thought.

But she will not give up. She will keep trying, although *nobody* believes her – they all take the queen's word over hers. How to convince them?

How to get through to Sita?

She may not get her son back this way, by camping beside the palace gates, but at least there is a chance she might see him. At least she is near him.

She cannot bear to leave here. How can she, when all she cares for, all she loves, all that is hers in the world – her son – is inside the palace. So close. And yet, inaccessible.

Chapter 72

Sita

Good Genes

1937

'My grandson's naming ceremony is set to be even grander than your wedding and that was spectacular, the biggest celebration to grace this kingdom,' Sita's mother declares, eyes glowing.

Sita notes her mother's barely restrained joy and pride and wishes the woman had held *her* as effortlessly and naturally as she holds the child she thinks of as her grandson. She wishes she could hold her son, love him, as naturally as her mother does, as her husband can.

'You don't do things by halves.' Her mother plants a soft kiss on her grandson's forehead. 'The child you've produced at long last is so fair and easy on the eye. As if he has been blessed by the gods.'

He is blessed by the gods, Christian and Hindu – who made our paths cross, mine and Mary's, as children, and again recently, when I desperately needed a child.

This is what Mary does not understand: that it is her son's destiny to be king.

Stop thinking about Mary. You'll learn to love your son – your son – only when you forget her.

But Mary is not proving easy to forget or ignore. She has set up camp outside the palace gates, not leaving, even at night.

Why doesn't she take my advice and go to England? Why can't she see sense and accept her fate? She's been recompensed well enough and her son will be king.

*

'It appears there's a woman outside the palace gates who claims you've stolen her son,' the queen mother states when she comes to see her grandson.

'Since when have you started paying heed to all the mad people who grace the kingdom?' Sita asks coolly.

'I just wondered why she might be saying that. Apparently she hasn't shown any signs of madness before this.'

'Having just given birth, I can assure you that the pain can drive anyone mad.'

'I know. I gave birth to two sons – twins at that – myself.' The queen mother's voice sharp.

The queen mother peers at her grandson, who lies swaddled in his diamond-encrusted cradle, a present from his adoring father. She makes no move to touch the boy, unlike Sita's mother, who had held out her arms for him the moment she arrived and who was loath to let him go when she left. In this way, the queen mother is like Sita, who also cannot bear to handle, or even look at, her son.

'He's dreadfully pale, isn't he? Almost white-skinned.'

'He has good genes,' Sita says.

The queen mother looks up at Sita, her gaze probing. 'You look remarkably well for a woman who had a traumatic birth and had to be sequestered away for a couple of days.'

'What can I say? I recover well from setbacks.'

'That you do.'

Priests from all over the kingdom congregate to bless the heir to the kingdom. Generals and wise men, sultans and nizams, princes and kings from every corner of India come bearing gifts and imparting blessings. They are put up at the palace, their every wish pandered to. The Viceroy of India sends a message of congratulation.

Sita and Jaideep decide to call their son Arjun.

'Arjun meaning white, clear. Like his complexion. So pure.' Her husband's voice bubbling with pride.

'No, I wanted to name him Arjun after the hero warrior in the *Mahabharata*,' Sita says. 'I was reading stories from that epic when I saw a car coming up the drive of my father's house, bearing royal insignia and carrying a proposal that changed my life for ever.'

Chapter 73

Mary

Vigil

1937

On the fifth day of her vigil outside the palace gates, Mary wakes from where she is hunched beside her bag to see a bud on the hibiscus plant.

Is this a sign?

'Here,' the guards say, placing upma and tea in front of her.

'Mary,' says a voice.

She looks up, hope warring with excitement. Could it be…?

But the voice did not come from the palace. It came from the carriage that, she sees now, has pulled up beside her: it is Sister Catherine.

The nun folds Mary in her arms as Mary sobs. 'We just heard. It took a few days for the nuns from the refuge to let us know and another few for us to find out where you were.'

'The queen has my son.'

Sister Catherine does not look at her in disbelief. There is no pity in her eyes. Only compassion. And love.

'Come to the school. Your room is waiting for you.'

'But I-I thought my job…'

Sister Catherine colours.

And Mary understands. They think, like the nuns at the refuge, that her son is gone – stolen by that maid. That he's not coming back.

They don't believe her. Nobody does. She sinks to the ground, hopeless.

'The children…' Sister Catherine is saying.

Mary looks up, hopeful. 'My son?'

Sister Catherine colours some more. 'The girls you teach have missed you. They wait, hopeful, looking at every visitor, wishing for it to be you.'

Waiting like I have been, she thinks. *I have waited here for five days now but I haven't seen my son.*

'I'm not going anywhere without my child.'

'Mary—'

'I cannot abandon my son.'

'You'll not be abandoning anyone. You'll be on the outskirts of town and if you want, you can come here every evening.'

'But my son…'

'Mary, living like this, being labelled a madwoman—'

'Is that what everyone's saying?'

'Yes. That's why it took us so long to find you. We could not equate a "crazy white memsahib" with you.'

'Oh.'

'Living here, like this, is not helping anyone. And sooner or later, the king will take action.'

'That's what I want.'

Sister Catherine's eyes flash. 'To languish in prison?'

'Queen Sita should be in prison for taking my child.'

'Shush,' Sister Catherine says, alarmed. 'You cannot speak like this, here.'

'Do you believe me?'

'I care for you, Mary. We all do.'

She deflected my question.

'Please come back. The children need you.'

My son needs me. I need my son.

The guards feel sorry for her, but they will not let her in. *I have no plan. I am denied entry into the palace. My son is safe for now – well, as safe as he can be with a thief.*

Sita wants me to go away, to England. She thinks I'll meekly accept what she did, like when she appropriated The Wind in the Willows, *my birthday present. That time I couldn't prove anything and I can't this time either. I cannot camp outside these gates for ever… but I'm not going far. I'll stay at the school and haunt her, the fallout from her crime. The other mother of her child.* My *child.*

I love you and I will wait, my son, for as long as it takes.

She looks at the hibiscus bud, the representation of hope. Crimson as a bleeding heart.

And then she leaves with the nun, thanking the guards, looking back at the palace, inside which her infant son lies.

Chapter 74

Sita

Regard

1937

Sita watches her husband with the child he thinks of as his, the ease with which he handles him, the pride on his face, the unconditional love.

My parents were never like this with me. Their love – if it was that – came with conditions, and they only showed that love when I was betrothed to royalty, set to become queen.

Several times over the previous days, Sita has been tempted to return the child she cannot bear to touch or even look at to his grieving mother camped outside the palace gates. But she backs out every time, feeling more bound now than ever.

I've done all of this for power, for regard. I've done it because I want my parents' continued adulation and pride, want evidence of their love for me. Surely if their love was unconditional, like Jaideep's is for the child he thinks of as his, like Mary's, then they would love me anyway, even if I was revealed as a liar, a cheat, a woman who will stop at nothing, even stealing her friend's child, to get what she wants.

It fills her with despair, the thought that she has done this for her parents' fickle approval, among other things. Once upon a time she used to stand up to them to get their attention. Now, she has learned the diplomacy her mother so favours; she has learned to lie with a straight face, to steal another woman's child and pass it off as her own with a glowing smile.

The only truly valuable thing I had, she thinks, as Jaideep gives the child to an ayah – not bothering any more to hand the boy to her – and leaves her chamber without touching her – *was my husband's love and now, in my desire to keep my queendom, in my pursuit of my parents' ephemeral affection, their sanction, I am losing that too.*

She sinks back into bed and closes her eyes. Interminably tired.

'Maharaniji, shall I—' her maid begins.

'Go away,' she snaps with such vehemence that the maid recoils and, across the vast room, the child she has appropriated, who ties her to all of this, starts to wail.

Chapter 75

Mary

Love

1937–1938

The children at the school chant, 'Welcome back.'

They say, 'We missed your stories and the games you play with us.'

The nuns envelop her into their warm midst; they are, as always, kind, gentle and soothing.

While teaching Mary is able to hold her yearning for her son at bay, but she lies awake at night choking with longing, concocting elaborate ways in which she will ambush the palace, steal her son back. Her pillow is sodden in the mornings when, sleepless and groggy, grieving and spent, she cannot bear to face another day without her son. But then she thinks, *He is alive. He is nearby. I need to be strong. I need to keep going, for his sake, so I am ready for him when I get him back.*

Every child she teaches is in some part her son, the love she pours out to them the love she has been storing for her child. The care she gives them the care she cannot give to her own son.

Gradually, the yawning, gaping wound within Mary, if not heals, then at least scabs over with the plaster of love that the nuns and the children apply.

*

Mary writes to solicitors all over India and even to some in England. But none of them will take her on as none of them believe her.

She writes to the British Resident, requesting an audience. He doesn't reply. She writes telling him about what has been done to her. Again no reply. She travels to the city, to the courts, to law offices, to the British Residency, but no one will give her the time of day. When one of them does pay heed, their eyes drop away from hers as soon as she comes to the part where the queen invites her to the palace, asks for her child.

She returns to the school exhausted but determined. She will not give up until she holds her son in her arms again.

'Leave it, child,' the nuns say.

'How can I stop fighting for my son?'

Although they too don't believe her, the nuns pray for her and she prays too. In the chapel. In the garden of the school while she works the soil. Under the mango trees as the children play. In the classroom while the children labour on the work she has set.

On her day off, she travels to the city, keeping vigil outside the British Residency. And after she has waited outside the Residency one day every week for a couple of months, the Resident agrees to see her.

He listens impassively to her story, only a muscle twitching in his jaw giving him away. He does not avert his eyes when she tells him the queen has her son, how she arranged to have him stolen from the refuge.

When she has finished, he looks coolly at her. 'You're saying you were with the queen while your son was taken from the refuge across the lake.'

'Yes, but she called me there to say—'

'So the queen did not actually, physically, take your child. She invited you to the palace and while you were there, someone took your child.'

'It *was* her. She arranged for that maid—'

'You cannot prove any of these preposterous accusations you're levelling at the queen. We have a mutually beneficial relationship with the royals, and we mean to keep it that way. Even if, and it is a *big* if, what you're saying is true, isn't your son better off with the queen than with you, a divorced, disgraced woman?' He sighs. 'Go back to the life you have, Miss Brigham. Try to put this behind you.'

As if it were that easy. 'You don't—' she begins.

'I've heard enough, Miss Brigham. Don't come back.'

She blinks back tears, walks out of the room, her head held high, two words from his speech echoing in her head: *your son.*

My son. Mine.

And therein lies the crux: nobody believes her and even if they were inclined to, they agree that her son is better off with Sita. How can they decide what's best for *her* child? What gives them the right? What gives Sita the right to take her son because she assumed he would have a better life with her?

Every evening, after the children have gone home and the nuns are at prayer, Mary walks the mile into town and another mile up the hill to the palace.

The first evening she is greeted by a red hibiscus, smiling at her from the spot where she has kept vigil the past few days.

The guards greet her like old friends, sharing their spiced tea with her.

'Did you see my son?' she asks and their gazes falter as they blush on her behalf.

You don't look mad any more – you're clean and well dressed, not careworn and dirty – and yet you haven't rid yourself of your delusion, they're thinking, she can see. She doesn't care. What does it matter what anyone thinks when the person most precious to her is inside the palace?

'Did he come out? Did the queen bring him?'

'No, memsahib.' They sip their tea quietly, not meeting her gaze.

'Oh,' she says. 'And how are your children, Suresh? And yours, Raju?'

She has a chat with the guards, she tends to her smiling hibiscus, thriving despite the harsh conditions. All it needed was love.

Over the next few months Mary continues to go to the palace every evening. She is denied entry inside the gates, and doesn't see her son, but she tends to the hibiscus and plants flowers procured from the school, creating a garden in the area where she had kept vigil, mourned and longed for her son.

Sometimes, as she works the garden outside the palace gates, she thinks of Charles.

I trapped Charles, married him so I could give my child legitimacy. I used him.

Sita has done the same with me. She hasn't given a thought to my feelings, instead doing what she thought was best for her, and for my child.

I deserve everything I have received, she thinks as she pulls out weeds from the hard, packed earth. *It is karma.*

On her son's first birthday, Mary plants climbing roses and bougainvillea in her garden in front of the palace gates. Hopefully, with time, these plants will creep up the wall and cascade down the other side. She is denied entry into the palace, but the flowers she has planted will get inside, greeting her son, a secret message, in riotous colour, from his mother, whose real identity is also a secret.

Chapter 76

Sita

Insomnia

1938

The guilt that plagues Sita manifests as insomnia. She paces the palace at night, stopping, always, outside her son's room, her head resting against his door, thus waiting out the long, dark hours of night. It is the only place where she finds some peace from her nagging conscience, which is at its worst at night and takes the form of a woman – Sita's childhood friend and the mother of Sita's child.

That woman. The woman she wants to forget but who will not let her do so. She is still teaching at the school – the school that *Sita* started for the girls of the kingdom. The school because of which Mary returned to India in the first place and because of which this kingdom has an heir.

Sita tried to get Mary removed from the school when Mary went back there after having camped outside the palace gates during Arjun's naming ceremony, becoming a ghastly spectacle for all to see and comment upon.

She summoned Mother Ruth to the palace. 'I believe the madwoman who claims I stole her child is working at the school as a teacher. Is it wise for her to be with children when she's so unhinged?'

Mother Ruth flinched at her words, but covered it up admirably with a smile. 'It was grief that turned her head briefly, when her child… when she lost her child.'

Sita noted the pause after 'child', wondering at Mother Ruth's choice of words. Did she believe Mary?

You're getting paranoid.

'She's absolutely fine now and a fabulous teacher. The girls love her.'

'Nevertheless, I don't want a madwoman teaching at one of our schools.'

'Dr Kumar checked her out and pronounced her well, Your Majesty.'

'Is he a psychiatrist?'

'No, but—'

'Well then. Get rid of her.'

'With all due respect, Your Majesty, we need Mary desperately. Sister Hilda and Sister Theresa are retiring from teaching and travelling back to England in a couple of months. That leaves just myself, Sister Catherine and Mary. Hiring a new teacher will take months. And Mary has come into some money recently, which she's putting towards the school, so you'll not need to fund us for another year at least.'

Sita had dismissed Mother Ruth, barely concealing her frustration, her rage. Mary had bought herself a place at the school with the money Sita had given her to start a new life in England. It was as if she was laughing at Sita, trying everything she could to inconvenience her. The king, who had the final say in these matters, would not agree to letting Mary go, however much Sita tried to sweet-talk him into it – her sweet-talking had worked once, but not any more, not when he wouldn't come near her bedchamber, just visited his son and left without looking in on her. The one pure and precious thing in her life, Jaideep's love, how he looked for the best in her, made her into a woman better than she knew herself to be, had died a death when Sita would not hold their son, be the mother he had expected her to be.

Although Jaideep still bowed to Sita in matters where he knew she was right, in this one he would see that she wasn't making financial sense. And, if she insisted on Mary's dismissal, he would wonder why she wanted the woman to leave so desperately. Sita didn't want to draw attention to Mary. She had already caused enough talk by creating a scene at the palace gates during the naming ceremony. Sita didn't want anybody, not least her husband, and certainly not his mother, asking questions about Mary and the wild claims she had made when she was camping outside the palace.

Chapter 77

Mary

Happy

1939

Mary hears from Dr Kumar that Charles has remarried and is moving to England. There's a baby on the way.

And finally the guilt she has been carrying for the way she treated him lifts. *You deserve to be happy, Charles.*

I'm sorry for what I did. I will always be sorry.

When Mary's son is two, there is a procession like the one at which she first saw Sita. Then, she had fainted and the townspeople had pronounced it an omen.

I should have heeded them.

But how could I have seen it coming?

It is the first time she has seen her son since he was stolen from her, sitting in between the king and queen in a gold-embossed, jewel-studded howdah atop an ornately decorated elephant. The babe she had held in her arms and fiercely vowed to protect, who had suckled from her, whose minuscule fingers and toes she had counted and kissed, whom she had gazed upon in wonder, in awe, who had mesmerised her, is now a compact, sturdy, beautiful boy.

He takes her breath away. Perfect. Precious.

Unattainable.

He looks happy.

He is decked in splendorous clothes; he sits regal and dignified in between the people he knows as his parents, waving at the adoring crowd.

The townspeople gasp, 'The little prince, how cute he is, how delightful, how like his mother!'

'*I* am his mother,' Mary wants to shout.

But seeing him there, looking completely at home atop the elephant, seated between the king and queen, the king's face softening when he looks at the boy he thinks of as his son, Mary knows she has lost her child.

Even if she were to get him back now, would he be happy? Would he want her, when he is accustomed to luxury, any material thing he desires, the fawning of a kingdom? He is the adored only son and heir of the royals. Groomed to rule. Destined to be king.

Mary's son is no longer hers.

Sita has won.

As if she has read her mind, the queen's regal glance sweeps the crowd, and it widens when it lands on Mary. Sita's lips lift in a small smirk. *Look at what he has. Look at the toadying crowds. Look at what I can give him*, she is saying.

Mary holds her gaze and smiles. *You might have taken my son from me. But you will not bend me to your will*, her smile conveys. *I'll be here, every year, watching my son parade through the streets on the occasion of the day you have determined as his birthday, one day after his actual birth. And every evening of every day I'll make my way up to the palace gates to tend to the garden I've planted there. You'll not get rid of me.*

As if she has understood every word of Mary's silent vow, the queen's face falls and her gaze falls away.

Chapter 78

Sita

Promise

1960

I'll learn to love you, Arjun, Sita vows to her sleeping child, as the priests chant mantras at his naming ceremony. *I will protect what you represent – this kingdom. I've won it for you and, by extension, for myself. I will defend it with my everything.*

Through the years to follow, through the upheaval of India's freedom from British rule, through the integration into independent India of the kingdom Sita lied and stole to keep, through the gradual stripping of their power and their wealth, Sita upholds the promise she makes at her son's naming ceremony.

Sita grows to love her son, although it is from a distance. She still cannot bear to touch him. He, in his turn, learns not to run to her, throw his arms round her, like he does with his father. His face falls, lips trembling with hurt, when she flinches at his touch, when he comes to her bawling, knees scraped and bleeding, and she turns away, and her husband looks at her as if she were a stranger, with something close to dislike on his face.

Sita tries not to recoil from her son's timidity, his gentleness. His fear of attempting new things. The shyness he exhibits. She tries not to see his mother in him.

His mother… *Sita* is his mother.

But Mary is there, always, a thorn in her side. Stabbing, poking. Reminding.

The nuns have all gone back to England – Mother Ruth and Sister Catherine returned when India became independent. Mary now runs the school, which *Sita* started – oh the irony! – and which, like the kingdom, has reverted to the Indian government, so Sita no longer has the power to sack Mary, much as she wants to. As far as Sita can see – she still keeps tabs on her – Mary is allowed complete freedom in the running of the school. But she has not stopped there, of course. She has talked the government into opening an orphanage right next to the school, which she manages with the aid of local women, many of whom she taught as children. The woman has made herself indispensable and it grates on Sita. Even when Sita used to wield power, yet she could not do what she wanted most – get rid of the woman who reminds her of the one action that she would like to forget, the woman whose continued presence will not let her believe the fiction that her child is hers.

And to top it all, Mary has claimed the land just outside the palace gates and fashioned a garden there. Those flowers, riotous colour, thriving, mocking Sita: *Was it all worth it?*

When Sita first realised what Mary was doing, she'd been incensed.

'That woman can't do that! Claim a piece of land and grow things on it.'

'Why not?' Jaideep had asked, coolly. 'She's creating something beautiful. She's not harming anyone.'

Sita did not want her husband, or his mother – who seemed to have a nose for any intrigue concerning Sita – to wonder why she was interested in Mary's doings. So she had to let it go.

But every time she comes out of the palace she shuts her eyes. She does not want to look at the garden, the vibrant flowers singing accusations at her.

'Ma, you should look at the flowers instead of closing your eyes. They are so beautiful. Why aren't they inside the palace?' her son once asked.

She had bitten her lip so hard it bled. 'There are more beautiful flowers inside the palace,' she managed, after a bit, her voice tight.

Arjun, as perceptive as Mary had been as a child, never brought up the flowers or the garden again.

Sita and her husband grow apart, living in opposite wings of the palace, tended to by their own covens of servants. Sita is in the east wing that she appropriated from her mother-in-law all those years ago, Jaideep in the west wing.

The queen mother grows frail, a bitter, ranting old woman (no change there) and dies.

Sita's parents succumb to heart attacks within two years of each other. Her brother Kishan and his family settle in New York.

Sita stops visiting the Lake Palace. Her son loves it but she cannot bear to be there. She takes him to London instead, to Paris. Never the Lake Palace.

Sita's son grows into a quiet, gentle and yet determined boy, close to his father, distant from his mother. Reserved and wary where Sita is concerned.

Sita becomes a woman who lives and breathes the kingdom, because this is all she has to show for her questionable decisions, the guilt that sits bitter in her throat so that everything she eats, everything she breathes, everything she does, is spiked with it. Even when the Indian government no longer recognises princely states, when it dissolves kingdoms, she fiercely holds on to the idea of it: a kingdom that no longer exists.

*

Sita cannot sleep and, at night, she paces the long corridors of the palace. The only place she finds some respite is outside her son's room, her head resting against his door, and even then, she hears Mary: *If you'd known that ten years after you stole my child, India would be independent, that you would be queen in name only, would you have done anything differently?*

Go away, Mary, she replies, wearily, to the voice in her head. *Stop plaguing me. Arjun has a good life, a life he wouldn't have had if he stayed with you. He's happy. He does not want for anything. I cannot countenance a different life, a life without him.*

I couldn't either, Mary mocks her. *But because of your actions, I've had no choice. He will never be yours. He is mine. Mine.*

She jerks awake, gasping, opening her son's door gently so she can make sure he's there and when she has taken in the sprawled, snoring reality of him, closing it again.

'Uncle Praveen has offered me a job at his company,' her son declares. 'I'll be one of the managing directors alongside my cousins.'

Sita stares at him, aghast, not wanting to believe what she's hearing.

Jaideep's twin, Praveen, his wife Latha and their children – three strapping boys – have moved to Bangalore to be near Latha's family. Praveen started a jute business after Indian independence and it has proved very successful.

'Baba has given his blessing,' Arjun announces, his gaze meeting hers, afraid and yet defiant, showing that same steely core that Mary had displayed when she told Sita, stroking her bump, that she was keeping her baby, that day at the library of the refuge when they met again as adults.

'I thought you'd stand for election and govern the kingdom in this way, like your father,' Sita bites out, her voice sharp to hide her upset.

'There is no kingdom, Ma.' Her son's voice patient and frustrated at the same time, as if she is a senile old woman talking nonsense.

'This is our kingdom and nobody will convince me otherwise,' Sita snaps.

Her son sighs. 'I'll not be moving away,' he says, a peace offering.

'As royals, we don't work for ourselves. Our duty is to our people.'

Her son continues as if she hasn't spoken. 'I'll be heading the branch of Uncle Praveen's company in this state.'

Sita turns away, acknowledging that in losing to her brother-in-law the son she appropriated to keep the kingdom from the same man, she is getting what she deserves. His vengeance has been a long time coming but it is here now.

Chapter 79

Priya

Legacy

2000

'You're much too thin, you need feeding,' Priya's grandmother huffs. But her eyes are soft and her gaze takes Priya in hungrily.

Although her grandmother is trying her best to seem normal, she is wan, a shrunken version of her old strident, domineering self, and Priya is glad her father persuaded her to return home.

When her father said her grandmother was dying, Priya had not quite believed it of her dadima, who always gave the impression of great strength. Surely even Death would be cowed by Dadima's formidable will, give in to her, like everyone else she has dealings with?

But now, Priya can, and it is sobering, distressing.

Priya and her grandmother are in a taxi, heading towards the palace that was once their family home. Her father has gone to his offices in the city to touch base: 'I'll join you this evening. I want to make sure things are running smoothly in New York in my absence.'

It had been his idea to stay at the palace.

'Your grandmother never really got over having to sell her home…' he'd mused as he booked their tickets. 'What if we arranged for her to stay in the rooms she used to occupy at the palace?'

'You think she'll like that?'

Her father had shrugged. 'Who knows? I've never been able to read your grandmother's mind, her moods.'

'It's a nice gesture, Baba. I'm sure she'll appreciate it.'

'I hope they've retained its character,' Priya's grandmother sniffs as they approach the town that she used to rule in the not so distant past. 'It was one of the conditions of sale.' Her voice acrid, dripping disdain.

To hide her nervousness, Priya understands, suddenly. Dadima is worried that the palace will have changed beyond recognition. At any other time, Priya would have been annoyed at her grandmother's brusque tone, but now, her anguish over her failed marriage seems to have opened her eyes to the emotion the older woman is hiding behind her brittleness. If her grandmother was open to affection, Priya would pat her hand. But she is a prickly old woman and any display of affection would only make her suspicious and more interested than usual in Priya's affairs.

And Priya definitely doesn't want that.

She cannot deal with the judgement, on top of everything else. Her grandmother never warmed to Jacob, and Priya can't bear to hear her crow, 'I told you so.'

And sick as she is, Dadima will have no qualms about doing so.

The taxi is climbing up the hill now, the palace coming into view. As glorious and opulent and forbidding as ever.

When Priya told friends about her childhood, they would exclaim, 'Wow, how lucky, to grow up in a palace!' They didn't get it and she didn't want to sound spoilt, moaning about growing up in the lap of luxury, wanting for nothing. But it had been lonely, all those rooms, sad and fraying, tarnished grandeur, cobwebbed glory, and only ghosts from past lives for company.

They pass the municipal garden outside the palace gates. Boisterous blooms, kaleidoscopic, abundant colour. Laughing children. Picnicking families.

This garden has always been joyously riotous, making the gardens inside the palace gates appear sedate and dull in comparison. Too perfect. Monochrome.

Perhaps this is why when her counsellor had asked Priya about her happy place, this garden was what she thought of. It is what comes to mind when she looks at its hotchpotch rainbow beauty: a happy space.

There's an old woman sitting on one of the benches, vaguely familiar. Her face turned towards the palace. 'Is that—' Priya begins, but her grandmother cuts her off.

'Can you believe it?' the older woman snaps. She is looking straight ahead, sitting very still. Her aged, disease-riddled body is alert, radiating nerves as she breathes the palace in, her keen eyes missing nothing, it seems, no corner or crevice exempt from her scrutiny as the gates are opened for them and the taxi creeps up the stately drive, lawns on either side stretching away. 'They've painted it white!'

She says 'white' as if it is the worst kind of crime.

'Wasn't it white before?' Priya ventures.

'Cream,' her grandmother bites. 'The pink-stained cream of dawn when it parts ways with night.'

'The palace inspires the poet in you, Dadima.' Priya tries for levity.

'It was my *home*,' her grandmother spits. 'They've ruined it,' she snorts as they are welcomed into the large, elegant foyer with spiced green mango juice and barfi wrapped in crêpe paper.

'All fake. Cheap trinkets. Not antiques like we used to have.'

Priya bites her lower lip, weary. Of her grandmother. Of life. She wants to go to the room assigned to her, shut the door, pull the curtains and sleep. Forget.

'Please come with me,' a smartly dressed woman with a polished accent says.

'I know the way, thank you. This was once mine,' her grandmother says regally. 'My maid will take me.'

Her grandmother has brought her maid along, of course. The one maid left now of the posse she took with her when she left the palace.

'The decor is ridiculous. Pretentious and vulgar. They've stripped the place of character,' her grandmother sighs when they reach the east wing. 'Your father has booked the entire suite of rooms; at least that's something.'

'I know being slim is the fashion now but honestly, Priya, you've gone too far. Have you not been eating at all?'

Her grandmother is draped across a divan overlooking the decorative pool, which is deserted but for them. They are having afternoon tea in the courtyard of the east wing: nimbu pani and spiced chai, churmuri and chaat, pakoras and jalebi, none of which her grandmother touches.

It shocks Priya, how reduced her grandmother looks, as if the life force is leaving her.

Lily pads float on the calm surface of the pool, interspersed with fountains and a small temple in the centre.

It is an idyllic paradise and it is indoors, the courtyard that leads into the east wing of the palace. The palace where they all used to reside, her grandmother in her suite of rooms in the east wing, Priya, her parents and her grandfather, when he was alive, in the west wing.

Priya lies back down on the lush grass in the shade of the palm trees, her feet in the silky water. It's a world away from Jacob and his pregnant mistress. She bites her lip until she tastes iron and salt, to keep sorrow at bay.

She is exhausted, both from the journey and from keeping her upset from her grandmother. The older woman is also trying hard to be her usual self, unravaged by illness, but Priya can see how much it takes out of her.

Her grandmother knows that Priya and her son, Priya's father, are here because she is dying, but she'll not admit it, demanding in her imperious, entitled way that they take their cue from her.

'Our heritage as rulers of the kingdom now a lodging for tourists…' Her grandmother spits, the word 'tourists' mired in scorn.

Priya looks at the sky, a brilliant white, haloed honey gold by the sun. 'We haven't been rulers for a long time, Dadima.'

'Perhaps not in the eyes of the government, but we certainly still are in the eyes of the people. And your grandfather was still ruler, in every sense, until he retired from government. Your father would not put himself forward, insisting on working for his uncle instead – a travesty, such selfishness! And here we are now, visitors at our own residence!'

'Baba did offer to help save the palaces.'

'I refuse to take a paisa of your great-uncle's money,' her grandmother snaps vehemently.

'It's Baba's hard-earned money…' Why, when she's with her grandmother, can they not go two minutes without arguing with each other? Although there is some comfort in the fact that nothing has changed there. Her grandmother is a shell of her previous self physically, but just as sharp as always. And in the few minutes they've been talking, Priya hasn't once thought about Jacob.

'The Lake Palace and this one, part of a hotel chain!' Her grandmother says 'hotel chain' as if she is speaking about rubbish festering in a dump.

'They've restored it passably…'

Her grandmother is moved to sit up and glare at Priya. 'This was our legacy. Yours too.' The older woman's voice harsh, her words the bruised violet of nostalgia.

Priya notices the new lines peppering her face. She looks fragile – a word Priya would never before have associated with her indomitable grandmother.

And on the heels of that thought grief surges, for her grandmother, for the dissolution of her marriage, her empty womb, the relentless passage of time.

'I'm tired, I'll rest now,' her grandmother says and her maidservant leads her gently away, supporting her now insubstantial weight.

Priya roams the many rooms of the palace; she knows every nook and cranny, having explored them growing up, witnessed by the host of spirits she has always sensed lingering in these musty, timeworn rooms. She was a solitary child, haunting the vast rooms bereft of people but stuffed with antiques, the decrepit souvenirs of bygone greatness serving only to underline the loneliness, the stark emptiness, the clamour of entombed phantoms.

Now, the aging grandeur, the mildewed chill of old ghosts and past lives trapped in the unravelling tapestries, the stale-oil-and-spice scent of ancient revelries captured for ever in the numerous paintings, the threadbare carpets that had serviced myriad feet, sultans and rulers, subjects and servants alike has been replaced with sparkly furnishings, gaudy, in-your-face splendour. The character is gone but so too are the spirits, the chill stale air thick with the ethereal breath of spectres from generations past whose whispers had haunted Priya, baying to be heard, given voice, restored to greatness again.

The mirrored screens throw up images of a hollow-cheeked woman, swollen eyes ringed by dark circles, holding herself together as if with effort.

In her documentaries, she has railed against women who define themselves by their men, who go to pieces when they find themselves on their own.

I am no different.

When the women she interviewed protested that they did not know how to live without their men, Priya had said, blithely, 'Then learn to do so. Discover yourself. Love yourself. You have that opportunity now.'

She has called herself a feminist. She has preached about self-worth, women power. Easy to do so, of course, when she had Jacob's backing, his love bolstering her, his belief in her reinforcing her belief in herself.

The women in the many mirrors cringe, even as their sunken cheeks bleed with colour. They push their shoulders back and their mouths work as they say, out loud, 'I will not let what happened defeat me. I will be like this palace, reinvented, given a new lease of life. I will look to a future sans Jacob – he is my old ghost, his time is past, he needs to be put to rest.'

Priya smiles, with effort, until she can detect a glimmer of her old self in her many ravaged reflections. And out loud, she makes a promise to herself, 'You've claimed quite enough of my life, Jacob. No more.'

Afterwards, she finds herself on the landing at the curve of the stairs, with its view of the long, stately drive, the landscaped lawns and fountains, the gates and the garden just outside, with its wild profusion of flowers, in glorious contrast to the sedate precision of the neat flower beds inside the gates.

Priya used to stand here after fraught sessions with her grandmother and looking at the untamed and carefree garden outside the gates, her racing heart would settle, her anger, at her grandmother and at herself, for allowing her grandmother to rile her, would gradually dissipate and she would find a semblance of calm.

This is why she has come here now, almost without thinking. Her legs, of their own accord, leading her to view her happy place.

The garden is just the same, if not wilder, more beautiful than she remembers. She almost expects to see the woman too, sitting on one of the benches haphazardly dotting the garden...

Mary. She was there, Priya realises. Older and yet unmistakably her, sitting on a bench as their taxi had driven past...

She's not there now. But as Priya looks at the garden, reiterating the promise she made to herself, not to allow her husband's actions to destroy her, to look forward to a future without him, a germ of an idea sprouts.

Chapter 80

Mary

A Visitor

1940

One morning, Mary is cooking with the children – it is Mother Ruth's birthday and they are attempting a cake, flour on faces, on surfaces and on the floor – when Sister Catherine says, 'Mary, you have a visitor.'

Her heart jumps, hope budding despite all the setbacks.

Sister Catherine, seeing her face, says, 'No. Sorry, Mary.'

Her heart sinks.

She knew of course that it wouldn't be Sita or one of her maids handing Richard over, but there's always hope Sita might change her mind, come to her senses. If there wasn't then Mary might as well give up.

It is irrational but for Mary the garden she has planted outside the palace gates represents the promise that her son will one day be returned to her. As long as the garden thrives, there is hope.

She strides into the visiting room, wiping her hands on her apron, pushing her hair from her face, which is sweaty from the heat of the kitchen.

A man is standing at the window looking out at the school garden that she works on in her spare time, with its vegetable patch and medley of flowering plants and fruit trees.

He is thin and tall, with a slight hunch as if apologising for his height. Gangly arms hang by his sides. Long fingers. Something about the way he holds himself...

She clears her throat.

He turns.

Thick curls framing an angular, bearded face. Laughter lines around his mouth and eyes. Hooked nose. Eyes looking at her, taking her in. Eyes she has known sparkling with laughter, and pouring tears that fateful day when her life changed irrevocably for the first time. A face that colours her happiest memories.

'Amin.'

His eyes shine and he smiles, dimples flashing, and it is the Amin of her childhood standing before her. She will not think of her other childhood friend, revealed to be traitor and thief, the worst sort of betrayer. She will not.

'Missy Baba,' he says.

The name she lost when she stepped on board the ship that took her to England.

'I recently heard about this woman who's as good with plants as she is with children. She can coax both into doing anything she wants, it is said. I had to come and see for myself!'

She laughs, and is startled by the sound. When was the last time she laughed?

The nuns clearly are too, for they poke their heads around the door and smile gratefully, approvingly, at Amin.

'I've heard you're doing so much good for the children of this town that you've transformed into a saint! Is this your way of doing penance for the way you treated me in childhood?'

She laughs some more and he joins in.

Laughing still, he taps his nose. 'There's some white stuff just here. Is it your halo? If so, it needs readjusting. Isn't it supposed to rest upon your head?'

'Flour, you monkey!' she says and, giggling, she experiences the first taste of unadulterated happiness in a long while. The echo of long-ago contentment and joy and the reckless abandon of childhood.

'The dirt road leading to the river, the water tower. They're all here. Unchanged.'

'Yes,' Amin says.

He has brought her to their hometown where Mary once roamed the streets, secure in the knowledge that life would never change. That she was safe and loved.

Amin lives in his childhood home with his toddler, Jahid, and his mother, old and blinded by cataracts. She touches Mary's face all over, kisses her forehead. 'Look at you, all grown up.'

Jahid flashes her a gummy, toothless, spit-bubble grin, and Mary tries to suppress the pangs of grief and yearning for *her* boy. Will she ever be a part of his life?

Amin is a boatman, ferrying people across the river.

'It's what you said you'd do.' She smiles.

'When I'm on the boat, I think of us as children. Skimming stones, racing kites and paper boats. How happy we were then, eh?'

'Yes.'

Amin wanted to be a boatman, while Mary's ambition had been to marry a handsome man like her papa and have many children…

You've achieved your ambition, Amin, but mine has changed. I'd like my son back, that is all.

She bites her tongue until she tastes blood, bitter iron.

'I hear the echo of our laughter, see our childhood selves and wish we were children again. But then, well, I wouldn't have Jahid.'

'Jahid's mother…?' she asks tentatively.

They're sitting on the rope bridge, where they were the day Mary's world changed direction for the first time. The water ripples below and the bridge, wobbly as ever, sways gently in the breeze. This time, she did not even so much as blink as she climbed onto the bridge.

'You're not afraid any more,' Amin observed.

'No.' She had lost everything dear to her, what did she have to be afraid of?

'My wife died giving birth to Jahid. My mother and I look after him, as best we can,' Amin says.

Mary closes her eyes, turns her head to the sun. So much sadness running slipshod over lives, fate ironing out differences and also bringing them to the fore.

On the bank, a cow's plaintive moos, a girl's laughter. The smell of stewed tea and frying onions.

'What happened to your sparkle, Missy Baba?'

She has asked him to call her Mary. But, 'You'll always be Missy Baba to me.'

And sitting there, the river whispering secrets it has garnered over centuries, she tells him.

He listens quietly, intently.

When she has finished, he sighs deeply. 'I'm so sorry.'

She turns to him. 'You believe me.'

His eyes glitter brightly with the ache she has tried to hide. 'Missy Baba, you were always so trusting of Sita. But I... the Sita I knew would stop at nothing to get what she wants. She hasn't changed.'

She tears up then, and he moves to comfort her, stopping before he touches her, holding the rope instead. They can no longer be friends with the same casual abandon of childhood. They are a grown man and woman, she white, he Indian. And so they sit there, side by side, not touching, Mary trying and failing to hide her sniffles.

Amin hands her his handkerchief.

She takes it and blows her nose. It smells of him, lime and mint.

'I cannot imagine the anguish, the agony of it. I cannot imagine life without my Jahid,' he says softly.

Somehow, after she is all cried out, as they prepare to leave the town of her childhood in his bullock cart, she feels better. Just having Amin believe in her has been enough. It is a gift she tucks into her heart.

'Let's make a small detour,' he says.

And then they are pulling up at the cemetery and he is taking her to the graves of her parents.

She looks at her parents' names, side by side, together in death as in life, and once again she has to borrow Amin's handkerchief.

Richard. Her father's name. The name she gave her son.

'Back then, the adults making decisions on my behalf decided that I was too young to attend their funeral. I meant to look up their graves once I came here, settled in. But then I found out I was pregnant and then…' She takes a breath. 'I think attending their funeral would have helped me come to terms with my loss more. As it was, I never quite believed they could disappear just like that. They were there one day and then just gone.'

Like my son. But I'll get him back, I will.

'Perhaps that was why I buried my past, my life here, when I went to England. I just couldn't accept they were dead.'

Her parents' graves are cared for, she notices. There are plants here. Flowers nodding in the breeze.

'Who tends their graves?'

Amin flushes, scuffing the earth with his toe. 'I come here every week, have done so since you left.'

'You planted the flower bushes?'

'My mother suggested it, when the flowers I brought here wilted.'

'Thank you.'

*

'I'll be back when I can,' Amin promises, when he drops her off at the school.

'That would be lovely,' she says and he smiles, winsomely, the boy who was her childhood friend.

Chapter 81

Priya

A Family Again

2000

'Here we are, a family again,' Priya's grandmother says, holding up her glass, her eyes twinkling, the beautiful young woman she must have been once shining briefly through her wrinkled face.

Supper is being served in the banquet room in the east wing, but where there was once a long table, now there are hosts of smaller ones, Priya, her grandmother and father occupying the one at the far end.

The evening before Priya was leaving for England to do her film-making course, this was where they had sat, the three of them, all that was left of their family; her grandmother at the head of the long table, her father on one side and Priya on the other, chandeliers glinting, crystal and silver sparkling, all the empty place settings mocking them.

And now, here they are again. But this time, their silence is masked by the pleasant murmur of conversation from other tables. Guests in their finery being served by smartly dressed, obsequious staff.

It must have been like this in its heyday, Priya imagines, when her grandmother, as queen, would host durbars. She looks up at her grandmother and reads the memory in her nostalgia-suffused eyes.

Her father raises his glass and smiles at Priya, before downing his whisky, the colour of sunset reflected on water, in a long gulp. His skin glows in the light from the chandeliers. He has always been very light-skinned, with his amber eyes, his reddish brown hair.

'Like me,' Dadima likes to say.

But while Dadima has tawny eyes and is pale-skinned, Priya's father is even more so. Dadima's side of the family intermarried with the British and somehow, her son is almost white. *Genetics*, Priya muses.

'You eat up now,' Dadima urges Priya. 'You're shockingly thin.' She gestures to the waiters. 'Serve her, go on. She needs more of everything.'

Priya bites her lower lip. *I'll not lose my temper.*

She says, evenly, 'I've quite enough on my plate, I'll finish this first.'

It's always like this when she's with her grandmother, their wills clashing, her grandmother's overpowering one winning much of the time.

After dessert – kheer, rasgullas, jalebis, kala jamun – has been served, after her father has retired to his rooms, her grandmother asks, 'Shall we sit by the pool in the courtyard?'

In the yellow light she looks fatigued, ashen. The dinner seems to have wiped her out.

Although Priya longs for bed, feeling wrung out and tired from the journey and from trying to act normal for her grandmother's sake, she cannot refuse this request. Her grandmother is shrunken, a shell of her former self, and Priya is acutely aware that there won't be many more moments like this with her.

Faced with her grandmother's imminent mortality, Priya realises that she cares for this cantankerous old woman more than she'd like to admit. She has fought with her, wilfully stayed away from her, but nevertheless, she cannot bear to lose her. Her grandmother is infuriating; she drives Priya up the wall with her antiquated opinions and her posturing. But... She's the only grandmother Priya has.

They claim their favourite places in the courtyard – which is, once again, blessedly empty but for them; her grandmother in her divan, Priya, sandals off, legs in the pool, lying back on the tiles and staring up at the sunset-splashed orange and rose sky, smudged occasionally by the green and black shadows of parrots and crows flying home to nest.

'What're you not telling me?' her grandmother says, direct as always, astute despite her illness, her uncanny instinct for rooting out secrets as sharp as ever.

'Where do you want me to start? I haven't seen you in ages,' Priya says dryly, staring at the rippling water, kaleidoscopic with the rainbow reflection of the darkening sky.

'Is it that feckless man you married making you miserable?'

Tears bite sharp and stinging, along with a rush of anger towards her grandmother and an urge to defend her husband.

She swallows both down. Her anger towards her grandmother is misplaced, for Dadima – who had disliked Jacob on sight and had tried to dissuade Priya from marrying him, which had made Priya all the more determined – is right. Jacob *is* feckless, he *is* making her miserable.

Not any more, she thinks, resolute, recalling her promise to herself when she was looking at the garden by the gates. Her happy place.

The garden. Her idea...

Her grandmother's maid hands out tall glasses of cold spiced green-mango panna, sweating with condensation, along with cashew-nut barfi and almond halva flecked with plump raisins.

Her grandmother takes a barfi and bites into it, looking discerningly at Priya. 'It *is* that man. What's he done?'

Priya takes a gulp of her juice and, wanting to distract her grandmother from Jacob, says, 'I'm planning on doing a documentary on the garden outside the palace gates and the woman who created it – Mary.' Doing the documentary will consume Priya, stop her dwelling on Jacob. It will be the first step towards the new future she's promised herself. Ever since Priya first laid eyes on the garden it has fascinated her, as has Mary, its architect. She's always had the feeling that there was a story behind the garden, something Mary is trying to convey. And Priya wants to find out what it is. 'I want to look into Mary's motivation and—'

Dadima spits out the barfi, white crumbs littering the divan and the patterned mosaic tiles at the edges of the courtyard, beyond the grass, where the divan rests. She coughs, a seemingly unstoppable volley, and her maid rushes up with water, holding it to her lips while also massaging Dadima's back.

When Dadima has finally finished coughing, as the maid wipes her streaming eyes, she yells, 'I must complain to the management about those barfis. They're disgusting.'

'Dadima—'

Her grandmother holds up a palm. 'You know that I'm very ill.'

There it is. Out in the open. The reason Priya and her father are here. Why is her grandmother bringing it up now, after skirting around the subject since she and her father arrived?

'Yes?' Her voice raised at the end in question. Her grandmother never does anything without an agenda.

'I don't have much time.'

'Oh, Dadima—'

'I have one request.'

Priya waits.

'Don't do the documentary or contact Mary. At least not until I'm gone.'

'What? Why? How is your illness connected with what I want to do? Why do—'

Her grandmother clutches her arm. 'Please.'

Priya shuts up, completely stunned by the uncharacteristic word coming out of her grandmother's mouth.

'This is all I ask.'

Priya fumes, feeling manipulated by her usually strident, feisty grandmother, now vulnerable and begging.

She *hates* this. She feels played, first by Jacob and now Dadima.

Her grandmother will do anything to get her way. Priya has watched her formidable will in action many times. But why this request? Why doesn't she want Priya to do this documentary? What has she got against Mary? Why doesn't she want Priya to contact her?

She looks at her grandmother, skin yellow, shockingly pallid. Dying and yet as wily and determined to get her way as ever.

'Please,' she says again.

Priya nods, her mouth not working enough to speak. Bile rising in her throat.

'Thank you.' Her grandmother looks spent. A bit like Priya feels. Completely and utterly spent. Used. To suit her grandmother's needs.

Chapter 82

Mary

A Bond

1947

Mary opens the door of the school, which she now runs, in the middle of the night, to Amin.

He is with his son, and carrying a bag of clothes.

'People I've known all my life have turned against me, just because I'm not Hindu, a fact that never mattered before,' he says. 'They want me to go to the Punjab, which is now going to be Pakistan under Mr Jinnah. I'm worried for Jahid.'

Jahid peers at her with his father's wide, earnest eyes.

'Can he stay here?' Amin asks.

'Of course,' she says, ushering them in. 'Will you go to Pakistan?'

'This is where I was born and raised, where my family has lived for generations. I'll not leave. But I don't want my son to see his neighbours, his friends, shun him just because he's of another religion. Can you keep him here until it all calms down?'

'Yes, of course,' she says again.

Amin kisses his son, squeezes her hand and leaves, ushering his bullock cart into the night.

Mary never sees him again. He is killed in the religious riots post-independence. It is another wound she will nurse all her life, another loss she will carry.

Jahid, an orphan, and she, another, form a bond. She takes the place of the parent he never had – the mother who died giving birth to him – and he eases her ache and longing for her son.

Chapter 83

Priya

Solitary

Priya finds her father in his room, playing chess against himself. Deep in thought, his head bent, bald spot showing, a sprinkling of grey in his thinning hair. So solitary it makes her chest ache.

Her father in his room, her grandmother in hers, issuing orders, manipulating lives from her deathbed, and Priya, alone after fifteen years of being part of a couple, having given up hope of becoming a family...

Tears assault and she brusquely rubs them away. No more self-pity, only action. She will make that documentary, deathbed promise or not, which is why she is here. Losing herself in work is the only way she can think of to move on, drag herself out of this fever of upset that ambushes her when she least expects or wants.

When her mother died, her father had pushed her to continue her studies even though it was the last thing she felt like doing when her world was askew, one half of the pillars bolstering her gone.

'It will help, Priya, I promise,' he had said. And, 'Your mother would have wanted you to achieve your ambition. She would be upset and disappointed if her dying stopped you from following your dreams. You've set your sights on doing that film-making course in England. Well, for that, you need to get the requisite marks. Come on, you can do it.'

And so she had put her head down and she had worked. And just as her father promised, it had helped her wade through the lake of sorrow, pull herself out of the swamp of loss and grief she was floundering in.

'Baba...'

Her father looks up, bishop in hand. 'Ah, hello.' He smiles. 'Sit.' He pats the seat next to him.

'Shall we go to the courtyard? It's hot in here.'

In the courtyard, she folds herself into one of the loungers beneath the palm trees.

'How are you?' her father asks, lowering himself into the chair beside Priya.

A simple question. Requiring a straightforward answer. She opens her mouth to say she is fine, but... 'I-I'm angry.'

Her father nods. 'As you should be. He's not worth any more of your time, Priya.'

She laughs, harsh, raw. 'I know. But tell that to my heart.'

'You're precious, Priya. Loved so very much.'

She stares at the sky, luminous golden-white, dotted here and there with parrots, green silhouettes flying across the courtyard before alighting on the trees scattered around the pool, until the tears stabbing her eyes stop their attack.

'Don't let what Jacob did undermine who you are,' her father says.

His words reminding her of the promise she made herself. The garden. The documentary. Her promise to her grandmother... Her grandmother. 'Dadima looks so emaciated.'

'I cannot imagine her as anything but invincible,' her father says.

'And bent upon getting her own way,' Priya says bitterly. 'What does Dadima have against the woman who created the garden outside the gates, Mary, do you know?'

'Oh, you picked up on that too?' her father asks, rubbing his chin, looking surprised. 'I think your grandmother felt threatened by Mary.'

'Threatened? But how? They're very different and...'

'Your grandmother wanted to be the only important woman in the state, the only one spoken about with reverence and respect, the only one looked up to and admired.'

'And yet,' Priya muses, comprehension dawning, 'people would do that with Mary.'

'Yes. Your grandmother had wealth, once. Status. Family name. People respected her and looked up to her because of these things, not because of anything she had achieved. Mary, on the other hand...'

'People revered her, loved her, even went to her with their problems.'

'They still do, I think. I don't know if you recall that time the board voted for Mary to be given a commendation in honour of the work she was doing in the community?'

'I think I do.'

'Your grandmother had tried to oppose it, exerted her considerable influence, but your grandfather stood firm. He too admired Mary greatly.'

'I remember,' Priya says. 'I must have been about seven...'

Chapter 84

Priya

Another Day

1972

Another day, preparations for another party. There's always some celebration or other happening at the palace, it appears to Priya.

But this one, she notes, is different. This time, her grandmother is not the one directing the palace servants and the temporary labourers hired for the occasion, who are setting up marquees in the grounds. Her grandmother is not discussing the menu with the head cook, and her vast retinue of helpers. She's not grumbling about the bunting not being the kind she ordered, the marquees not being in palace livery colours, the uniforms of the staff not being smartly ironed. Instead she is in her rooms, resting, and Priya's grandfather and parents are managing it all, looking harassed and put-upon, so Priya knows to keep out of their way.

'Is Dadima ill?' she asks her mother.

'You could say so, yes.'

'What do you mean by "You could say so"?'

'Forget I said anything.'

Priya is still mulling over her mother's cryptic words the next day when the award ceremony takes place. Her grandmother sits rigid next to her husband, looking flawless but with no smile gracing her features. Priya sits sandwiched between Dadima and her mother, her father sitting beside her grandfather on the other side.

'Don't fidget or slouch. Show them you've as much right to sit here as a boy. That you can sit *better* than a boy,' her grandmother has reiterated many times. 'When I was young no woman sat in a durbar. They had a separate seat up there in the gallery.'

'But this is not a durbar. We don't do that any more. This is a—'

'Pshaw,' her grandmother waves Priya's words away. 'Same thing, different name.'

The ceremony starts. Her grandfather gives a speech. 'We're gathered here today to honour an amazing woman who has done so much for our community…'

As the speech progresses, her grandmother goes more and more rigid, and Priya worries that if she holds herself any tighter, she might explode. Priya is also listening to the speech and the more she hears, the more she wants to meet this woman whose virtues her grandfather has been listing for many minutes now.

When she comes forward, Priya lets out a gasp of surprise and recognition. It is the woman from the garden by the gates, that magical garden that Priya saw from the top of the roller coaster…

For her seventh birthday, the palace grounds had been transformed into a fairground.

It was when Priya was at the very top of the roller coaster about to plunge down the slope, her stomach dipping in anticipation, her mouth open and ready to scream, that she saw the garden. It was spectacular. A riot of colour. Not neat and arranged in perfect rows like inside the gates, but a wild feast for the eyes.

A woman was tending to the garden, a boy squatting beside her, pulling up weeds. From the roller coaster, Priya could see that the woman was English. She was wearing a dress with the skirts bunched up and showing something to the boy, who had brown hair and dark skin and was unmistakably Indian.

The roller coaster started moving and Priya was dipping, falling, the scream she had been holding in escaping.

When the ride ended, among the crush of people dismounting and waiting to get in, Priya had managed to give the maid looking after her the slip. She ran, pigtails flying, all the way to the front gates.

She held on to the railings, smelling the tang of iron and rust. 'Watchman, why is there a garden outside the gates?'

The man guarding the gate had smiled at her. 'Because it does not belong to the palace.'

'Then who does it belong to?'

The man scratched his head.

'It is my grandmother's garden,' a young voice called from behind the watchman.

It was the boy Priya had seen from the roller coaster, his hands muddy, clutching weeds, his face glowing with exertion.

'It's not mine, Ahmad,' said a gentle voice, with a faint accent. 'I just tend to the garden. It is everybody's.' The woman Priya had seen alongside the boy came into view. She was old, her hair flecked with grey, and yet beautiful. Her eyes smiled at Priya and she looked kind. Something about her warmed Priya from inside.

'Hello,' she said, eyes twinkling. Her smile lodged right in Priya's heart. 'I won't shake your hand, mine's dirty.'

'I don't mind a bit of mud.' Priya had an urge to touch the woman. She thrust out her hand just as her maid caught up with her, panting.

'There you are, I've been looking all over for you. Don't run off like that again, you gave me quite the fright.'

Priya had been reluctantly led away and admonished severely, ordered not to speak to strangers. But the woman had not felt like a stranger at all…

Some days later, Priya discovered the landing at the curve of the stairs from where she could see the garden and, sometimes, the woman and the boy. It made her happy, both the garden and the woman tending to it.

Mary. Priya rolls the woman's name around on her tongue as she comes forward to receive her award from Priya's grandfather. She is wearing a simple white dress, her greying hair loose over her shoulders. No jewels, but she wears a wide smile and she looks beautiful. Even more so, Priya thinks, than her glamorous, jewel-bedecked grandmother.

As she puts her hand out to accept the plaque her grandfather is giving her, Priya sees that there's still some mud crusted around her nails, too ingrained to be scrubbed away.

Priya likes Mary all the more for it.

'Thank you for this honour,' she says. 'I'll use the money to improve the facilities in the orphanage and, if there's any left over, the school.'

Priya's parents and grandfather chuckle but beside Priya, her grandmother stiffens even more.

Mary smiles widely, encompassing Priya in her gaze. It is a soothing deep brown with streaks of orange, beautiful and fathomless as the horizon at sunset.

'Thank you, son,' Mary says, nodding at Priya's father.

At this, at last, her grandmother speaks. '*Your Majesty* to you,' her voice harsh and prickly as a thorn drawing blood.

Priya is aglow with embarrassment. Even *she* knows that her grandfather is no longer king, that her father never was, so why does her grandmother insist on this? Why is she making a scene in front of this wonderful woman?

But Mary only smiles, even as a whisper runs through the audience, rippling across the assembled people, and Priya's grandfather lays a calming hand on his wife's.

'Let the celebrations begin,' her grandfather calls and the string orchestra starts up and dancers take to the stage and her grandmother, looking forbidding and grim, walks away, not making an appearance for the rest of the celebrations, not for the peacock dance, not for the elephant parade, not for the children of the orphanage singing the song they've prepared for Mary.

Chapter 85

Priya
Side By Side

2000

Priya and her father sit side by side, lost in memories, as the afternoon fades into evening.

'Does it get any easier?' she asks after a while.

'Hmm?' He looks at her from over the top of his glasses, which are balanced on his nose.

'Losing the love of your life.'

Her father places a hand on hers. It is comfort. And love. 'There will be another more worthy of your love.'

'Have you moved on, Baba?' she asks.

'Ah.' He rubs a hand across his eyes. 'You've put me on the spot, Priya. Your mother, she was quite special.'

'She was.' Her eyes prick and sting. 'I... I thought my special one was Jacob.'

He squeezes her hand. She waits until the press of tears against her eyelids eases, until her vision clears.

'You're young. You have your life ahead of you, waiting to be seized. The love of your life waiting to be claimed.'

She sniffs, pushing aside her misery. 'And right now, a documentary waiting to be made.'

Her father looks at her, keen. 'Yes?'

'I'd like to do a film about Mary and her garden. I've always been fascinated by it. I want to explore Mary's motivation for creating it.'

'What a fabulous idea!' Her father beams. 'I've always been captivated by the garden and the woman behind it too.'

'Dadima doesn't think so. She's extracted a promise from me not to do the documentary or contact Mary while she's still around.'

'What? Why?'

Priya shrugs. 'Who knows why Dadima takes against something or someone?'

'But to ask you not to do the documentary...' Her father raises his eyebrows. 'How will you get round it?'

She smiles, properly, for what feels like the first time in a long while. 'How do you know I won't just give up?'

'I know you, Priya, don't forget. Your mother and I have always been fiercely proud of your formidable will, even during your terrible teens—'

'I wasn't that bad!'

'That's right. You were worse.'

She chuckles, feeling lighter all of sudden.

'You'll not let a small obstacle like a promise to your grandmother stand in your way. In fact, it will have made you even *more* determined to get your way. Am I right?'

'You are.' She grins. Feeling almost like her old self. Fired up. Ready to take on the world. *Jacob, watch me.* 'The only way I can think to move on is through working. And that garden – I just know there's a story there. Now that I've found my subject, I'm raring to begin but my hands are tied because of my promise to Dadima.'

'So what's your plan?'

'Well, it involves you.'

'Me?' Her father's eyebrows shoot up. 'Ah. That's why you came to find me. Here I was pleased you'd come to chat, but all the while you had a hidden agenda.'

'Yes.' She smiles. 'Will you help me, please?'

'When you ask so nicely, what choice do I have? What would you have me do?'

'You don't have to sound so resigned.'

'I'm a tad apprehensive. Can you blame me?'

'Dadima asked me not to contact Mary, so I'd like you to interview her instead. I'll write out the questions for you. This way I'm honouring my promise to Dadima, not contacting Mary myself and not doing the documentary – yet. But if I have Mary's answers, I can start researching and laying the ground for how I want to go about the film, where to begin…'

Her father smiles at her and she recognises pride in his gaze. Love. 'I hope your mother is watching.'

Priya's eyes prickle as they've taken to doing without warning lately, but this time, it is gladness she feels and gratitude towards her father. The melancholy that has engulfed her is slowly but surely lifting.

She realises that right now, she's fuming at what Jacob has done, a part of her still misses him and longs for him, but she's not devastated, crushed as she was in the early days after his leaving.

Part 7

Hope and Love

Chapter 86

Mary

The Same Soil

2000

Mary sits on the swing seat in the veranda of her room at the school, looking out at the garden where the children play, their delighted squeals drifting up to her. Innumerable children have frolicked in the garden, passed through these doors. They come and visit, children who are now grown and have families of their own. Some of them work at the school, others at the orphanage.

So many children. And yet none of them her own.

Was it worth it? she asks herself often.

Yes, without a doubt it was.

Amin's son, Jahid, Jahid's wife, Noor, and their children, Ahmad and Athiyah, have taken over the management of the school and the orphanage. The garden up at the palace gates is now the property of the government, a municipal garden, open to and enjoyed by the public, unlike the exclusive gardens inside the palace, which are only enjoyed by the rich patrons of its new incarnation as a five-star hotel. Mary still goes every evening to the garden she created when at her lowest, sitting on one of the benches that have been installed and admiring the blooms. She cannot walk there any more, so Jahid drives her up in his car.

It was Amin leaving Jahid in her care that spawned the idea of building an orphanage in the empty field next to the school.

India's independence had caused so much bloodshed, created so many destitute children, and the orphanage quickly filled.

After the war she'd written to her aunt, just to check if they were all right. Her aunt had written back, asking her to come home; all was forgiven. The war had levelled everything, wiped her anger away. The huge house had been converted into a hospital during the war. Rose lost her husband, Lily and Iris their beaus.

Over the years she's kept in touch. Her uncle died in 1947 and her aunt in 1956. Her cousins are grandmothers now, Iris a great-grandmother. They invite her to England in every letter. But, although she has felt tempted several times, she has never been back. She never will.

For how can she leave? Her sons are here, both the one she lost to one childhood friend and the one she gained from the other.

Mary will die here, be buried in the same soil that nourishes her sons and their families.

She did not fight for Richard enough. She was young then and scared, alone, overwhelmed. Nobody believed her. She tried, but not hard enough. But she has fought for all the other children who've been in her care, in his stead.

It's still not enough, her inner voice whispers.

She's weary now. Weary to her bones. Two things give her joy: the gardens, this one in front of her and the one in front of the palace, a gift and burden of love, lost and found; and the children. All her children.

Once a week, Jahid takes her to her parents' cemetery. She has talked to the priest there, made arrangements to be buried beside them.

I've lived a long life, a productive life. I've watched Richard grow, and Priya too. That should be enough.

And although she tells herself this, sometimes in those fallow hours of darkest night before dawn pushes fancy away, she aches for a chance to hold her son and his daughter, her granddaughter. Just once. She imagines the feel of them in her arms – her son's broad shoulders, his handsome face bearing the grooves of a life lived without her in it; her granddaughter with her angel wing shoulders, her fragile, beautiful face. So precious. Of her. But not hers.

A knock.

'You have a visitor,' Jahid's wife. Breathless. Her cheeks flushed with excitement. 'A very important one. The prince himself!'

Although he's not a prince any more, everyone still accords him the respect afforded their ruler. For them, this is what her son will be, always.

Mary's hand goes to her heart.

She's heard that Sita is dying, that Richard and Priya are visiting with her and that they are staying up at the palace, paying guests at what was once their residence.

But her son, here?

This is what she's been waiting for, wishing for, fantasising about. Her son, somehow finding out that she's his mother, gathering her in his arms, saying, 'Mama, I love you.'

Stop it, she chides her overarching imagination.

Why now? Why is he here, after all these years? Has he found out?

Well, she'll know soon enough.

She looks in the mirror, pats her hair, like silver down. Brushes her dress. Her hands shaking. *Silly woman.*

Richard. My Richard. Although he knows himself as Arjun.

He's not yours. He's hers, has been for almost all of his life.

'Arrange for tea and snacks,' she says as she walks, very carefully, to the front room.

Her son stands as she enters. His face, the face that occupies her dreams, the face whose features she traces in her fantasies, so familiar. So beloved. Yet not hers to claim.

He smiles.

His hair speckled with grey. Her son, her baby, is getting old.

His smile shy, tentative. Like one he would give a stranger. He doesn't know. Her heart falls, disappointment acrid in her throat.

'Forgive me intruding on you like this,' he says.

His voice brings back memories of sitting on a salty, wind-battered deck with a man whose features are replicated on this beloved stranger.

'It...' She clears her throat, says, with effort, 'it's my pleasure to have you visit.'

It is indeed. I've been waiting all your life for this.

'My daughter...' he begins.

You're my son and yet I've never been able to claim you as casually, as easily as you claim your daughter. Oh son, my son.

'She'd like to make a documentary about you and she has a few questions.'

So why is he here then, in Priya's stead? Priya, such a beautiful name for that beautiful, spirited girl. Priya meaning 'beloved'. Mary has looked it up. Said it over and over again. Priya. Does *she* know? Is that why she's sent her father?

Mary doesn't think so. Priya is straightforward, from what she's seen and heard of her. If she knew, Mary is convinced she would come herself, raising a hue and cry. Priya reminds Mary of her father (how he would have loved his great-granddaughter) and of the girl who slept with a man on a ship and set in motion events that culminate in the here and now.

'Priya... she's not very well.'

'What's the matter with her?' Mary cannot help herself.

Her son colours. Looking at him, so bashful, Mary yearns to gather him in her arms, set him at ease. She wants to trace the lines of grief and experience that have been wrought on his face, learn the narrative of each one.

She fists her hands and holds them close by her sides, in case they follow the call of her heart.

Priya is not well. And yet she wants to do this, a documentary about *her*.

Mary feels warmed.

'Are you okay with this? My daughter is passionate about what you do and she'd very much love to know more about you, as would I.'

'Yes, of course,' she says, once again clearing her throat to get words past the lump that has lodged there. 'It would be my privilege and great honour.'

Chapter 87

Sita

Recovering From Night

2000

When her maid – the only one she has left now, the last of the royal servants who had accompanied her from the palace when she had to sell it – enters Sita's chamber, her face pale as the cream awning that dawn drapes over a drowsy sky still recovering from night, Sita knows.

Her past, what she did, what she's been carrying, the guilt biting at her so that she bites at people, snapping at her so that she snaps at everyone, especially those closest to her, has finally caught up with her.

'Your son has been to see Mary Memsahib,' her trusted maid says.

Mary. That woman never went away. Instead she became Sita's conscience, she and that unruly, obscenely colourful garden, pricking and poking, prodding and eating away at her.

She closes her eyes.

They know.

But how? They cannot.

Only *she* knows. She and Mary.

And even if Mary tells – and why would she, why now? – why would *her* son believe the woman?

Must be Priya's doing. Her beloved, feisty granddaughter, too smart for her own good. Priya, fierce and spirited, who knew her mind right from the start, standing up to Sita with a determination and stubbornness that has amazed her and terrifies her now that Priya's fascination centres on Mary.

When Priya announced that she wanted to do a documentary on Mary, Sita had been stunned, blindsided by upset.

And so, backed into a corner, she had extracted a promise from her granddaughter to wait, knowing even as she did so that it might backfire on her, given Priya's indomitable determination. Knowing there was a risk she would disregard the promise, her inquisitiveness driving her straight into the lair of the woman Sita has wished off the face of the earth.

But her granddaughter, cleverer even than Sita gave her credit for, is honouring her promise to Sita while also getting her own way, by, presumably, making her father approach Mary, an outcome Sita had not foreseen and did not want.

'Why're you living in the past?' Priya would ask as a child. 'Why do you keep referring back to the time when you were queen?'

'It is my identity,' Sita would reply.

'It *was* your identity,' Priya, her dynamic, go-getting, firecracker of a granddaughter would huff.

'We're not kings or queens in the political sense, but to our subjects, we're still rulers.'

Priya would roll her eyes. She reminded Sita of the girl she herself once was. The girl who thought she could do anything, be anyone.

'Dadima, the world has moved on. No one thinks that way any more.' Priya would sigh. 'You say that as a little girl you had great ambitions.'

'That's right.'

'But what you became, a queen, that was through marriage, not through any actions of your own.'

Her granddaughter, so young and yet so wise.

*

Sita is proud of her son and her granddaughter. So very proud.

But they don't know this. Sita has never been able to tell them.

Her granddaughter's beautiful almond eyes go hard when she looks at Sita; her son is reticent, unforthcoming with her. Both have put as much distance as possible between themselves and her – her son, after his father and wife had passed away, travelling all over the world for his uncle's company, Priya moving to England.

I don't like myself, so how can I expect anyone else to like me?

When they returned upon hearing of her illness, when her son booked her into the rooms that had been her chambers in the east wing, she was touched by his thoughtfulness, but she did not know how to show it. And so she reverted to type, doing what came easily to her, honed through years of being queen. She had been sharp and biting, critical and haughty and watched their faces freeze, the familiar expressions of put-upon sufferance taking the place of their smiles.

Sita had thought her mother-in-law cold, power-hungry, ruthless, but she turned out to be just as conniving, as manipulative, as heartless as her. If not more so.

And for what?

She uttered the first lie to save the Lake Palace, keep it for herself rather than give it to Prince Praveen and his son. But the joke was on her. Once she had done what she did, she could never go to the Lake Palace again.

She stole her friend's child to keep her kingdom and her status as ruler. But just some few years later the kingdom for which she'd sold her soul was no longer being recognised. She was no longer ruler of a kingdom, lording it over everyone else.

How would her life have turned out had she helped Mary instead of stealing her child, cultivated her friendship again? Mary, the first person to have really seen *her*, the idealistic girl she was before she became the immoral queen.

Perhaps then, Sita would have had friendship, love, and not this perpetual loneliness, clotted violet with guilt. She would have been able to look at herself in the mirror. She would have been able to love Arjun, in his true avatar as Mary's son, the way he deserved to be loved. She would have earned the love of Arjun and Priya, in place of their withdrawn distance, their irritated, dutiful tolerance of her. And perhaps she would have been able to preserve the love of her husband.

But what use ruminating now, when what she did is, finally, catching up with her?

Her son might just be doing Priya's bidding, meeting Mary for the sake of his daughter's documentary. But sooner or later, during this continued association, the truth will out.

Inevitable, Sita knows. She's been waiting for this ever since she crossed a line by stealing her friend's child. Much as she didn't want it to happen, she's prepared for this eventuality.

'Tell me when my son comes back,' she says to her maid. Then she picks up her pen and starts to write.

The maid returns an hour later. 'Your son is home.'

My son. And that is how I want it to remain.

Sita takes out the pouch from her jewellery box where it has rested, beside her dwindling jewellery, all these years.

She will not die in shame. She cannot bear to see her son and granddaughter turn against her even more than they are already, look at her as if she is scum, blame her, point fingers at her.

She will die with dignity.

She will die a mother.

She will die a queen, surrounded by her son and granddaughter, in her rooms in the east wing of the palace from where she had once reigned. *Thank you, son, for making this possible.*

'Bring me some milk,' she says.

She empties the pouch, all the pills she's collected over the years, and swallows them down with the milk.

She clutches her stomach, fighting the urge to be sick.

'Fetch them,' she whispers, the letters she wrote while waiting for her son to return to her after visiting with Mary in her hand.

Chapter 88

Priya

The Crux

2000

'Mary grew up in India, but when she lost her parents, she was taken to England to live with her aunt and uncle. She came back to India years later and never left,' Priya's father says.

Once again, they're in the courtyard, sipping tea and catching up on her father's encounter with Mary.

'Mary started teaching at the school, married a doctor. But the marriage wasn't happy. She separated from her husband and she lost a child. She said that was what prompted her to create the garden. For her it represents hope and love.'

'That is what I feel whenever I look at it,' Priya says.

'A remarkable woman,' her father says. 'Anyway, all her answers are here.'

He hands Priya a sheet filled with his messy handwriting.

Mary fostered beauty through her garden, and love through her school and orphanage, doing so much good despite her misfortune. I will too.

Returning home has been cathartic. Already Jacob, what he did, is not hurting as much as before. The pain, although always there, is not as intense. It still throbs but not so fixedly.

One day it will go away, she understands. *I'm not going back. India is home and here I will stay.*

I'll show him, my husband the traitor. I'll make the best docu-
mentary of my life and do so without using a penny of his company's
funds. And if I cannot have children then I'll adopt them, work in
orphanages, like Mary.

Priya doesn't understand her grandmother's aversion to Mary.
Yes, what her father said – that Dadima wanted to be the alpha
woman, the one everyone respected and looked up to – makes
sense, but… Why make Priya promise not to film a documentary
about Mary?

Then, something that her father said, something that has been
niggling at her – 'Why at the palace?'

'I'm sorry?'

'Why grow a garden at the palace gates? Why not near the
school? The palace is more than a mile away from the school, at
the top of a hill. Why here?'

'I didn't think to ask. It wasn't on the list of questions you
gave me.'

How did Mary lose her child? Priya had assumed when her
father said Mary *lost* a child that it had died. But what if it didn't?
What if she means 'lost' literally? Is it somehow connected to the
palace? Is that why the garden is here, at the gates? Is that why it
represents hope and love? The hope that her child will be found
again, and Mary's love for it?

A thrill takes Priya over, goosebumps erupting, that same
feeling she gets every time she unearths the crux of the documentary she's working on. The hinge, the turning point…

She opens her mouth to share her thoughts with her father, but
her grandmother's maid is tumbling into the courtyard, breathless,
panting. 'Please come. Your grandmother… she is…'

Priya and her father exchange terror-filled glances.

Then they are running, behind the maid, to Priya's grandmother's chambers.

*

Dadima is having convulsions, gasping for breath. Her eyes bloodshot.

They soften when she sees Priya and her son, Priya's father.

'The doctor,' Priya says to the maid.

'He's on his way.'

'Too late,' her grandmother pants.

Priya sits on one side of her, her father on the other.

'I'm so proud of you,' her grandmother whispers, holding Priya's gaze.

Priya does not heed the tears that are cascading down her cheeks. She squeezes her grandmother's hand.

Dadima turns to her father.

'I love you, forgive me.'

He looks at her askance, his tears too falling unchecked.

'Ma…'

'Letters,' she gasps. 'Here.'

She hands one to him and one to Priya.

'I love you,' she says. 'I'm sorry.'

And then she is gone.

Chapter 89

Priya

A Confession

2000

My dearest Priya,

I have a confession to make. A secret I've harboured for the past many years. A wrong I have wrought that I haven't had the courage to right.

Over the years, you've asked me about the garden outside the palace gates.

Oh, Priya, that garden mocks me. It is my conscience. It asks of me 'why?'. It berates me and it does not allow me to forget what I did, even for a moment. When I lived at the palace, my rooms did not overlook it. And yet I knew it was there. I close my eyes and the flowers bloom in front of them, the red of blood, the white of lies, the yellow of remorse, the purple of guilt.

Mary. I have wronged her.

You are fascinated by her, wanting to make a documentary on her and that garden. I've stopped you from reaching out to her, thus perpetuating what I did, making it worse.

I am afraid, child. I am a coward. I am guilty.

Before I go any further, know that I love you. I love your father. What I did... I did not have the purest motives...

Priya stops reading, her gaze blurring, her grandmother's words swimming before her eyes.

Her grandmother's animosity towards Mary had a deeper reason, a hidden motive…

What is she about to learn? Does she want to? Her grandmother was fierce and strong, indomitable and yet beloved. Does she want her opinion of her to change?

I want to know the truth.

She reads the rest of the letter.

She cannot get her head around it.

She reads it again. And again.

Mary lost a child while her grandmother gained one. Mary, in her grief, started a garden.

But why start it at the palace gates, why not near the school? Priya had wondered, knowing somehow that there was more to this than she was seeing.

Mary was showing the woman who stole her child that she was waiting. Watching. That she was there. That she wouldn't go away.

She was creating something beautiful for her child. A labour of love. Sending him a message. Showing her yearning, her love for him through the flowers. The garden representing the hope that her son would one day be hers again.

And it served its purpose. While Priya and her father loved it, for her grandmother – or, not her grandmother, the woman who claimed to be her grandmother – it was the manifestation of her guilt. The reminder of her crime.

'Son,' Mary had called Priya's father at the award ceremony where she was honoured and Priya's grandmother had bristled. Lashed out.

Son.

Mary's son, stolen by the queen. How must it have felt, to watch her son grow and yet not be able to claim him? Watch him from afar, knowing that he was hers, but not being able to do anything about it.

And the strange bond Priya felt with Mary. The bond that was always there. Blood…

She wants to keen. Yell. Throw something. Break something.

She wants her grandmother alive so she can rail at her, break her, destroy her, make her account for what she did.

But then her father…

Her father had a letter too.

She stands, and then she is running.

He's sitting in the courtyard, the letter in his hand, tears streaming down his face, staring at nothing.

'Baba…'

He looks up at her and she sees he is ravaged. Devastated. Old.

'How could she?' he says, softly. 'How dare she?'

She kneels beside him, takes his hand in hers. It is cold, so cold. She rubs some warmth into it.

'Mary. My mother…'

He chokes on his words. Swallows. 'And all these years, she was so close. Living with the wrong done to her. Growing that garden. So close and yet…'

She holds him. They hold each other.

After a bit, he sniffs, wipes his eyes. 'I'm ready now,' he says.

And she knows just what he means.

'Come,' Priya says, 'she has waited long enough.'

Chapter 90

Mary

Complete

2000

Mary is sitting in the garden she created when she had lost everything, the garden that started with the first hibiscus blooming, offering hope, when she sees activity at the palace – she can't think of it as a hotel.

She squints against the sun, the better to make out what is going on. Her eyesight is good for her age, her doctor – Dr Kumar's grandson – has declared.

Two figures are running across the lawns.

Something's happened. Nobody runs anywhere within the grounds of the palace, and they certainly do not dash across the grass when there are neat paths along which to amble.

The figures come closer.

Her son and her granddaughter. Sprinting. Urgent.

What's happened?

Please God.

They come to the gates. Pull up short when they see her, breathless.

And the look in their eyes. A cornucopia of emotions. Grief, sorrow, hurt. Love.

She starts to shake. They know.

They *know*.

Her son comes to her, and there, in the garden she created when all hope was lost, the garden that was her salvation, he calls her by the endearment she never expected to hear from his mouth, although she never gave up hope. 'Ma.'

She envelops him in her arms. 'I held you for a few hours when you were born. I named you Richard after my father. And then I lost you.'

Then his daughter is there, nestling into the embrace.

And standing in the garden into which she poured the love she couldn't show her son, holding her family, Mary feels, for the first time since she gathered her baby boy in her arms, complete.

A LETTER FROM RENITA

I want to say a huge thank you for choosing to read *Beneath an Indian Sky*. If you did enjoy it, and want to keep up to date with all my latest releases, just sign up at the following link. Your email address will never be shared and you can unsubscribe at any time.

renitadsilva.com/e-mail-sign-up/?title=beneath-an-indian-sky

What I adore most about being a writer is hearing from readers. I'd love to know what you made of *Beneath an Indian Sky*, and I'd be very grateful if you could write a review. It makes such a difference and helps new readers to discover one of my books.

You can get in touch with me on my Facebook page, through Twitter, Goodreads or my website.

Thank you so much for your support – it means the world to me.

Until next time,
Renita

 RenitaDSilvaBooks

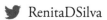 RenitaDSilva

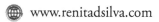 www.renitadsilva.com

ACKNOWLEDGEMENTS

I would like to thank all at Bookouture, especially Abi Fenton, for the advice and support. Thank you, Abi – you are the best. Thank you also to Lauren Finger, Jacqui Lewis and Jane Donovan for your wonderful eagle-eyed scrutiny of the manuscript.

A million thanks, Jenny Hutton, editor and seer, who always manages to tease out the story I am trying to tell from the mess of my drafts – I cannot thank you enough.

Huge thanks to Lorella Belli of Lorella Belli Literary Agency for your brilliant efforts in making my books go places. Thank you also to Milly and Eleonora. Lorella, I am honoured and humbled to have you championing my books.

Thank you to my lovely fellow Bookouture authors, especially Angie Marsons, Sharon Maas, Debbie Rix and Rebecca Stonehill, whose friendship I am grateful and lucky to have.

Thank you to all the fabulous book bloggers who give so freely of their time, reading and reviewing, sharing and shouting about our books. I am grateful to my Twitter/FB friends for their enthusiastic and overwhelming support. An especial thanks to Jules Mortimer and Joseph Calleja, book bloggers extraordinaire, who I am privileged to call my friends, and who are the best cheerleaders one could wish for.

I am immensely grateful to my long-suffering family for willingly sharing me with characters who live only in my head. Love always.

And last, but not least, thank you, reader, for choosing this book. Hope you enjoy.

10278626R00240

Printed in Great Britain
by Amazon